DEATH, TAXES, AND A SKINNY NO-WHIP LATTE

"Readers will find Kelly's protagonist a kindred spirit to Stephanie Plum: feisty and tenacious, with a self-deprecating sense of humor. Tara is flung into some unnerving situations, including encounters with hired thugs, would-be muggers, and head lice. The laughs lighten up the scary bits, and the nonstop action and snappy dialogue keep the standard plot moving along at a good pace."

—*RT Book Reviews*

"Readers should be prepared for a laugh fest. The writer is first-class and there is a lot of humor contained in this series. It is a definite keeper." —*Night Owl Romance*

"A quirky, fun tale that pulls you in with its witty heroine and outlandish situations . . . You'll laugh at Tara's predicaments, and cheer her on as she nearly single-handedly tackles the case." —*Romance Reviews Today*

"It is hard not to notice a sexy CPA with a proclivity for weapons. Kelly's sophomore series title . . . has huge romance crossover appeal." —*Library Journal*

"An exciting, fun new mystery series with quirky characters and a twist . . . Who would have ever guessed IRS investigators could be so cool!" —*Guilty Pleasures Book Reviews*

"Kelly's novel is off to a fast start and never slows down. There is suspense but also laugh-out-loud moments. If you enjoy Stephanie Plum in the Evanovich novels you will love Tara Holloway!" —*Reader to Reader Reviews*

"Diane Kelly gives the reader an action-packed thriller bursting at the seams with humor." —*Single Titles*

DEATH, TAXES, AND A FRENCH MANICURE

"Keep your eye on Diane Kelly—her writing is tight, smart and laugh-out-loud funny."
—Kristan Higgins, *New York Times* and *USA Today* bestselling author

"A hilarious, sexy, heart-pounding ride, that will keep you on the edge of your seat. Tara Holloway is the IRS's answer to Stephanie Plum—smart, sassy, and so much fun. Kelly's debut has definitely earned her a spot on my keeper shelf!"
—*New York Times* bestselling author Gemma Halliday

"The subject of taxation usually makes people cry, but prepare to laugh your assets off with Diane Kelly's hilarious debut." —Jana DeLeon, author of the Ghost-in-Law series

"Quirky, sexy, and downright fabulous. Zany characters you can't help but love, and a plot that will knock your socks off. This is the most fun I've had reading in forever!"
—*New York Times* bestselling author Christie Craig

"With a quirky cast of characters, snappy dialogue, and a Bernie Madoff-style pyramid scheme–hunting down tax cheats has never added up to so much fun!"
—Robin Kaye, award-winning author of the Domestic Gods series

Death, Taxes,
and Silver Spurs

DIANE KELLY

St. Martin's Paperbacks

DEATH, TAXES, AND SILVER SPURS

Copyright © 2014 by by Diane Kelly.

For information address St. Martin's Press, 175 Fifth Avenue, New York, NY 10010.

ISBN: 978-1-250-04831-8

Printed in the United States of America

St. Martin's Paperbacks edition / August 2014

St. Martin's Paperbacks are published by St. Martin's Press, 175 Fifth Avenue, New York, NY 10010.

10 9 8 7 6 5 4 3 2 1

*To Jenny Elliott and Paula Highfill, two great friends
who are thoughtful, generous, and lots of fun!
Thanks for cheering me on all these years.*

Acknowledgments

Thanks to my wonderful editor, Holly Ingraham. It's always a pleasure working with you!

Thanks to Sarah Melnyk, Paul Hochman and everyone else at St. Martin's who played a part in getting this book in the hands of readers. You're a fantastic team!

Thanks to Danielle Fiorella, Monika Roe, and Iskra Design for another fun and eye-catching cover. Y'all rock!

Thanks to my agent, Helen Breitwieser. I appreciate everything you do!

Thanks to authors Angela Cavener, Hadley Holt, Cheryl Hathaway, and Sherrel Lee for your feedback on my drafts. I'm so lucky to have you in my life!

Thanks to the hardworking and talented Liz Bemis-Hittinger and Sienna Condy of Bemis Promotions for your work on my Web site and newsletters. You two are awesome!

Thanks to the many members of Romance Writers of America, as well as the national office staff. I am proud to be part of such a professional and powerful organization!

And, finally, many thanks to my readers. Enjoy your time with Tara and company!

chapter one

Groomed

At two o'clock on a Saturday afternoon in early February I spent a full minute pulling forward and back, forward and back, trying to maneuver my plain white government sedan into a space at the curb. I could put a bullet into a bull's-eye at three hundred yards, but I'd never mastered the art of parallel parking.

My partner cut his brown eyes my way. Eddie was tall, talented, and tough, a black father of two and a political conservative, more Clint Eastwood than Kanye West. Though he said nothing, his expression spoke for him. It said, *Wow. You really suck at this.*

I cut my gray-blue eyes back at him, hoping he'd read the reply contained therein, which was, *Pffft.*

"Close enough," I muttered, turning off the engine. The car sat farther than the recommended six to eight inches from the curb, but if Dallas PD issued me a ticket I could pull rank and get it dismissed. Working for Uncle Sam definitely had some benefits.

We climbed out of the car, made our way up onto the sidewalk, and pulled open the glass door that led into

Doggie Style. Nope, the place wasn't a sex shop. It was a pet groomer. Get your mind out of the gutter. Or at least six to eight inches from the gutter.

An alarm on the door announced our arrival with a short, sharp beep.

The place was small and smelled like a rank yet refreshing mix of wet dog and oranges, probably from some type of citrus-based flea shampoo. A pegboard along the side wall displayed an assortment of bows, collars, barrettes, and other fashion accessories for pets. A bulletin board on the back wall featured snapshots of the groomer's kitty and canine clientele in cute costumes, including a white poodle in a pink tutu and a brown tabby in army fatigues. A notation under the cat's photo identified him as Chairman Meow.

Eddie eyed the photos. "Dressing up your pet? That's just wrong."

"I think it's cute."

"You would."

An open door behind the service counter led to the groomer's workspace. Through the door we could see an elevated table currently occupied by a golden-red chow. A nooselike apparatus hung from a pole, encircling his fluffy neck and immobilizing him. A big-boned woman with a blond ponytail circled the dog, examining him closely, occasionally reaching out with the clippers to perfect his lion cut. *Bzz. Bzz.* Something tiny, black, and furry peered up from a pillow in the corner, opening its mouth in a wide, pink yawn. Being adorable was exhausting.

"Be right there!" the woman barked without looking up.

Why was I here? Because I worked as a criminal investigator for the IRS and the groomer had not only shaved dogs and cats but had shaved well over a hundred thousand off her reported earnings as well. The audit department had issued an assessment, but Hilda Gottschalk had refused to pay up. On three separate occasions, an agent from the collections department had come by and seized the contents of the cash register, netting a mere two hundred dollars for his efforts. Not an efficient process, obviously.

Hilda still owed thirty grand and was making no attempts to settle her tax bill. The IRS had put a lien on her house and levied the small balance in her checking account, but it was clear the woman was hiding her cash somewhere, like a dog hiding a bone, secreting it to savor later.

When the collections department had no luck tracking down her hidden profits, they'd booted the case over to criminal investigations. That's where I came in. I'm Special Agent Tara Holloway, a law enforcement agent for the IRS, a tax cop if you will. I had the same powers as the collections agents to seize assets, but I also had a gun, handcuffs, and the legal right to kick tax-evader ass. Often, when cases were escalated to criminal investigations, tax cheats finally realized their days of playing games were over. Many cooperated at that point. A few, however, chose to go down fighting.

I hoped Hilda wouldn't be the latter type. I had front-row seats for a concert tonight and I'd prefer to save my energy for dancing to the tunes of my favorite country crossover star.

Brazos Rivers.

The mere thought of his name made me want to sigh and swoon and shine his belt buckle with my panties. Yep, I had it bad for the guy. A major celebrity crush that would put any tweener with Bieber fever to shame.

Hilda removed the noose from the dog's head. With a grunt, she lifted the big beast from the table, set him on the floor, and led him to a large cage to await his owner's return.

Clippers still in hand, she stepped into the foyer, her hazel eyes flicking to Eddie before meeting mine. "What can I do for you?"

Might as well cut to the chase. I needed the rest of the afternoon to primp and preen and wax my upper lip. "You can tell us where you've hidden your assets."

Hilda frowned as she took in the badges Eddie and I held up. "Who the hell are you?"

"Special Agents Tara Holloway and Eddie Bardin," I said. "We're from IRS criminal investigations. Your case has been escalated." Saying her case had been *escalated* was the polite way of letting her know she was in deep doo-doo.

She crossed her arms over her chest, flicking the clippers on and off with her thumb. *Bzz. Bzz.* "You can't make me talk."

Ugh. So that's how she wanted to play this, huh?

I put a hand on my waist and pushed back my blazer, revealing the Glock holstered at my waist. Her eyes went to my gun and back to my face. The expression in them read, *Fuck you and the horse you rode in on.* Her eyes were very ill-mannered.

Eddie chimed in. "The government means business, Miss Gottschalk. Either you tell us where your assets are or you go to jail."

She seemed to ponder his words for a moment, clicking the clippers on and off once more—*bzz-bzz*—before glancing back into the workroom. "I can't leave these dogs here."

Eddie cocked his head. "You won't have to if you tell us where you've hidden your cash."

Bzz. Bzz. She looked the two of us over as if sizing us up. She had a good six inches over my five-feet-two-inch frame and, with her stout build, likely weighed as much as Eddie. Still, there were two of us and only one of her. *Neener-neener.*

"All right," she said finally. "I've got some cash in my safe in the back room."

"Got anything else in that safe?" A gun, perhaps? I'd learned—the hard way—never to assume someone would be unarmed.

"That's for me to know!" she called out in a snarky, singsong voice. "And you to find out!"

I rolled my eyes. What did she think this was, a third-grade playground spat?

Eddie and I followed her to the back room. I glanced around. The black puppy was curled up in a tiny ball on his pillow now, snoozing away. The floor in front of the porcelain tub glistened with water droplets, having yet to dry after the chow had taken his bath. Clumps of reddish-gold dog hair lay on the floor around the grooming table.

Hilda led us to a small storage closet in the corner and pointed at the door. "The safe is in there."

"I'll open it," Eddie said.

That meant I'd be standing guard, making sure Hilda didn't pull a fast one. You might think it would've been better to have Eddie on guard, but you'd be wrong, even if you are one of those geniuses who knows how to parallel park. Eddie was bigger and stronger than me, sure, but he didn't have my quick-draw gun skills. They didn't call me the Annie Oakley of the IRS for nothing. I put a hand on the butt of my gun, ready for action.

Eddie opened the door to the closet. A stack of white towels sat on the top shelf, bottles of pet shampoo on the next one down. On the floor was a mop bucket. That was it. No safe in sight.

"Where's the—"

Eddie hadn't gotten his words out before Hilda lunged toward the back exit door.

Oh, hell, no.

This woman is not getting away.

I sprang toward her and grabbed her thick arm. She flung me aside with little effort. All those years of lifting dogs had given her some solid arm muscles.

"Crap!" I slipped on the wet floor and landed on my butt, my head banging back against the tub. Damn, that hurt! My brain rattled, I sat helpless for a moment as I tried to gather my wits. Unfortunately, my wits were all over the place, like a litter of lively puppies. Before they could be fully corralled, Eddie blocked Hilda's escape route and she decided to seize the moment and come at me with the clippers.

Bzz! Bzz!

The clippers buzzed like a ferocious swarm of hornets around my head. *Bzzzzz! Bzzzzz!* Before I could slap Hilda's hands away, a harsh tug began at my forehead and ended at the crown of my head. A four-inch strip of my chestnut hair fell into my lap.

"Stop that!" I yelled, leveraging my back against the tub and kicking out at her with my steel-toed shoes.

I landed two solid kicks to her meaty calf but my actions didn't scare her off. They only seemed to make her madder. She came at me again, her face red and blotchy with anger and adrenaline.

With a primal cry, Eddie grabbed the woman from behind and pulled her away from me, shoving her up against the wall. But it was too late. My hair was now styled in a reverse Mohawk.

I reached up to touch the bald landing strip on my head, igniting in an instant fury. How dare this woman ruin my two-hundred-dollar cut and color! Especially when I'd be meeting Brazos Rivers in person tonight.

My body launched from the floor like a bitch-seeking missile, hurtling toward its target. I body-slammed the woman from behind, smashing her face and torso against the wall. The clippers fell from her hand with a thunk.

On instinct, I yanked my gun from my holster only to shove it back in when I had second thoughts. I'd just recently got back my job with the IRS after being fired for shooting a target four times in the leg. Long story, but suffice it to say the bastard deserved every one of those bullets and then some. Still, I knew that using my gun now would get me in even deeper doo-doo than Hilda Gottschalk. I'd have to even the score some other way. Hmm . . .

An eye for an eye.

A tooth for a tooth.

A hair for a hair.

chapter two

What a Tangled Hair
We Weave

I grabbed the trimmer from the floor and flipped the switch. *Bzzzzz.*

Eddie slapped cuffs on Hilda, who yapped a string of repetitive and ineffectual threats like an overzealous lapdog. "Screw you! Screw you! Screw you!"

Too bad we couldn't muzzle her.

"Hold her still," I ordered.

Eddie eyed the device in my hand, looked into my eyes, and shrugged. "Have at her."

God love 'im.

I set to work. By the time I was done with Hilda, her blond ponytail lay on the floor and her bangs were history, shaved back to the hairline at the top of her forehead.

That'd teach her to mess with Tara Holloway.

Once Hilda had been hauled off to jail and the owners of the chow and black peekapoo had picked up their pets, Eddie and I returned to my G-ride. I took one look at my hair in the rearview mirror, gasped when it looked even worse than I had imagined, and fought the urge to dial

911. If my hair disaster didn't constitute an emergency I didn't know what did. Still, I doubted Dallas PD had a stylist on staff. I settled for returning to the groomer's shop and grabbing a red plastic barrette from the display. Sweeping one side of my hair over the top of my head, I clipped it in place on the other side with the barrette. The Mohawk was now replaced with a comb-over. Lovely.

I dropped Eddie back at the office so he could retrieve his car, and drove to my usual salon. I took one step in the door and removed the barrette. My hair flopped back into place, revealing the hairless stripe down the center of my skull.

My hairdresser, Amber, turned my way and shrieked. "Oh, my God!"

After I ran through the events at Doggie Style, Amber shook her head. "This could only happen to you."

"I know, right?" Something about me brought out the inner nut job in people.

Luckily, Amber had had a last-minute cancellation and was able to squeeze me in for a weave. I emerged an hour later with my bald spot strategically covered and made a stop by the pharmacy for the biotin she'd recommended for fast hair growth.

My boyfriend, Nick, arrived at six-thirty to pick me up for the concert. Nick was a fellow special agent, though he'd been with the IRS long enough to achieve senior status. I was still a relative rookie, having yet to put a full year under my belt.

Nick stood a manly six-two, with rock-hard pecs and broad shoulders a girl could lean on, cry on, and bite into. Trust me. I'd done all three. His dark hair was currently cut in a short, businesslike style. He wore a western shirt, jeans, and boots, standard Nick off-duty attire. The white felt cowboy hat I'd given him sat on his head, tilted back enough to reveal those whiskey-colored eyes that never failed to drink me in.

Those eyes went straight to my head. "Get your hair done?"

"In a manner of speaking." I gave him the rundown.

When I finished, he groaned but grinned at the same time. Nick found my escapades amusing. Sometimes I think he stuck with me for the entertainment value. "It never ends with you, does it?"

He stepped close and gave me a soft, warm kiss that sent a tingle from the tips of my toes up to my shaved scalp. When he released me, his gaze backtracked down my body, taking in my fitted red sweater dress and hand-painted boots, sexy Southern chic. "Look at you, all prettied up."

He dipped his head in acknowldgement and appreciation, apparently assuming I'd gotten myself all gussied up for him. Truth be told, I'd wanted to look good for Brazos. The star hadn't paid taxes—*ever*—but surely it was an accidental oversight, right? Heck, with all the money Brazos Rivers and the Boys of the Bayou raked in, he'd probably write me a check on the spot tonight. Case closed.

I grabbed my cute knit shawl and we drove in Nick's pickup to a Mexican restaurant not far from the American Airlines Center. We sat on opposite sides of a small booth and shared a platter of loaded nachos. I sipped a frozen margarita while Nick nursed a Shiner bock.

The alcohol did nothing to numb my senses. I felt giddy with anticipation, virtually bouncing on the springy seat of the booth. "I can hardly wait to meet Brazos Rivers!"

Nick chuffed. "You won't. You'll be meeting Winthrop Merriweather the seventh."

Obviously, the name Winthrop lacked sex appeal, and his last name sounded like it belonged on a set of bedsheets or one of the good fairies from *Sleeping Beauty*. The singer, like many celebrities, had chosen a fitting pseudonym, naming himself after the longest river in Texas. The Spanish called the river *Río de los Brazos de Dios,* which translates as the River of the Arms of God. The Brazos flowed from a headwater in New Mexico all the way through the Lone Star State to the Gulf of Mexico. The waterway was featured in John Graves's classic book *Goodbye to a River,* as well as James Michener's *Texas* and even in a book by Cormac McCarthy. The river was also mentioned in songs by Lyle Lovett, John Hiatt, and Bruce Springsteen. Both the river, and the singer who'd named himself after it, had made quite a splash.

Brazos had clearly taken pains to ensure the general public had no idea that his real name was Winthrop. As an IRS employee, I was privy to this bit of secret information. The tax records showed that Brazos Rivers was an assumed name for a business operated by Winthrop Merriweather VII. He'd filed for an employer identification number to be assigned to his professional alias, Brazos Rivers, so that he wouldn't have to use his real name and personal Social Security number for business purposes. Standard procedure for individuals running a business.

Truth be told, it was titillating to know I had an inside scoop on the star that few others had. Brazos had also been quiet about his childhood and vocal training, evading reporters' nosy questions, leaving his background a mystery. He'd popped onto the country music scene several years ago as if materializing out of nowhere.

"Who cares what his real name is," I replied to Nick. After all, a rose by any other name . . . right? "He's incredibly talented."

The fact that Nick responded with only a draw on his beer told me he didn't agree. I was nothing if not stubborn, though. I'd make Nick see the light.

"*People* magazine called Brazos a modern-day poet." They'd also named him the sexiest man alive last year.

But no sense mentioning that, right? Besides, Nick was damn sexy himself. I mean, if I had to choose between the two . . . I'd take them both. Maybe even at the same time. Hee-hee!

"Brazos Rivers a poet?" Nick raised a dark, skeptical brow. " 'Baby, if you're willing, let's do some horizontal drilling?' You call that poetry?"

"Not that particular song," I said in my defense, fishing among the nachos for one with extra guacamole. "I was referring to the one that goes 'you left without saying good-bye, your love was an illusion, your love was a lie, it's enough to make a cowboy cry.' "

"It's enough to make a cowboy puke." Nick removed his hat and pretended to urp into it before placing it back on his head.

Nick was entitled to his opinion, but if he wanted this debate to end he should've kept his thoughts to himself. After all, I kept my mouth shut when he extolled the virtues of the Dallas Cowboys, several of whom had landed themselves in jail in recent years for one offense or another.

"All three of Brazos Rivers's albums have gone platinum," I pointed out. Can't argue with a fact like that, right? "He's a huge crossover star. Like Taylor Swift."

"There's nothing swift about Brazos Rivers. The guy's an overrated, oversexed man-whore who can play a little guitar, that's all."

I bristled at Nick's comment. Okay, so Brazos Rivers was rumored to have a girl or two in every port, maybe even three or four. Who could blame him? He was young, hot, and single. He'd also been a centerfold in *Stud Farm,* a short-lived publication intended to compete with *Playgirl.* The spread showed the star floating in a river on an inner tube wearing nothing but his trademark leather boots and silver spurs, his straw cowboy hat covering his crotch, a naughty grin on his oh-so-kissable lips.

While the other men featured in the magazine had been shown full frontal, Brazos offered only his waxed chest, his six-pack abs, and some upper thigh. When female stars posed for boudoir photos but didn't want to do full nudity, they'd at least show their fans some side boob. Too bad Brazos hadn't followed suit, done a profile pic, maybe reveal a little side ball.

Despite the fact that the photo spread had left me wanting, I had a dog-eared copy of the magazine hidden in my purse right now. But who could blame me? Brazos had sex appeal out the wazoo.

Besides, Nick saying that Brazos wasn't swift was just plain wrong. The guy was a marketing genius. He and his music were featured in a commercial for a pickup truck. He endorsed everything from electric razors to toothpaste. He'd launched his own line of guitars and barbecue grills, even a men's fragrance called Whitewater. The guy was drenched in the sweet smell of success.

But no sense arguing with Nick. *I* knew I was right even if he didn't. I sipped my margarita, said nothing, and pitied his ignorance.

Nick seemed to realize he'd taken things too far and reached a hand across the table, chucking me gently and affectionately on the chin. "Sorry. I shouldn't poke fun at the guy. After all, you never put down Carrie Underwood."

My eyes narrowed. "You have a crush on Carrie Underwood?"

"Oops." Nick offered an expression that was half grin, half cringe. (A *gringe*?) "Did I forget to tell you about that?"

chapter three

$\mathcal{R}$ed Lace and a Washtub

Nick and I showed our tickets to the security guard at the entrance to the floor seats and made our way to the front row. Our little disagreement at the restaurant was forgotten now, all of it, even the part where Nick called Brazos overrated and admitted to being hopelessly in love with Carrie Underwood. I wondered if it was too late to phone in to *American Idol* and rescind the vote I'd cast for her.

Okay, maybe the argument wasn't *entirely* forgotten.

The warm-up band was an up-and-coming local group who'd gotten their start playing Johnnie High's Country Music Revue in the nearby city of Arlington. They weren't bad, but they were no Brazos Rivers and the Boys of the Bayou.

When they left the stage, it felt as if someone had sucked the bones and organs out of my body and replaced them with one hundred percent pure helium. In minutes— *mere minutes!*—Brazos Rivers would be standing on the stage right in front of me.

The road crew brought out three guitars and positioned them in stands only a dozen feet away. The crowd, which was a least three-quarters women, began to murmur in anticipation as additional lights on tall stands were wheeled onto the stage. The Jumbo Tron screens were turned on, the image showing a dark floor. The lights dimmed, signaling the crowd that the show was ready to start.

A high-pitched sound somewhere between a squeal and a roar (a *squoar*?) rose from the crowd as the Boys of the Bayou strutted out onto the stage, waving their cowboy hats over their heads. All four of the Boys were shirtless, with suede leather chaps and six-pack abs, which, if you did the math, adds up to one orgasm-inspiring view.

My eardrums vibrated with a high-pitched shriek I didn't realize was coming from my mouth until Nick looked my way and chuckled. He might not be a fan of Brazos and the Boys, but at least he was being a good sport about things now.

When the crowd calmed a bit, an image popped up on the oversized screens, a black boot with silver spurs, the heel tapping out a slow rhythm, the spurs jangling with each tap. The crowd roared again, even louder this time if such a thing were possible.

That boot belongs to Brazos.

The tapping grew faster and harder, faster and harder, until it became an outright stomp. The boot suddenly disappeared and the camera panned up, showing a smiling Brazos running toward it. He emerged from between two towering amplifiers, his hat held high in his hand. He ran toward the front of the stage—*toward me!*—stopping just three feet back from the edge where I stood at my seat, trying not to self-combust from the heat of my lust.

At twenty-two years old Brazos was my junior by half a decade, but that didn't stop me from fantasizing about his young, fresh flesh. Besides, these young stars grow up fast, right? Men had no qualms about marrying women half their age. It was only fair for women to do the same. I'd happily rob any cradle containing Brazos Rivers.

The blond-haired, blue-eyed superstar looked out at the audience, waved his cowboy hat, and hollered his signature greeting. "Hey howdy, y'all!"

"Hey howdy, Brazos!" we all yelled back.

Brazos wore an unbuttoned plaid shirt with the sleeves ripped off, revealing his waxed chest, perfect pecs, and the Lone Star flag tattooed on his firm bicep. Like the river he was named after, he had the arms of a god.

My hands flew into the air as if by their own accord, and I found myself jumping up and down and screaming. Sheesh. What a fan girl, huh?

Without further ado, Brazos jammed his hat onto his head, stepped back, and grabbed a guitar. He and the Boys launched into their first song, which just happened to be "Horizontal Drilling."

Heck, yeah! I was willing!

The crowd whooped it up, the excitement infectious. When I caught Nick singing along halfway through, I jabbed him in the ribs with my elbow and pointed a finger at his face.

Busted.

He smiled and raised his palms in surrender.

While the Boys of the Bayou sang backup and performed choreographed dance maneuvers behind him, Brazos went on to sing his hits "Roughnecks and Rednecks," "Let's Get Rowdy Now," and a romantic ballad called "Riverbank Blues." Nick draped his arm around my shoulder and pulled me close during that one, rubbing a warm thumb over my shoulder. *Eat your heart out, Carrie Underwood.*

When the song was over, Brazos put a hand over his eyes to shade them from the spotlights and called out to the audience, "Who wants to get down and dirty?"

We knew our line and shouted it in response. "We do!"

"All righty, then!" he called. "Time to bring out the washtub!"

Two girls in tight blue jeans and skimpy halter tops sauntered onto the stage, carrying a large metal tub and an old-fashioned washboard. Brazos reached behind a speaker and pulled out a lasso, twirling the thing over his head for a moment before stretching the rope between the towers of amplifiers and tying it to handles on the sides, improvising a clothesline.

Brazos and the band launched into song now, singing about wanting to get down and dirty, fast and filthy, lusty and dusty. Okay, maybe I could see where Nick got the oversexed man-whore thing. But that wasn't going to stop me from worshipping the ground Brazos walked on.

As Brazos sang, a blitzkrieg of bras and panties bombarded the stage, thrown from nearly every row in the place, some fluttering down from the balcony. The crowd tossed the undergarments forward until they landed on the stage, where the Boys rounded them up and filled the washtub.

A purple bra landed on Nick's head. Holy guacamole! The cups looked big enough to shelter two people in the event of a tornado. My 32As were no match for the mammoth mammary glands that bra had housed.

Nick raised a brow. "That's more woman than I can handle!" he called over the music. A lie, probably, but one intended to let me know I was all the woman he needed even though I had the tiny breasts of a chubby adolescent boy. Nick took the bra from my hand, balled it up, and threw it football style onto the stage where it sailed over Brazos's head and was snatched out of the air by one of his backup singers.

Brazos let his guitar hang from its strap and clapped his hands over his head. The audience followed suit. His fingers free now, he headed over to the full washtub, plucked a pair of silky black panties from the top, and held them up with a sexy grin. One of the girls on stage handed him a clothespin and he pinned the panties to the clothesline. In minutes, the clothesline filled with black bras, pink bras, white bras, and strapless bras, in every size from 32A to 44DD. Panties, too. Polka-dot panties, striped panties, thong panties, crotchless panties.

All Brazos needed now was *my* panties.

Caught up in the excitement, I wriggled my red lace panties down over my hips and pulled my feet out of my boots to get them off. I might not have much up front, but thanks to regular squats at the gym I had a tight little rear. I wadded up my panties, pulled my arm back, and threw as hard as I could. The undies flew through the air, unfurling in an arc as they sailed toward the magnificence that was Brazos Rivers. Was it my imagination, or had Brazos cut a glance my way? I couldn't be certain.

Nick looked my way, too, appearing annoyed at first, but when he glanced down and realized I now wore nothing under my dress he understood the situation had its advantages. He gave me his own sexy grin.

Onstage, Brazos continued to hang the undergarments, laughing into his mic when he reached into the tub and discovered a pair of white men's boxers printed with red hearts. He held the boxers up for all to see, then hung the undies on the line next to a pair of ruffled pink panties.

When the tub was empty, he launched back into song, strutting up to the front of the stage with his guitar, his chest glistening with sweat now. *What I wouldn't give to work up a sweat with him . . .*

The concert continued until, after three encores and a standing ovation, the lights came up and the crowd began to stream out of the center. Nick and I stepped into the hallway and headed to the backstage area, sticking close to the wall since we were going against the flow. At first I felt a little naughty walking around in public without undies, but the titillating feeling waned when I realized half the women in the hallway were bare-assed or bare-breasted under their clothes, too.

When Nick and I finally managed to reach the corridor leading to the dressing rooms, the crowd had thinned out. Five security guards with Brazos Rivers concert tees stretched tight over their massive chests stood shoulder to shoulder, a wall of muscle blocking the entryway. Three twentyish girls with long hair, tight jeans, and stilettos worked a guard with sleeve tattoos and a shaved head, begging him to let them backstage.

"Come on!" one of the girls pleaded. "Be cool."

The guard shook his bald head.

The girl leaned in, poking out her chest suggestively and putting a hand on the guy's shoulder. "We'll make it worth your while." She winked and gave him a coy smile. "If you know what I mean."

Oh, we all knew what she meant, all right.

He brushed her hand off him. "Not interested."

Gotta say, I might not think much of his skinhead look but I admired his personal ethics.

Insulted but undaunted, the girl reached into her purse, pulled out her wallet, and retrieved a hundred-dollar bill. "Does this change your mind?"

The guard's lip twitched. "Not in the least."

The girl shoved the money back into her purse and glared at the man now. "Can I at least get my bra back? I paid fifty dollars for it at Victoria's Secret."

"No," baldie said. "Get lost."

Huffing in frustration, the girl turned and stormed away, her friends following behind her, their heels click-clacking on the tile floor.

I almost felt sorry for the girl. Who wouldn't want to meet Brazos Rivers face-to-face? As federal agents, Nick and I would have no trouble getting backstage. I couldn't wait to meet my favorite star! The two of us whipped out our badges and showed them to the bearded bouncer in front of us.

"We're with the IRS," I told him. "We need to see Mr. Rivers."

The guard crossed his ham-hock arms over his gorilla chest, glanced at my badge, and snorted. "Where'd you get that thing? A box of Cracker Jacks?"

Nick and I exchanged glances. Neither of us had faced a situation like this before. Our badges normally worked like a key to the city, granting us entrance into virtually any venue. People tended to fear the IRS and would rather cooperate than risk our wrath.

I reached into my purse and pulled out my driver's license. "See?" I said. "The name on my license matches my badge."

I held my license out to the man but he didn't even look at it. He merely lifted a shoulder. "That proves nothing."

I pulled out one of my business cards and held it up in front of his eyes. "How about this?"

Again he lifted the shoulder. "You coulda ordered those cards online."

Nick and I exchanged another glance. I knew exactly what he was thinking, because I was thinking the same thing. We could take out our guns and force the men to let us back to the dressing room. But our weapons were intended to be used sparingly and defensively. Too many risks involved otherwise. No way could we justify the use of force in this situation.

"Look," Nick said, an edge to his voice as he took a

step closer. "We're members of federal law enforcement. You're obstructing justice here."

"You want to see Rivers?" The guy narrowed his eyes at Nick, made a fist, and cracked his knuckles. "Come back with a real cop."

chapter four

a Dam in the River

Fuming, Nick stepped to the side, pulling his cell phone from his pocket to summon a uniformed U.S. Marshal to the scene. Meanwhile, I stared the guard down, fighting the urge to put my knee in his nuts. *Real cop.* Grrr. We *were* real cops, even if nobody else seemed to get that. Then again, Nick and I were dressed no different from the other concertgoers. Perhaps we would've been more convincing in our ballistic vests and raid jackets.

A commotion down the hall behind the guards drew my attention past them. Three roadies came in a back entrance and headed to the main dressing room door. One raised a meaty fist and knocked. Six raps to the tune of "Baby, if you're willin'."

The door swung open.

"The bus is ready," the roadie called into the room.

A murmur of voices drifted into the hall. Did one of those voices belong to Brazos?

"Beat it," the bouncer said, stepping toward me. Though he didn't touch me he came within inches. Obviously, he expected me to retreat. Just as obviously, he hadn't met

Special Agent Tara Holloway before. I grew up with two big brothers and didn't scare easily.

I stepped toward the man, closing the space to mere millimeters. I looked up into his flaring nostrils. "Go tell Brazos we're here. He needs to talk to us. For his own good."

He snorted hot breath down at me. "Not gonna happen."

The phone call completed, Nick rejoined us. "A U.S. Marshal is on his way."

The guard snorted. "He better get here quick, 'cause we ain't waiting."

Behind the guard, a stream of people began to exit the dressing room.

The girls in the halter tops.

The Boys of the Bayou.

And last, but certainly not least, Brazos Rivers himself, in all his gorgeous glory.

A zing electrified my nether regions and his name ejected from my mouth like a bullet from a gun. "Brazos!"

Brazos turned his head my way. His eyes, as blue and sparkling as a Texas stream in summer, locked on mine.

My head went dizzy and I felt myself wobble. I could barely force my words out between panting breaths. "I need to . . . talk . . . to you!"

"I got this," the security guard called over his shoulder to Brazos. He turned his attention back to me, stepping to the side to block my view. No matter. The image of Brazos gazing at me would be forever etched in my mind.

The guard leaned down into my face, glaring into my eyes. "I said 'beat it.' "

As I mentioned, having two older brothers made me relatively fearless. It also made me a crafty fighter.

"All right," I lied. "We'll go." I took a step back then faked a left. When the guard shifted his bulk to the side, I rushed forward, slipping through the space between him and the guard next to him. Being petite, agile, and sneaky had its benefits.

"We need to talk about your taxes!" I cried, sprinting toward Brazos.

His brow creased in confusion. "My what?" he asked in his smooth, Southern-accented voice.

"Your taxes!" I was a mere five feet from the shining star that was Brazos Rivers when the guards caught me from behind, grabbed my arms, and yanked me to a stop.

"Taxes?" Brazos frowned. "Who are you?"

"Special Agent Tara Holloway." I struggled to free myself from the tight grips of the bouncers. "I'm with the IRS."

Brazos eyed me a moment as if processing the information.

The bearded guard tightened his hold on me. "Don't fall for it," he warned the singer. "It's just another bullshit gimmick to get back here to meet you."

The guards began to pull me backward, away from Brazos. Though I tried to dig in with my heels, the tiled hallway offered nothing for them to dig into.

The singer raised a hand. "Hold on a minute. Why would anyone in their right mind pretend to be an IRS agent?"

Good point. Brazos wasn't just sexy and talented, he was perceptive, too.

He jerked his chin upward. "Let her go."

"Whatever you say, boss."

The guards released me. Unfortunately, my body was angled backward and with no more support from the sentries my ass hit the floor. *Fwump.*

Brazos smiled his beautiful smile, lighting up the dim hallway like a human floodlight. He strode up to me, his spurs jingle-jangling as his closed the distance between us. He towered over me, his denim-covered crotch perfectly framed by the leather chaps, his open shirt giving me an up-close-and-personal glimpse of those well-defined abs and pecs. I stared up at him, simultaneously frozen in place while experiencing a hot, full-body blush.

The man is just so . . . damn . . . sexy.

Chuckling, he reached down. "You look like you could use a hand."

I looked at the hand in front of me, at the fingers that strummed the guitar, plucking number one hits. Dare I touch this sacred flesh?

Oh, hell yeah, I dare!

I grasped Brazos's warm hand in my own. The Texas flag on his bicep flexed as he pulled me to a stand directly in front of him.

"Come on back to my bus," he said. "We can talk privately there."

Privately . . .

Still holding my hand, he turned and headed down the hallway. I trailed along like a helpless stray puppy following a kid home from school, hoping to be taken in.

"Tara!"

On hearing Nick's voice behind me, I dropped Brazos's hand and looked back. *Oh, my God.* I'd totally forgotten about Nick. What was wrong with me?

Two of the security staff continued to block Nick's way. With his jaw set firm and his eyes ablaze, Nick looked none too happy about it.

Brazos looked from me, to Nick, and back to me, a grin tugging at his lips as he leaned toward me and whispered under his breath. "He your boyfriend?"

Yes, of course, Nick was my boyfriend. But at the moment our personal relationship was irrelevant, right? We weren't here as a romantically involved couple. We were here as IRS special agents to negotiate a tax settlement with Brazos.

"He's my partner." Despite my words being true, my gut clenched with guilt. Nick was my partner, sure, but he was also so much more than that.

"Your partner, huh?" Brazos ran his eyes from the top of my hair to the tip of my boots and back up again. "You look like a woman who's capable of handling me all by yourself." His pupils flashed darkly before he looked down the hall and addressed Nick directly. "She'll be back." His eyes narrowed in challenge. "When I'm done with her."

chapter five

Whispers and Kisses

When he's done with me . . .

What, exactly, did Brazos plan to do with me? And why was I going along so easily, helpless to resist, like a witless, innocent lamb being willingly led to slaughter?

Brazos ushered me out the back doors of the arena and into the crisp air of the parking lot, the cold air snapping me back to reality. Sure, Brazos was an internationally renowned songwriter and country-western star. Sure, he had one of the finest asses ever to sport a pair of chaps and the bluest eyes a girl could dream of. Sure, he had an income an Arab sheik would envy. But those things didn't make him superhuman. And they didn't exempt him from paying his due to the U.S. government.

His enormous tour bus stood waiting in an enclosed area, the engine idling. The transport bore the name BRAZOS RIVERS in large red letters along the side underneath the windows. A vertical panel near the back featured an enlarged photograph of the star leaning back against a red barn, wearing his trademark cowboy hat, boots, and silver spurs. The specially equipped tour bus was valued at \$230,000 according to the documentation provided by the collections department. Quite a ride.

The doors swung open, operated by unseen hands, as Brazos approached.

Brazos ascended the first step, then turned to offer a hand down to me. "Watch your step. The first one's a doozy."

"Thanks."

My red boot had barely touched the first step before Brazos hoisted me up to the floor of the bus and encircled me with his arms. The fan-girl in me nearly swooned. The federal agent in me thought he was getting a little too personal. Still, too personal or not, I let myself enjoy his touch for a moment while I glanced around the bus.

The visible part of the vehicle contained an extended living area with three leather couches forming a semicircle around a coffee table. Farther back to the left was a built-in dining table with padded booths on each side, wide enough to seat six people comfortably. On the right was a small kitchenette and fully stocked liquor cabinet complete with a polished wood bar and built-in stools with a brass footrest. Between the dining area and kitchen was a closed door that presumably led back to the sleeping quarters. Per the article in *Stud Farm,* the bedroom contained a hot tub and a king-sized bed with black satin sheets.

"When I'm done with her . . ."

The roadies, the girls in the halters, and the Boys of the Bayou milled about the main space, grabbing beers from the minifridge, flopping back onto the couches, using a remote control to channel-surf on the big-screen TV mounted on the wall.

Brazos grinned down at me. "You're awfully cute, you know that?"

Had he seen my hair right after Hilda had groomed it this afternoon, he'd have surely felt differently.

I took advantage of our proximity to give him an up-close-and-personal once-over. He was damn fine, no doubt about it, but up close like this a few minor imperfections became apparent. For one, he smelled a little sweaty. But who could blame him? He'd spent the last two hours dancing and singing and playing his heart out under hot spotlights. The sweat had washed away some of his stage makeup, and the skin underneath was a little ruddy. Not a problem. He was still sexy as hell. And I wasn't naïve. I'd known the magazine photos of Brazos were airbrushed. Nobody's pores were totally invisible like that. I also noticed that the roots of his sunny blond hair were a mousy brown. So the guy had his hair colored. No big deal, right? You'd expect a celebrity to try to look his best. These realities did nothing to dampen my infatuation. In fact, meeting Brazos in the flesh, feeling his hands around me, only made him seem less like a fairy-tale prince and more like a real man, a real possibility.

Yet, as much as I enjoyed his touch, I had to put an end to it. I was here as a special agent now, not an adoring fan. I put a hand on each of his wrists and eased his arms back. "Let's talk about your taxes."

He took a step backward. Though the grin had left his mouth, his eyes still twinkled with merriment. "What's the matter? You don't mix business with pleasure?"

"It's not allowed." Getting involved with a taxpayer who was the subject of a tax-evasion case was a huge no-no. We'd been warned against such entanglements in our special-agent training, and the manual strictly prohibited agents from working any case in which they might have a real or perceived personal interest. That said, a silly celebrity crush wouldn't disqualify me from pursuing the taxes Brazos owed, so long as I didn't let my infatuation cloud my judgment.

Brazos cocked his head. "What if it were allowed?"

I'd boink your brains out!!! I offered him a beguiling smile. "Let's not go there."

With a chuckle, Brazos stepped over to the bar, pulled a glass from a shelf, and poured three fingers of bourbon into it. "Can I get you something?"

I was intoxicated just drinking him in. "No, thanks."

"Let me guess. Alcohol's not allowed on the job, either?"

"Right."

He raised his glass in salute. "Here's to our faithful public servants."

A few of the others raised their glasses and beers, too, calling out, "Here-here," or, "Bottoms up!"

Brazos tilted his head to indicate the booth. When he slid into one side, I slid into the other. The star set his glass down on the table and looked at me expectantly.

I pulled a file from my oversized purse and pushed it across the table. "Our records show you've never filed a tax return."

He cocked his head. "You putting me on?"

I shook my head.

His blue eyes went wide. "That can't be right."

He opened the file and flipped through the contents. A transcript showing the earnings reported to the IRS by the various companies he'd done endorsements for. Reports for royalties earned on the sales of his CDs and music downloads. Summaries of concert revenues, every show a sellout. All in all, he'd earned $43 million in the five years since he'd launched his singing career, the majority of it in the last twenty-four months as his popularity gained momentum.

I pointed to a spreadsheet at the bottom of the stack. "As you can see, the estimated tax due is nearly twenty million dollars with interest and penalties." What's more, interest was continuing to accumulate at the rate of

$2,191.78 per day. Luckily for Brazos, current rates were low, only 4 percent.

Brazos closed the file and sat back, a dumbfounded look on his face. "This is the first I've heard about a tax bill. My CPA was supposed to take care of my taxes. Something must've fallen through the cracks somewhere."

"You didn't get the notices the collections department sent you?" They'd sent a dozen or more.

He shook his head. "With me being on the road so much, I have all my mail sent to a forwarding service. I don't recall receiving anything from the IRS. Of course, I get so much fan mail the notices could have gotten lost in the shuffle."

I could understand where the guy was coming from. After I'd pursued both a charismatic televangelist and the leader of a secessionist group, I'd received mail by the tons, too, from outraged parishioners and infuriated separatists. Though I supposed calling the letters "fan mail" would be inaccurate. It was unlikely the letters to Brazos began with *Die, bitch, die!*

The fact that Brazos had been nonresponsive and impossible to access was part of the reason the collections department had turned his case over to the criminal investigations division. Like most celebrities, the man was insulated by layers of staff and managers and bodyguards, a whole regiment of gatekeepers. The collections agent had never been able to break through the barriers and speak directly with the star.

What's more, despite the fact that Brazos had millions in assets, collecting the taxes due proved impossible. He maintained only nominal cash balances in U.S. banks, and his hard assets—his tour bus, his private jet, his sixty-eight-foot yacht dubbed the *River Rat*—were mobile, constantly on the move, their whereabouts impossible to pinpoint at any given time.

"Who's your CPA?" I asked.

Normally we expected the taxpayer to take action to resolve outstanding tax issues, but in this case I'd be willing to cut Brazos some slack and contact his CPA myself for information. After all, the poor guy toured virtually nonstop according to the schedule on his Web site and, looking at him across the table, at the confounded expression on his face, it was clear the guy had no clue how to handle this problem. He might be a talented singer and songwriter but, like many celebrities, he seemed to have no idea how to run the business end of things. He'd relied on others, and those others had let him down. It wasn't the first time such a thing had happened. Besides, the tax bill didn't take his expenses into account. It was only fair to get the data from his CPA so his bill could be adjusted downward to account for his costs. Heck, the gasoline for this behemoth bus alone probably cost fifty grand a year or more. What's more, the penalties were negotiable. If he cooperated, the penalties could be significantly reduced or eliminated entirely.

Brazos shrugged in response to my question. "Honestly? I don't know who my CPA is. My agent said he'd hire someone for me." He leaned forward across the table. "Look, Tara—"

Oh, my God! He said my name! Ugh. Guess I couldn't totally quell the fan-girl in me.

"I want to straighten this out," he continued. "Let me get this information sent over to my agent so he can take care of things. Sound good?"

I looked into the depths of those river-blue eyes and found myself nodding like a bobblehead doll in a car driving over a cattle guard.

"Great." Brazos flashed his hundred-watt smile before looking back down at the file, noticing the magazine underneath and pulling it out. "What's this?" When he realized it was a copy of *Stud Farm* he laughed, a rollicking, natural laugh, like water flowing over rocks in a stream. "Want me to autograph this?"

"Would you?"

"For you, Tara? Anything."

Take me, Brazos! Now! Right here in this booth!

"Got a pen?"

"Sure." *Anything else you'd like to put your hands on, just let me know.*

I retrieved a pen from my purse and handed it to him, embarrassed to notice my hand trembling. Brazos scrawled something on the centerfold page, then closed the magazine and handed it back to me. "I'll walk you out."

When I stood from the booth, he put a hand on the small of my back to guide me to the door of the bus. I found myself slowing my pace to increase the pressure of his touch. A desperate move but, hell, *Brazos Rivers was touching me!*

We reached the exit and descended the stairs to the parking lot.

"It was wonderful meeting you," he said.

"You, too."

It had been more than wonderful. Meeting Brazos had been a dream come true.

He glanced around before reaching into the front pocket of his jeans and easing my red lace panties out. He leaned his head down until his lips were mere inches from my cheek. "Want these back?" he whispered, his breath soft and warm on my skin. "Or can I keep them to remember you?"

As a federal agent pursuing him for unpaid taxes, I probably should've been mortified that he'd realized I'd been the one to throw the red lace panties. But as a female fan, all I could think was, *Brazos Rivers touched my panties!* Would've been more fun if I'd been in them at the time, but I'd take what I could get. I gazed back into his eyes. "Keep them." *And, please, don't ever forget me.*

He offered me a sexy grin and leaned in even closer, his mouth—*those lips!*—aiming directly for mine.

Holy shit! Brazos Rivers is going to kiss me!

At the last second, I turned my head away. As much as I adored Brazos, as much as I worshipped the very ground upon which he walked in those boots with their jingle-jangling silver spurs, my heart simply wouldn't let me betray Nick. Brazos might have seemed more real to me tonight than ever before, but the chances of the two of us developing a relationship were laughably low. Besides, what I had with Nick was close to perfect. No way would I risk that, even for my celebrity crush.

Chuckling, Brazos pressed his lips softly to my temple. "You're acting awfully shy for a girl who wears red lace panties."

"I'm an enigma." An enigma wrapped in a mystery going commando.

"Everyone on board!" A thirtyish, dark-haired woman with a clipboard and a headset marched toward the bus, waving an arm to round up the stragglers. "We're heading out!"

With a final grin, Brazos Rivers stepped away from me. "Bye, Tara."

"Bye, Brazos."

chapter six

$\mathcal{F}$inished

I made my way back into the arena, feeling simultane-ously proud that I'd managed to resist Brazos's many charms and stupid that I'd passed up a once-in-a-lifetime opportunity to suck face with the superstar. Maybe I could have taken a sample of his saliva to the biology depart-ment at SMU to get a clone made. If the scientists in *Jurassic Park* could bring dinosaurs to life after billions of years of extinction, surely creating a Franken-Brazos from fresh spit should be no problem, right?

The hallway where Nick and I had had our standoff with the security guards was empty now. I walked up the corridor and spotted Nick and a uniformed marshal just outside the glass front doors. Nick leaned back against the building, his arms crossed over his chest, a scowl on his face. The marshal stood nearby, smoking a cigarette and looking up at the Dallas skyline.

When I stepped outside, Nick cast a disgusted look my way. "Brazos all done with you now?"

The marshal's gaze lowered from the skyline to us, traveling from Nick to me and back again, assessing.

I forced a smile and raised a hand in greeting to the marshal, then turned my focus to my boyfriend and partner. "Look, Nick. Neither of us would have gotten any face time with the guy if I hadn't gone to the tour bus with him. I did what I had to do. For the sake of the investigation."

He snorted. "Remind me to nominate you for special agent of the month."

The marshal stepped up. "Am I still needed here?"

"No," Nick told him. "But thanks for coming out."

"No problem."

As the marshal headed off, Nick turned his whiskey-warm eyes on me. Like Brazos, Nick had a few imperfections. A small scar on his cheek. A slightly chipped tooth. A tendency to be a little overbearing. But none of those things were deal breakers. Hell, I wasn't perfect, either. I was short, lacked curves, and tended to be a little stubborn. Okay, make that *a lot* stubborn. But despite our flaws, Nick and I worked well together, both professionally and personally.

"Did Brazos agree to pay the taxes?" Nick asked.

I nodded. "He's going to send the information to his agent."

"His agent? Why?"

"His agent has all the documentation. He was supposed to hire a CPA to get the taxes done."

"Obviously he dropped the ball." Nick frowned. "When is the agent supposed to contact you?"

Um . . . "When he's had a chance to look into things."

"You didn't set a deadline?"

Um . . . "No, but I'm sure it will be soon."

"Who's the agent?"

Um . . . I didn't have a clue who Brazos's agent was. It hadn't even crossed my mind to ask. My brain had been a little too preoccupied with the singer's sculpted, hairless chest and dazzling blue eyes.

Shit.

Shit, shit, shit!

Nick's upper lip quirked in condemnation. "At least tell me you got a direct phone number for Brazos."

The collections agent had been unable to obtain the number for Brazos's personal cell phone. None of his staff would give it to her. Neither would his parents. Not without a court order, anyway. I'd been an idiot not to ask Brazos for the number.

I gave Nick the most intelligent response I could, which was "Ummm . . ."

Nick's jaw flexed with barely restrained rage. "Do you know what hotel Brazos is staying at?"

I shook my head.

"Jesus Christ, Tara. This makes no sense!"

Nick was right. It didn't make sense. If the target had been anyone but Brazos Rivers I never would've agreed to the flimsy arrangement. I would've issued demands, set firm deadlines, locked things down.

"Come on!" Nick barked, grabbing my hand.

He pulled me after him, heading in the direction of his truck. I had to jog to keep up with his long strides.

"What are we doing?"

"We're going to follow Rivers's bus to his hotel," Nick said. "And *I* am going to deal with the guy this time."

Humiliation heated my cheeks. The spot where Brazos had kissed me no longer felt sacred and special. Instead, it felt like a mark of shame. I should have to wear a scarlet letter *S* for *Stupid*.

I'd screwed up. Royally. No ifs, ands, or buts about it.

As we approached Nick's pickup, he bleeped the door locks. He jumped into the driver's seat, while I climbed in the passenger side. Normally, he'd open my door for me but this was no time for niceties. I'd barely clicked my seat belt into place when Nick hit the gas and roared around to the back of the arena.

The tour bus was pulling out a gated exit. Nick floored his gas pedal, hurtling across the expansive parking lot, racing time as the gate began to slide closed behind the bus. But we got there an instant too late. The gate clanged into place, blocking the exit.

Nick slammed a palm against his steering wheel. "Dammit!"

Short of ramming the gate with his bumper, we were out of options here.

Nick shook his head and muttered, "Guess we'll find out which hotel he stayed at when the police report is filed tomorrow."

Nick's jibe was a reference to the rumors that Brazos had trashed several hotel rooms along his tour route. He'd allegedly pulled a chandelier from the ceiling of a suite in St. Louis when he'd drunkenly tried to swing from it. In Little Rock he'd purportedly thrown a serving platter at the wall, shattering a piece of expensive framed art, when room service had mistakenly brought him bacon strips rather than Canadian bacon as ordered. In Houston, he'd supposedly poured a bottle of bubble bath into the outdoor hot tub just for kicks. The tub had to be drained, cleaned, and refilled with fresh water. Whether this childish behavior was fact or fiction was anyone's guess, but I chose not to believe any of it. After all, my mother had always said not to believe anything I heard and only half of what I saw. My mother was a pretty smart lady. Not smart enough to catch me climbing out my bedroom window at two A.M. back in high school to attend an impromptu keg party in a pasture, but still.

I waved a hand dismissively. "You know how people

like to gossip about celebrities. All that talk about Brazos trashing hotel rooms is probably made up." At least I hoped it was. I'd hate to think he was really that immature. I also chose not to believe the rumors about his sex life, that he had multiple girlfriends along his tour route and, when none of them were available, he supplemented their services with expensive call girls. After all, if any of this were true, we'd have seen photos and videos online, right?

Ignoring me, Nick said, "Maybe we can catch up with the bus if I take another exit."

He threw his truck into reverse, backed up, and hooked a hard left, hightailing it to the nearest public exit. Unfortunately, traffic on the street was bumper to bumper with concertgoers heading home. Out the side window we saw the bus turn right onto North Houston Street. Then it disappeared from sight, taking Brazos Rivers and his luscious lips and sculpted abs with it.

Where the band was headed was anyone's guess. The Anatole? The Magnolia Hotel? The Renaissance? Phone calls to the hotels would be futile. The staff were trained not to reveal whether a celebrity guest was in residence. To prevent fans from flocking to the hotel, the bus driver would surely park the bus off-site. We were out of luck, at least for the moment.

Nick cast another disgusted glance my way. It chapped my ass even though he had every reason to do so.

Though I had *no* reason whatsoever to do so, I tossed him a disgusted glance right back. "I can get the name of Brazos's agent from the Internet."

At least I prayed I could.

A quick search on my phone produced the information. *Thank goodness.* I was tired of feeling like an idiot.

I held up my phone and pointed to the screen. "See? I've got the info right here. His agent's name is Quentin Yarbrough. His office is on St. Paul Street."

Nick's jaw flexed again. "You got lucky."

"Why are you being such an ass?" The more appropriate question would be, *Why am I being such a ditz?* But I certainly wasn't going to ask that question of myself. I knew why I was being such a ditz. Because Brazos Rivers and his blue eyes and his sexy smile had gotten my nerves as jingle-jangled as his silver spurs.

"You think *I'm* the one being an ass?" Nick cut me an incredulous look this time.

Neither of us said anything more on the ride home. I knew I should apologize, but frankly, I was embarrassed to have acted like such a star-struck schoolgirl. Maybe Nick would just forgive me without my having to grovel. He obviously had a high tolerance for ridiculous behavior or he would've traded me in long ago for a girl with better manners and more decorum.

When Nick pulled his truck into the driveway of my town house, he left the engine running and didn't bother getting out of the truck to see me inside. He looked straight ahead at my garage door. "See ya."

Okay, looked like he wouldn't be granting any reprieves. Swallowing my pride, I reached a hand over and laid it on Nick's arm. "I'm sorry, Nick. I was . . ." We both knew what I was. *An absolute moron.* No need to say it out loud, right? "Come inside."

When he still made no move to turn off the truck, I reached over and turned the truck off myself. He didn't stop me, a sure sign he'd begun to forgive me. I pulled the keys from the ignition and dropped them into my purse. I pushed out my 32As and batted my eyes at him, like the girl in the stilettos had done earlier to the security guard. "I'll make it worth your while if you know what I mean."

The look Nick cast me now was one of unfettered lust. Sheesh. Men are so easy.

Nick slid out of his truck and headed to my front door.

I met him on the porch, unlocking the door and grabbing his hand to pull him upstairs to my bedroom. Fortunately, my roommate, Alicia, was out of town for the weekend visiting her folks and working on plans for her upcoming June wedding. Other than my two cats, Nick and I had the place to ourselves.

In less than a minute, Nick and I were naked on top of my patchwork quilt and I was riding him like a twenty-five-cent mechanical pony in front of a grocery store, though without the passing foot traffic. As I threw my head back in ecstasy, words spewed from my mouth, naughty nouns and vixenlike verbs, astonishing adjectives and evocative adverbs, words I am much too mortified to repeat here so you'll just have to use your imagination. Suffice it to say that my close-call near-kiss with Brazos had me wanting to get down and dirty, fast and filthy, lusty and dusty. My creamy cat, Anne, watched from the doorway, her head tilted as she tried to make sense of the unfamiliar words streaming from my mouth.

My exuberance and dirty talk brought Nick to the brink in no time at all. He grabbed my hips, stilling me as his climax overtook him. I was near the brink myself, teetering on that edge of excruciating ecstasy.

"Don't stop!" I cried, shoving Nick's hands away and resuming the ride. *Put another quarter in the pony! I'm not done yet!*

Nick reached up and grabbed me by the arms, flipping me over onto my back on the bed.

"Yes!" I shrieked, arching my back. "Take me!"

"Nah." Nick released me. "I think I'll leave you instead."

My eyes sprang open. "What?"

Nick stood, tossed the used condom into the trash can, and slipped back into his boxer-briefs. "I'm done here."

"What!" *I was almost there! This type of torture has to be against the law!*

I sat up in the bed as he grabbed his jeans from the floor and slid them on. "You can't do this to me, Nick!"

He zipped his fly. *Zzzzzip.* "Watch me."

I grabbed a pillow and hurled it at him. "Get back in this bed! Now!" Can a woman get blue balls? Blue ovaries, perhaps? I was dying here!

He yanked his shirt and boots from the ground and headed out the bedroom door.

Naked, I sprang from my bed. Nick was halfway down the stairs when I launched myself from the upper landing onto his back. The force of my impact sent him stumbling down the remaining stairs, but luckily for both of us Nick managed to stay on his feet. All those years of playing high school football had taught him how to take a hit.

I squeezed him between my bare thighs, hanging on for dear life like a barrel racer rounding a turn. "You need to finish what you started, Nick!"

He eyed me over his shoulder. "I didn't start this. Brazos Rivers did. He can finish it."

Using his elbows, he eased me off his back and headed to the front door.

"Nooooo!" I launched myself at him again, this time staying low and taking him out at the knees.

Nick folded and collapsed to the floor of the foyer, laughing as I rolled him onto his back and fumbled with the button on his jeans. "I'm afraid you're going to be disappointed, darlin'. I'm done. At least for the next ten minutes or so."

"Aaagh!" I let go of his pants and sat back, bare-assed, on my cold tile floor. I crossed my arms over my naked chest and pouted.

"I don't know what you see in Brazos Rivers, anyway," he said. "The boy's got no hair on his chest. It's like he hasn't even reached puberty yet."

"He waxes," I spat. "Lots of men do it."

"It's unnatural."

"It would be natural for me to have hair on my legs and in my armpits," I said. "Want me to stop shaving?"

"Yuck." Nick grimaced. "Point taken."

I curled up, wrapping my arms around my legs to try to stay warm. The heat was set to sixty-eight degrees, which wasn't bad if you were fully dressed or under the covers in bed. But if you were sitting buck-naked on the floor, it was damn chilly.

Henry, my fluffy brown Maine coon, cast me a look of derision and jumped down from my TV cabinet, his tail swishing as he headed for a midnight snack in the kitchen.

A smile tugged at Nick's lips. "You look pathetic."

"I'm freezing and unfulfilled." I tilted my head. "Take some pity on me?"

He exhaled a long breath. "Oh, what the hell. Why ruin my one hundred percent satisfaction rating over a little jealousy? Give me some more of that dirty talk and I bet I can take care of you."

Two minutes later he stood to go, leaving me panting and pleased and no longer cold.

Mmm. I was definitely one hundred percent satisfied. Maybe I should write Nick a review on Yelp.

chapter seven

Don't Tell Me You Told Me So

First thing Monday morning I stopped by Quentin Yarbrough's office, a small office suite on the twenty-seventh floor of the One Dallas Centre building. The walls of the reception area sported framed photos of Yarbrough's famous clients, serving as a veritable who's who of local music talent. A female folk trio called Fiddle Dee-Dee who'd been featured on *The Today Show*. An Asian pianist who'd recently won the Van Cliburn competition in nearby Fort Worth. A married duo who sang sappy but profitable easy-listening love songs. And, of course, Yarbrough's biggest claim to fame, Brazos Rivers and the Boys of the Bayou.

Brazos had autographed the photo. "To Quent—Keep us in high cotton. Hey howdy! Brazos and the Boys."

The words he'd written in my copy of *Stud Farm* were far more suggestive. "Tara—Let me show you what's under the hat. XXX, Brazos."

Yarbrough's receptionist, a pretty yet professional-looking blonde, completed her call, jotted a message on a pink phone slip, and added it to a sizable stack accumu-

lating in a bin on the corner of her desk. She looked up at
me. "Good morning. How may I help you?"

I stepped up to her desk and handed her my card. "I'm
Special Agent Tara Holloway. I need to speak with Mr.
Yarbrough."

Her eyes scanned my card before returning to my face.
"Mr. Yarbrough's on vacation in Europe. He'll be back in
the office on Friday."

Dammit! I'd hoped to firm things up today. Not only
did I want to collect the money owed to the IRS, but I'd
hoped to get this resolved to spare Brazos the expense of
additional interest. Heck, since Friday alone his outstanding bill had accrued another $6,575.34.

"May I tell him what it's regarding?" she asked.

I wasn't sure whether she was doing her job or just being nosy, but either way it couldn't hurt to tell her. "It's
about Brazos Rivers."

She smiled an odd little smile, maybe even a *wry*
smile. What did that mean?

"Please have Mr. Yarbrough call me as soon as he returns," I said. "It's urgent."

She placed my card in the bin. "I'll let him know."

"Thanks." I turned to go, but on second thought decided to take my chances and returned to her desk.
"There's something you can do for me now."

"Yes?"

"I need a direct phone number for Brazos."

She eyed me suspiciously. "You work for the federal
government. Don't you have access to that information?"

Despite all the hullabaloo about the NSA illegally reading the general public's e-mail, law-abiding government
employees had far less access to personal data than people
might expect. Certain information could not be legally
shared across agencies, or even within an agency. My

exhaustive search had turned up no landline or cell number registered under the Brazos Rivers pseudonym or his real name. Either Brazos used one of those untraceable prepaid cell phones or the number for his phone had been registered in someone else's name.

"There's no listing for him in any database," I said.

The woman shook her head. "I'm sorry. I'm not authorized to give out personal information about our clients."

I'd figured as much, but it never hurt to try. Sometimes people feared repercussions if they failed to cooperate. Others assumed they were legally required to give out information when requested by a federal agent. Of course I did nothing to persuade them otherwise, though, when asked, I told them honestly that they had a right to refuse to provide the information unless directed by a court order. Fortunately, most didn't think to question me.

"Understood," I told the woman. I'd just as soon wrestle the woman to the floor and search her files for the information I sought, but no sense jeopardizing the job I'd only recently got back. "Have a nice day."

Frustrated and ashamed, I headed over to my office at the IRS, hoping Nick wouldn't grill me. No such luck. The second I reached my office door he looked up from his desk across the hall.

"How'd it go at Yarbrough's office?" he asked. "Did you set a firm deadline for him to file Dusty Boogers's tax returns?"

"His name's not Dusty Boogers," I said, rolling my eyes. "It's Brazos Rivers."

"Actually it's Winthrop Merriweather, remember?" Nick emitted a half grunt, half chuckle (a *grunkle*?). "Frankly, I'd prefer Dusty Boogers to Winthrop any day."

My fingers tightened around the handle of my briefcase and I exhaled a long breath. "Yarbrough's out of the country until Friday."

Nick's expression was smug. "I hate to say I told you so—"

"Then don't!" I snapped, my ass freshly chapped by Nick's smirk. "Besides, Friday's only four days from now and I've got other cases that need my attention."

It was true. Though none of my other investigations were nearly as big as the case against Brazos, there were several on my plate. In fact, I had a meeting scheduled for six o'clock this very evening with a woman named Katie Dunne, a bookkeeper who worked at Palo Pinto Energy. PPE was a privately held company involved in natural gas exploration. Katie had called the IRS a week ago to blow the whistle on some shady goings-on at the business. Though she'd been at work when I called her back and was thus forced to be cryptic in our phone conversation, she assured me she'd give me all the details tonight.

Nick raised his hands in surrender. "Whatever you say."

Him acting like I was being unreasonable and irrational chapped my ass even more. Much more of this ass-chapping and I'd need to coat my butt in Vaseline.

I stormed into my office and slammed my door shut behind me. I wasn't about to look at his smug face all day, even if it was a handsome smug face.

I spent the rest of the morning and the early afternoon stewing at Nick and looking over documentation in a case against a middle-aged man who detailed luxury cars. He made a pretty penny washing, waxing, and vacuuming the vehicles. With a fairly regular clientele, he pulled down sixty Gs a year, but had reported none of those Gs to the IRS. Not only had he failed to pay his taxes due, he'd also filed fraudulent claims for disability benefits from Social Security, food stamps, and housing assistance from HUD. With me on the case, his days of illegally sucking on the public teat would soon be over.

By three that afternoon, my chair and butt had nearly

become one, and I feared if I didn't get up and move around my buns would become flat as pancakes. I decided to head out for my meeting in Palo Pinto a little early. It would be a two-hour drive, and I might as well beat the traffic, right? Besides, according to the documentation in my file on Brazos Rivers, his parents owned a ranch just west of the town of Mineral Wells. The ranch was roughly on my way to Palo Pinto. No harm in taking a look-see, even if it was primarily just to satisfy my personal curiosity.

I packed up my briefcase, grabbed my purse, and tiptoed to my office door, cracking it open and peeking out. I waited a few moments before heading out of my office, strategically timing my departure while Nick was tied up with a phone call. Didn't want him asking where I was going. What he didn't know he couldn't get jealous about, right? No sense giving him another reason to withhold sex. After all, a woman has needs. Besides, Valentine's Day was coming up shortly and I didn't want him upset with me when he picked out my gift. Otherwise he might go with something I had no interest in or use for, like a frying pan, a vacuum cleaner, or a subscription to *Popular Science*.

I'd already bought Nick's Valentine's Day gift. A bottle of Brazos Rivers's Whitewater cologne. In retrospect, maybe that hadn't been the best choice. Then again, maybe I could slap a fake label on the bottle so he wouldn't know the difference.

I made my way down to the parking lot and climbed into my red convertible BMW. Still too chilly to put the top down. Rats. Nothing like the wind in your hair to make a person feel alive. After spending most of the day at my desk, I needed to live a little. I had to settle for cracking the window a couple of inches.

I headed out of downtown, traveling west on I-30.

Knowing both that it would be a long night and that swimsuit weather would be here soon, I picked up a skinny no-whip latte on my way. The drink would provide enough caffeine to keep me safely awake for hours, while containing few enough calories to keep a roll of fat from developing around my belly.

I cranked up the Brazos Rivers CD in my stereo and sang along as I drove.

> *Let me be your bronco, baby,*
> *I will buck you, take a ride,*
> *No need for a saddle, baby,*
> *I will buck you, hang on tight.*

Yeah, yeah. I know. Oversexed man-whore. But what about this ballad?

> *I'm not half the man I used to be,*
> *Because I'm only whole when I'm with you.*
> *Now that you're gone, there's a piece of me missing,*
> *There's just no me without you.*

Nick was wrong. There was much more to Brazos than met the eye. This song was deep and moving, like a river after a hard rain.

I continued on until I-30 merged with I-20, and drove a few more miles before taking the exit for Weatherford. As I entered the town, my GPS told me to turn onto US-180. Obeying, I headed down the road, passing through the town of Mineral Wells and emerging into the rural area to the west.

My heart beat as fast as a drum in my chest. *Almost there.*

One turn onto a country road and two miles later, a white pipe fence appeared ahead, enclosing the twenty-acre

riverfront spread dubbed the Brazos Bend Ranch. I
slowed to a crawl.

Though the deed to the property was in the name of
Brazos's parents, Marcella and Winthrop Merriweather
VI, we suspected that Brazos had paid for the acreage and
custom-built house. Fortunately for his mother and father,
the property had been purchased before the IRS had issued its tax assessment. Although gifts made while an assessment was outstanding could be set aside, the fact that
the deed had been recorded years ago insulated the property from seizure. The fact that the IRS couldn't legally
get its hands on the place wouldn't stop me from checking it out, though.

The place was what Southerners call a gentleman's
ranch, meaning it wasn't really a ranch at all, but rather
an estate in the country where wealthy folk could play
cowboy. Though the ranch comprised sufficient acreage
for cattle or horses, there was no barn on the property and
no livestock to be seen unless you counted the jackrabbit
hopping along the fence line.

A hundred yards back from the road sat the main residence, a two-story gray stone monstrosity that looked more
castle than house. The design included a towering turret
on one end, a breezeway between the expansive main house
and generous guest quarters, and a wraparound balcony
with views of the countryside in front and the river in
back.

As I eased past, my eyes spotted the tour bus parked
beside the detached five-car garage. Looked like the singer
and his band were taking advantage of their time in north
Texas to visit his folks. The fact that Brazos was a family
man only made me adore him all the more.

At the back of the lot sat an expansive dock and boat-
house in the same gray stone as the house. While the Brazos River was too narrow and shallow at this point for

motorized boats, the waterway was perfect for the canoes and kayaks stacked on the dock.

On the far side of the house lay an asphalt airstrip complete with a nylon wind sock on a pole. I was no expert, but the runway looked long enough for the singer's private jet to land on.

All along the front fence-line sat teddy bears, flowers, and notes left by fans for Brazos. Ridiculous, really. What was a twenty-two-year-old man going to do with a teddy bear? And what straight man gave a rat's ass about flowers? He might be interested in the risqué boudoir photos a few of the women had left, though.

The sounds of multiple motors caught my ear and four all-terrain vehicles popped up over a rise near the far end of the property. Looked like some of the gang had decided to get their redneck on. From this distance it was impossible to identify the riders with certainty but, given that all were dark-headed and similarly sized, my guess would be the Boys of the Bayou. They raced down the incline and across an open area, whooping it up.

I made a U-turn on the narrow road, my tires spinning momentarily in the gravel at the edge before regaining traction. I drove past the ranch again, a little faster this time lest someone mistake me for a stalker.

When I'd passed the ranch, I slowed to a stop on the road and typed Katie Dunne's address into my GPS. I never would've gotten away with such a thing in Dallas, where there were always two or three people riding your bumper. But out here there wasn't a car in sight. Well, other than the black Ferrari Spider sailing up the road toward me.

Hmm.

A pricey sports car wasn't the type of vehicle you'd expect to see out here in cattle and oil country, where pickup trucks and SUVs ruled the day.

As the car drew near, my eyes caught the word on the personalized plates.

BRAZEN.

Brazos sat at the wheel, sporting mirrored sunglasses and his cowboy hat. Just as quickly as I'd recognized him he was gone, the car having blown past me. My eyes watched Brazos in my rearview mirror. He pulled up to the iron entrance gate, unrolled his window, and typed a code into the keypad. A few seconds later the gate slid open. He gunned the engine, the tires squealing and kicking up a cloud of dust. The car streamed along the inside drive, screeching to a stop at the garage.

Okay, so maybe Brazos was a little immature. But who could blame him? He'd barely reached the age of eighteen when he'd recorded his first hit. The fantasy life he lived on the road probably hadn't helped, either. Besides, if I had a Ferrari, I'd drive like a bat out of hell, too. Otherwise you might as well own a Yaris, right?

Retrieving my tablet from my briefcase, I searched the DMV records to see who owned the Ferrari. If the car belonged to Brazos, it would be fair game. Hell, I'd offer to seize the thing myself just so I'd get a chance to drive it.

The information popped up on the screen. Sure enough, the car was registered to Winthrop Merriweather VII. The data indicated the car had been purchased only a month ago.

I whipped out my field glasses, turned around in my seat, and took visual aim at the ranch. By this time, Brazos had gone into the house and there was no activity outside other than a squirrel digging up a long-forgotten pecan hidden in the front flower bed.

I supposed I shouldn't feel disappointed that I didn't get to see more of Brazos. After all, I hadn't expected to see the guy at all. But the quick glimpse I'd gotten made me feel a little heartsick. His love ballads touched me, moved me. He seemed to understand love, to feel it in his soul, to acknowledge it openly in a way that most men, including Nick, wouldn't.

Don't get me wrong. I knew Nick was crazy about me. But the L-word? It had yet to pass his lips—other than when directed at his mother's barbecued chicken.

Did Nick love me? To be honest, I wasn't entirely sure. The two of us got along great, enjoyed many of the same activities, had had similar upbringings. Other than our little spat Saturday night, our sex life was spectacular. We approached life with the same attitude, that our time on earth was an opportunity to be seized and savored. We applied the same gusto to our work.

Of course we had our differences, too. While I loved to indulge in exotic ethnic foods, Nick was a meat-and-potatoes man. My roommates included two cats, while Nick shared his town house with a sweet, half-blind old dog. And while I thought Brazos Rivers hung the moon, Nick considered him nothing more than a prepackaged marketing gimmick. These differences were minor, though. None were deal breakers.

Did I love Nick? I was pretty sure I did but, to be honest, I was afraid to acknowledge it. Love made a person vulnerable, and vulnerability made me uncomfortable. I liked to feel in charge, under control. Looked like Brazos Rivers wasn't the only one with some growing up to do, huh?

chapter eight

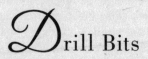

Drill Bits

My scenic tour now complete, I set off for Palo Pinto, an unincorporated town with a population of 425 according to the most recent census data.

On the drive over, several natural gas rigs caught my eye. While rigs within the city limits of Dallas and Fort Worth were enclosed to protect surrounding homes and businesses in the event of a blowout, the wells out here in the boonies included no such precautionary structures. Apparently they weren't required by law. No surprise, given that the oil and gas industry had a powerful lobby, labor unions were virtually nonexistent in Texas, and the risks of collateral damage were significantly less out here in the country. After all, what's the worst that could happen if a blowout occurred in these wide-open fields? A few cows would be grilled earlier than intended, but that's about it.

Several years ago, when a large gas reserve had been discovered under the land in north Texas, energy companies had flocked to the area, each trying to be the first to secure leases from the landowners. Thrilled by the unexpected boon, landowners were happy to sign away their rights in return for a sizable option payment and future royalties. Heck, if it worked for the Beverly Hillbillies, why not other folks? It seemed like a win-win.

But Texans' relationship with oil had always been a love-hate relationship, a cycle of boom and bust, fortune and failure. Things proved no different with natural gas. When companies began fracking in the area, the love affair between the landowners and energy companies began to sour.

The normally seismically calm area experienced a startling series of earthquakes. The fracking process produced an enormous amount of wastewater, which was injected deep into the ground for disposal, causing the earth to destabilize. Nine earthquakes struck an area in Johnson County in a five-week period. Texans could face down an F-5 tornado and not blink an eye, but set the ground shaking under them and you'd have them quaking in their boots.

As if the earthquakes weren't bad enough, the wastewater also contained a number of toxic chemicals, including uranium, hydrochloric acid, mercury, and formaldehyde. Once the residents learned this disturbing bit of information, they began to fear the health risks posed by the toxins.

The wells also posed the risk of explosion. A blast at a well in Buffalo, Texas, killed two workers and injured five more. More recently, a blowout in a well near Granbury killed one gas company employee and injured multiple others, shook up both houses and residents, and spouted a geyser of flame visible for miles. Numerous other wells had caught fire, too, with nearby residents exposed to smoke and toxic gases.

The love affair over, many landowners wanted a divorce but found themselves bound by the contracts they'd signed. Several filed lawsuits, alleging property damage

and exposure to hazardous chemicals. Others had appealed
to the Environmental Protection Agency for help. But
big oil had big bucks and fought the allegations, claiming
they were fallacious, inaccurate, and overstated. I, on the
other hand, feared a race of six-legged, hundred-pound
horned toads would rise up and attack Dallas. But perhaps I'd watched too many Godzilla movies with my
brothers when I was young.

As the sun began to set, my GPS directed me to turn
down various country roads, then ordered me onto an un-
marked, one-lane road. Shortly thereafter, the voice ordered
me to turn left into a rain-rutted dirt driveway.

I pulled to a stop in front of the Dunne home. The place
could not have been more different from the Brazos Bend
Ranch. Rather than stone, the Dunnes' house was constructed of aluminum. Instead of a five-car detached garage that housed ATVs and a new Ferrari, the single-wide
mobile home sported an attached drive-thru carport that
contained a Ford pickup and a Kia Sportage, both of
which were older models. In lieu of the pipe fence and iron
gate, this place featured a small backyard enclosed with
chicken wire. But what the place lacked in luxury, it made
up for in hominess. The yellow siding and the purple pan-
sies in the flower bed were cheery and bright, even in the
dim evening light. What's more, the white poodle mix in
the front window barked happily and wagged its tail as if
to welcome me to her humble home.

With the dog having announced my arrival, I didn't
have to knock on the door. Katie opened it as I ascended
the two steps to the threshold.

Katie's hair was the reddish-brown color of chili powder and hung in loose, long waves down to her waist. Her
skin sported approximately two hundred freckles per
square inch. Her brown eyes bore only one coat of mas-
cara and her lips were left natural. She wore jeans, scuffed

boots, and a green cable-knit sweater. She was younger than I'd expected, only in her early twenties. With a crease between her brows and her lower lip clamped between her teeth, she appeared anxious and upset.

As we women sized each other up, a skinny young man, hardly more than a boy, stepped up behind Katie. His dark hair was shorn short in an easy-care style. He wore patched canvas cargo pants and a heavy-duty cotton work shirt. His clothes and face were smudged with grease. He must've just arrived home from work. His teeth were crooked but his smile was warm.

I held out my hand. "Hi, Mr. and Mrs. Dunne. I'm Special Agent Tara Holloway."

Katie shook my hand. "Call me Katie."

"Doug," said her husband, likewise shaking my hand.

I reached down to pet the curly-haired dog, who had jumped up on my leg and begun to sniff my pants, probably smelling my cats. "Hey, there, pup."

Katie held the door open and gestured for me to come inside. The door opened directly into the small living area. Three boys, ranging in age from twelve months to four years, played with plastic army men on the floor. All three had their mother's reddish hair and freckles.

"Bang-bang!" hollered the oldest boy as he aimed his soldier at another. "Bang-bang!"

A cheap particle-board bookcase took up one wall. On top of it was a photo of Katie and Doug dressed in prom attire. Next to it sat their wedding photo, clearly not taken by a professional photographer but charming and touching all the same. The two hadn't aged a bit from one photo to the next.

"High school sweethearts?" I surmised.

Doug grinned. "Got married the first weekend after graduation."

Wow. The two hadn't even been old enough to drink

champagne at their own wedding. Heck, before reaching
twenty-one, they'd given birth to at least one of their boys,
maybe two. The government wouldn't trust them with a
beer, but they could raise a kid. Ironic, huh?

The boys hardly noticed as we stepped over them and
went into the kitchen. Katie offered me a drink but I declined. The three of us took seats at the dinette table.

"Cute kids," I said.

Katie smiled. "They keep us busy, that's for sure."

"Pains in the butt is what they are!" Doug called to his
boys in an exaggerated voice, his smile belying his words.

The oldest boy pointed his army man at his dad, a grin
on his face, too. "*You're* a pain in the butt, Daddy!"

Doug stood, putting his hands on his hips and narrowing his eyes at his son in feigned fury. "Do you need a
whooping?"

His son stood, too, likewise putting his hands on his
hips. "I'd like to see you try."

Doug hurled himself toward his son, scooping the
child up in his arms and spinning around, the boy squealing with glee all the while. Clearly, the interaction was a
ritual for the two.

While I pulled a legal pad from my briefcase to take
notes, Katie retrieved a slightly bent manila folder from a
tote bag. She laid the folder on the table between us and
stared at me, still chewing her lip. Doug returned to the
table, slipping back into his seat.

Katie leaned back, as if afraid to get too close to me.
"Everything I tell you is confidential, right?"

I didn't want to scare her off, but I didn't want to lie,
either. "At this point, yes. But depending on how things
go, you could be asked to provide an affidavit or testify in
court." Honest but nonthreatening. No sense throwing out
the word *subpoena* or she might clam up.

She bit her lip again. "I'm afraid I could lose my job

for talking to you. Doug works for Palo Pinto Energy, too, as a roughneck. If we both end up out of work . . ."

She didn't finish her sentence, but she didn't have to. The fearful glance she sent her sons' way finished it for her. There wasn't much in the way of industry out here in the sticks. If she and her husband both lost their jobs, they'd be unable to provide for their three young sons.

I reached across the table and put a reassuring hand on her arm. "I'll do my best to make sure your family doesn't suffer any repercussions."

Katie and Doug exchanged glances. He nodded for her to continue.

Scooting her chair closer to the table, she opened the folder and pulled out copies of bank statements for PPE's operating account. She laid the documents in front of me. "See the entries I've circled?"

I looked through the paperwork. The circled entries showed a $7,500 cash withdrawal made from the account each Friday. The first had taken place seven months ago, in July of the preceding year. My mind quickly did the math. The accumulated withdrawals totaled over two hundred large so far.

When I looked back up, Katie continued. "My boss, Larry Burkett, has me make a cash withdrawal every Friday. When he first asked me to do it, I asked him what the money was for. He said he got a special cash-only deal on drill bits from a new supplier."

I didn't know squat about the oil and gas industry, but in many lines of business cash discounts were common. "Did the arrangement seem strange to you?"

"Yes," she replied. "If Mr. Burkett was supposedly getting such a great deal on bits from the new company, why did he continue to order from Hughley-Baker, our existing supplier?"

Good question. "Had drilling activity picked up?"

Doug provided the response to that question. "No. If anything it had slowed down by that point."

"Interesting." I turned my attention back to Katie. "Tell me more about the cash. Does someone from the supplier pick it up when the bits are delivered?"

"Supposedly," Katie said, "but I've never actually seen the cash change hands. I work Monday through Friday, but the deliveries from the new supplier always take place on the weekends. Mr. Burkett has me lock the cash in the safe. When I get to work the following Monday the cash is gone."

"What's the name of the company that sells the discounted bits?"

"My boss claimed it was a company called Ector Oilfield Supply out of Odessa, but when I tried to look them up on the Internet nothing came up. No Web site. No address. No phone number. Nothing."

"Wasn't the contact information printed on the shipping receipts?"

"Mr. Burkett never gave me any shipping documents. That's part of the reason why I'm worried. I don't have any documentation in the file to prove where the money went."

"Nothing?" I asked. "Not a purchase order or an e-mail confirmation or anything?"

She shook her head. "Mr. Burkett said he placed the orders by phone. He claimed the company was a small outfit that operated on handshakes and trust."

Not entirely implausible, especially in a good ol' boy business like oil and gas. Despite the fact that it was an enormous industry, the number of key players was surprisingly small and tight-knit. Heck, back in 1934 a group of oilmen founded the Dallas Petroleum Club, a private club exclusively for oil and gas executives. The club continued to thrive today, providing a place for oil execs to network.

Forth Worth, Houston, Midland, San Antonio, and other major cities had their own Petroleum Clubs, as well.

"Were you able to verify whether the bits had actually been delivered?" I asked.

"No," Katie said. "Mr. Burkett or one of the foremen always takes care of the deliveries. There's all different types of bits, diamond bits and roller cones and a bunch of others. Doug could tell you about them, but I wouldn't know one from another."

Diamonds, huh? Given their strength, I supposed it made sense to put them on drill bits. Still, it seemed a shame to waste a precious stone on digging a hole when it could just as easily have graced my finger or ears imbedded in a nice gold setting. I made a note on my pad. "Where are the bits stored?"

"All of the equipment and tools are kept in a locked warehouse behind the office until they're needed on the drilling sites."

"Can you access the warehouse?"

She paused a moment as she seemed to consider my question. "Mr. Burkett's never given me authority to go into the warehouse. The equipment is worth a lot of money so he's real picky about who goes back there. He only issues keys to the foremen."

Nothing she'd told me so far sounded necessarily unusual. It wasn't uncommon for employees to steal supplies or equipment from their employers, so nobody could blame the man for taking precautions.

Katie continued. "But he did give me a spare set of keys to all the buildings and the locks at the drilling sites. You know, just in case he or one of the foremen loses theirs. I keep them locked in the safe in my office."

Interesting . . . "You said Mr. Burkett never gave you permission to go into the warehouse," I said, "but did he ever give you explicit instructions *not* to go in there?"

She chewed her lip again. "Well, no. Not exactly."

A potential loophole. I wondered if I could exploit it. "Did you tell your boss you couldn't find any information on Ector Oilfield Supply?"

"Yes," Katie said. "He told me that sometimes companies have divisions or subsidiaries that operate under different names and there was no need for me to worry myself over it."

Again, his explanation could make sense. Then again, it could have been complete and utter bullshit.

"To be honest," Katie said, "I was afraid to push the issue. Mr. Burkett's been on edge lately, what with the lawsuit and all."

"Lawsuit?"

Doug jumped in now. "It's a big 'un. One of them class action things. Bunch of ranchers from all over north Texas claiming that fracking has polluted their water wells and caused cancer and all sorts of other bad stuff."

I eyed Doug. "You think there's any truth to that?"

He looked away, as if not wanting to face the fact that he might have played an inadvertent part in contaminating the environment and making things rough for area ranchers. After a moment, he turned back to me and shrugged. "Hell if I know. I'm not a scientist." He paused a moment, took a deep breath and, in a softer voice, went on. "That said, I wouldn't be at all surprised. Oil and gas is dirty, dangerous business."

A dirty, dangerous business that paid for the roof over their heads and put food on their table. I had to admire the Dunnes for coming forward, especially when it wasn't entirely clear that anything wrong had taken place. Still, I'd learned to listen to my gut and apparently Katie had, too. The situation hadn't sat right with her and my gut was telling me she might have reason to feel uneasy. Nonetheless, I had to know her motives. A good informant could be critical to an investigation. On the other hand, a disgruntled employee with a vendetta could use the IRS as an unwitting weapon, siccing us on their employers, wasting our valuable time and making us look like overeager witch hunters for going after an innocent party.

"Please don't take this the wrong way, Katie," I said. "But what's in this for you? Why tell the IRS? And why now instead of when the cash transactions started last summer?"

She looked taken aback, which told me her motives were pure. Cheaters and con artists didn't offend so easily.

Katie swallowed hard. "What finally got me to call was when Mr. Burkett made me responsible for the tax returns PPE filed this year. He hires a CPA to prepare the returns based on the records we provide, but I was the one who had to sign the form stating that the return was accurate to the best of my knowledge. That made me nervous. I don't know much about taxes. How was I supposed to know whether the return was computed right or not? And I can't really say what happened to the cash I left in the safe, whether it was really spent on drill bits or not. I didn't want to end up getting in trouble myself." She glanced over at her boys, tears filling her eyes. "I don't want to end up in jail."

"Don't worry, Katie." I offered what I hoped was a reassuring smile. "With you coming forward like this and cooperating there's little chance of that happening." Assuming, of course, that everything she'd told me so far was true, which I suspected it was. Besides, it wasn't even clear that anything untoward had happened here. Everything Mr. Burkett had told her could be true. Where there's smoke, there isn't always fire. Sometimes there's just a hippie in Jesus sandals and a tie-dyed T-shirt sucking on a bong.

"What kind of accounting training do you have, Katie?"

"I took one bookkeeping course at a trade school

several years ago. They taught us how to use the Quick-
Books software and some basics about recordkeeping,
but that's the only formal education I've got. The woman
who had the job at PPE before me trained me for a week
before she retired."

"Do you handle the payroll and payroll taxes?"

"No. We outsource that."

"Royalty payments?"

"Those are outsourced, too."

Neither of those facts surprised me. PPE probably had
hundreds of oilfield workers on staff and thousands of
landowners receiving royalties. Handling those payments
would overwhelm a single accounting clerk.

"What about PPE's bills?" I asked. "Do you decide
who gets paid and when?"

"No. Mr. Burkett tells me which bills to pay and when
to send the payments. I'm not authorized to issue any payments without getting his okay first."

"Not even routine bills, like phone and electricity and
water?"

She shook her head.

"What about income?"

She explained that PPE's only source of income came
from retail providers who bought gas from PPE to resell to
their customers. "The payments to PPE are deposited elec-
tronically. I look over the bank records online to make
sure the payments have been received and then I update
the customers' accounts in our system, but no payments
are run through the office."

From what Katie had told me I gleaned that she served
primarily as a data entry and file clerk, with no real authority over financial matters. In most situations like this,
where the in-house accounting staff had only nominal
education and served a limited role, the owners of the
company were the ones to verify the tax returns. The fact

that Burkett had put the responsibility on Katie could be a sign that he was trying to protect himself, to put himself in a position to shift blame should the tax return contain questionable information. Katie could easily become a scapegoat. Then again, Mr. Burkett was undoubtedly a busy guy. Maybe he'd simply delegated the duty to Katie to get the task off his plate. And since she input the numbers into the system and prepared the reports, he might have figured she'd be more in touch with the financial data.

"If Burkett isn't spending the cash on drill bits," I said, "what do you suppose he might be spending it on?"

Katie lifted her shoulders. Doug raised his palms. I supposed two young parents who were probably just making ends meet couldn't imagine what a person with an excess of money would spend it on.

I tossed out some possibilities. "What about gambling?" I asked. "He ever take trips to Vegas? Shreveport? Those Indian casinos up in Oklahoma?"

"Not that I know of," Katie replied. "He doesn't take much time off. He's kind of a workaholic."

"Any chance he's got a drug problem?" He could be snorting the cash up his nose or smoking it, maybe popping pills.

"I doubt it," she said. "I've never seen any signs that he might be on drugs."

"No red eyes?" I asked. "Jittery behavior? Moodiness? Sniffles?"

Katie shook her head. "Not that I've noticed. But we don't interact a lot. When he's in the office he spends most of his day at his desk with the door closed."

"What about a secret second family?"

Another shake of the head.

"Maybe he's a cross-dresser and he spends the cash on Prada shoes and Kate Spade handbags?"

Katie didn't bother to shake her head this time. She just stared at me as if I were crazy, which maybe I was.

Might as well eliminate as many possibilities as possible. "Could he have a health issue? Had some plastic surgery?" He could've gotten a face-lift. After all, if Jerry Jones, the owner of the Dallas Cowboys, could do it, why not other men? Or maybe Burkett had gone for a penis enlargement. We'd seen it all at the IRS. Not much would surprise me.

"I don't see how," she said. "He hasn't taken more than a day or two off from work since last summer."

"And he's still as wrinkled as ever," Doug said.

Looked like whatever Burkett was spending the money on was for him to know and me to find out. Part of me hoped it really was drill bits. I had a large caseload and would love to put a quick close to this investigation. Still, another part of me hoped this case would turn into a public scandal. I thrived on action, after all, and after my embarrassing excessive-force trial I could use a big win.

I thanked Katie for the information, stood, and handed her my business card. "I'll be in touch."

chapter nine

$\mathscr{D}$rive By

Evening had settled in by the time I left the Dunnes'
home. I found myself grateful to be born in the age of
technology, knowing I'd be hopelessly lost out here in the
middle of nowhere without my GPS, especially in the dark
where landmarks and road signs could easily be overlooked.

Before heading back to Dallas, I decided to take a detour by the headquarters for Palo Pinto Energy. Might as
well after driving all this way, huh?

The administrative office was in a small, one-story brick
building six miles north of town on Farm to Market Road 4.
I drove slowly past, taking things in. Security cameras were
mounted on each corner of the building. Behind the brick
building was a large prefab warehouse well lit by floodlights. Security cameras were mounted on each corner of
the warehouse, too, as well as over each door. Various types
of trucks and trailers were parked alongside the warehouse.

The warehouse and truck lot were surrounded by a
ten-foot reinforced fence topped with barbed wire. In
case thieves weren't scared off by the sign that read

WARNING—ALARM WILL SOUND IF GATE IS OPENED, a
trio of Dobermans lay in front of their doghouses in an
open pen near the warehouse doors, ready to tear any in-
truders limb from limb.

PPE's closest neighbors were an Angus rancher a half
mile to the north and a feed store a quarter mile to the
south. Though I chose to live in the city now, I'd grown up
in a small town in east Texas and could appreciate these
wide-open spaces. The stars were brighter out here, the air
cleaner, the nights quieter, the pace slower.

Just for grins, I pulled over at a historical marker a mile
south of the PPE complex, cut my engine, and climbed
out. Stopping at an unknown place in the dark of night
might seem unwise, but it's not like there would be muggers or serial killers lurking around out here. Of course
there could be a rattlesnake or coyote, but with my Glock
holstered at my waist I could easily dispatch either should
they set their sights on me.

I took a deep breath, filling my lungs with the cold,
fresh country air and looked up at the sky. The stars twinkled overhead, along with the lights of a jet bound for the
Dallas-Fort Worth airport eighty miles to the east.

Baaaa.

A shriek tore from my throat and instinctively I jumped
backward, yanking my gun from its holster. The source
of the sound was a black nanny goat in the pasture a few
feet away. She'd stepped up to the fence to check me out
and had issued the sound in greeting.

I shoved my gun back into the holster, walked over to
the fence, and reached over it to scratch her back. "You
liked to scare me to death," I told her. "You're lucky I
didn't shoot you."

Three or four other goats wandered over, curious about
the woman at the fence and hoping to get their backs
scratched, too.

"Hey, y'all." I reached out with both hands to deliver maximum scratching.

One of the goats nibbled on my sleeve, realized I was neither tasty nor edible, and wandered off, disappointed. Another sampled my shoe with the same result. A third lowered his head and butted another in the ribs, shoving him aside and stealing his place in line for scratching services.

When the herd had been scratched to their satisfaction and left me at the fence, I wandered back to the marker. Curious about the significance of this remote place, I stepped up to the plaque, punching the flashlight app on my cell phone to illuminate the words.

The marker provided a quick history lesson. This land had once been the homestead of a man named George Webb Slaughter, who served as a courier for General Sam Houston in the Texas War for Independence. Slaughter's claim to fame was that he'd once taken a dispatch to Colonel William B. Travis at the Alamo in San Antonio. Slaughter's marriage to Sarah Mason in 1836 was the first sanctioned under the laws of the Republic of Texas. The couple went on to have eleven children. I could see why. Didn't seem like there was much to do out here in the way of entertainment but scratch goats or fornicate. Slaughter later served as both a preacher and a practitioner of saddlebag medicine. His family survived several Indian attacks. No surprise there. With eleven kids they had their own army regiment.

My history lesson complete and my toes numb from the near-freezing outside temperature, I climbed back into my car and headed home.

My cell phone rang the next morning as I dug into my usual breakfast, a heaping bowl of Fruity Pebbles. Wheaties might be the breakfast of champions, but these colorful flakes looked much more cheerful in the morning. Alicia sat across the table from me, sipping coffee in her shiny satin robe and looking like death warmed over. Her normally sleek platinum hair stuck out at odd angles, and her eyes were puffy and underscored with shadows.

Alicia worked in the tax department at Martin & McGee, a downtown accounting firm where I'd worked for four years, too, before joining the IRS. Gotta say, I didn't miss the long workdays of tax season. Not that I didn't put in a lot of overtime in my job as a special agent, but at least my current job didn't keep me chained to a desk all day. In some ways I was a kid who'd never grown up. I still liked to go outside for recess.

The readout on my phone indicated Nick was calling. I punched the button to accept the call and put the phone on speaker. Unable to talk with the crunchy blob of cereal in my mouth, I offered a grunt in greeting.

"Good morning to you, too," Nick said.

I swallowed my bite. "You caught me in the middle of breakfast."

"Any chance you're naked?"

Alicia snickered into her coffee.

"Nope," I replied to Nick. "I'm showered, shampooed, and fully dressed."

"Damn. Too late for a quickie, huh?"

"Yeah," I said. "But you can put me down for a nooner in the supply closet."

Alicia groaned and left the table, taking her coffee upstairs to my guest room where she was currently squatting rent-free until her nuptials this summer.

"Pencil me in for the nooner," Nick said. "For now, bring me a couple of fried baloney sandwiches. Nutty's being finicky this morning."

Nick lived in a town house on the same block as me. The arrangement was perfect given the current state of our relationship—serious and exclusive, but with each of us retaining a modicum of independence for the time being. Nick's dog, Nutty, was a golden retriever mix. The two had been best buddies since Nutty was a pup and Nick was a teenager. Despite the top-notch care Nick provided, old age could only be held at bay for so long. The elderly dog had cataracts, bad breath, and a flatulence problem, as well as a rapidly progressing case of arthritis. He'd also become much more picky about his meals, turning up his nose at the steaks and hot dogs Nick tried to feed him by hand. But the one thing the dog would never refuse was one of my homemade fried baloney sandwiches. Nick had tried frying them up himself, following my exact directions, but Nutty knew the sandwiches Nick offered him weren't mine. The dog was a canine connoisseur.

"Will do." I could never refuse that sweet dog. "I'll be down in ten."

I wolfed down the rest of my cereal, stuck my bowl in the sink, and retrieved the butter and baloney from the fridge. I slung a spoonful of butter into the pan and waited for it to melt before slapping two slabs of baloney into the pan, too. In a few seconds the lunch meat began to curl up and quiver on the hot surface. Using a spatula, I flipped the meat over to ensure it was cooked on both sides. When the baloney was done, I placed each piece between two slices of white bread thickly spread with mayonnaise. Martha Stewart would surely cringe, but me and Nutty happened to like this white-trash food.

After wrapping the sandwiches in foil and gathering up my purse and briefcase, I stepped to the bottom of the stairs. "Bye, Alicia!"

A muffled reply came from the bathroom. "See you later!"

I hopped into my car and motored down the block to Nick's place. He met me at the door, his face puckered with worry. Nick was normally a pragmatic, stoic guy. Seeing him looking so anxious made my heart clench. That cinched it. I'd buy a pair of Mavericks tickets for Valentine's Day. That would take Nick's mind off his dog's rapidly declining condition. I'd see if Alicia and her fiancé, Daniel, wanted to go with us. Christina and Ajay, too. Christina was a DEA agent I'd worked with on previous cases and with whom I'd developed a lasting friendship. Ajay was her smart-ass boyfriend, a doctor who had treated me for multiple ailments including a burn caused by an errant cigarette that had been part of an undercover outfit, a stab wound inflicted by a cockfighting rooster, and a skin rash caused by a sexual-enhancement product. A triple date would be fun.

I glanced around as I stepped inside Nick's town house, looking for Nutty but not seeing him anywhere. "Where is he?"

"Kitchen floor."

I walked to the kitchen to find Nutty lying on his side on a folded nylon sleeping bag Nick had laid on the floor for him. A full bowl of food sat in front of him, as well as another bowl filled with his favorite treats. Neither had been touched. My heart squeezed in my chest.

Nutty lifted his head and his wagging tail brushed against the sleeping bag with a *swish-swish*. He made no move to get up, however.

"Hey, boy." I knelt down on the floor and gave the dog a kiss on the snout. "Not feeling good today?"

His nose twitched as he scented the fried baloney sandwiches. I quickly unwrapped them and tore the first into small bites. With a little help from Nick, Nutty rolled onto his belly and eagerly took each morsel from me. Halfway through the second sandwich, he turned his head away, refusing to eat the rest.

Nick took the remainder of the sandwich from me.

"No sense letting this fine cooking go to waste." He finished it off in two big bites.

With a final scratch behind the ears and an admonishment for Nutty to be a good boy while his daddy was gone, Nick rounded up his jacket and briefcase and the two of us headed out to work.

After checking my voice mail and e-mails at the office, I decided to do some cybersnooping on Larry Burkett, see if I could dig up some dirt on the guy.

An hour later I'd found some data but no dirt, not even a tiny dust speck. The guy appeared to be sterile, squeaky clean, sanitized for my protection.

Per my research, Burkett owned a fifty-acre spread near Palo Pinto. The place had an agricultural exemption and thus showed a value of only $175,000 for property tax purposes. No doubt the actual market value would be much higher. He and his wife, Patty, had five kids, all of them grown and on their own with addresses in various towns and cities across Texas. The couple owned three vehicles. A Dodge Ram pickup, a Yukon SUV, and a Cadillac coupe. I assumed his wife drove the latter. A photo in the online version of a newspaper showed a smiling Burkett posing with the Wildcatters, a girls' softball team PPE sponsored. Another showed him receiving an award from the local chamber of commerce for bringing much-needed jobs to the area. By all accounts the guy was a stand-up family man who ran a successful business.

Doug had been right, though. The guy was wrinkled. The shallow, narrow wrinkles were likely from age, but the deep crags could only have come from spending excessive amounts of time under the brutal Texas sun. Not surprising, I suppose. Someone who worked in the oil and gas industry probably spent a lot of time outside checking on their wells. He might want to apply some sunscreen next time.

A couple of entries regarding the lawsuit showed up online, but the curt reports told me little more than Doug had. Although the lawsuit had originally been filed in Palo Pinto County, defense lawyers had claimed PPE could not get a fair trial there and sought a change of venue. The case had been transferred to the Dallas County Court. The plaintiffs alleged that benzene and other toxic chemicals had seeped through the ground and polluted their well water. The suit alleged a total of $13 million in damages.

Though I empathized with the ranchers, I knew the lawsuit didn't necessarily mean that Burkett was a bad guy, even if the allegations were true. The wastewater disposal methods were standard in the industry, and did not always cause damage. PPE's operating methods were no different than those of other natural gas companies. And, really, was there any good way to dispose of contaminated water? Perhaps I was naïve, but it seemed to me it would simply be best not to contaminate it in the first place. Hopefully scientists would soon develop better solar power methods or some other clean type of energy source. After all, if Willie Nelson could develop biodiesel fuel from vegetable oil and waste fats, why couldn't someone invent an energy source powered by expired pudding cups and toenail clippings?

Nothing in the Burketts' tax returns or those for PPE immediately caught my eye, either. PPE's corporate charter was in good standing with the Texas Secretary of State's office, meaning the business was current on all state tax filings, too.

Despite my best attempts, I found nothing online for Ector Oilfield Supply. This tidbit was the only piece of the puzzle that didn't seem to fit. Like Katie, I came up with nothing to indicate the business existed, not even an assumed-name certificate filed with a county clerk. I did find an Ector Oil & Gas Equipment Company, however, as well as an Ector Gas Well Servicing, Ltd. Perhaps Katie had gotten the name wrong.

Frankly, this investigation looked like a waste of my time. Still, I couldn't totally discount Katie's gut feeling that something was awry. My brain told me nothing was wrong, but it couldn't hurt to get a second opinion from my own gut, too. I decided to go check out Larry Burkett for myself.

chapter ten

*P*ants on Fire

Friday morning, I swung by Quentin Yarbrough's office bright and early, not bothering to wait for his phone call. In fact, I beat the man to his digs and had to wait in his reception area until he arrived a few minutes after nine.

Since I'd stopped by on Monday, Brazos's account had accrued another $8,767.12 in interest. It wasn't fair that Brazos would be hit with the additions to his bill when none of this was his fault. I'd be sure to point that out to his agent.

Yarbrough was a tall, narrow-shouldered man with the slightly rounded belly common to middle-aged men who worked from a chair. His dark hair was slicked back over his head, the ends curling up under his ears. Though dressed in a black business suit, he had an artsy look, partly due to the longish hair, partly due to the silky gray-and-white-striped shirt he wore under his suit jacket and the matching pocket square.

He blew into his office like a gust of wind, heading straight for the stack of pink phone message slips on his receptionist's desk. "God, it's good to be back," he told the woman seated in the chair. "If I had to eat one more crepe I'd slit my wrists."

As I stood and stepped up beside Yarbrough, the woman looked up apologetically. "Mr. Yarbrough," she said, raising a hand to indicate me, "this is Agent Tara Holloway from the IRS."

I stuck out a hand. "Good morning."

Yarbrough ignored my hand and looked down at me, his lips pursed in displeasure. "I'm a busy man. The IRS doesn't have the courtesy to make an appointment?"

"Sorry." I offered a contrite cringe. "My mother would be very disappointed in me." So would Miss Cecily. I'd attended her charm school as a young girl, but often found it hard to practice what she'd preached.

Yarbrough glanced back at his secretary. "What's on my schedule today?"

"You've got a ten o'clock teleconference with a producer from the *Today* show, an early lunch with the art director at Gladstone Advertising, and a three o'clock with a prospective client."

Yarbrough turned back to me. "Looks like it's now or never. Come this way."

He dipped his head toward his office door and I followed him inside. He closed the door behind me and gestured for me to take a seat in one of the low, boxy chairs that faced his enormous desk.

He took a seat, too, sitting stiffly and raising a brow. "What's up?"

"It's about Brazos Rivers," I said. "His tax returns haven't been filed."

"Ugh." Yarbrough slumped back in his chair. "Why am I not surprised?"

Huh? "I'm a little confused. He told me that you were supposed to hire a CPA to file the returns for him."

"Why would I do that?" Yarbrough said. "I'm his agent, not his bookkeeper."

I was at a loss. Brazos was the first performer I'd pursued for taxes. I really had no idea how the agent relationship worked. My confusion must have been spelled out on my face, because Yarbrough went on to clarify things for me.

"My job as an agent is to get Brazos gigs for performances and endorsements and to negotiate the contracts, not to babysit him or wipe his ass. I help him *make* money. But as for his recordkeeping and accounting and whatnot, that's up to him." He swiveled around in his chair and opened a drawer in the filing cabinet behind him. After thumbing through several files, he pulled out a document and tossed it onto his desk. "Take a look. That's the agency contract between me and Brazos. You see anything in there about filing his tax returns?"

I picked up the document and quickly scanned it over. Per the agreement, Yarbrough was entitled to a percentage of revenues from the concerts and promotions he arranged for Brazos. Nothing in the contract obligated him to file tax returns on behalf of his client. I noted, too, that nothing in the contract addressed the Boys of the Bayou.

"Do you represent his band, too? And the backup singers and dancers?"

Yarbrough shook his head. "Can't. Potential conflict of interest. Brazos brings them along for the ride but it's my understanding they work on an at-will basis."

In other words, the boys worked for Brazos and he decided how much to pay them and when.

"Brazos has been a pain in my ass since the day he set foot in this office," Yarbrough continued. "The kid's never satisfied, never thinks he's getting paid enough even though I always get him every dollar he deserves and then some. If he hadn't made me millions I'd dump the ungrateful little shit."

Wow. This wasn't what I'd expected at all. "You got a number where I can reach him?"

Yarbrough pulled out his cell phone and consulted his contacts list. He rattled off a number. I figured the smartest thing I could do was call Brazos right then and there to straighten this matter out. When I tried the number, though, I got a recording telling me the number was no longer in service.

"That doesn't surprise me, either," Yarbrough said. "That boy is always breaking his phones or losing them." He consulted his contacts list again. "I've got his parents' home number. They can tell you how to reach him."

He rattled off a number in the 940 area code. When I tried the Merriweathers' number I got a recording. *Damn.* I'd hoped to leave Yarbrough's office having made some real progress. Looked like that wasn't going to happen. I left a message for Brazos' parents, giving my callback number and asking them to inform their son that I needed to get in touch with him as soon as possible.

As I stood to go, Yarbrough raised a finger. "Hold on just a minute. If memory serves me right, Brazos has a photo shoot coming up in Fort Worth. You might be able to catch him there." He turned and riffled through the file again, pulling out another document. "Here it is. He's got a shoot on Monday for a print ad for boots."

I took the contract from him and made a note of the time and location of the shoot. I also noted that Brazos would be paid $300,000 for the one-hour job. I felt both impressed and annoyed. I worked my ass off trying to collect past-due taxes, risked my very life, but Uncle Sam didn't pay me in a year what Brazos would make in an hour. Kind of hard not to feel a little irritated by that fact. "Thanks, Mr. Yarbrough. I appreciate your cooperation."

He slid the contract back into his file cabinet. "My pleasure."

For the second time this week, I slunk into the IRS office with my tail between my legs.

Unfortunately, Nick and my boss, Lu, were talking in the hallway as I approached my office.

Nick arched a brow. "So? Dirty Undies gonna pay up now?"

"It's not Dirty Undies," I said. "It's *Brazos Rivers*. And for your information I'm going to meet with him in person next Monday."

Okay, so maybe calling my plan to crash the photo shoot a "meeting" was an overstatement. But better to fib a little than for Nick to know that Brazos had lied to me and that I'd fallen for it.

"Want me to go to the meeting with you?" Nick asked.

"No!" I snapped. He'd given me enough crap about how I'd handled this investigation. I'd rather leave him out of it and take care of things all by myself.

Lu crossed her arms over her ample chest, squinted at me through her false eyelashes, and cocked her pinkish-orange beehive toward me. "Someone should go with you to make sure the job gets done."

What? My jaw fell slack.

"Lu came by to check on things when you weren't here," Nick said, a defensive tone in his voice. "She asked me for an update."

The glare I aimed at him was so intense it wouldn't have surprised me to see flames shoot from eye sockets. Obviously he'd told her about my less-than-stellar performance in this case, how Brazos had manipulated me like a kid with a fresh can of Play-Doh. I felt embarrassed and betrayed. Nick wouldn't be getting any for a while. Tara's Fun Factory was temporarily closed for business.

Beyond furious, I threw my hands in the air and turned my attention to my boss. "After all I've done for this agency, you're going to treat me like an incompetent idiot?"

"You're not incompetent, Tara," Lu said, the placating tone in her voice annoying me even further. "You're just a little star-struck. It's understandable. Heck, this is partly my fault. I should've known better than to assign you to go after Brazos. Tell you what, I'll go with you on Monday. It's been a long time since I've been out in the field. I wouldn't mind getting out of the office for a bit."

Great. Now *I* was the one with a babysitter.

chapter eleven

Friday Night Lights

Eddie rode out to Palo Pinto with me Friday afternoon. We'd taken my government-issued fleet car, a white sedan with no bells, whistles, or personality.

"Talk about Hicksville," Eddie said as we rolled through what little passed for a town out here. The city boy was definitely out of his element.

Eddie and I had partnered on many cases since I'd begun working for the IRS last spring. Though we shared neither gender, political views, nor skin color, we did share a mutual respect. When I'd asked him to accompany me, he'd readily agreed. His twin girls were having a sleepover tonight and he'd been looking for an excuse to stay away from his house.

"Ten preteen girls?" he said. "The shoot-out in the truck yard was less scary."

Eddie, Nick, and a new agent named William Dorsey had taken fire recently and took cover on top of the cab of an eighteen-wheeler. I'd climbed a tree and, with my expert marksman skills, kept the bad guys at bay until Dallas SWAT could take them down and round them up. My heroism and sharpshooting skills seemed to have been forgotten in the wake of my getting all goggle-eyed over Brazos. What I needed now was a chance to redeem myself.

When we reached Mineral Wells, I pulled into a 7-Eleven parking lot and texted Katie from my cell. *Heads-up. I'm coming in undercover with partner. Remember, u never saw me B4.*

Her response came seconds later. *Ok.*

We continued on, pulling into the PPE headquarters and parking next to Burkett's Yukon. There were only two other cars in the lot, Katie's Kia and a red Prius. Eddie and I grabbed our briefcases and headed inside.

A sixtyish woman with wispy brown hair sat at the receptionist desk, sorting through the day's mail. In recognition of the upcoming holiday, the front of her desk was decorated with pink heart cutouts and the candy dish on the corner of her desktop was filled with conversation hearts. On the credenza behind her desk sat a small aquarium, the filter giving off a barely audible hum. Inside were two goldfish, one of whom swam to the glass and hovered in the water, moving its tiny fins as it seemed to eye us. Behind the woman were two doors, one opened, one closed. The open door led to Katie's workspace, a tiny office lined with filing cabinets. She glanced up as we walked in, but quickly turned her attention back to the mountain of paperwork in front of her.

"Hello," I greeted the receptionist, reaching over to her dish to snag a yellow candy heart that read BE MINE. "I'm Sara Galloway." The name had become my go-to alias, similar enough to my own to be memorable, but different enough to be distinguishable. I gestured to Eddie. "My associate, Teddy Martin. We'd like to speak to Mr. Burkett, please."

I popped the candy into my mouth as the receptionist

picked up her phone and pushed the intercom button. "Mr. Burkett, there's a Sara Galloway and Teddy Martin here to see you." She listened for a moment before putting a hand over the mouthpiece. "What company are you with?"

"Um . . ." I said the first thing that popped into my mind. "Bits, Bolts, and Beyond."

The woman's brows formed a confused V. "Haven't heard of that company before."

"We're a start-up," I replied.

Eddie discreetly cut his eyes my way and shook his head. Yeah, maybe I should've thought this through better on the way over.

The woman removed her hand from the phone. "She says they're with Bits, Bolts, and Beyond." She listened for a couple more seconds, then returned her receiver to the cradle and gestured to the closed door behind her. "Y'all can go on in."

"Thanks." I went to the door with Eddie following along behind me.

After a quick rap on the door, I opened it to find an office nicely appointed with oversized leather and walnut furniture. Mr. Burkett stood behind his desk. Though his face bore the same craggy wrinkles from the Internet images, it also bore a pleasant smile. He was dressed in a gray business suit that looked well made, if slightly out-of-date.

Eddie and I introduced ourselves under our aliases and offered our hands. After shakes were exchanged, Burkett motioned for us to take a seat in the leather wing chairs facing his desk.

He plopped down in his high-backed chair and folded his hands over his belly. "What can I do you for?"

"We're sales reps for a new metal fabrication company," I said. "We plan to corner the market on drill bits."

"Bolts, too," Eddie added. "And . . . uh . . . beyond."

Burkett chuckled. "Nothing wrong with ambition."

"We'd like the opportunity to work up a bid for your drill bit needs." I prayed it sounded like we knew what we were talking about and that Burkett wouldn't realize we were just making things up as we went along.

Eddie chimed in. "We might be able to save you some money."

Burkett dipped his head. "I like the sound of that."

"If you could provide us with the prices you pay to your current suppliers," I said, "we'll see about beating them."

Burkett cocked his head. "Tell you what. You want my business? Fix me up a price sheet with your best quantity discounts and we'll take it from there."

Rats. He wasn't biting. I'd hoped he'd give us some specifics so we could tell whether he really was using the cash to buy bits.

I leaned forward in my seat. "How will we know what price to beat if we don't have your current cost information?"

"You won't," he replied, the smile seeming more shrewd now than pleasant. "And maybe you'll go even lower than you would if I gave you the information."

I forced a smile. "You're a tough negotiator, Mr. Burkett."

He raised his palms to indicate the cushy office around him. "That's how I got here, hon." With that, he stood, letting us know in no uncertain terms that our unscheduled meeting was over.

We thanked him for his time, shook hands good-bye, and headed back out to my G-ride. It was after five now and much colder than it had been earlier. Dusk was setting in and the outdoor floodlights had come on. Two of the three Dobermans paced along the fence surrounding the warehouse, watching me and Eddie with wary eyes, steam snorting from their nostrils as if they were some type of canine dragon. The third guard dog lay in front of his doghouse in their daytime pen, presumably on a coffee break.

"What did your gut tell you?" Eddie asked once we were seated in the car.

I reached back to grab the strap of the seat belt and clicked it into place. "My gut's being silent." Well, other than the gurgling caused by the latte I'd downed on the drive over.

On one hand, Burkett hadn't been forthcoming with the information we'd requested. On the other hand, who could blame him for keeping his proprietary information private? He hadn't been overly friendly, but he had been polite and professional. Perhaps he was exactly what he appeared to be—a savvy businessman and nothing more.

I started the engine. "What's your take on him?"

Eddie lifted a shoulder. "Honestly? I'm not getting any strange vibes. I'd bet he's using the cash for drill bits."

Eddie was probably right. He had years of experience as a special agent and good instincts, as well. Still, I wasn't entirely ready to throw in the towel just yet. Call me overzealous, but I felt like I owed it to Katie and Doug not to give up until I was one hundred percent sure Burkett wasn't involved in any shenanigans. After all, they'd put their jobs on the line to contact me, put their livelihoods at risk.

Though my gut wasn't saying much, it did tell me the $7,500 in cash Katie had withdrawn from the bank earlier today and placed in PPE's safe wouldn't likely remain there overnight. It wasn't a good idea to leave such big sums of cash on-site at any workplace and, as a seasoned businessman, Burkett would know that.

"As long as we've driven all this way," I told Eddie, "let's hang around for a while, follow him when he leaves. Maybe we'll learn something."

"Yeah," Eddie said. "Like maybe we'll learn just how boring it can be to sit in a car out here in the middle of nowhere."

"You want me to drive you back to Dallas for the slumber party, then?"

"Heck, no! I'd rather be bored than listen to all that squealing and shrieking."

To use up some time, we drove back into town and stopped for a quick, early dinner at a small Chinese restaurant on the main road. The food was surprisingly good, if a bit on the spicy side.

On the walk back to the car, I cracked open my fortune cookie, shoved the dry bits into my mouth, and consulted the white paper slip.

"Things will soon heat up."

Eddie glanced over at me.

"What do you think that means?" I asked him.

He shrugged. "Maybe there will be some developments in one of your cases. Or maybe you'll get some kind of skin rash."

Once we were seated in the car again, Eddie cracked open his own cookie. His fortune was identical to mine. "Things will soon heat up." Looked like someone in quality control at the fortune cookie factory needed a swift kick in the pants. Really, mix 'em up a little!

"I feel cheated." Eddie tossed the slip into the car's ashtray. An instant later, he put a hand to his mouth to stifle a peppery burp, then banged a fist on his chest. "What do you know?" he said. "The cookie was right. I can feel the heartburn already."

After the feed store down the road from PPE closed up for the evening, I pulled into the gravel lot at the rear, parked facing the PPE headquarters, and retrieved a pair of field glasses from under my seat. Eddie had brought his binoculars, too. Unfortunately, neither pair had night-vision capabilities so visibility was limited in areas that were not illuminated.

As we watched, we saw both the receptionist and Katie leave the office. We continued to sit there until seven o'clock, occasionally turning the engine on and running the heater to warm up the car when it became too cold to bear.

"I don't know which is worse." Eddie hugged himself in an attempt to keep warm. "The boredom or the fact that I can no longer feel my balls."

"Wimp." Easy for me to say. I was wearing the beautiful cobalt-blue coat Nick had bought me for Christmas and had also wrapped myself in the car's reflective window screen, which radiated my body heat back at me. I'd offered to share it with Eddie but he'd told me I looked ridiculous. What the heck did I care? There was nobody to try to impress out here unless you counted the goats or the Dobermans.

Eddie shook his head. "I'm getting frostbite here. That fortune cookie was way off."

Movement at PPE caught my attention and I put my field glasses to my eyes. In the glow of the floodlights, Burkett could be seen exiting the office, tucking a large envelope under his arm, and turning back to lock up the building.

"Looks like he might be taking the cash somewhere," I told Eddie, who was also watching through his binoculars.

"Think he's taking it home?" Eddie said. "For safe-keeping?"

"Maybe. Or maybe he's taking it to his second family. Maybe he has a secret son or daughter who needs an organ transplant."

"And what? He's taking them money to buy a heart or a lung on the black market?"

"Yeah. Or maybe a kidney."

Eddie rolled his eyes. "You watch too much crap TV."

As we spied, Burkett climbed into his Yukon, started the engine, and pulled out of the parking lot, heading in our direction. To avoid being spotted, Eddie and I ducked down in our seats as Burkett drove up the road toward the feed store. Once he'd passed us, I gave him a ten-second lead then reached out to start my engine.

Keeping his sights on Burkett's car through the back window, Eddie put his hand on mine, stopping me. "He's slowing down."

I turned to take a look. Bright red brake lights illuminated the road behind the SUV as Burkett pulled over.

Eddie put his binoculars to his eyes again. "What is he doing?"

"Is he stopping at the historical marker?" I raised my glasses to my eyes again, too. Sure enough, Burkett climbed out of his car, leaving the door open. With the interior light adding illumination, we could get a better visual. "Why would he stop there?"

"Maybe he's going to take a leak," Eddie suggested. "Old guys like him have to pee twenty or thirty times a day."

"That's not his penis in his hand," I pointed out. "It's the envelope."

As we watched, Burkett set the envelope down at the base of the marker. When he was done, he climbed back into his car. He flashed his bright headlights three times in quick succession.

"What's that all about?" I asked. "You think it's some kind of signal?"

Before Eddie could respond, Burkett made a U-turn and headed back in our direction. We ducked down once again as he drove by. When we sat back up, we saw headlights coming up the road from beyond the marker. The car slowed to a stop at the marker. Unlike Burkett, this driver cut his headlights and closed his door after climbing out. Though it was impossible to tell given the darkness, it was a good guess that he'd stopped to pick up the envelope.

"I've changed my mind," Eddie said. "I'm getting weird vibes now."

"Me, too." Burkett appeared to be up to something. The only question now was *what*.

A moment later, the car's headlights came on again. The car pulled a U-turn, too, shining its beams on the curious crowd of goats at the nearby pasture fence before heading back in the opposite direction.

"Let's roll." I started the engine, cranked the heater on full blast, and pulled onto the highway to follow the car. I drove slowly, leaving my headlights off for a minute so as not to alert the driver that he or she was being followed. When I felt it was safe, I switched on the headlights and sped up, catching up to the car when it stopped at an intersection.

The car was a basic black Toyota Corolla with a student parking sticker for Lamar High School on the back window. It was too dark for us to tell much about the person at the wheel, but judging from the height the driver appeared to be male.

"I've got the plate number," Eddie said, jotting the number down on a napkin I'd left in the car.

While I continued to follow the driver at a safe distance, Eddie ran the license plate on his tablet. He looked up when he had the data. "The car belongs to a Gregory Michelson in Arlington."

He ran Michelson's name through the driver's license records next. "The address on his license matches the one on the vehicle registration."

Rather than raise Michelson's suspicions that he was being followed, I took a right turn down a country road.

Meanwhile, Eddie searched the man's name on the Internet.

"He's listed as a member of the building committee for the Seventh Day Adventist Church," Eddie said, reading from his screen. "He's a runner, too. He placed twenty-third in the Dallas marathon last year."

"Not bad."

"I'm finding a LinkedIn profile, too. It says Michelson's a respiratory therapist at HealthSouth Rehabilitation Hospital." Eddie looked up from his tablet. "What's this dude doing way out here in the boondocks? And why would Burkett be giving him cash?"

My gut was talking now. Loud and clear. "You said Michelson works at a hospital, right? He's getting that kidney for Burkett's secret son. He's planning to steal it from a coma patient." Okay, so my gut was talking smack. I couldn't help it if my gut was a smart-ass.

Another eye roll. "Get real, Tara."

"Okay. How's this for real? Michelson potentially has access to drugs such as painkillers. Maybe a doctor's prescription pad, too."

Eddie raised a brow. "You think Burkett's paying the guy for Vicodin or oxycodone?"

"Well, I don't think he's paying for Band-Aids, bedpans, or Jell-O."

"So?" Eddie said. "What's next?"

"What's next is I approach this from the back end. Put some eyes on Michelson."

But what would those eyes see?

chapter twelve

Thin Mints Is an Oxymoron

When I returned home Friday night, I was tempted to go down to Nick's place. The light in his living room was on so I knew he was home, but I was still angry at him for ratting me out to Lu. Instead I stayed at my place and watched a double feature of romantic comedies on Netflix. Then I logged onto Facebook and changed my status to show that I was in a relationship with Poo-Poo Head. That would show Nick. If he ever logged onto Facebook, that is.

After a good night's sleep, I woke early, feeling more forgiving today. After all, I wasn't entirely sure what Nick had told Lu. Chances were she'd read between the lines and figured out why I hadn't done a better job nailing Brazos down. Dating a coworker, mixing business with pleasure, came with this type of potential pitfall. One of the things I admired about Nick was his strong work ethic. No sense in me punishing Nick for doing his job, right?

I took a quick shower, threw on a pair of yoga pants, a sweatshirt, and sneakers, and drove to the bakery around the corner to pick up some lattes and cronuts, the new half-donut, half-croissant craze. Frankly, I was still waiting for someone to make sconuts—a half scone, half donut. Or maybe a waffnut—half waffle, half donut. Really, what could be more yummy than a donut covered in maple syrup?

I let myself into Nick's place with my key. The place was still dark and quiet. I shut the door behind me and tiptoed upstairs.

Nick lay facedown in his bed, his head turned to the side, his arms arched over his head like a ballerina with arms in fifth position. Trust me, though, this bad boy was no ballerina. The covers were bunched down around his waist, his muscular, naked back exposed. I fought the urge to cover his body with my own. Doing so would only lead to a morning of lovemaking and, as much as I'd enjoy getting busy with Nick, I had work to do. In fact, that's why I was here. To see if Nick might be willing to keep me company as I spied on Michelson. Stakeouts were incredibly boring regardless, but doing one alone was like being put in solitary confinement. Besides, I needed someone for backup so I could take the occasional pee break. I was a dedicated agent, but not dedicated enough to wear an adult diaper.

Nutty lay next to Nick in the bed, snoring softly in his sleep. The dog looked quite a bit thinner than he had only a few weeks ago. His fur had lost its luster, too. Poor thing. He clearly wasn't long for this world. I wondered if Nick had accepted that reality yet. At least the dog had enjoyed a long and loving life, with a doting daddy who catered to his every whim.

I put Nick's latte on the night table and gently sat down on the bed.

He opened one eye halfway and groaned in greeting. "Is it morning already?"

"Yep." I held up the bag. "I brought coffee and cronuts."

He frowned and sat up. "You brought *what*?"

"Cronuts. They're part croissant, part donut."

He took the bag from me, opened it, and peeked inside. "They're an abomination is what they are. What's next? Some type of half bacon, half sausage meat called bausage?"

When it came to food, Nick was a traditionalist. I, on the other hand, enjoyed experimenting with new things, so long as I didn't have to cook them myself. I had mad gun skills, but I had no idea what to do with a casserole dish. "Just shut up and eat one. You'll change your mind."

Nutty woke, too, struggling to sit up on the bed. I reached over, helped him onto his belly, and offered him a pink frosted cronut.

"That thing'll rot his teeth," Nick said, fishing out a blueberry pastry for himself.

"Have you smelled Nutty's breath?" I replied. "That ship sailed a long time ago."

Nick reached out to stroke his dog's back. "Don't listen to her, boy. You're as good-looking as ever."

Nick was obviously in denial, but I couldn't blame him. I didn't want to think about Nutty's worsening health issues, either. Despite his halitosis, I couldn't imagine life without the sweet dog. He made Nick's relatively spartan bachelor pad feel like a real home.

Forcing those thoughts aside, I scratched Nutty at the base of his tail and took a sip of my latte. "I'm going on a stakeout this morning. Want to come with me?"

"What's in it for me?" Nick retorted.

"My undying gratitude."

He tilted his head and raised a brow. "Toss in some nooky and it's a deal."

A half hour later, when I'd kept up my *end* of the bar-

gain, so to speak, Nick took a quick shower, dressed, and
headed out with me to my G-ride. He took the wheel, leaving me to navigate.

Nick glanced my way as he started the car. "So you
think this Michelson's dealing in prescription drugs?"

"I don't know what to think," I said. "But that's the only
connection I can see, the only obvious reason why Burkett
would be slipping cash to the guy." Other than the secret
family and the black-market kidney, of course.

I pulled out my cell phone and called Christina Marquez, my friend at the DEA. She might have some insights
on the situation. She answered on the third ring.

"It's only nine-thirty," she said, her voice gravelly with
sleep. "Somebody better be dead."

"Nobody's dead," I said, "but I could use your help.
Any chance I can convince you to come on a stakeout with
me and Nick?"

"What's it in for me?"

"You're as bad as Nick. He demanded nooky before
he'd agree to come with me."

"I'll pass on the nooky," Christina said, "but I'm in for
a mango smoothie."

"Done."

I directed Nick to the Jamba Juice near Christina's
apartment, bought her a smoothie, and carried it to her
door. She, too, wore yoga pants and sneakers, though she'd
topped hers with a long-sleeved tee and a hoodie. She'd
pulled her long black hair back in some type of quick and
easy twist and secured it with a plastic clip. She wore no
makeup, but despite the sloppy hair and bare face still
managed to look drop-dead gorgeous. She'd be an easy
person to hate if she weren't such a fun and loyal friend
who was always willing to lend a hand.

While I slid in the passenger door, she climbed into the

back, kicked off her shoes, and stretched her long legs out along the seat. "Who we after here?" She put the straw to her lips and took a sip of her smoothie.

I met her gaze in the rearview mirror. "Respiratory therapist named Greg Michelson." I gave her the rundown on Larry Burkett and the cash envelope he'd left at the marker last night. "Think Michelson could be dealing painkillers?"

Christina shrugged. "Could be. Or maybe he's got some dirt on Burkett and is blackmailing him." She paused for a moment, her brow furrowed as she appeared to think. "How would Burkett and Michelson have met?"

It was my turn to shrug now. "Maybe Burkett had a procedure at the hospital where Michelson works."

Nick joined in now. "But Burkett lives way out in Palo Pinto. If he needed some type of specialized medical treatment, it seems like he would have gone someplace in Fort Worth rather than driving farther to Arlington."

"True," Christina replied. "And it's possible that even if the envelope contained cash, it wasn't part of the $7,500 Katie withdrew. Maybe Burkett's got a personal issue here. Maybe the envelope didn't even contain cash. Maybe it was the results of a paternity test or something."

"Maybe Michelson is Burkett's illegitimate son," Nick suggested.

Christina arched a brow. "Or his lover."

I was tempted to put my fingers in my ears and sing, *La-la-la!* The more they talked, the more convoluted and complicated this case became. The possibilities were endless, but what was it they say? The simplest answer is usually the right one.

But which answer was the simplest? That Burkett was using the cash to buy drill bits and that the envelope he'd transferred to Michelson contained something of a personal nature rather than cash?

When we arrived in Arlington, we drove slowly down Michelson's street, eyeing his house as we drove past. The residence was a single-story brown brick home, a traditional ranch model with white shutters and a two-car garage. The driveway was empty, the garage doors closed. Was the Toyota parked inside the garage? The garage had no windows. There was no way to tell.

We parked a block down where we could keep an eye on Michelson's house without being spotted. Then we sat and waited.

And waited . . .

And waited . . .

Luckily, the day was warmer than usual, in the low sixties, so at least we weren't freezing to death out here. We entertained ourselves by playing games on our phones and catching up on our favorite television shows online.

Around noon, the front door of Michelson's house swung open. A man dressed in running shorts and a T-shirt came outside. He had curly gray hair, along with the hard leg muscle and gaunt build of a marathon runner. He stopped halfway down the driveway to set a timer on his watch and took off running in the opposite direction.

"Is that Michelson?" Nick asked.

"I think so." The man looked like the photo Eddie had found online.

"Let's follow him," Christina said.

"Might as well," I agreed, though it seemed doubtful he'd be doing anything more than going on a simple run. After all, there were no telltale bulges under his tee or shorts to indicate he'd stashed the cash—or whatever had been in the envelope—on himself.

Nick started the car and we followed the man, careful to hang back and hug the curb lest he spot us. He didn't once look back, oblivious to the fact that three armed federal agents had set their sights on him.

A half hour later he circled back to his house and went inside. He remained there for the rest of the afternoon.

When five o'clock rolled around we decided to call it a day. My ass had already grown numb. Much longer and my glutes would begin to atrophy.

"For what it's worth," Christina said as we pulled away from the curb, "I don't think Michelson's dealing drugs himself, at least not on a big scale. Nobody came to his house today. Drug houses normally get lots of traffic."

More food for thought. My brain was having a virtual feast.

Sunday morning I repeated the routine, going down to Nick's with breakfast in an attempt to recruit him for another day of staking out Michelson's house. Unfortunately, I found his bed empty. Nutty was nowhere to be seen, either. I texted Nick to find out that his mother had beat me to the punch, inviting him over to attend church and have lunch. I wanted to be mad, but how could I begrudge a widow some time with her only son?

Christina had mentioned that she and Ajay had planned to see a movie today, so I headed over to Arlington alone, this time parking four houses down on the opposite side of the street just to shake things up a bit. I checked my e-mails. I painted my fingernails. I Skyped with my parents back home in Nacogdoches. Per my mother, everyone back home was doing fine, though my favorite niece, Jesse, had skinned both her knees chasing after one of the barn cats. By mid-afternoon I was going nuts cooped up in this car.

No one came to Michelson's house today, either. I wondered if Christina was right. That he wasn't dealing drugs. But if that were the case, then where did that leave me? With nothing to go on, that's where.

I climbed out and took a walk down the block to get

my stagnant blood moving. When I turned the corner, I spotted two young girls in green uniforms up ahead, accompanied by a woman who was likely their mother. The girls pulled a red Radio Flyer wagon stacked with cardboard cases.

Girl Scouts!

Cookies!

"Hey!" I ran after them, pulling my wallet from my purse and waving it in the air. "Wait for me!"

The girls turned and waited as I ran the rest of the way.

"Got any Thin Mints left?" I asked.

The older girl rummaged around in the wagon and came up with a carton. "We've got one case left. How many boxes would you like?"

"I'll take the whole case." Sheesh. I was as bad as a crack addict, huh? But I figured if I froze the cookies and paced myself, I could eat one box a month and be fully supplied until next cookie season. How's that for thinking ahead?

The girls seemed to think nothing of my purchase. Apparently I wasn't the only one who bought Girl Scout cookies by the gross.

"Thanks!" I paid for my cookies, tucked the carton under my arm, and returned to my car and my stakeout. Three hours later, I'd eaten nearly through to my August supply of cookies, ingested enough calories to fuel an army regiment, and seen no movement at the Michelson house. What were they, a family of hermits?

Just when I thought my stomach would explode, the garage door began to roll up. I sat bolt upright in my seat. The back tires of a vehicle became visible, then a bumper. But when the door ascended fully it revealed only a silver Mitsubishi Outlander parked in the garage. The black Toyota was nowhere to be seen.

Fed up—and overfed—I climbed out of my car. As I

walked toward the house, a lanky teenager in knee-length basketball shorts and a wrinkled T-shirt emerged from the garage with a plastic tub of recyclables. Aluminum cans. Glass bottles. Newspapers and ad circulars. A few plastic bottles that had once held juice, shampoo, and cleaning products, but no small plastic pill bottles. *Hmm . . .*

The kid rounded the side of the house, opened the larger rolling recycling can, and upended the tub. Cans, glass, and paper clinked, clanked, and fluttered into the can.

"Hey," I called to the boy as I approached.

He looked up.

I stopped. No sense getting too close and making him feel wary. "Does your family have a black Toyota?"

"Used to," he spat, slamming the lid to the can.

"Used to? What do you mean?"

"My dad got rid of it." He followed this revelation by muttering, "Asshole."

I had an accounting degree. I could put two and two together. These people no longer owned the car Eddie and I had seen at the historical marker, and I'd just wasted two days of my life. *Ugh!* "It was your car, huh?"

The kid jerked his chin up once in affirmation. "Dad sold it after I flunked algebra and history."

"When was that?"

The kid squinted at me, as if trying to determine whether he knew me. "Who are you, anyway?"

Looked like I'd asked one question too many.

"I'm Tara Holloway. I work for the government." I pulled my badge out of my purse and held it up for a moment before slipping it back into the inside pocket. "Is your father home?"

Rather than answer me, the kid gestured to my face. "You've got something all over your mouth."

When I stuck my hand in my purse this time it was to

retrieve my compact. I whipped it open to take a look in the mirror. Sure enough, remnants of chocolate covered my lips.

"Girl Scout cookies," I explained, adding, "Thin Mints," as if that excused my gluttonous behavior. I quickly licked off what I could and used a finger to wipe off the rest.

"Got any more?" the boy asked. "If you give me a box I'll go get my dad."

Seriously? This kid had no respect for authority. "I'm a federal agent," I reminded him. "I carry a gun."

"So?" He snorted. "You're not gonna shoot me."

"Don't count on it. I've shot people before."

A brow went up. "Really?"

"Really." I'd shot the left nut off one guy and shot a set of twins and a strip club owner in the legs. Set someone on fire once, too. But I probably sound like I'm bragging now, huh?

The boy considered my words for a moment before crossing him arms over his chest. "My dad never answers the door. We get too many solicitors. Either you give me some cookies or I won't tell him you're out here."

Jeez. First the nooky, then the smoothie, and now the cookies. Did nobody do anything out of the goodness of their heart anymore? "You're a little shit, you know that?"

He cast me a smirk. "It's the one thing I'm good at."

I went to my car and retrieved a box of cookies. I held them out, but whipped them back out of his reach as he extended his hand. "No cookies until you bring me your father."

"Done." He trotted into the garage, opened the door leading into the house, and hollered at the top of his lungs. "Dad! There's some chick from the government outside who wants to talk to you!"

When Greg Michelson stepped outside, I tossed the

box of cookies to the boy. Michelson was dressed in a pair of sweats and a tight-fitting workout shirt that was the same gray color as his hair. I introduced myself, passing him one of my business cards and offering him a hand to shake.

He held the card in his left hand, looking it over while shaking my hand with his right. "What can I do for you, Agent Holloway?"

"I have some questions about the Toyota you sold."

He cocked his head. "Is there a problem?"

"The title is still showing up in your name," I noted. "When did you sell it?"

He closed his eyes, apparently thinking back.

"It was on a Sunday at the end of October," the boy said testily, answering for his father. "The day I became a dork who has to ride the school bus with all the other dorks."

His father cut a glance his way. "You had fair warning, son. You're the one who chose to spend all your time playing video games rather than hitting the books."

"Hitting the books?" the boy parroted back as he opened the box of cookies and tore open the foil sleeve. "The school doesn't give us books anymore. Everything's online. You want me to hit my iPad?" He shoved three cookies in his mouth at the same time. Crude, but at least it shut him up.

Mr. Michelson turned to me. "You got kids?"

"No."

He hiked a thumb at his son. "You want one?"

I looked over at the kid, who was wiping his hands on his tee, leaving a chocolate smudge. "I'll stick with cats for now, thanks." I forced a smile before getting back to the business at hand. "Who did you sell the car to?"

"Heck," he said, shrugging. "I've got no idea. I put an

ad in the paper and a sign on the car in the driveway. A guy called, came by to take a look, and paid me cash on the spot. I signed over the title and that was that."

Texas law required people who purchased used cars from private parties to pay sales tax. They were also required to change the title into their own name within thirty days of the sale. Whoever had bought the car from Michelson had done neither. I suspected the buyer may have purposely neglected to put the car in his own name to avoid being identified.

"The man who bought the car," I said, "what did he look like?"

"A skinny elephant," the boy said before shoving another three cookies into his mouth.

"You're right." Michelson turned back to me. "The guy had big ears and a long, narrow nose. He was friendly, but a little odd looking."

"What kind of car was the man driving?"

"He was on foot," Michelson said.

Arlington was the largest city in the U.S. without a regular public transportation system. Instead, the city had put its tax dollars into building a stadium for the Texas Rangers baseball team. Although a few buses had recently been put into operation for a trial run, the routes were limited. To my knowledge none ran close to the residential area in which Michelson lived. A hunch told me that the buyer had had another person drop him off to buy the car, or maybe he'd taken a taxi.

"Anything else you can tell me about him? Dress? Height? Distinguishing characteristics?"

Michelson shrugged. "Seemed like he was just wearing jeans and some kind of everyday, casual shirt. He was medium height, if I remember right. That's really all I can recall. It's been a while."

"You've got my card," I reminded him. "If you think of anything else, give me a call."

"I sure will."

As I stepped away, the boy lifted a chocolate-fingered hand in good-bye.

chapter thirteen

*H*orsing Around

I'd hoped to hear back from Brazos or his parents before Monday, but nobody bothered to return my call. I wasn't sure what to make of that. Had his parents received my message and ignored it? Had his parents passed the message on to Brazos and he'd blown me off?

I supposed it was possible the Merriweathers hadn't even heard my message yet. After all, they could be traveling. Or perhaps, like many people, they relied primarily on their cell phones and didn't often check their landline. Regardless, I'd be able to nail things down in person today when I saw Brazos at his photo shoot.

Lu came to my office after lunch on Monday. In recognition of the upcoming Valentine's holiday, she'd dressed in a red polyester pantsuit accessorized with a Cupid-print scarf.

"Festive," I noted.

She put a hand to her neck. "Carl gave me this scarf as an early Valentine's gift."

Carl was Lu's sexagenarian boyfriend. Despite his white bucks, leisure suits, and bizarre, basket-weave-pattern hairstyle, the guy was quite the charmer. Lu had recently met him through an online dating service and the two had been going strong ever since.

I'd purposely dressed as plainly as possible today, to prove to Nick and Lu, and maybe even to myself, that I could be completely professional where Brazos Rivers was concerned. My navy blue suit and brown loafers could not be more boring, and other than a small pair of gold studs, I was bereft of accessories. Heck, Brazos probably wouldn't even recognize me as the same woman he'd met after his concert, especially since I'd be wearing panties today.

Nick looked up from his desk as I followed Lu out into the hall. "Off to see Stinky Sewers?"

Nick could just not let this go, could he?

"It's *Brazos*," I growled. *"Rivers."*

Nick gave me a mirthless grin. "Whatever. Just make sure he signs an agreement to get his taxes filed and paid."

With an executed agreement in place, it would be easier to get search warrants later should Brazos fail to abide by the terms. A judge was less likely to grant a search warrant when it wasn't clear whether a taxpayer had willingly ignored the IRS or was merely absentminded and disorganized. I knew that. I didn't need Nick reminding me. Really, why did he have to act like such a jerk? "I don't need you to tell me how to do my job."

A brow lifted now. "You sure about that?"

I crossed my arms over my chest. "One more word out of you and I'll ask Brazos to go with me to the Mavericks game on Valentine's Day."

Nick stood, a real smile on his face now. "You got seats to the game?"

"Lower level center court. Alicia and Daniel and Christina and Ajay are going, too." I'd paid nearly two hundred bucks each for our tickets. The least Nick could do is stop acting like a jealous teenager, right?

"Hot damn!" He clapped his hands. "I could kiss you right now!"

A frown creased Lu's bright red lips. "Need I remind you two that you're at work?"

With that, she took off down the hall. I gave Nick one last warning glance and pointed my finger at him. "Cut the crap."

He gave me a stiff salute. "Yes, ma'am."

Lu and I headed down I-30 aiming for Fort Worth, which lay thirty miles to the west of Dallas. We pulled up to the photography studio to find half a dozen cars in the lot. One of them was the black Ferrari with its BRAZEN license plate.

The front door of the studio was locked and guarded by two of the same beefcakes who'd blocked the hallway at the concert. Lu and I stepped up to the glass and held up our badges.

"Federal law enforcement." I pushed my jacket back with my elbow to reveal the gun holstered at my waist. "We need to speak with Brazos Rivers. Open the door."

The men looked from me to Lu, said something in a low voice to each other, and fought a grin. I could hardly blame them. Lu did look a bit clownlike in her bright red getup.

One of the men stepped to the door and turned the dead bolt. He didn't bother opening it for us, though, he merely stepped back. The ass could stand to learn some manners. I pushed the door open and held it for Lu.

"Where's Brazos?" I asked, disappointed to feel my heart begin its pitter-patter in my chest. *Brazos isn't a god,* I told myself. *He's just a man. One who lies, at that. Nothing to get worked up about.* Unfortunately, my attempts to calm my beating heart were ineffective. Love might be blind, but lust was downright stupid.

The guard jerked his head to indicate the end of the hall. "He's down there."

At the end of the corridor a door stood ajar. A shaft of blindingly bright light shined from within, as if the door were the portal to heaven. Maybe Brazos was a god, after all. A soft murmur of conversation drifted out into the hallway. I started down the hall with Lu following behind.

When we reached the door, we glanced inside. Brazos sat in a high director's chair in front of a mirror lit with a dozen bulbs. He wore a blue western shirt with pearl snap buttons, along with jeans and chaps. The only thing missing were his boots and spurs. A female makeup artist in a white smock flittered around him, applying powder to his face with a brush as if he were a work of art. *Damned if he isn't.* With those blue eyes and soft, pink lips, he was a sculpture of flesh and bone.

Brazos looked into the mirror and his beautiful blue eyes met mine in the glass. A smile played about his lips as he gazed at my reflection. "Hello, again," he said, "Tara."

My heart melted in my chest. It was a wonder I didn't collapse to the floor. My voice came out high-pitched and airy. "Hi, Brazos." Geez. I sounded like a chipmunk.

In the mirror, his gaze shifted from me to Lu. He offered her his irresistible smile. "Who's this gorgeous creature you brought with you?"

Lu's hand fluttered around the scarf at her neck and a giggle escaped her lips. I was used to my boss barking orders and issuing demands. I hadn't known she was capable of a giggle. Her false eyelashes fluttered, too. Was she having some sort of seizure?

Oh, my God.

Lu is as star-struck as I am.

"Give us a minute?" Brazos raised a finger, signaling the makeup artist to leave the room.

"No problem." She took one last dab at his nose. "I'm all done here. Hard to improve on perfection." She shot Brazos a wink and slid the brush into a cup on the countertop. As she stepped out of the room, she closed the door behind her, giving us privacy.

Brazos stood, hooking one thumb in the pocket of his jeans and stretching the other up a support beam in the center of the room as if already posing for a photo. He leaned in and offered us an irresistible smile. "To what do I owe this pleasure?"

Beside me, Lu emitted an odd sound that was part gulp, part squeal. *Guhweee!*

Brazos chuckled.

"I spoke with your agent," I said. "He told me that he wasn't responsible for filing your tax returns."

"My *agent*? Is that what I told you?" Brazos pulled his hand from his pocket and slapped his palm against his forehead, fingers splayed. "That must've been the exhaustion and the liquor talking. It's not my agent who was supposed to file my returns. It's my manager."

Relief flooded through me. So Brazos wasn't a liar, after all. Thank goodness. I'd hate to think I'd spent the last couple years lusting after a loser. "Is your manager here today?" I hoped so. It sure would be nice to put an end to this matter.

"No," he said, "but I can give you her card. It has all of her contact information on it."

He turned around, treating us to a nice, close view of his perfect ass. Again, Lu made the sound. *Guhweee*. Brazos squatted down and pulled a leather duffel bag from under the makeup bench. He fished around in an outside pocket, retrieving a business card. He stood and stepped toward me.

He stopped a mere foot in front of me and Lu. She made the odd noise a third time. *Guhweee*.

Brazos held the card out. Our fingers touched when I took it from him. His skin was soft and warm, leaving a sensation where he'd touched me that I was much too aware of.

"Thanks," I somehow managed. My throat had closed tight.

I looked down at the card. It read:

SIERRA BEHR, MANAGER
BRAZOS RIVERS AND THE BOYS OF THE BAYOU
(555) 453–1576
SBEHR@BRAZOSRIVERS.COM

"Let her know I'll be calling, okay?"

"No problem." He hiked a thumb toward the door. "Now that we've got this tax thing resolved, want to come watch the shoot?"

Lu responded for us. *Guhweee!*

Brazos must've taken her response in the affirmative. He slid his straw cowboy hat onto his head, opened the door, and offered an arm to Lu.

Smiling so broadly she risked fracturing her face, the Lobo wrapped her forearm around his and let him lead her down the hall and into the studio space. I followed along, a sharp knife of jealousy stabbing me in the gut. Brazos and I had only touched fingers, yet Lu was basically having elbow sex with the guy. So not fair.

Brazos grabbed two folding chairs from the wall and pulled them open for us. "Have a seat, ladies."

As Lu and I sat down to watch, the room erupted in a flurry of activity. Two people brought in a painted ply-wood backdrop that looked remarkably like a real barn door. They stacked three bales of hay against the door and hung an old-fashioned lantern over it. When the set crew finished, the photographer's staff set up a variety of lights and reflectors around the perimeter of the scene. Finally, a representative of the Buckin' Bronco Boot company approached Brazos with a new pair of black cowboy boots, filling the room with the scent of leather and polish. The rep held the boots still while Brazos stepped into them. A moment later, the rep added a shiny new set of the singer's trademark silver spurs.

Brazos stepped onto the set, his spurs jingling.

One of the set designers called down the hallway to the other. "Bring in the horse!"

Lu turned to me. "They're going to bring a live horse in here? What if it poops?"

"I'm prepared." I pulled the bottle of Whitewater cologne from my purse and spritzed the air.

Lu lifted her nose in the air and sniffed. "That's some fine-smelling stuff."

"Here." I handed her the bottle. "Give it to Carl." No way in hell would I give the bottle to Nick now. He'd probably just pour it on some charcoal briquettes and take a match to them, maybe grill some burgers.

"Thanks. I've gotten awfully tired of Carl's Aqua Velva."

Holy crap, did they still make that stuff? My grandfather had worn it back in the day.

A moment later one of the set designers led a light tan horse into the room. Only the horse didn't walk in. It rolled. Yep, the beast was a taxidermied horse on wheels, posed in a rearing position, his front legs pawing the air. Forget Mr. Ed. This was *Mr. Dead*. Jeez, this creepy thing was sure to give me nightmares.

"Was that a once real horse?" Lu called to the woman rolling it into place.

"No," the woman replied. "It's a good likeness, though, isn't it?"

Damn straight and thank God. I could avoid the nightmares now.

The woman plunked a saddle on the oversized stuffed animal and cinched it tight. "We have to use a fake. It's too dangerous to use a live horse. The flash could spook it. We can't risk Brazos being injured."

Part of me understood. Another part of me felt cheated. Seeing Brazos atop a real muscular, well-hung steed would have been much more titillating than this phony pony prop. He might as well be riding a broomstick horse.

Once everything was in place, the women put a stool next to the horse and Brazos used it to climb up onto his mount. If Brazos weren't so gorgeous, this scene might have been comical.

Once Brazos was seated on his stuffed steed, the photographer grabbed a camera and began issuing instructions. "Chin up. Now down a little. Turn your head to the right. Back just a touch. Arm up over your head. Great. Now fist your hand. A little looser. You want it tight but not clenched."

The photographer snapped a dozen photos in quick succession. *Click-click-click.* After sliding a foot to the right, he snapped another set of shots. *Click-click-click.* He rose up on his toes. *Click-click-click.* He bent down on one knee. *Click-click-click.* All the while Brazos smiled more, then less, then more again, at the photographer's direction.

Noise from the entrance doors caught my attention. One of the security guards headed our way. "Bad news, Brazos. We've got trouble."

chapter fourteen

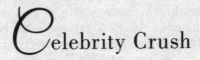

Celebrity Crush

"Trouble?" Instinctively, I stood. As a member of federal law enforcement, I dealt with trouble as part of my job.

"What's the matter?" Brazos asked his bodyguard.

"Bunch of fans gathering outside," the guy said. "Word must've gotten out that you were shooting here."

Brazos turned his eyes my way.

I raised my palms in innocence. "I didn't tell a soul where you'd be." Why would I? Hell, if I could, I'd want Brazos all to myself. "They probably spotted your car."

The Ferrari with the personalized plates wasn't exactly subtle. The car screamed, *Look! Here comes Brazos Rivers!*

Brazos stepped to the doors to take a peek outside. Lu and I followed him. At least fifty women had gathered in the lot, most of them dressed in low-cut tops and short skirts despite the frigid temperatures. Apparently, they thought putting the goods on display might draw the eye of their favorite singer, especially since the cold temperatures had brought the nipples out in full force. Several held CDs in their hands, no doubt hoping Brazos would

personally autograph them. A few others had brought the
singer gifts in colorful gift bags. One had even brought a
bouquet of helium balloons, as if the star were a five-year-
old child. A woman who appeared to be about Lu's age
held a foil-covered pie tin in her hand. No doubt she'd
made Brazos's favorite cinnamon apple pie. The article in
Stud Farm had noted the pie was the star's guilty pleasure
and provided the recipe. Despite the woman's advanced
age, she was dressed just as scantily as the younger girls,
the only difference being that her low-cut top had to hang
a little lower to show off the gravity-ravaged goods.

Brazos turned to address his security detail. "I don't
have time for personalized autographs. Pass out some of
my signed headshots while I wrap things up in here."

One of the team retrieved a manila envelope from Brazos's duffel bag and headed out the door, while the other
remained just inside the door to keep watch. Brazos returned to the studio to finish his shoot.

As the guard passed out the photos, I took another look
outside. The women eagerly accepted the signed headshots from the security guard, but made no move to leave
afterward. Looked like they preferred to wait for at least
a glimpse of their favorite star. The older lady with the
pie had strategically moved to the edge of the group
where she'd be better able to see the star when he emerged
from the studio.

Ten minutes and three hundred thousand dollars later
the shoot was over. Sheesh. I'd gone into the wrong line of
business, hadn't I? Then again, I couldn't carry a tune and
got stage fright. I probably would've been a horrible failure as a singer and would never have gotten this kind of
lucrative endorsement deal. Still, maybe I could've made a
name for myself in a sharpshooting show on the rodeo cir-
cuit. After all, if Annie Oakley had done it, why not Tara
Holloway?

Brazos rounded up his bag and handed it to the guard at the door. He turned back, putting a hand on Lu's shoulder and issuing one last smile meant only for us. "You beautiful ladies take care now."

When Brazos removed his hand, Lu reached up to touch the place on her shoulder where his fingers had been. Yep. She was smitten.

Brazos hiked his head at the door and his guard led the way out. Lu and I followed the singer out into the lot. When the women outside realized Brazos was in their presence, the crowd offered a concerted shriek even the Beatles would envy. My eye involuntarily twitched, the high-pitched noise threatening to give me an aneurysm. The cool breeze carried the overwhelming scent of River Rain, Brazos's fragrance for women. These fans must have bathed in the stuff.

"Hey howdy, y'all!" Brazos offered the screaming women a smile and raised a hand in a passing greeting as he made his way to the Ferrari.

Thirty feet away, his two security guards spread their arms out to create a barrier to restrain the women. Unfortunately, two men, no matter how meaty, were no match for fifty horny women intent on copping a feel of their favorite star.

The guards managed to stop only four of the women before being plowed down and trampled over. Now it was the security detail who were shrieking.

"Get off me, bitch!"

"Ow! My fingers!"

The rest of the women stampeded past the bodyguards, rushing toward Brazos as if a dam had broken. The women's heels click-clack-click-clacked along the asphalt like an out-of-control train rushing along at five hundred miles an hour. The helium balloons bounced along among the heads of the women in the crowd before being batted away, breaking free from the hand that held them, and soaring skyward.

"Brazos!" cried a woman in a red leather miniskirt and matching bustier. She held up her CD. "Sign this!"

"Wait!" hollered another, holding up a book trimmed in red satin ruffles. "Look at the scrapbook I made for you!"

My gaze followed the women as they raced toward Brazos who, in turn, raced as fast as he could to his car. He'd just reached the Ferrrari and put his hand on the door handle when, with a final, desperate yelp, he disappeared under a tsunami of thighs and cleavage and Creative Memories. The women piled on as if they were defensive tackles for the Dallas Cowboys, one even leaping upward before coming down on the stack. The women wailed and writhed, each trying to wriggle her way down to the singer at the bottom of the pile.

"Holy crap!" I cried. Brazos would be smothered under all that perfumed flesh! My celebrity crush would be crushed!

Lu rushed forward. "Come on! We've gotta help him!"

Lu and I ran to the pile of women and began pulling them off. I grabbed one by the hair and yanked her backward. She landed on her butt on the asphalt.

"You bitch!" she cried, her eyes flashing with fury. Before she could get up and come after me, I'd slung another woman her way, knocking her back onto her ass once again.

Lu grabbed two by the waistbands of their skirts and dragged them aside. Not bad for a woman in her sixties. Looked like those workouts were paying off.

The next woman I pulled off the stack began slapping at me, windmill style. With her hands moving in front of her, she didn't see my foot coming. I hooked my loafer around her ankle and gave her chest a shove. *Fwump!*

She, too, fell back on her ass, joining the other women on the asphalt.

The older woman with the pie made it to the car just as a young woman on top of the pile threw her leg up behind her. The girl's stiletto hit the bottom of the pie plate with a resounding *ting!* and sent the dessert soaring into the air.

"Nooooo!" The woman who'd baked the pie could only watch in horror as the plate reached its pinnacle, gave in to the forces of gravity, and fell back toward earth, turning top down on its descent. *Spluck!* The pie landed on the roof the Ferrari, sending up a splatter of apple pieces, gooey cinnamon-scented filling, and buttery crust. The woman's face contorted in rage and she grabbed the girl who'd kicked the pie plate by the calves, tugging her from the fray and onto the pavement.

The rest of the women were making no effort to get off Brazos, like football players fighting over a ball. Lu and I exchanged glances. We were running out of steam, but if Brazos didn't get out from under this crush of bodies right away, he would be both squashed and torn to pieces, a bloody smear and dismembered limbs in the parking lot the only things left of him.

I was just about to pull my gun from my holster when Lu beat me to the punch, aiming her gun at the sky. *BANG!*

A few of the women at the top of the pile screamed, gave up their quest to touch Brazos and ran off, their hands curved protectively over their heads.

BANG!

Lu's second shot scared off the next layer of women, but at least half a dozen diehards still remained.

Brazos wasn't yet visible, though we could hear his terrified gasps. "Get . . . off . . . me! I . . . can't . . . breathe!"

I pulled my gun and joined Lu, each of us getting off one shot.

BANG!
BANG!

Several more women scattered, running for their lives. Two stubborn women hung on, though, yanking Brazos back and forth like a rag doll, his head tossing first one way then the other. Both Brazos and one of the women had bloody noses, while the other woman sported a split lip and a raw cheek that had been scraped from her chin to her brow bone.

Brazos looked up at me and Lu, his blue eyes alight with desperation. "Help me!"

"Don't worry, Brazos!" Lu cried. "We've got 'em!" With that she raised her gun and slammed the butt of it into the side of the closest woman's skull. The woman's head spun for a moment before she collapsed forward, falling face-first into the Ferrari's back tire hubcap. *Ping!*

Lest she suffer the same fate, the other woman threw up one hand to shield her head and used the other to push herself to a stand. She took off running, her pace impeded by the broken heel on her left shoe. *Click-thud-click-thud-click-thud!*

While Lu and I slid our guns back into our holsters, Brazos lay back against the door of the car, his eyes wide, his jaw slack, and his chest heaving. His blue western shirt was ripped to shreds, both front pockets and one sleeve missing, a tear in the front revealing a waxed pec and a pinkish nipple. His belt was gone, his jeans pulled down several inches, revealing a pair of blue striped boxer briefs and barely concealing his naughty bits. Both of his brand-new Buckin' Bronco boots were gone, though the spurs had fallen off and lay on the ground near his feet.

Now that all of the women, other than the unconscious one at our feet, had fled, the two members of the security detail rushed over. Spotting the prone woman, one phoned an ambulance, while the other summoned local police.

When Brazos had gathered his wits, he looked up at the four of us. "Those bitches nearly killed me!"

I reached down an arm to help him up and Lu did the same.

He took our hands and pulled himself to a stand. After looking down at what remained of his clothes, he dusted himself off, hiked his pants up, and reactivated his charm, turning those dazzling blue eyes on us. "I sure was lucky you two were here." His eyes gazed into mine for a moment, then traveled down my body and back up again, the resulting smile telling me my moves today had gotten his attention and that he was duly impressed.

Those same blue eyes cut to his bodyguards, treating them to a look that was more disgusted than dazzling. His trained protection detail had been bested by two women, one in her sixties and one who stood only five feet two inches.

Neener-neener.

Brazos knelt down to retrieve the spurs, then offered one set to me and one to Lu. "A little memento of all the fun we've had here today."

The three of us shared a laugh. It was a special, intimate moment.

As Lu and I tucked our souvenir spurs into our purses, the police and ambulance arrived, sirens wailing and lights flashing. A male medic tended to the woman Lu had pistol-whipped, while a female medic treated Brazos's nose and felt him up all over.

"Checking for broken bones," the EMT claimed as she ran her hands over his rib cage.

Seemed to me she was just taking advantage of the situation to cop a feel of celebrity flesh. There were no bones in his ass, after all.

The female fan, now conscious but dazed, was taken to the hospital for observation.

The police officers took statements from each of us. When they finished, one turned to Brazos. "Any chance I can get an autograph?"

"Me, too!" said the other. "And one for my girlfriend?"

Brazos nodded. "Be happy to oblige."

When the autographs had been signed, the cops set about gathering evidence, sliding the dented pie pan, the broken heel, and an earring into evidence bags.

As the officers were wrapping things up, a news van roared into the lot. In the front passenger seat sat Trish LeGrande, a bosomy reporter with hair the color of butterscotch or ear wax, depending on your viewpoint. I was in the ear wax faction. Trish had reported on various cases I'd been involved in, and she rarely made the IRS look good. She'd also relentlessly pursued Brett Ellington, the guy I'd dated before Nick. Needless to say, I abhorred her.

Trish must have caught the action on a police scanner. The van had barely screeched to a stop when she leaped out onto the pavement. She wore a fitted suit in her trademark pink, along with gray high-heeled boots and a pearl choker around her neck.

"Mr. Rivers!" she called, raising a hand that held a wireless microphone. "I've got some questions for you!"

Her cameraman joined her and began shooting footage of her impromptu interview.

"I understand that a group of fans attacked you here only moments ago," she said in her typical breathless, bedroom voice as she stepped up close to Brazos, accidentally on purpose brushing her boob against his bicep.

Tramp.

"That's right." Brazos aimed a brilliant smile at the

camera. "I'm lucky to have a following of dedicated fans, but this particular crowd was a little overzealous," he teased, "as you can see." He gestured from his shoulder to his hips, indicating the torn clothing.

Trish put a concerned hand on his shoulder and, though the camera couldn't pick it up, I noticed she ran her thumb over his shoulder blade in a flirtatious, far-too-personal gesture. "I, for one, am glad you survived this terrifying incident."

"That makes two of us." Brazos chuckled, then waved me and Lu over to stand beside him. "I owe it all to these two lovely ladies."

When Trish saw me, her eyes flashed with revulsion. She felt the same way about me as I did about her.

Without waiting for Trish's prompt, Brazos continued speaking. "Miss Holloway and Miss Lobozinski pulled the women off me and fired their guns into the air to scare the more determined ones off. If not for them I'd be in much worse shape."

Trish skewered me with her eyes. "Tara Holloway shooting her gun again. Why am I not surprised?"

Brazos looked from Trish to me, his brows lifting. "You two know each other?"

"She's reported on my previous cases," I said before Trish could open her plumped pink lips. *And she hadn't reported fairly.*

Trish turned away from me and cocked her head coyly. "Tara tends to push the limits of the law. The public has a right to know."

Brazos looked again from Trish to me, the expression on his face telling me he was both amused and intrigued.

When Trish wrapped up the interview, she slipped her business card into the front pocket of Brazos's jeans and looked up at him, her lips parted seductively. "Just in case you need to reach me."

She might as well have said, *Call me if you want an easy lay.*

Lu and I bade Brazos good-bye.

He gave us each a warm hug. "You two are one of a kind."

It might have been my imagination, but I thought I heard Trish mutter, "Thank God!" under her breath.

chapter fifteen

$\mathcal{D}$on't Fence Me In

Nick cornered me and Lu when we returned to the office. "Well? You two get a firm commitment from Brazos?"

Luckily, Lu responded for me. "We got something better!" she cried. "His spurs!" She pulled her set from her purse and jingled them in front of Nick's frowning face.

"Really?" he snapped. "That's all you got?"

"'Course not." Lu dropped the spurs back into her open purse. "We got his manager's number. She's the one who was supposed to file the returns."

Nick grunted. "Same song, second verse." He narrowed his eyes at Lu. "Don't tell me you fell for that little tax-cheatin' cowboy, too?"

Lu crossed her arms over her chest. "If I didn't know better, Nick, I'd say you were jealous of Brazos."

Whoa! I tried not to laugh when Nick sputtered.

"Me?" he said. "Jealous of that pop-music punk? That'll be the day."

The bulging vein in his neck told me that Lu had struck a chord. Frankly, I was glad she'd put Nick in his place. Not because he'd been wrong about anything, but instead because he was absolutely right yet didn't have the sense to keep his mouth shut about it.

When I returned to my office I placed a call to Brazos's manager. Unfortunately, all I got was Sierra's voice mail. I left her a message, asking her to call me ASAP. "Interest is accruing at the rate of $2,191.78 per day," I told her. "So it would be best for everyone involved to get those taxes paid up right away." With that, I ended my message and hung up my phone.

I sat back in my chair. Now that I was away from Brazos, I could think clearly again. This case had dragged on longer than it should have without any sort of progress. Nick was right. It was time to get things moving along.

Nick and I ordered pizza in and ate dinner at his place, feeding our crusts to Nutty who ate only a small portion but licked the cheese and sauce off the rest. We spent the evening cuddling on the couch and watching sitcoms, with Nutty lying between us. The dog's head was in Nick's lap, his butt aimed in my direction. Nutty glanced back at me with his cataract-clouded eyes and gave a soft but demanding woof.

"Okay, buddy." I reached out to scratch his hindquarters with both hands. "How's that?"

He thanked me with a quick wave of his tail.

I didn't bring up the issue of Brazos Rivers and neither did Nick. It felt good to relax and not think about work for a while.

When the ten o'clock news came on, we flipped through the channels to watch Trish's report. Though she spent a full minute detailing the attack on Brazos, she made no mention of his rescuers. Lu and I had ended up on the cutting-room floor. *Grr.* I wouldn't mind taking a pair of scissors to Trish someday, too, maybe lop off those shiny golden locks of hers and shove them down her throat.

"Lu and I saved Brazos's ass," I lamented. "I can't believe Trish didn't mention us at all."

"Don't let that ditz get you all hot and bothered." Nick slid me a sultry grin and nuzzled my neck. "That's my job."

Mmm. I tilted my head to give him more skin to work with. "If this is your job, I should give you a raise."

"You already did." Nick gestured to the sizable tent in his sweatpants.

"Wow," I said. "That's going in your performance review."

I spent the night at Nick's. Alicia and my cats could take care of themselves. Besides, things between Nick and me had been strained since the concert. I was crazy about him, and I didn't like it when we were at odds. With any luck, Sierra Behr would call me tomorrow, she and I would get things sorted out, and I could finally put my case against Brazos Rivers to rest.

Despite my leaving her four more voice mail messages, Sierra Behr did not call me on Tuesday or Wednesday. Things did not get sorted out. And I still couldn't put the case against Brazos to rest.

Dammit, I thought as I toyed with the silver spurs the singer had given me. *Dammit, dammit, dammit!*

When I hadn't heard from Sierra by five o'clock, I wasn't merely embarrassed, I was frustrated and annoyed and out of patience. What part of "call me back immediately, this is extremely urgent" did she not understand? Due to her failure to return my call, Brazos had racked up $4,383.56 more in interest. I felt sorry for the guy. I mean, I knew the people working for him must be busy. But they were supposed to be helping him *make* money, not *waste* it.

I sat back in my chair, pondering my options.

One, I could give Sierra another day or two to return my call. Maybe she'd been tied up with work or a personal issue. It happens. Was I being too impatient?

Two, I could call Quentin Yarbrough and find out when and where Brazos would be making his next appearance in the area. But that could be weeks away and I was ready to take action *now*.

Three, I could drive out to the Brazos Bend Ranch. There was a good chance Brazos was still staying out there with his parents. I could take an agreement with me, get his signature on it. That way it would be his problem to figure out who was supposed to get his returns filed and why they hadn't done it. I felt stupid that I'd let him put that task on me in the first place. I never did such a thing with other taxpayers with past-due bills. I'd simply advise them that they had to get their returns filed by a specific date or they'd be hauled off in handcuffs. I'd trusted Brazos, assumed he'd been on the up-and-up with me about his returns. But I was beginning to fear he'd fed me a line of bull.

I pulled up a form agreement on my computer and filled in the blanks, giving Winthrop Merriweather VII one month from today to file his delinquent tax returns and pay up. After printing out the form, I slid it into my briefcase and stormed out of my office, a woman with a purpose.

Two hours later, I drove up the country road toward the ranch, passing one of PPE's gas rigs. The lights surrounding the rig lit up the dark evening sky. A number of workers milled about the rig with equipment and tools, earning some overtime. I wondered if one of them might be Doug Dunne.

As I approached the ranch, I spotted more lights up ahead, what appeared to be a single headlight flanked by a smaller red light on one side and a green light on the other.

A plane.

Was Brazos flying out?

No!

I pushed the gas pedal to the floor, flying down the road at eighty miles per hour, then ninety, then a hundred. But it still wasn't fast enough. Just as I reached the gate to the Brazos Bend Ranch, the singer's private jet barreled down the asphalt runway and soared into the sky, leaving a cloud of exhaust hanging behind it in the cool evening air.

I banged a fist on the steering wheel in frustration, inadvertently honking the horn. I kept screwing this case up, over and over. Ugh. Maybe the IRS shouldn't have given my badge and gun back to me after all. I rested my head against the wheel and closed my eyes, not wanting to face myself even if it was only in the rearview mirror.

When I finally lifted my head, I caught another flash of light. Someone had come out the front door of the Merriweathers' house. From this distance and in the dark it was impossible to tell who it was, even through my field glasses. Was it possible that Brazos could still be here? Maybe his pilot had flown the plane somewhere for maintenance or refueling. Or maybe Brazos had given his pilot a few days off and the pilot had decided to fly home, wherever that might be. The tour bus wasn't in the drive, but perhaps the bus driver had taken it elsewhere, maybe driven the Boys of the Bayou and the roadies to a hotel. Rather than speculate, I might as well drive on up to the gate and find out for myself whether Brazos was around, right?

I drove up to the gate and pushed the button with the picture of a speaker on it. *Bzzt*.

When nobody had responded in twenty seconds, I tried the buzzer again, holding the button down a little longer this time. *Bzzzzzt*. Still no answer. Just for kicks, I buzzed out the tune to "Baby, If You're Willin'." *Bzt-Bzt Bzt Bzt Bzzt-bzt*. Nobody came to the intercom. Apparently, nobody was willin'.

It dawned on me then that if the person had come outside, there might be nobody in the house to respond to my summons. I eyed the gate in front of me. It topped out at eight feet, but that was no match for the east Texas tree-climbing champion. I turned off the engine, tucked my keys and the agreement in my pocket, and took a running leap at the fence. Grabbing the upper bar, I used my feet for leverage and eventually managed to straddle the gate. Swinging my outside leg over, I dropped to the ground. *Plop*.

I headed across the field, using the flashlight app on my cell phone to light my way. As I drew close to the house, I noticed a man and woman sitting on the front porch, sipping white wine from sparkling stem glasses.

The two looked nothing at all like the parents of a country-western star. The woman was dark haired and olive skinned, with a voluptuous build à la Sophia Vergara. She wore a loose-fitting tunic top over fitted pants with ridiculously high heels. She looked to be in her mid-forties. The man was noticeably older, around sixty or so. He was tall and trim, with white hair and pale skin. He wore a starched dress shirt and dress pants with sleek polished dress shoes. The two seemed unusually chic for country folk.

I stepped up to the porch railing. "Hello. Mr. and Mrs. Merriweather?"

Brazos's mother let out a scream and reflexively raised

her arm, inadvertently tossing most of her wine over her shoulder.

Brazos's father flew out of his seat, stepping in front of his wife in a protective gesture. "Leave these premises now or I'll summon the police!"

Wait a minute. His words were neither Southern nor spoken with a Texas accent. A Texan would've said, *Get your sorry ass off my property or I'll fill you with lead.* If I didn't know better, I'd say this man's accent had come from somewhere north of the Mason-Dixon line.

I raised both hands. "No need. I'm federal law enforcement." I could understand their reaction. No doubt an overzealous fan or two had stalked their son out here. I pulled my badge from my pocket and displayed it. "I'm Special Agent Tara Holloway from the IRS. You're Winthrop and Marcella Merriweather, right? I left you a voice-mail message a few days ago."

The two exchanged glances but said nothing.

"Brazos and I have been in negotiations regarding his taxes. I have something I need to discuss with him in person. I was hoping to catch him here."

Marcella stood, raising a finger to point at the sky. "Our son just left in his jet."

Her accent was neither Southern nor Yankee. Rather, it sounded foreign. Like Spanish but not quite. Italian, probably, given her first name. How could this be? Brazos dressed in boots and jeans and sang songs about Southern life and Southern people, yet his father sounded like a New England WASP and his mother sounded like a character from *The Sopranos*.

I looked from one of them to the other. "When will Brazos be back?"

The two exchanged glances again.

"I'm not certain," his father said.

I stepped closer to the rail and rested my hands on it. "Why didn't you return my phone call?"

"We didn't get your message," Winthrop VI replied at the exact same time Marcella said, "We accidentally erased your number."

"Which is it?" I gave first one, then the other a pointed look. "Did you not get it or did you erase it?"

Neither responded for a moment. When Winthrop finally did, it was without conviction and didn't answer my question. "You're trespassing."

"And you're not shooting straight with me."

We stood in silence for a moment.

"Look," I said, "your son's account is accruing interest of over two grand per day. That's not exactly chump change. If Brazos agrees to get his returns filed and his taxes paid, I can work with him, maybe get some of the penalties waived. But he's got to cooperate. First he told me his agent was supposed to file his returns, but that turned out to be false. Then he told me that his manager was supposed to file his returns, but I've left her multiple messages and she hasn't called me back. It's starting to look like he's jerking me around. You don't want him to get in trouble, do you? Maybe end up in jail?"

The two said nothing. Sheesh. What would it take to break these people? Sleep deprivation? Thumb screws? Waterboarding? Unfortunately, none of those techniques was legal now that a Democrat was in the White House. Perhaps I could contact the NSA, though, see if they had any of the Merriweathers' e-mails in their databanks. Surely they would. After all, they had recordings of Angela Merkel calling out for a delivery of schnitzel and strudel. If that didn't work, maybe I could order up a drone, have it buzz the house occasionally, scanning for Brazos.

"Unless you two want to be implicated for obstruction

of justice," I said, adding some bluster, "you'll give me your son's current cell phone number."

The two exchanged a final glance before Marcella went inside and returned with her mobile phone. She dialed up her son's name on her contacts list. I noticed she'd entered his name as "Winnie." A cute name for a girl, but the only male Winnie I knew was the pantless bear whose oversized butt got stuck in the window after he'd indulged in too much honey, whose raspy voice and slow, halting speech made him sound as if he'd smoked too many funny little cigarettes out there in the Hundred Acre Wood. It made sense. After all, that donkey he hung out with was obviously hooked on downers. And that bouncing tiger? A speed freak if ever there was one.

I entered Brazos's number into the contacts list on my phone and forced a smile and nod at the Merriweathers. "Thanks for your cooperation. Enjoy the rest of your evening."

I'd made it ten steps before I realized I'd have to jump the gate again to get out. "Any chance you can open the gate for me?" I asked as I turned back. But it was too late. The Merriweathers had gone back inside. I'd have to scale the thing one more time.

After stalking back across the field, praying there were no rattlesnakes out and about tonight, I pulled myself up and over the gate once again.

"Dang it!" I landed hard, jamming my left ankle and falling back on my rear, scraping my palms on the asphalt. I pushed myself to a stand, leaving a layer of my skin on the pavement, and kicked the gate. The jangling of the iron bars only jangled my nerves all the more.

The instant I was seated in my car I placed a call to Brazos. My call went straight to voice mail. Had his parents already warned him I'd be calling? Maybe. Maybe not. I supposed it wasn't necessarily suspicious that the

call went to the messaging system. After all, he was air-
borne. Any use of his cell phone could screw up the pilot's
controls and send them crashing into Possum Kingdom
Lake. Brazos wouldn't be the first famous singer to die in
a plane crash. But I wasn't so sure we'd be singing bye-bye
to American pie this time. In the case of Winnie Merriweather, perhaps an Italian pizza pie would be more
appropriate.

Who the hell is Brazos Rivers?

chapter sixteen

Mission Possible

I sat in my car for a few moments, thinking, frustration setting me on edge. My efforts to collect from Brazos had all been for naught so far. All I had to show for my efforts was a silver spur and a sprained ankle. I hadn't gotten anywhere in the PPE investigation, either. Heck, I still wasn't even sure Larry Burkett had done anything illegal. I'd looked over PPE's and the Burketts' personal tax returns and nothing had immediately jumped out at me as unusual. Was he spending the cash on drill bits or not?

There was only one way to know for certain. I needed to get into the PPE warehouse, determine if bits had, in fact, been delivered. And there were only two ways to get into the warehouse. One, I could break in. Or, two, I could use the spare key Burkett had given to Katie.

Breaking in held little appeal. I'd set off the alarm and have only limited time to look over the bit inventory before the sheriff's department would send someone out. Besides, like Katie, I knew nothing about drill bits. How would I be able to tell one from another? Was there even a way to distinguish what company had made a particular drill bit? I had no idea. And what if I got caught doing an illegal B and E? I'd be fired and any evidence I found would be inadmissible in a court case against Burkett.

Spare key it was.

I drove to Katie's house and phoned her from the driveway. "That's me outside," I said, flashing my lights. "Can I come in for a minute?"

She sounded surprised and tentative. "Okay."

Again she met me at the door, putting a finger to her lips, indicating I should speak quietly. "The boys are already in bed."

"I'll be quick," I whispered, following her inside.

As she closed the door behind me, Doug emerged from a bedroom dressed in a pair of pajamas that were two inches too short in both the legs and sleeves, an old pair he'd obviously outgrown but still found comfortable. Their fluffy white dog followed him.

"Have you found out anything?" Katie asked, keeping her voice low.

I shook my head and knelt to give the dog a scratch behind the ears. "I followed a lead, but it appears to be a dead end." I stood and the dog sauntered off, jumping up onto the couch. I told Katie and Doug about the envelope Burkett had left at the historical marker, that it had been picked up by someone driving a black Toyota, and that my attempt to identify the driver hadn't panned out. "Any idea who the driver of the car could be?"

Katie mulled it over for a moment. "I don't remember seeing anyone with a Toyota."

"Me, neither," Doug said. "'Course I'm usually out at the drilling sites. I only go to HQ when my foreman asks for help loading equipment."

"Keep an eye out for the car," I advised. "Call me immediately if you see it."

Both indicated their agreement.

I turned to Doug. "If someone went into the warehouse and took a look at the drill bit inventory, would they be able to tell whether the bits were from the usual supplier or whether they were delivered by another vendor?"

He nodded. "Every bit I've ever seen was from Hughley-Baker. The letters *HB* are engraved on the base of the bit, followed by the model number."

"Hughley-Baker has their own in-house sales force," Katie added. "Each sales rep has an exclusive region. Nobody else would be able to sell Hughley-Baker bits to oil and gas companies in this area."

"How do you know this?" I asked.

"The sales rep had car trouble once when he'd come by to call on Mr. Burkett. I fixed him a cup of coffee and we talked briefly while he waited for roadside assistance."

Doug cocked his head and raised a suspicious brow. "Was he good-lookin'?"

Katie tossed a flirtatious grin at her husband. "Not half as good-looking as you."

Helpful info. The part about the exclusivity, I mean. Not the part about who was better looking than whom. "So if Mr. Burkett is buying bits from another supplier, they'd have to be from a different manufacturer?"

Katie was all business again. "Right."

I looked from Katie to Doug, wondering whether I could convince them to let me into the warehouse to take a look around. What's more, even if I *could,* I wondered if I *should.* What if we went in, found bits that had not be made by Hughley-Baker, and realized Burkett had been telling the truth all along? There was a chance our snooping would be discovered and the two of them would lose their jobs. Was I willing to take that risk?

After some thought, I realized it wasn't my decision to make. Katie was obviously concerned about her exposure if she continued to make the cash withdrawals from the bank, enter unsubstantiated data into the accounting system, and affirm under penalty of perjury that PPE's tax returns were true and correct to the best of her knowledge. It was up to her and her husband to decide.

"I have an idea," I said. "It could put an end to this investigation right now and give you some peace of mind."

"What is it?" Katie asked.

"Mr. Burkett gave you a key to the warehouse. And he never explicitly forbade you from using it, right?"

She gave a tentative nod of her head.

"I'm not a lawyer," I said, pulling up what little business law I could remember from my class in college. "But it seems arguable that when Burkett gave Katie the keys without imposing specific conditions on their use, he gave her implied authority to access the warehouse and to grant access to others."

Katie nibbled nervously at her lip, apparently mulling things over.

I looked from her to Doug. "How would you feel about you and I going to the warehouse tonight? We could take a look at the drill bits and determine whether there's inventory that's not from Hughley-Baker. That way we'd know whether Mr. Burkett has been telling the truth, that he's been buying bits for cash from a second supplier, or whether he's been lying and spending the money on something else."

The two exchanged glances.

"It's pretty much the only option left," I prodded, though I supposed that wasn't exactly the case. I could always stake out PPE again this Friday and follow the Toyota if it showed up then. But frankly I was out of patience, desperate to either move this case ahead or call it quits and move on to my other pending investigations. It took me half a day on the road just to drive out here and back, and I couldn't continue to invest this type of time in a case that might be moot.

The sound of creaking bedsprings came from a room down the hall, drawing Katie's attention. When she turned back, she said, "I can't leave the boys."

Doug looked from me to his wife. "Agent Holloway and I can go alone," he said. "I can get the keys out of the safe if you give me the combination."

Katie hesitated, continuing to gnaw her lip.

Doug reached out a hand and took hers in it. "I think it's the right thing to do. This situation has been eating at you. Something's gotta change."

Katie exhaled sharply but stopped worrying her lip. "What about the security cameras?"

His wife now seemingly on board, Doug pulled his hand back. "I can turn off the electricity at the fuse box." He turned to me. "I don't think there's any cameras on the back of the administrative building where the box is located."

"But the fuse box is padlocked," Katie said. "The key is in the safe."

"I'll take my bolt cutters," Doug said, "and my soldering iron to fix the lock afterward."

"What about the Dobermans?" she asked. "They'll eat you alive."

I glanced toward the kitchen. "Got bread, mayonnaise, and baloney?"

Katie cocked her head, her eyes narrowing. "Yes. Why?"

"Dogs love my fried baloney sandwiches," I said. "I can use the sandwiches to lure the dogs to their pen so that Doug and I can get into the warehouse safely."

Katie exhaled a longer breath this time and closed her eyes for a few seconds. When she opened them, she said, "All right. Let's do it."

While Doug went to their bedroom to change into more suitable clothes, Katie led me to the kitchen. I melted butter in the frying pan while she rounded up a loaf of white bread, mayonnaise, and an open package of baloney. The baloney was a little dry around the edges, but I doubted the dogs would mind.

When the sandwiches were ready I fed one to the Dunnes' dog, who'd hopped down from the couch and come sniffing around. Katie and I wrapped the rest of them in foil and stashed them in a plastic grocery bag.

"Ready?" I asked Doug.

He'd changed into a pair of dark coveralls and a black knit cap. "Ready as I'll ever be."

Katie looked at her husband, worry contorting her face. "You should wear some kind of disguise in case the cameras pick you up or someone drives by and sees you." She stepped to a bedroom and slipped inside, returning a moment later with two cheap plastic masks that must have been from her boys' Halloween costumes. One was a storm trooper from *Star Wars,* the other was Darth Vader.

Doug took the masks, keeping Darth Vader for himself and holding the other out to me.

I took the white and black mask from him. "Thanks."

Katie jotted down the combination to the safe on a piece of paper. She handed her husband a set of keys and the combination, along with two pairs of yellow latex gloves she'd retrieved from under the kitchen sink. Having properly equipped the team, she followed us to the door. When she spoke, her voice was hesitant and tinged with trepidation. "Please be careful, okay?"

"Don't worry, honey. We will." Doug leaned in, cupped her chin, and gave her a kiss.

I hoped their next kiss wouldn't be during a conjugal visit at the county jail. If we got caught . . .

Ugh. I didn't even want to think about that possibility.

chapter seventeen

*I*t's a Dog-Eat-Baloney World

"Let's take my truck," Doug said. "I've got all my tools in the back."

We climbed in and drove off. Minutes later, he pulled the truck onto the grass at the edge of PPE's property, cutting his headlights and proceeding with only the parking lights on until he reached a couple of scrubby cedar trees. He parked the truck behind the trees for cover, cut the engine, and climbed out to retrieve the bolt cutters and soldering iron from his bed-mounted tool case. I climbed out of the passenger side and slid my mask into place. Doug followed suit. Next we donned the bright yellow latex gloves.

Doug glanced over at me. "Not exactly James Bond, are we?"

He was right. We looked like some type of costumed cleaning crew.

Still, goofy looking or not, we had an important job to do. "Time to boldly go where no man has gone before." I'd quoted *Star Trek* rather than *Star Wars* but Doug had the graciousness not to correct me.

We picked our way across the field to the administrative building, careful to stay well out of range of the security cameras mounted on the warehouse. Masks or not, we'd rather not be videotaped if we could avoid it. No sense raising suspicions. The ankle I'd jammed jumping over the Merriweathers' gate throbbed a little, but the pain was manageable.

I shivered in the cool air, but I think my quivering had more to do with my nerves being on edge than with the frigid winter temperatures. This mission was one of the more risky things I'd done in my job. I wasn't entirely sure it was legal or prudent. But we'd come too far to turn back now.

While the fenced-in space around the warehouse and the parking lot of the office were lit by floodlights, the back of the office was dark. We slipped behind the structure, squinting through our masks in the dark. The Dobermans stepped to the chain-link fence behind us, watching our moves, emitting low warning growls. *Grrrrr.*

"Here we are," Doug said, his voice muffled slightly by the black mask. He stopped in front of a metal box mounted on the back of the building. He reached out, positioned the lock for easy access, and raised his bolt cutters. Emitting a quick grunt, he forced the handles together. The severed lock fell to the dirt with a clunk.

One of the dogs emitted a short, sharp bark in response. *Yap!*

I turned to look at them and put a finger to my lips. "Shhhhh."

Doug flipped the switches inside the fuse box. *Snap. Snap. Snap. Snap.* The floodlights on the warehouse went dark. We stepped around to the front of the administrative building to find it dark, too.

Using Katie's key, Doug unlocked the front door and we slipped inside, closing the door behind us. I activated the flashlight app on my phone and used it to light our way to Katie's office. I found myself instinctively tiptoeing despite the fact that there was nobody around to hear our footsteps—nobody other than the goldfish, that is. One of them swam to the edge of the aquarium again, seeming to watch us as we crossed the room, as if it were some type of sophisticated high-tech spy equipment.

Wait. It isn't, is it?

Josh, my techie coworker, once told me that military contractors had developed a miniature spy drone that looked like an insect. A goldfish wouldn't be much more of a stretch.

Sheesh.

I mentally chastised myself for thinking such a ridiculous thought. My nerves were just getting to me. Nobody would put a hidden camera in a fake goldfish. It was a ridiculous thought, right? Right?

I tamped down my anxiety and tried to focus on the tasks at hand. Once we were in Katie's office we glanced around, looking for the safe.

"Where is it?" I asked Doug.

He shrugged. "Forgot to ask."

Doug texted Katie, who directed us to the safe's location. We found it behind a framed painting of a drilling rig. Ironically, or perhaps appropriately, the artist had painted the rig with *oil* paints. The frame had hidden hinges along the right side. Doug swung the picture outward, revealing a small safe built into the wall.

I stepped up behind Doug as he turned the dial. "I thought they only hid safes behind pictures in the movies."

He shrugged again, turning the combination lock to the final number. The lock released with a soft click. He pulled the door handle. Once the safe was open, I shined my phone light inside.

The only thing inside the safe was the spare set of keys. They hung from a key chain imprinted with a quote from John Paul Getty. "Formula for success: rise early, work hard, strike oil." So it was that easy, huh?

Doug snatched the keys, left the safe open, and walked back outside with me trailing along behind him. When we reached the fence that surrounded the warehouse, the dogs stalked up on the other side, growling and snarling at us. One of them drooled, as if he could already taste our flesh. I wondered what human meat tasted like. Chicken?

I'd faced down men armed with guns and box cutters, but these dogs were something entirely different and, frankly, far more frightening. Their fangs appeared to be six inches long, their toenails as sharp as knives. These dogs could tear any intruder to shreds in seconds.

"Hi, boys!" I said in the friendliest voice I could muster given the cold sweat that had broken out over my entire body. "Got a special treat for ya!"

While Doug unlocked the gate, I unwrapped the foil from the first sandwich and waved it in front of the fence to give them a good smell of the food. When I had their attention, I tore the sandwich into large bites, tossing them over the fence into their pen. With a reluctant and distrustful glance back at me, they ambled into their pen and wolfed down the sandwich, two of them engaging in a brief squabble over one of the bites. Yep, you could always count on fried baloney.

The gate unlocked now, Doug returned to my side. I handed the other sandwiches to him and pulled my weapons from my holster. With my gun in my right hand and my pepper spray in my left, I pushed the unlocked gate open and stepped inside, my stomach clenched tight in fear. I had no intention of shooting the dogs even if they attacked. After all, they were only doing what they'd been trained to do and I knew I could never bring myself to kill an animal. But a shot fired into the air might scare them off like it had scared off the rabid fans at Brazos's photo shoot. As for the pepper spray, though, I'd have no qualms using that. It might burn and sting for a few minutes, but the dogs would fully recover.

Doug continued to toss pieces of sandwiches over the fence and into the pen, distracting the dogs as I quietly slunk toward the open gate of their enclosure.

When I was five feet from the gate, one of the dogs turned, spotted me, and bolted toward the open gate of the pen. A scream ripped from my throat as I fought the instinct to turn and run but instead forced myself to bolt toward it, too. I reached the gate a half second before the dog, managing to slam it shut and lower the hinged handle to hold the gate closed just as the dog hurled himself at it, shaking the entire structure as he tried in vain to get at me.

"Holy shit!" Doug cried from the other side of the fence. "I thought you was a goner!"

"Me, too!" Thank God I hadn't wet myself.

The dogs secured in their pen, Doug entered the larger enclosed area and we made our way to the warehouse door. After a few tries, he found the key that fit the lock to the sliding doors of the equipment storage area. He slid it open just enough for us to squeeze through, then slid it closed behind us.

Using the light from our cell phones once again, we stepped over to the area where the drill bits were stored.

Doug looked over the numerous boxes and peeked inside to verify their contents. "Hughley-Baker. Hughley-Baker. Hughley-Baker." He glanced over at me. "There's no other bits here."

"So Katie was right. Larry Burkett's been lying to her."

That was good news. I'd hate to think I'd risked being

ravaged by savage dogs for nothing. But what had I risked my life for? What, exactly, was Burkett up to?

After Doug and I exited the warehouse, he turned to lock up. When the building was secured, we headed toward the open gate. My plan was that once we got outside I'd use the crowbar I'd seen in Doug's toolbox to open the latch on the dog pen and release them back into the bigger enclosure. I could stick the crowbar through a hole in the chain-link fence and safely nudge the latch from outside the fence. Yep, Tara Holloway knows how to get things done.

Apparently the dogs had a different plan, though, one that would make the fried baloney a mere appetizer and me the main course. When Doug and I came around the corner of the warehouse, we found ourselves face-to-face—or should I say face-to-muzzle?—with the three dogs. Apparently they'd figured out how to nudge the latch too.

I spread my legs and arms to block the dogs as well as I could. "Run!" I screamed to Doug. "Save yourself!" It had been my stupid idea to come here. If anyone was going to get hurt—or killed!—it should be me. He had a wife and three young boys counting on him. All I had were a couple of cats, only one of which would mourn my loss.

While Doug tore out the gate and yanked it closed behind him, I engaged the dogs and backed slowly toward it. "Nice doggies," I said in what I hoped was a soothing voice as I slowly readied my gun and pepper spray again. "Good boys!"

While Nutty would've wagged his tail in appreciation of these compliments, these dogs seemed to realize that my tone and words were complete falsehoods, intended merely to placate them. They continued to snarl and show their teeth, their upper lips and nostrils twitching. With each backward step I took toward the gate the dogs took a step forward, stalking their prey.

"You're sweet doggies," I lied. "Good, good doggies!"

A beard of foamy drool formed on the frontmost dog. *Yikes!*

When I reached the closed gate, I counted down. "One. Two. Three!"

Doug slid the gate open just enough for me to get through. I turned and darted out, the dogs on my heels.

Bam!

"Aaaaaaaagh!" I fell forward to the asphalt, losing both my gun and pepper spray, screaming in terror and agony.

Doug had closed the gate too soon, slamming it on my already sore ankle. While most of my body had made it through the gate, my left foot was still inside the fence, being mauled by the dogs. Thank God I'd worn my Doc Martens. With their thick leather and steel toes, the shoes proved difficult for the dogs to bite through, though they did manage to quickly cover the shoe with drool and tooth marks.

Grrr!

Snap!

Snarl!

I kicked backward, managing to loosen the dogs' hold just long enough to pull my foot free from the shoe and through the gate to safety.

This time the *BAM!* as the gate slid closed was followed by the metallic rattle of the fence. Foam-beard picked up my shoe and shook it violently in his teeth. If my shoe had been a small animal its neck would have broken. Wagging the tiny stub he had for a tail, the dog trotted back toward its pen with the prize.

I turned to Doug. "What should we do about the shoe?"

"Not a problem," he replied, gesturing toward the pen. "There won't be anything left of it by morning."

I glanced back to see that the dog had already ripped the laces from their grommets and pulled the tongue free, too. Losing a pair of hundred-dollar shoes made me none too happy, but I decided to count my blessings. After all, that could've been my foot he was chewing on.

chapter eighteen

$\mathcal{M}$y Furious Valentine

Nick was out of the office all day on Thursday. Frankly, it was a relief not to have him hovering over me, asking whether I'd heard from Sierra yet. He'd never shown this much interest in my other cases and his attempts to micromanage this one irked me. That said, on a personal level, I was looking forward to spending the evening with him. He'd left a bouquet of red roses on my desk before heading out this morning, and they'd greeted me with their sweet scent and gorgeous blooms upon my arrival.

The card he'd left with the flowers was typical no-nonsense Nick. It read: "Happy Valentine's Day. Go Mavs!"

I used my lunch hour to make a run to Nordstrom for a new pair of my signature red Doc Martens. Luckily for me the store was having a Valentine's Day sale. I used the money I saved to buy myself new red lace panties to replace the pair Brazos had kept after the concert.

Given that my attempt to speak face-to-face with Brazos yesterday evening had been a bust and the fact that I still hadn't heard from him or his manager by the end of the workday on Thursday, I decided to track Sierra Behr down myself. I found an address for her in the DMV database indicating she lived in the Dallas suburb of Carrollton. I'd pay her a visit bright and early tomorrow morning.

That evening, Nick and I joined Alicia, Daniel, Christina, and Ajay for dinner at a Moroccan restaurant near the American Airlines center before the Mavericks game. Nick would've preferred a steak and baked potato, but he was outvoted five to one.

"I don't think Nutty's gonna be too excited about couscous in his doggie bag," Nick complained, looking down at his plate.

"I'll fry him some more baloney," I said. "He likes that better than steak anyway." Nutty was a dog of simple tastes.

Alicia raised her cocktail. "Dear God, I needed this drink. I'm not sure I can survive another tax season."

As she took a sip, her engagement ring caught the light, the diamond sparkling brightly, almost as if it were taunting me. Both she and Christina had received rings and were in the midst of planning their weddings, while I had yet to even hear the L-word from Nick. Of course, he hadn't heard it from me, either, but that was beside the point.

"Come work with me at the IRS," I suggested to Alicia. "It's way more fun than preparing tax forms all day."

"Only *you* would think chasing down criminals and getting shot at is fun," she returned. "Then again, maybe I should apply. It's not every job that lets you get up close and personal with celebrities."

I tried to shush Alicia with my eyes, but she was looking down at her drink, not at me, and didn't see the warning.

"I can't believe you met Brazos Rivers's parents," she

added. "I hear they keep a really low profile and refuse all interviews."

Nick's head turned my way. "You met his parents? When?"

Dang it! I should've never mentioned it to Alicia. But when she'd arrived home late last night I'd still been up, searching every database I could access, trying to find more information on Brazos and his family. My knowledge of his real name led me to sources the media hadn't accessed. I'd learned some intriguing tidbits unknown to the general public.

According to my exhaustive search of the state vital records, Brazos was the Merriweathers' only child. He'd been born in Burlington, Vermont. Dear Lord, he was a Yankee! Not that there was anything wrong with that, of course. It's just that Southerners liked their country-western music the same way they liked their salsa, made by someone born south of the Mason-Dixon line. As for bagels, however, Southerners conceded a total lack of skill and only trusted a bagel vendor from a Northeastern state. I wondered if Northerners felt the same way about barbecue?

Even if Brazos hadn't been born and raised in Texas, I supposed I couldn't fault him for having Texas's Lone Star flag tattooed on his bicep. Texas was by far the largest state down this way, with the greatest number of potential music buyers, and in many ways symbolized the South. Besides, the white star on the blue background flanked by single red and white stripes was far more simple than the Vermont flag. Per my glance at Wikipedia, that state's flag included a deer, a cow, a pine tree, three sheaves of wheat, mountains, the state's name, and the state's motto, Freedom and Unity. That's a lot of detail for one arm. It might fit on a butt cheek, though.

Brazos's father, Winthrop VI, had come from old money, sticky money earned in the maple syrup industry. He'd served as chief financial officer of the family syrup business in Burlington. He'd sold the company to a food conglomerate three years ago and eased into an early retirement, moving down to the Texas ranch though retaining a ski chalet in Stowe.

Per the information on her son's birth certificate, Marcella's maiden name was Abbiati. Though there was no record of Brazos attending any public or private school in Vermont, the Web coughed up a reference from the early nineties noting that his mother, a minor opera star in Italy, had traveled to her home country to star as Violetta in *La Traviata.* According to the article, Marcella Abbiati Merriweather had been accompanied by her child, who was being schooled by a tutor in Milan. Presumably Brazos had been taught by private tutors throughout his childhood. The lack of interaction with other children could explain his tendency to childish behavior. Perhaps his social skills had not properly developed under a pair of doting parents and paid instructors.

I'd found three other articles indicating that Winthrop Merriweather VII had sung roles in various performances in summer stock musical theater performances in Vermont. He'd once played Kurt, the "incorrigible" son of Captain von Trapp in *The Sound of Music,* and performed as Oliver in *Oliver Twist.*

His name popped up in several articles written in Italian. I didn't know the language, but I could make out some of the words. *Il barbiere di Siviglia.* I was pretty sure that was *The Barber of Seville. Don Giovanni* and *La bohème* needed no interpretation. My best guess after reading the articles through several times was that Brazos had been cast in secondary roles in these operas. Judging from the dates, he'd been in his mid to late teens at the time, after his voice had changed but not long before he'd launched his country-western career.

Surprisingly, I found no speculation that Brazos and Winthrop Merriweather VII were one and the same. No one he'd performed with back then seemed to have clued in that the brown-haired boy in their acting troupe was now the blond-haired country star with the silver spurs.

By all accounts, Brazos's parents had initially been raising him to follow in his mother's classical opera footsteps. But at some point Winnie had instead decided to pursue a career as a country-western singer rather than as an opera star. I wondered what had made him change directions. Had he discovered a love for the musical genre? Or had he simply been chasing the almighty dollar, jumping on a trend?

My mind swirled and churned like river water after a hard rain. I wanted to believe it was the former, that Brazos had fallen in love with the country music I liked so much, that he'd chosen to sing his songs because they appealed to the common man and spoke to a sense of simplicity. To believe otherwise would mean Brazos was a phony, a fraud, a made-up man who didn't really exist other than in the minds of his fans. Not wanting to believe it, I pushed the ugly thought from my head.

"I met his parents last night." I poked the food on my plate, avoiding Nick's stare. "Brazos's manager still hasn't called me and I thought maybe I'd find him at his parents' ranch."

"*Thought* you'd find him?" Nick snapped. "Or *hoped* you would?"

I turned my eyes on Nick now. "I *hoped* I'd find him so I could get him to sign an agreement. Geez. Don't get your panties in a wad."

Nick huffed. "At least I'm wearing underwear."

Touché. Or should I say tush-é?

His reference to the panties I'd thrown on stage at the concert was the final straw. I'd only been trying to have a good time. I dropped my fork onto my plate with a clatter. "First you tell me I'm not moving the case along fast enough, then when I do something to try to get the case resolved you get mad about that, too." I rolled my eyes. "Make up your damn mind."

Nick looked away, his jaw clenched in anger. "That kid is making a fool out of you, Tara! Can't you see that? Worse, he's making a fool out of—"

Nick stopped himself, but I knew the guy well enough to know what he'd been about to say. That Brazos was making a fool out of *him,* too. That my fawning all over the guy when I was supposed to be committed to Nick made him feel like he was playing second fiddle.

So that's what this was all really about, huh? Nick's ego. Sheesh. The guy stood well over six feet tall and had played on the defensive line on his high school football team. He'd since maintained the tight abs and ass and well-developed pecs he'd formed back then. He kicked butt on a regular basis, had one of the best records of any special agent within the entire IRS. He had every right to strut around like a proud peacock, yet his ego was as fragile as spun sugar.

My first impulse was to tell him to sack up, that he was acting like a damn baby and to get the hell over it. But I knew that would only make matters worse. One of us had to swallow their pride, and it looked like it would have to be me. Of course my pride would be much harder to choke down than the delicious food we were eating.

The other couples watched us across the table, their expressions revealing their discomfort at our spat. I felt uncomfortable, too. I didn't want to be arguing at all, especially in front of our friends. Yet it seemed no matter what I did where Brazos was concerned, Nick didn't like it. I could do no right.

I exhaled a long breath. "It's Valentine's Day," I reminded Nick. "Let's just have a good time, okay?"

"Don't you worry." Nick tossed back the remains of his drink and slammed his glass down. "I'm not gonna let Teeny Weenie stop me from enjoying myself."

"Good." I scooted my chair over and snuggled up to him. "'Cause you're twice the man Brazos Rivers will ever be."

I thought my compliment would thaw Nick's frosty attitude, but instead it only seemed to piss him off more. Perhaps I'd inadvertently sounded patronizing.

Fortunately, he seemed to let go of his anger once we arrived at the game, even draping his arm around my shoulders and playing with my hair during the second quarter. The Mavericks' win put him in even better spirits, and the ride home was pleasant and conflict-free.

After the game, we headed to Nick's place. When we entered, we found Nutty lying in a puddle by the back door. The poor old dog hadn't been able to get out the doggie door Nick had installed for him. Nutty wagged his tail, slinging fluid all over the floor and wall.

Instantly, the two of us gelled, rushing to the poor dog.

"You all right, Nutty?" I asked, laying a hand on his side.

"It's okay, boy." Nick lifted Nutty up without regard to the mess the dog would make of his clothes. "I know you tried."

In that instant I knew, without a doubt, that I loved Nick. He might be a stubborn ass sometimes but, hell, so was I. How could I not love a man who was so patient with an old dog, who was capable of such caring and compassion?

I opened the back door for Nick and he carried Nutty out into the yard. While the two of them were outside, I grabbed a bottle of spray cleaner and a roll of paper towels and cleaned up Nutty's mess, feeling tears prick at the back of my eyes. A few minutes later, Nick carried Nutty back inside. Nick's eyes looked misty as he took the dog upstairs to give him a bath. I ran down the street to round up my blow-dryer, and returned to Nick's. When Nutty had been washed and dried, Nick laid him in the center of the bed where'd he be comfortable and couldn't accidentally roll off.

Nick stripped off his soiled clothes, took a quick shower, and changed into a clean pair of boxer briefs and flannel lounge pants. I put on the silky red sleep shirt I kept in Nick's dresser drawer and the two of us climbed in on either side of the bed with Nutty sandwiched between us. Our gazes met over his furry back, communicating without words. There'd be no nooky tonight. Both of us were too concerned about Nutty to even think of carnal desires.

The dog's health was rapidly declining, noticeably worse nearly every day. Still, I couldn't bring myself to suggest that the dog should be put out of his misery. Nutty was suffering, sure, but he still seemed to get some joy out of life. He still wagged his tail when Nick came home and enjoyed the fried baloney sandwiches I made for him. That was something, wasn't it?

"I almost forgot." Nick climbed out of bed and went to his closet. "I got you something for Valentine's Day." He opened the door and pulled out a tall, narrow gift bag and large box wrapped in pink paper with white hearts and topped with an oversized pink bow.

"Wine?" I guessed, taking the bag.

He grinned. "Nope."

I yanked out the tissue to find a night-vision rifle scope.

The device would be perfect should I ever need to use my long-range rifle in the dark. It would also be useful in keeping an eye on PPE and the historical marker. I'd mentioned to Nick that Eddie and I had trouble seeing much in the dark when we'd driven out to Palo Pinto last Friday. Apparently, Nick had listened. That in itself was romantic. In my experience, most men didn't pay much attention to anything that didn't involve sports, beer, or sex.

"This will come in handy, Nick. Thanks." I gave him a smooch on the cheek before turning to the box. "Wow. That looks big." I swung my legs over the side of the bed and walked over. Starting at the top, I tore into the wrapping. When I was done, I found a gun cabinet, custom-painted in my signature red. The cabinet was big enough to hold my entire collection of handguns and rifles, as well as a sizable stash of ammunition. "I love it! You always find the perfect thing to get me."

He shrugged, a soft smile playing about his lips. "I know you a little."

The cabinet had both a key lock and a programmable number pad for extra safety. I currently kept my guns and ammo in a trunk in my bedroom closet. This cabinet would make the guns more difficult to access. It would be perfect for the days ahead when, if my life went according to plan, I'd have a rug rat or two running around. I eyed Nick. I hoped those rug rats would be his rug rats, too.

Nick cocked his head, his eyes narrowing. "Why are you looking at me like that?"

Obviously, I couldn't tell him I was envisioning the two of us starting a family or he'd run for the hills. Or would he? Maybe. Maybe not. Regardless, I wanted him to know how I felt about him. "I . . ."

Ugh. I can't do it. I couldn't say the L-word even

though I knew without a doubt that I loved him. I supposed I feared that he might not be ready to say it back. What a chickenshit, huh? Love is risky. We all know that going in. Nonetheless, I decided to go with, "You're a great guy, Nick."

"Hell, yeah." He gave me a wink. "And don't you forget it."

chapter nineteen

$\mathcal{M}$ismanaged

It was only 7:15 in the morning when I knocked on the door to Sierra Behr's condominium. She lived on the first floor of a three-story building painted maroon and gray and topped by numerous chimneys. Her car, a bright yellow Camaro, was parked directly in front of her unit.

I had a number of questions for Sierra, the first of which was, *Why didn't you return phone calls from a federal criminal investigator? Was it because you're stupid or because you've got something to hide?* Hmm. I guess that's two questions, huh? And now I've asked three. Maybe I should just stop while I was ahead.

A few seconds later a groggy voice came from behind the door. "Who is it?"

I looked directly at the peephole, knowing Sierra would be looking out at me. I held up my badge. "Special Agent Tara Holloway with the IRS. Open up." I didn't say *or else,* but my tone implied as much.

She hesitated a moment. "This isn't a good time."

"Tough."

Another hesitation. "I'm not dressed yet. And . . ." She

seemed to have realized that not being dressed was a lame excuse and one that could readily be remedied. "I'm not feeling well. I think I've got the flu." The sound of a forced cough came through the door.

"I'll take my chances. Throw on a robe and let me in. You're not leaving this condo until you talk to me." If she didn't voluntarily open her door, I'd sit out here all day if I had to.

A few seconds later the door opened, revealing the woman I'd seen with the clipboard and headset at the tour bus after the concert. Sierra was dressed in rumpled light blue pajamas and fluffy socks. Her black hair was squished on one side, fluffy on the other in a bedhead style. Her eyes, which were crusty with sleep, stared at me, bright with anxiety. Still, though she was hardly at her best, she exhibited no signs of having the flu. Her nose wasn't red and raw and she wasn't hunched over with achy muscles.

I stepped forward, positioning my brand-new steel-toed shoe in the doorway to prevent her from shutting the door should she change her mind about talking to me and try to close it. "I've left you a half-dozen messages. Why haven't you returned my calls?"

She looked up, as if trying to come up with a credible response. "I'm sorry. I've . . . been busy."

"Too busy to get Brazos Rivers's tax returns filed?"

Her eyes darkened and she put her thumb to her mouth, chewing nervously on the nail.

I was tired of being jerked around. "You've got one month from today to get the returns filed. Better get crackin'."

Sierra's brow furrowed and she pulled the thumb from her mouth. "What happens if the returns aren't filed by then?"

"Then I arrest him for tax evasion and you for aiding and abetting. But don't worry. Your dark hair would look great with a bright orange jumpsuit." I turned to go. "Have a nice day."

"Wait!" She grabbed the sleeve of my blazer, then glanced out the door, looking to see who might be around, as if afraid to be seen consorting with the enemy. "Come inside. Please!"

"No funny stuff," I told her, stepping inside. "I'm armed." Not to mention cranky. Getting up extra early to come by here hadn't exactly put me in a friendly mood.

I glanced around quickly as she let me in. Her place was a two-bedroom unit. Both doors were open, one revealing an unmade bed, the other revealing a room being used as an office. The office contained a small desk with a laptop and printer sitting on top of it, a four-drawer filing cabinet, and a large bookshelf.

Sierra led me into her kitchen and gestured for me to take a seat at the table while she made coffee. I noticed her hands were shaking as she poured the grounds and water into the machine. I doubted the shaking was the result of the flu, though. More likely it was nerves. This woman seemed to realize she was up shit creek without a paddle and that a waterfall lay dead ahead.

Once she had a steaming mug in hand, she slid into the seat opposite me. "I . . . I don't know where to start."

"The beginning is a good place," I suggested.

She gazed down into her coffee for a moment before looking up at me. "I don't know why Brazos told you I was supposed to file his tax returns. That's not part of my job as his manager. I handle his schedule, make hotel arrangements, make sure the bus is gassed up and stocked with food and drinks. When he's got a concert I go to the venue early to set up his dressing room the way he likes it. I run errands for him. I also hire and manage the crew and make sure they get paid and that their earnings are reported to the IRS. I even respond to his fan mail, post tweets for him, and maintain his Facebook fan page. But I don't take care of any personal financial matters for Brazos."

"He's never asked you to hire a CPA to prepare and file his taxes?"

She shook her head. "There's no way I could. Brazos doesn't share his financial information with me. I have no idea what he earns. I just know it's a lot."

I sat back in my chair. "I'm beyond frustrated here. First, Brazos told me his agent was supposed to take care of his taxes. Then, after his agent denied it and I confronted Brazos again, he told me the taxes were your responsibility. Is the guy just forgetful or is he pulling a fast one?"

I feared he was trying to buy himself some time. Time he could use to hide his assets or spend his cash, leaving me with nothing to seize to satisfy his tax debt. A stupid strategy, really. I might not be able to seize his assets, but I could seize *him,* throw his sweet ass in jail. Perhaps he was thinking of moving in with relatives in Italy, beyond the jurisdiction of the U.S. Treasury. He could always resurrect his opera career. Maybe he'd land the role of Figaro this time.

"I don't know what to tell you," Sierra said. "I really have no idea what he's thinking."

"How do you pay the roadies and staff?" I asked. "The hotels and restaurants and all that?"

"Brazos set up a business account for me to use for paying expenses. He keeps just enough in it to cover the bills. When the account runs low, I tell Brazos and he wires money. He also gave me a business credit card to use."

Sounded like Brazos had received advice from someone with financial savvy back when he'd set up these accounts. Why hadn't that person advised him about his taxes? Or perhaps that person had told Brazos to get his taxes paid and Brazos had ignored him or her. Unfortunately, just like people sometimes ignored the advice of their doctors, they also sometimes ignored the advice of their accountants. I'd run into that type of client back when I'd been a practicing CPA. They'd pay for my advice, then refuse to follow it. Dumb butts.

"Do you know whether Brazos hired someone to advise him on his finances? On setting up the accounts?"

"I have no idea," Sierra said. "Brazos is pretty tight-lipped about that kind of thing. For someone who's so well known he's actually a very private person."

I was beginning to think that Brazos's public persona might be more marketing ploy than reality. It wouldn't be the first time a singer had reinvented himself in pursuit of the almighty dollar. Sexpot Jessica Simpson had started out singing Christian music. When she realized her boobs were made for gawking, she changed her tune to "These Boots Are Made for Walking." As the culture changed in the sixties, the Beatles changed, too, giving up their black suits and ties and the clean, comprehensible lyrics of songs like "I Want to Hold Your Hand," exchanging them for Nehru jackets and ankle boots and the incomprehensible tune "Lucy in the Sky with Diamonds." More recently, Snoop Dogg transformed into a cat, changing his name to Snoop Lion. Allegedly inspired by Rastafarian priests, he switched his style from rap to reggae. It was reasonable to assume that Brazos might have followed suit and chosen to pursue country music over opera.

"Do you provide Brazos with financial reports?" I asked Sierra.

"Yes," she said. "I give him a monthly report of all the expenses, as well as copies of receipts, bank statements, and credit card bills. What he does with them I have no idea."

"Can you give me copies of the reports?"

She bit into her thumb again, clearly uncomfortable with my request. "Am I legally required to? I'd like to clear it with Brazos first. He is my boss, after all."

"If you refuse I'll get a court order."

She gnawed the thumb again. "Let me talk to him and get back with you. How's that?"

It wasn't what I'd hoped for. But I'd take what I could get. I retrieved a card from my pocket and handed it to her. "Call me the instant you hear from him."

"I will."

It dawned on me then that if she kept his schedule, she'd know where the guy was supposed to be and when.

"You mentioned that you handle his schedule," I said. "Can you tell me where he is?"

"He's taking a few days off," Sierra said. "I haven't spoken with him in a couple of days, so I'm not sure exactly where he is. Sometimes he stays at his parents' ranch, other times he stays on his boat. Sometimes he flies off on a whim and spends a night or two in Paris or London or Acapulco."

"When's his next engagement?"

Sierra stood, went to her living room, and pulled a planner from her tote bag. She returned to the table, sat down, and looked at his schedule. "He's filming a commercial next Wednesday afternoon at the Fox TV studio in Dallas." She showed me the entry on the calendar.

I took a screen shot of the information and asked whether I could look through the rest of his calendar.

She chewed the thumb again. "I guess there's no harm in that. He's got nothing else on his schedule at the moment. He won't go on tour again for at least a year, until he finishes writing and recording his new album."

I flipped through the pages. Sure enough, each one was empty. I stood to go. "Will you be at the filming?"

"No," she said. "The film crews assign a runner to take care of Brazos, so I don't normally attend those type of things. I usually just send a couple bodyguards. Of course, after what happened at the shoot for Buckin' Bronco Boots, I might have to send the whole team this time."

I was tempted to issue her a bill for the ass-saving services I'd provided at the photography studio, but the woman looked upset enough that things had gone awry. "Maybe he'll leave the Ferrari at the ranch this time, travel incognito."

She shook her head. "God, I hope so."

chapter twenty

Come Fly with Me. Or Not.

Friday at 4:30, Eddie and I headed back out to Palo Pinto, taking a different G-ride this time in case Burkett had taken note of the car we'd driven last week. We parked at the closed feed store again, though this time we waited on the dirt along the side of the building, where the vehicle would be less visible.

The evening was considerably warmer than before, so we climbed out of the car and sat on a wide railing in front of the dark store, keeping an eye on PPE's building. Eddie used his binoculars. I used the new night-vision scope Nick had given me for Valentine's Day.

Eddie frowned. "I can't see shit." He snatched the scope from my hands. "My turn."

"Hey! That was a gift!"

"Too bad, so sad." He held the scope up to one eye, closing the other. "This thing works great."

"Maybe Sandra will get you some night-vision goggles for next Valentine's Day."

"That would beat the grout-cleaning kit she got me this year."

Sheesh. "Is that what it's like after you've been married a few years? The romance dies?" I hoped that would never happen with me and Nick.

Eddie shrugged. "Yeah. Some. But the nice thing is you get to take each other for granted."

I snorted. "That's a good thing?"

"Sure," he said. "It's a lot less work. Cheaper, too."

Eddie and his wife were as crazy about each other as Nick and I were. Though I hoped my relationship with Nick would always be romantic, Eddie had a point. Knowing someone would always be there, having that assurance, was worth much more than any material gift. Still, my scope was pretty darn awesome.

"Besides," Eddie added, "it's not like the romance is totally gone. I took her out for pizza last month and we made love afterward."

"For one, that's too much information," I replied. "For two, you haven't had sex since last month?"

"You try getting it on when one kid or another climbs into your bed every night. There are limited windows of opportunity."

I made a mental note not to have children until I was ready to give up sex. Then I realized my mental note made no sense because I wouldn't be able to have children if I gave up sex.

I snatched the scope back out of Eddie's hands. "Gimme."

Right at seven, Burkett exited the building, a glowing green apparition. "Jeez. The guy looks like an alien."

I handed Eddie the scope so he could take a look. "You got that right." He handed it back to me.

I put the scope back to my eye. "Wait. Is that a drill bit in his hand or an anal probe?"

As we watched, Burkett climbed into his car and headed our way.

Eddie and I scurried back to our car. Burkett drove past, making a stop at the historical marker again. As he'd done the week before, he dropped the cash envelope, flashed his lights three times, then made a U-turn. A moment later, a car came up the road from the other direction. The night-vision scope made the headlights unbearably bright and I had to remove the lens and blink several times to clear the spots from my vision. I exchanged the scope for my field glasses and watched as the car stopped at the marker. Sure enough, it was the same Toyota Corolla from the week before.

Once the driver of the Corolla had picked up the envelope, circled around on the highway, and driven back in the direction from which he had come, Eddie and I pulled out of the feed lot and followed the car. We were the only vehicles on the road.

"It's a little hard to be inconspicuous out here in the middle of nowhere," Eddie said.

"We might've been better off borrowing Nick's pickup," I said. "That would've fit in better out here than this Taurus."

Fortunately, once the Corolla pulled onto Interstate 20, traffic was heavier and we could blend in easier. The Corolla headed east, merging onto I-30 in Fort Worth, then exiting to drive north on 360.

"Where's he taking us?" Eddie asked.

"Apparently it's not Six Flags," I noted as we passed the amusement park, the bright lights from the roller coasters lighting up the sky.

Our question was answered five minutes later when the driver took the exit for the Dallas–Fort Worth Airport.

"What should we do?" I asked Eddie. "Stop him before he goes through security and question him?"

Timing was critical in an investigation. If an agent waited too long to make a move, a target might escape.

But moving too fast too soon could put a target on notice that he or she was being watched. The evidence could disappear and the case could fall apart. Knowing exactly when to swoop in for the kill was an acquired skill, and one that could never be completely honed. After all, each investigation and each suspect was different and unique.

Eddie shrugged, noncommittal. "We'll just have to play it by ear."

The man pulled into long-term parking and circled up three flights, bypassing several empty slots.

"Why hasn't he pulled into one of the available spots?" I asked. "You think he's on to us?" What if he led us up to the roof, blocked us in, then pulled out an AK-47? That would really suck.

Before Eddie could reply, bright red brake lights illuminated ahead and the Corolla pulled into an empty parking spot. Eddie quickly pulled into an empty space on our right and cut the engine.

The car next to us had tinted windows, impeding our view of the Corolla and its driver. I unfastened my seat belt, swiveled to a kneel on the front seat, and wiggled over into the back so I could keep an eye on things through the back window. As I watched, a Caucasian man exited the car. He was dressed in jeans, a loose-fitting dark sweatshirt, and a knit winter cap. The green cap covered his hair, so I couldn't tell what color it was. The cap only partially covered his ears, though. Heck, it would take *two* caps to cover those enormous ears. His nose was definitely long and skinny and trunklike. Despite the fact that it was nighttime he wore dark sunglasses.

"Michelson's son was right," I told Eddie. "This guy looks like an elephant."

The man slung a backpack over his shoulder and, to my surprise, headed neither for the elevator nor the sky bridge that led to the airport terminal. Rather, he began walking up the ramp.

"He's walking up to the next level," I told Eddie.

"I'll follow him on foot," Eddie said. "Get behind the wheel. Have your phone ready in case I need to contact you."

Eddie exited the car, slid into his suit jacket, and retrieved his briefcase from the trunk. He pulled his cell phone from his breast pocket and held it in front of him, pretending to be viewing the screen as he began his ascent up the row. His dress and behavior made him look like any other business traveler. Of course if anyone gave it much thought, the person might wonder why a businessman who'd only taken a day trip would have parked in long-term rather than short-term parking, but hopefully elephant man wasn't a deep thinker.

A minute later Eddie sent a text to my phone. *Dumbo got in a silver Mer.* He also sent me the license plate number.

I jumped onto my tablet and quickly ran the plate. According to the DMV, the Mercedes belonged to a Russell Cobb who lived on Amherst Avenue in Dallas.

Amherst Avenue. *Hmmm* ... Where was that? The name didn't sound familiar, though it did sound hoity-toity.

I was just about to plug the address into my GPS when movement in the rearview mirror caught my eye. The Mercedes passed behind me. I craned my neck to see the car turn the corner to go down to the next level. Better follow the guy in case this car was untraceable, too.

I cranked the engine and zipped back out of my parking place.

A simultaneous screech and honk filled the quiet space, echoing off the concrete walls and ceiling. An enormous SUV rocked back on its axles, its front bumper mere millimeters from the back fender of the G-ride. *Oops.* Guess I should've looked before I leaped.

With a conciliatory wave, I threw the car into drive and pulled forward, only to yank the gearshift into reverse and back out again a second later. *Honk!* A second car that had been obscured by the SUV had driven up now. Jesus Christ, didn't they know I had a criminal to pursue? Ugh!

Unlike the enormous SUV, this car was a little commuter car, one my G-ride could easily best if the two went head-to-head. Or should I say headlight-to-headlight? Rather than pull back into my space, I forced the driver to wait and continued backing out. Eddie ran up and jumped into the passenger seat. As I drove past the waiting vehicle the driver mouthed a word at me. From the way his lips first spread, then pursed, I surmised the word was *asshole*.

I took the curves and straightaways at breakneck speed in pursuit of the Mercedes, slowing only when a family in a minivan pulled out in front of me and took their time circling down the ramps.

"Come on, Daddy!" I cried. "Move it!" I tried to pass him but was blocked by a car coming up the ramp from the other direction. "Dammit!"

Unfortunately, we arrived at the exit line just in time to see Cobb drive out of the garage. Even more unfortunately, there were three cars ahead of us in line to pay their parking fee. The attendant, a gray-haired man with oversized glasses, seemed to be in no hurry, counting out the change first to himself, then to the driver. He pushed his glasses backward on his nose before taking the bill extended by the driver of the next car.

I turned my face to the ceiling of the car and screamed at the gods of fate. "Ugggggh!"

"That goes double for me." Eddie put his palms on the

dash, pushing against it as if the motion could somehow force the cars ahead of us to move forward.

I handed Eddie my tablet, which still displayed Cobb's address. "Figure out where his house is."

Eddie tapped the screen. "I'm on it." A moment later he looked over at me. "It's in University Park."

By the time we exited the garage, the Mercedes had a two-minute lead on us. What's more, we didn't know whether the driver had headed for the airport's north exit or south exit. If Cobb were heading home, he'd take the north exit. But if he were going somewhere else first, maybe dropping the cash somewhere or passing it off to someone, it was possible he could be headed to the south exit.

Eddie pulled a quarter from the cup holder. "Heads we go south, tails we go north." He flipped the coin. "Tails."

I floored the car and headed to the north exit. Still no sign of the Mercedes. We made it all the way out of the airport property and onto the freeway, using GPS to direct us to Cobb's residence. It took us on 635 to the Dallas North Tollway, then directed us to head south to the exclusive University Park neighborhood. No sign of Cobb's car anywhere along the route.

In minutes we were on Amherst Avenue. We pulled to a stop across the street from Cobb's house. The residence was traditional, part red brick, part whitewashed wood with black shutters. The house featured several gables, dormer windows, and a brick walkway. There was no garage door on the front of the house.

"Looks like these houses have rear-entry garages," Eddie said. "Go down the alley."

I drove to the end of the block, took a right onto the side street, then another right into the alley. Cobb's house was the third one from the corner. The garage door was shut. Unfortunately, the garage had no windows, so there was no way to tell if Cobb's Mercedes was already inside or not.

We parked on the street at the end of the alley, keeping an eye on things for the next hour. A car exited from the garage of the house next door to Cobb, but that was it.

While we sat, we used our phones and tablets to look up information on Cobb. According to our search, Russell Cobb was a named partner in Cushings, Cobb, & Beadle, a downtown public relations firm. Their Web site listed a number of high-profile and influential clients, including a former U.S. senator, several players for the Dallas Cowboys, a member of the city council, and a local writer who penned western sagas. A Web search indicated the firm had also been involved in repairing the reputations of a real estate mogul swept up in a cocaine bust and a local athlete who'd suffered fallout after assaulting his girlfriend.

Why would a PR man be surreptitiously accepting cash from Palo Pinto Energy under the table? If PPE was trying to mitigate the negative publicity resulting from the lawsuit, it could just hire the firm outright, no need for secrecy. Clearly a piece of the puzzle was missing.

We finally decided to call it a night. Even if we saw Cobb pull into his garage, we were unlikely to glean any pertinent information from that fact. After all, there'd be no way to tell where he'd come from. Besides, for all we knew his car was already in the garage, locked up tight. What's more, it was Friday night. Who wanted to be sitting in a cold car staring down an empty alley when we could be at home with our significant others watching TV and taking each other for granted? Besides, there was always next week. We'd make sure he didn't get away then.

chapter twenty-one

$\mathcal{T}$he Terminator

When I arrived home Friday night after following Russell Cobb, I gave my cats some kibble and attention, started a load of laundry, and walked down to Nick's place. Nick and I stayed up late watching movies on Netflix. We each picked one. I chose a romantic comedy, of course. Nick chose a blood-and-guts high-action thriller. We watched his first. I didn't need to go to sleep with visions of bloody knives in my head.

After the movies, Nick carried Nutty upstairs, though tonight he laid him on his doggie bed on the floor rather than on the bed. I took this as a sign that Nick wanted to be intimate, and I was glad about that. It wasn't the physical aspects of sex I'd missed, it was feeling close to Nick. Our relationship had experienced so many ups and downs lately it was as if we were on an emotional trampoline. I was ready to perform one final flip, make a soft landing on my ass, and climb off the ride.

Nick and I were fully engaged when Nutty let out a soft whine. Nick turned his head and stopped moving. "You okay, boy?"

"It's gotta be his arthritis," I said.

Nick dismounted. "I need to get him another pill." He climbed out of bed and left the room, fully erect and bare-assed, going down to the kitchen to fetch Nutty's Rimadyl.

I sat up and looked over at the dog. "Daddy's getting your medicine, sweetie."

Nutty didn't lift his head, but he did raise his tail in a single wag.

Nick returned with the pill. He'd wrapped the medication in a slice of cheese to entice Nutty to take it. Still lying on his side, Nutty sniffed the cheese but didn't attempt to take it from Nick.

"Come on, boy," Nick coaxed, kneeling down next to his dog. "It'll make you feel better."

Nutty closed his eyes and let out a shuddering breath. My heart contracted into a tight ball. I wasn't sure whom I felt worse for, Nutty with his joint pain or Nick with his breaking heart. I joined the two of them on the floor, putting one hand on Nick's shoulder, the other on Nutty's flank.

Nick scratched his dog under the chin. "Please, Nutty? For me?"

At the desperate sound in Nick's voice, Nutty opened his eyes and extended his snout, taking the cheese and pill from Nick.

"Good boy." Nick gave the dog another scratch and kissed him on the forehead before turning back to me. By now, his arousal was gone.

I stood, retrieved my nightshirt, and began to slip it on.

Nick reached out a hand to stop me. He cleared his throat as if to clear it of the emotions choking him up. "I need some lovin' even more now."

I understood. Nick was upset and frustrated that he couldn't do more for his beloved pet. He needed a release.

I gestured at his crotch. "Looks like we're back to square one."

Nick glanced down, then looked back up at me with a roguish grin. "Say those dirty things you said the other night and I'll be ready to go in five seconds flat."

"Good boy!"

We slept in late the next morning. While Nick whipped up some pancakes for breakfast, I phoned Katie Dunne.

"Does the name Russell Cobb mean anything to you?" I asked. "Or maybe the name Cushings, Cobb, and Beadle?"

"Is that a law firm?" she asked.

"No," I replied. "They do public relations."

She was quiet for a moment, apparently thinking. "It rings a bell, but . . . I can't quite place it."

"Keep mulling it over," I said. "If something comes to you give me a call."

After our late breakfast, Nick and I cleaned up and drove over to visit his mother, Bonnie, taking Nutty with us.

As we climbed out of Nick's truck, I reached down to grab the copy of the *Dallas Morning News* from the driveway. Nick's mother was traditional, still preferring her news in print form rather than reading it on the Internet. My parents were the same way. My mother liked to curl up in an easy chair with a cup of coffee and the newspaper, and leisurely peruse the news from our hometown and the world. My father would take the sports page and his coffee at the kitchen table.

Bonnie met us at her front door. She was tall, like her son, with the same dark brown hair, though hers had a hint of silver here and there. Unlike Nick's whiskey-brown eyes, Bonnie's were blue. She was a pleasant woman, down-to-earth and friendly. She doted on her son, but she didn't let him get away with much, either. She lived alone. Nick's father had passed away years ago, leaving her a widow.

Bonnie eyed Nutty as Nick led him in. The dog tripped over the small threshold, landing spread-eagled in her front hallway.

Nick was on him in an instant, lifting the big dog into his arms as if he weighed no more than a puppy. Nick cocked his head so he could look Nutty in the eye. "You okay, buddy?"

Bonnie gave her son a stern but empathetic look. "Nick, you're going to have to do something about that poor dog."

"Not yet," was all Nick said in reply. He carried Nutty into the living room and laid him down on the braided rug in front of the fire.

Bonnie's eyes met mine and she shook her head. "Losing that dog is going to break that boy's heart," she whispered.

Nick was hardly a boy, but there was no doubt the rest of what she said was true. Since Nick had returned home from a forced exile in Mexico last year, he and Nutty had been constant companions. They watched the Cowboys games together, sharing a bucket of wings. When Nutty's arthritis wasn't acting up, the two would take walks around the neighborhood together. Nick even took Nutty out with him on his bass boat. I knew I was special to Nick, but Nutty filled a space in Nick's heart that only a furry, four-footed creature could fill. I feared that space would soon be empty.

I handed Bonnie the newspaper and she tucked it under her arm. "Come see what's growing." She gestured for me to follow her into the backyard.

Bonnie and I shared a love of gardening, an interest I had little time for these days, unfortunately. Between work and helping Alicia prepare for her upcoming wedding, I had little time to walk the aisles at the nursery or dig in the dirt. I missed it. Gardening had always relaxed me. Something about working the soil just brought things into perspective somehow. Maybe once I got the cases against PPE and Brazos Rivers resolved, I'd take a day or two off and work on the flower beds in my yard, maybe buy a new hanging basket for the shepherd's hook near my front porch.

Bonnie showed me the vegetables growing in her garden. Spinach, broccoli, beets, and peas. Even a little kale.

"You've got quite a harvest," I noted.

She pulled a stalk of broccoli from the ground. "I'll wash this up, get some ranch dressing, and we'll have a snack."

My idea of a snack ran more along the lines of barbecue-flavored potato chips, but her suggestion was much healthier.

"Nick?" Bonnie called as we went back inside. "You want some broccoli?"

"Only if it's cooked and smothered in so much melted cheese I can't taste it," he called back.

"Some things never change," Bonnie said.

While she prepared the food, I poured us each a glass of her homemade peach sangria. The stuff was light and fruity. She'd been kind enough to share her recipe with me and I often whipped up a batch for me and Alicia.

My cell phone chirped and I checked the readout. The screen indicated the caller was Sierra Behr. I punched the button to accept the call. "Hi, Sierra."

The only sound that came through the speaker was a sob.

"Sierra? Are you okay?"

"He fired me! I told Brazos that you had come to see

me and—" She sobbed again for a few seconds. "He let me go!"

"That makes no sense," I told her. "He's the one who told me to contact you. He's the one who gave me your number."

She gulped and sniffled. "He asked me what I had told you. I said you asked why I hadn't hired a CPA, and that I'd told you he'd never asked me to take care of his taxes. He said that was a lie, that he had asked me to file his taxes and that he'd assumed I'd gotten them done every year."

How could Brazos have expected her to file his taxes if he never provided her with his income information? I was beginning to think Brazos was nothing more than a greedy jerk, who'd rather leave the tax-paying up to everyone else while he accumulated ranches and all-terrain vehicles, planes and boats and fancy cars.

Sierra sniffled again. "It's not true! Brazos never asked me to hire a tax preparer. I'm very organized. I would've remembered."

It looked like Katie Dunne might not be the only one being set up to take a fall for her employer.

"Any chance you're willing to give me copies of his financial records now?" I asked.

Another sniffle. "He told me he'd sue me if I gave you anything," she said. "He sent two of his bodyguards over to pick up my laptop."

"Did you give it to them?"

"Yes," she said. "I'd bought it with money from the business account, so Brazos said that meant the computer belonged to him."

"Did you happen to keep any hard copies of the records?"

"I tried," she said, "but the security guys went through my entire apartment and found them. They took everything.

All of the printouts. The checkbook. The credit card. The planner. Everything."

"You allowed them to go through your stuff?"

"I didn't want them to," she said, "but what was I going to do? Those guys weigh two fifty each. You don't say no to guys like that. Not if you like your teeth."

Clearly, Sierra felt betrayed and violated and perhaps even vengeful. I decided to use that to my advantage before she had time to rethink things.

"I'd like to come by in person," I said. "Ask you a few more questions." And get her to sign an affidavit. I needed to strike while the iron was hot.

"Okay," she agreed, issuing one last sniffle. "By the way, did you see the newspaper today?"

"No." My eyes scanned the kitchen, seeking the paper I'd handed to Bonnie earlier. It lay on the counter. I slid it from its plastic sleeve and rolled it open.

"I'm not the only one Brazos got rid of this weekend," Sierra said. "We can talk about it when you get here." With that, she ended the call.

I took a look at the front page. Sure enough, the headline was ROUGH WATERS FOR THE BOYS OF THE BAYOU. I quickly scanned the article. The report noted that Brazos Rivers had split ways with his backup singers and dancers, citing "creative differences."

I begged off, apologizing to Bonnie for having to leave early.

"I understand," she said. "Duty calls. Besides, that'll leave more broccoli for Nick."

"More broccoli?" Nick walked in from the living room and scrunched his nose in distaste. "Thanks a lot, Tara."

When I told Nick what Brazos had done, he was more than happy to hand me the keys to his truck. "I hope you and Sierra bring Stagnant Swamps to his knees."

I gave Nick a kiss on the cheek, Nutty a peck on the snout, and raised a hand in good-bye to Bonnie.

On the drive to Sierra's place, I ran through the evidence in my mind, building the tax evasion case against Brazos, then playing devil's advocate, trying to anticipate the defenses he might bring up should this case end up in court. Would he continue to claim that his manager was supposed to file his returns? If so, would a judge or jury believe it? Heck, could there be any truth to it? Sierra had seemed on top of things when I'd first seen her with her clipboard and headset at the tour bus, but it could be possible that she'd forgotten about the returns, right? Maybe had a miscommunication with Brazos about them? As busy as their schedule was it would be entirely plausible for a thing like that to slip his manager's mind, no matter how organized she might believe herself to be. Sierra took care of the other finances for the band, paying all of the expenses and salaries and filing their W-2s. It wasn't unreasonable to assume Brazos would've asked her to file his returns, too. But how did he think she'd get his income information if he hadn't given it to her?

Perhaps I was making this matter more complicated than it needed to be. Regardless of whether Brazos was guilty of criminal tax evasion, he still owed a buttload of taxes and interest. Maybe figuring out who was to blame wasn't as critical as collecting the money owed and ensuring he'd comply with his tax filing requirements in the future. Or maybe I was going easy on the guy because I wanted, *desperately,* to believe that he wasn't a creep. I'd had a crush on the guy for years, fantasized about him in intimate and compromising positions. I'd hate to think all of that energy had been wasted on a loser.

I parked next to Sierra's Camaro. She opened her apartment door right away and let me in.

I took one look at the place and let out a whistle. "Holy crap."

Brazos's security team had trashed her place. It looked as if she'd been robbed. All of the couch cushions had been flipped over and her mattress overturned. Every drawer in her dresser, desk, and filing cabinet had been pulled out, ransacked, and dumped. They'd even pulled the bookshelves away from the wall, as if to assure themselves that she hadn't hidden a copy of the financial records behind the unit.

Sierra dabbed at her eyes with a tissue. "They were thorough. I'll give them that."

Despite the fact that she hadn't been entirely cooperative before, I felt sorry for her. Having a bunch of overgrown thugs ransack your apartment had to be terrifying.

We sat down at her kitchen table.

"Would you be willing to sign an affidavit?" I asked. An affidavit loaded with condemning testimony could be helpful in convincing a defense attorney of the strength of our case, maybe encourage a quick settlement. I wasn't looking to put Brazos in jail. His actions, though far from exemplary, were not nearly as naughty as many of the targets I pursued. If he willingly paid up soon, I might agree to waive any criminal penalties. After all, the goal of my work was compliance and, if I could effectuate that without having to put Brazos behind bars, all the better. Besides, if he were behind bars, he wouldn't be earning the money he could use to get his taxes paid.

Sierra nodded. "Sure. I'll sign an affidavit."

We talked our way through the statement and I typed it up on my computer. Unfortunately, the goon squad had taken Sierra's printer with them. I had to settle for e-mailing the document to her and hoping she'd print it out, sign it, and mail it to me as promised.

"I'm going to buy a new computer and printer today,"

she said with a sigh. "I'll need them to look for a new job."

I gestured to the newspaper lying on her kitchen table. The paper was open, showing the front-page headline about the breakup between Brazos and his Boys. "What kind of 'creative differences' did they have?" I asked Sierra.

"I don't see how they could've had any real differences," she said. "Those guys did everything Brazos asked of them, without question. Brazos probably just got tired of giving them a cut of the earnings."

I tried to imagine the concert without the Boys of the Bayou. Sure, Brazos was the star, and he was the one all the women came to see. But the Boys added another dimension to the show. Their dance moves were fun to watch, even if their act was a little reminiscent of the cheesy eighties boy bands. Without them, Brazos would have to step things up a notch, find a way to fill the stage all on his own.

The question was, was he man enough to do it? I was beginning to feel like maybe I didn't know this man who'd been traipsing about in my dreams for years. No, I didn't think I knew him at all.

chapter twenty-two

$\mathcal{V}$oid

Monday evening, Katie called my cell with some interesting news.

"I remember now why the name of that PR firm sounded familiar," she said. "Mr. Burkett had me make out a check to them last May for $15,000. He never told me what the check was for, but I guess it was for a fee or retainer of some kind. He came back a few days later and told me to show the check as void in the system."

"Did he give the check back to you?" Good accounting practices dictated that voided checks should be retained in the records as proof that the check had not actually been issued.

"No," Katie said. "He told me he'd torn it up after he decided not to hire them. He also told me to delete their name from the computer files."

In other words, Burkett didn't want any type of paper or electronic trail linking him to Cushings, Cobb, & Beadle. But if he'd decided not to hire them, what were the cash payments for? Had he actually hired them after all, but didn't want anyone, including Katie, to know? If so, why? There was no shame in hiring a PR firm. Companies did it all the time. And why pretend that the payments were for drill bits instead?

None of this made sense. Of course it was my job to make it make sense. And I always got the job done.

Tuesday morning, I decided to take a stroll by the offices of Cushings, Cobb, & Beadle. Their office was only four blocks away from my office at the IRS, it was a sunny day, and I could use the fresh air. Why not?

I headed out and, in ten minutes, arrived at their building. The firm was located on the second floor. Their entire reception area was fronted with glass, the vertical blinds turned to allow those on the outside to see in and those on the inside to see out. A receptionist sat behind a built-in rectangular console to the side, while two clients sat on modern love seats, flipping through magazines while awaiting their appointments.

Brazos sure could use the services of a PR firm about now. His break with the Boys of the Bayou had been the only thing newscasters and entertainment shows could talk about all weekend.

Some of the reporters had been understanding, noting that it wasn't unusual for performers to part ways to pursue different interests or solo careers. The Beatles had done it. So had the Eagles, though they'd reunited for a concert tour, playing their classic hits for fans who refused to give up on them. Beyoncé and the other girls from Destiny's Child had parted ways to pursue individual callings, too. No big deal, right?

Others had condemned Brazos, painting him as a self-centered, egotistical jackass who cared about no one but himself. The Boys of the Bayou appeared on a local weekend talk show and had few nice things to say about the young man who'd employed them the last few years.

According to the Boys, Brazos never let them have any input on the music or lyrics and, until they'd taught him to dance, he'd had two left feet wearing two right boots. They vowed to move on, saying they already had plans in the works to hire musicians and form their own new "alternative Southern rock band with indie punk influences," whatever the heck that was. They planned to call this new band Armadillo Uprising. Hmm. They might want to give the name a little more thought . . .

Trish had landed an exclusive interview with Brazos, in which he'd claimed that his upcoming album would take his music in a new direction, one that was "less pop" and had more "artistic integrity and emotional purity."

"These new songs," Brazos had told her in the interview, putting his palm to his chest, "they came not just from my heart, but from my soul."

Nick had gotten a laugh out of that. "Sure they didn't fall out of your ass, Brazos?" he'd inquired of the man on the TV screen.

I'd thought Nick's comments were unfair, but I kept my mouth shut. Things between me and Nick seemed better lately and I wasn't about to get him riled up over Brazos again. Besides, as wonderful as Nick was, he was neither a creative type nor particularly in touch with his emotions. He simply couldn't understand a man like Brazos, one who looked deep within himself and drew on his experiences and emotions to craft beautiful songs of love and loss and feeling.

Oh, God. Nick was right. Brazos really did have me under his spell, didn't he? Even after he'd apparently misled me twice, I still wanted to forgive the guy, to think the best of him. *Ugh.* Was I really so weak? I didn't want to think so. But all of the evidence was against me. A silent shame burned within me.

Well, at least I could redeem myself somewhat if I

solved this darn PPE mystery. I discreetly watched through the glass of Cushings, Cobb, & Beadle, pretending to be talking on my cell phone in the outer hallway but in reality just muttering random gibberish into it—recipes, literary clichés, scenes from a romance novel I'd been reading. "Add two cups of sugar and a half cup molasses. Stir two hundred strokes by hand and then fold into a thirteen-by-nine baking dish. It was a dark and stormy night. And they lived happily ever after. Looking into his eyes, she took hold of his throbbing member and—"

Inside the PR firm, a door opened and a man in a business suit stepped out from the interior offices and into the lobby. He had a thick envelope clenched in his hand. Was it *the* envelope? The one Larry Burkett had left for Cobb at the historical marker? Hard to say. One bulging nine-by-twelve manila envelope looked just like any other. The man was followed by the elephant-faced man I'd seen at the airport.

My heart began to beat faster in my chest as adrenaline coursed through me. *What are you up to, Russell Cobb? What have you been doing with all the cash? Did you keep it for yourself or give it to someone else? And what about you, guy in the blue tie? Is that envelope in your hand from PPE? Are you the missing piece of this puzzle?*

Oops. I realized I'd just said those questions out loud into my cell phone. Duh!

The two men shook hands and the one in the business suit exited the PR firm. He didn't look familiar, but it couldn't hurt to follow him and try to figure out who he was and whether he was part of the PPE drill bits scam.

The man stepped to the elevator and punched the down-arrow button. I mentally crossed my fingers that he'd come here on foot. If he'd driven, he'd be heading down to the underground parking garage to retrieve his car.

Given that I'd walked here, I'd have no way of following him if he were in a vehicle. At least not for long. I could sprint for a couple of blocks, but after that I'd surely peter out.

I sneaked into the stairwell and dashed down the stairs to the first floor. I scurried across the lobby and stepped outside, positioning myself next to the garage exit to await him. If he came out on foot, I'd follow him. If he drove out in a car, I'd get his license plate and try to figure out who he was and the nature of his connection to PPE, assuming, of course, that there even was a connection.

A moment later, the man walked outside and turned left. *Good.* I followed him, keeping a discreet distance and pretending to be working my cell phone while surreptitiously watching him from under my bangs.

The man walked three blocks down and two blocks over, using a key to unlock the door of a downtown seafood restaurant. I knew this place. I'd heard on the news that the restaurant had been responsible for a recent salmonella outbreak. A dozen customers had been treated for gastronomical distress after eating at the place. *Ick.*

The man stepped into the restaurant but stopped just inside the door. As I slowly meandered by the front window, I saw the man hand the envelope to a young blond guy in athletic shorts, sneakers, and a hoodie. The young man had a canvas bag slanted across his chest. He tucked the envelope into the bag and came outside, slipping earbuds into his ears as he walked past me. Looked like I had new quarry to follow.

His head bopping in time to the music, the guy took only a few steps down the sidewalk before turning into the lobby of the skyscraper next door. I followed right on his tail, but the guy was oblivious, too absorbed in his tunes to even notice. The faint notes of the music drifted on the air, but I couldn't identify them as any particular song or artist. Perhaps it was a new release by Armadillo Uprising.

He punched the down button on the lobby elevator. *Damn.* He was heading down to the parking garage. Oh, well. Might as well follow him and get his license plate number, see if that information would get me anywhere.

I lagged behind as he stepped off the elevator, waiting until the doors began to close before forcing them back open with my hand and slinking after him. To my surprise, he didn't climb into a car. Rather, he pulled the thick envelope from his messenger bag, tore the end open, and removed a stack of papers. As I watched from behind a support beam, he began making his way down the row of cars, sliding what appeared to be a flyer under the windshield wipers of each vehicle.

When he'd rounded the corner to go down to the next row, I scurried up to the first car on the row and yanked the paper from the windshield. The flyer contained a cartoon fish with a conversation bubble that read:

Give us a second chance to earn your trust and tantalize your taste buds!
50% off your entire order with this coupon.
Void after March 15.

I'd come all this way for a stupid coupon? Sheesh. What a waste of time. Clearly, the owner of the restaurant wasn't involved in the PPE con. He'd hired Cobb's PR firm to come up with a campaign to rebuild its customer base after the salmonella scare. Good luck. With all of the restaurants downtown, competition was fierce. The seafood restaurant was likely sunk. I could only hope that my case wouldn't suffer the same fate.

chapter twenty-three

S ausage Fest

In the early afternoon on Wednesday, I headed to the elevators, trying to move as discreetly as possible. *Dang it!* Nick was at the end of the hall speaking with Lu's secretary, Viola. The last thing I wanted was for him to spot me. No doubt he'd give me a lecture if he knew I was on my way to see Brazos. The last thing I wanted right now was to be harangued, especially by him.

As I waited for the elevator car to arrive, Lu stepped out of her office down the hall.

"Where you going?" Lu called to me.

I'd been hoping nobody would ask. "Brazos is filming a commercial," I called back. "I'm going to swing by and see about getting him to sign an agreement to get his taxes filed and paid."

"I'd offer to go with you," Lu said, "but that young stud gets my blood pumping so fast I might have a stroke."

"Somebody ought to go with her," Viola said, giving me a pointed look over the top of her bifocals. "We all know what happened last time. *Nothing.*"

Gee. Thanks for the vote of confidence.

"Oh, for the love of God!" Nick snapped. "I'll go with Tara."

"Great," I said, though honestly, Nick coming with me was anything *but* great. On a personal level, I adored everything about Nick. On a professional level, Nick could be kind of overbearing sometimes. I didn't like Nick interfering with my cases, second-guessing my decisions, pointing out my mistakes. But I couldn't very well turn his offer down. He'd think it was because I wanted to go alone and get up close and personal with Brazos.

We bade Lu and Viola good-bye and headed down to my G-ride in silence. Once we were in the car, Nick cut angry eyes my way. "Were you planning to tell me you were going to see Brazos again?"

I cut angry eyes right back. "Why should I?" I added a derisive snort. "You don't give me every detail about your cases. For instance, you didn't tell me every time you got hit on by those gorgeous young girls at Guys and Dolls."

Nick and I had recently worked an undercover case at a strip joint. More than one of the dancers had attempted to work her charms on Nick, and she'd usually done it while wearing nothing more than a G-string and some glitter. I had been totally jealous, I'd just had the sense not to show it. Besides, I trusted Nick. He might have thought those girls were hot and sexy and enjoyed taking in some eye candy, but the fact that he was dating me told me that he wanted a woman who was more than a pretty face and long legs and huge honkers. He wanted a woman who could match him in guts and gumption, who challenged him and didn't kiss his ass, no matter how kissable that ass might be. Nick should show the same trust in me that I'd shown in him.

Nick didn't say anything in return. He just sat there, brooding silently, while I drove to the television station. Unfortunately, a crash on the freeway set us behind a good twenty minutes. Even more unfortunately, while we were stuck on the road, we'd been forced to stare at a new enormous billboard erected on the frontage road. A twelve-foot-tall Brazos smiled down at us from the back of a horse, his arm raised over his head as if he were riding the bronc. His spurs had been embellished with sparkly silver paint. The caption across the bottom of the billboard read: BUCKIN' BRONCO BOOTS. GREAT FOR SCOOTIN'. EVEN BETTER FOR KNOCKIN'.

I pretended not to notice the oversized ad.

Nick, on the other hand, rolled down his window, pulled his Glock from his holster, and aimed the gun at Brazos's oversized face. *Blam!* A hole appeared right between the singer's eyes.

I shook my head. "You're going to have to account for that bullet, you know."

Nick raised a shoulder. "Accidental discharge."

We arrived late to the commercial shoot. The Ferrari sat at the far end of the station's parking lot.

Nick took a glance at it as we pulled up. "That is *not* a cowboy's car," he said. Luckily, he left it at that.

We climbed out of the G-ride and went into the lobby. As we stepped up to the receptionist's desk, we held up our badges.

Before I could speak, Nick said, "We're with the IRS. We're looking for Flaming Brassiere."

The receptionist's face crinkled in confusion. "Who?"

I kicked Nick sideways in the ankle. "Brazos Rivers," I said. "It's my understanding he's filming a commercial here today."

"Right. Just a moment." The receptionist punched a button on her phone and summoned an intern to escort us to the studio.

We arrived to find the filming already in progress. This time, there was no stuffed horse on the set. Rather, the scene was designed to look like a backyard patio, complete with a wooden picnic table covered in a red-and-white-checkered tablecloth. Brazos stood before a shiny barbecue grill filled with dry ice to give the illusion of smoke. He was dressed in his trademark jeans, boots, and spurs, and held a two-pronged grilling fork with an enormous spicy summer sausage link on the end of it. Beside the grill stood a twentyish blonde wearing jeans and a red halter top so tight it was a miracle her blood could move through her veins. She was likely to develop a clot by the end of the day.

Two men in business attire stood off to the side. Probably representatives from the sausage company and its advertising firm if I had to hazard a guess. Next to them stood four of Brazos's bodyguards. Looked like he'd kept the muscle on the payroll. After what happened at the photo shoot for Buckin' Bronco Boots, he was wise to keep some personal protection in place.

A balding man with a fringe of fluffy brown hair stepped in front of the camera with a black-and-white-striped clapboard. "Schweiger's Spicy Summer Sausage Commercial take two." He slammed the top of the open board down. *Clap!*

On cue, Brazos raised the enormous sausage to the woman's lips. "Come on, honey, try a taste. You'll love my spicy sausage."

The girl opened her mouth wide and took the end of the sausage between her lips. She bit off a chunk before turning to the camera, closing her eyes, and emitting an elongated and sensual, *"Mmmmm."*

Nick covered his mouth with his hand and faked a cough that did little to mask his words. "Man-whore."

The man with the clapboard yelled, "Cut!," and shot Nick an angry look. "I don't know who you are, but if you can't be quiet you're going to have to leave the set."

Nick stiffened. "I'm federal law enforcement." He held up his badge and pushed his jacket back to show the gun holstered at his waist. "I'm not going anywhere until I've had a word with Brazos."

Until *he* had had a word with Brazos? *I* was the one who should be having words with Brazos, not Nick. Even if Nick was here as my partner and backup, this was still *my* case.

From the set, Brazos tossed Nick an eat-sausage-and-die look. In return, Nick shot Brazos a look so pointed I half expected to see a hole appear between Brazos's eyes, just like the billboard. The blonde, meanwhile, took a step to the side and spat the sausage bit into a bucket. No wonder she stayed so skinny. I bet she'd never had to un-button the top button of her pants.

The balding man turned his attention to Brazos. "Remember. It's not *try* a taste. It's *take* a taste."

"Take," Brazos repeated. "Got it."

The man turned to another college-aged girl waiting to the side. Probably another intern. "We need another sausage."

The girl nodded and pulled a cooked sausage from a Crock-Pot on a table next to her. Brazos held up his fork and the girl removed the bitten sausage, replacing it with the intact link.

"Okay." The director stepped in front of the camera again with his clapboard held open. "Schweiger's Spicy Summer Sausage Commercial take *three*." He slammed the top of the open board down once again. *Clap!*

For the second time since we'd arrived, Brazos raised the enormous sausage to the woman's lips. "Come on, honey, take a taste. You will love this spicy sausage."

The girl opened her mouth wide another time and again took the end of the sausage between her lips. She bit down and severed a bite, turning to the camera and emitting another elongated and sensual, *"Mmmmm."* Unfortunately, the *mmmmm* was followed by a gagging sound as the girl choked on the oversized bit of meat. She grabbed her throat with both hands, her mouth gaping open. *Hork. Horrrk.*

The director rushed over, performed a quick Heimlich maneuver on the bug-eyed blonde, and the sausage popped out of the girl's mouth like a baseball out of an automated pitching machine. The makeup artist, a thin man in a purple jumpsuit, stepped over with a tissue, dabbing moisture from the girl's eyes. "No harm done. You look great, darling. Fabulous!"

With a discreet cringe, the intern used a napkin to retrieve the errant sausage bit. She tossed both the napkin and the sausage into the bucket, returned to the Crock-Pot, and fished out a fresh sausage, replacing the one on the fork.

"Remember, Brazos," the director said, a hint of impatience in his voice. "It's not 'you will,' it's the contraction 'you'll.' We want this commercial to sound casual. It's also not '*this* spicy sausage.' It's '*my* spicy sausage.' That's, well, sexier."

Next to me, Nick shook his head and muttered, "This is all kinds of wrong."

The director stepped in front of the camera again with his clapboard held open. "Schweiger's Spicy Summer Sausage Commercial take *four*." He slammed the board closed. *Clap!*

This time, Brazos got the wording right and the girl didn't choke. When they were done, she spat the sausage bite into the bucket and asked, "How'd we do?"

The director and the two men who'd been standing along the wall watched a replay and huddled, quietly discussing the commercial. When they broke, the director said, "Let's do a few more takes so we can have some options."

Ten minutes and six sausage spits later they deemed the commercial "done."

Brazos glanced over at me and Nick and waved a hand, gesturing for us to follow him to his dressing room. When the four members of his security team attempted to follow us into the room, Brazos held up a palm. "Wait for me outside."

Brazos closed the door and turned, leaning back against the dressing table, his arms crossed over his chest. "I'm glad you two are here," he said. "We need to set some things straight."

chapter twenty-four

$\mathcal{S}$hooting Star

"Oh, yeah?" Nick spat, putting his thumbs in the front pockets of his pants. "Illuminate us."

Apparently deciding I'd be more easily convinced than Nick, Brazos turned his gaze on me. "If Sierra told you she wasn't supposed to get my taxes done, she lied. Way back when I first hired her I asked her to find a CPA to prepare my tax forms for me. I'm a singer and a songwriter—"

"A poet," Nick added, arching a brow. "Isn't that what they say?"

Brazos hazarded a glance at Nick. "Some do, yes." He turned his focus back to me. "At any rate, I don't know anything about taxes or running a business. That's exactly what I hired Sierra for. I didn't know she'd dropped the ball until you got in touch with me. I wish I'd realized it sooner."

His words instantly made me feel lighter, releasing a coil of tension inside me. This was all just a misunderstanding. Sure! What Brazos said made total sense. After all, as busy as he was, he couldn't be expected to take care of the business details himself, could he? Of course not. Sierra had been lying to me, covering her own ass. *She* was to blame. Not Brazos. Right?

Nick rocked back on his heels. "How'd you expect your manager to get your taxes done if you didn't give her your income information?"

Brazos addressed Nick's question, though his eyes were still on me. "Sierra had access to all of my income records. In fact, every time I received any kind of financial data I gave her a copy. She lied about that, too."

As he spoke, he scratched himself behind the ear. He might have just had an itch, but I also knew that scratching one's ear or nose or touching one's throat or face could be indicative that the speaker was lying. Was Brazos telling me the truth? Or had Sierra told me the truth? I had no idea whom to believe at this point. Brazos had previously claimed not to have received the letters sent by the collections department. Understandably, I now had trouble believing he was as on top of his financial paperwork as he'd just claimed. That coil of tension that had released only a moment ago began to recoil inside me, like a rattlesnake preparing to strike.

This case was coming down to a he said/she said situation. We special agents never liked those. We liked cases we could prove undeniably via paper or electronic trails.

People lied. Numbers didn't.

I felt Nick's eyes on me and turned to look at him.

His frustration was evident by the firm set of his jaw, the tightness around his eyes and mouth. "If everything you're telling us is true," he said to Brazos, "then you'll want to get this matter resolved and get your taxes all paid up."

Brazos dipped his head in agreement. "As soon as possible."

"Fan-damn-tastic." Nick pulled the agreement from the inside pocket of his jacket, where he'd stashed it after taking it from my briefcase on the drive over. He held it out to Brazos. "You'll have no trouble signing this agreement, then."

"It's to your benefit," I pointed out. "Your account is accruing over two thousand in interest per day."

The singer's eyes widened. "How much?"

"Over two grand. Two thousand one hundred ninety-one dollars and seventy-eight cents to be precise."

He blinked. "You're kidding, right?"

I shook my head.

Brazos took the paper from Nick and read over the one-page agreement. Now it was he whose jaw was set, who looked tight around the eyes and mouth. Brazos looked up, ignoring me now and setting his sights on Nick. "I'd be glad to get this back to you once I run it past my attorney."

Nick snorted. "Can't you read? That's one page of straightforward, black-and-white English. There's no room for misinterpretation. It says you'll have your returns filed within the month and make arrangements to get your taxes paid. That's all. It's not rocket science."

Brazos offered Nick a shrug. "I don't sign anything without my lawyer taking a look at it first. Surely you can understand that. You're not trying to deny me the right to an attorney, are you?"

If not for the smug, self-satisfied grin playing about the singer's lips, I might've still been willing to give him the benefit of the doubt. But in that instant I feared I'd been wrong to ever trust the guy.

Nick stopped breathing for a moment and I could sense him mentally counting to ten to prevent himself from snapping the singer's neck like a toothpick. Hell, I felt like doing it, too, but I knew I couldn't. The situation was clear to me now. Brazos had been playing me for a fool, stringing me along, toying with me. No doubt he'd already spoken with an attorney who'd suggested this very strategy, knowing it would temporarily tie our hands, give Brazos yet another reprieve.

Several years ago, a federal judge was forced to dismiss the biggest tax fraud case in U.S. history after the prosecutors on the case were held to have effectively denied the defendants their right to counsel by preventing the defendants' employer, one of the Big Four accounting firms, from paying legal fees on behalf of the accused. Since then, everyone working for Uncle Sam had been advised to be especially cautious when it came to defendants and their lawyers. No way would Nick and I risk the case against Brazos by interfering with his right to have an attorney look at the agreement, no matter how unnecessary that review might seem.

"Call your attorney right now," Nick suggested. "That's a short agreement. You can read it to your lawyer over the phone."

Though the smile remained on Brazos's face, his eyes flung sharp daggers at Nick. "I'm sure she'd rather see a hard copy."

"No problem," Nick said. "That's what technology is for. Snap a photo with your cell phone and attach it to an e-mail. She can print it out and take a look."

A frown flickered across the singer's face. He continued to balk. "My attorney is very busy."

"Surely not too busy for a star like you," Nick said. "Besides, you don't know if she's busy right now unless you call, right?"

Brazos said nothing, but the rapid rise and fall of his chest indicated he was secretly seething.

"Remember when we first met?" I said to Brazos. "You said you wanted to cooperate."

He had the nerve to snort then, and tossed a look my way that was so full of contempt it froze the blood in my veins. "What the fuck did you expect me to say?"

Both my stomach and heart clenched into tight little balls. How could I have been so wrong about him? So stupid as to believe his lies?

I supposed I should've been more annoyed that Nick had taken over here, but honestly, I was glad he had. I wasn't sure I could talk at the moment. Even though Brazos had misled me, even though he was being uncooperative, I still found it hard to overcome the long-held feelings I'd had toward the guy. No, not toward the guy, exactly, but toward the guy I thought Brazos had been. I'd been in awe of the Brazos Rivers I'd created in my mind. But the Brazos Rivers standing here in front of me? I supposed the most accurate way to describe what I felt for him was pity. This young man was clueless, and seemed intent on staying that way. The world had kissed his ass, fallen at his feet, let him get away with all sorts of bad behavior with impunity. Obviously, he'd expected the special treatment to continue.

"Tell you what," Nick continued, refusing to back down. "Since you seem so uncomfortable placing a call to your own attorney, I'll do it." He pulled out his cell phone and held a finger poised over it ready to dial. "What's her name and number?"

Brazos spoke slowly and deliberately, a sure sign he was fighting to stay calm. "I'd like to speak with her before I give you that information."

"I know bullshit when I smell it." Nick took a step closer to Brazos and looked down on him. "This stinks to high heaven."

Not to be outdone, Brazos took a step closer to Nick. "Do I need to call my bodyguards in here?"

Nick chuckled. "If this were a street fight, hell, yeah, you'd need those guys. But this is a battle of wits and legalities and honor. Those lame-brained thugs aren't going to be of much use to you."

Before Nick and Brazos came to blows, I figured I better put an end to this conversation. It appeared to be at an impasse anyway, and I'd finally overcome my shock enough to speak. "Look, Brazos," I said. "You're being . . ." An uncooperative ass is what he was being. But I couldn't very well say that, could I? I racked my brain for an appropriate choice and my mind spat up the perfect word. *"Incorrigible."*

The singer's head snapped my way, his eyes wide. "What the fuck did you just call me?"

Though I knew I shouldn't take it personally, his rude language and tone insulted me. My subtle reference to his summer stock performance in *The Sound of Music* had obviously surprised him. Was he actually so naïve as to think we wouldn't figure out who he really was? For a guy who was too big for his own britches, he had some growing up to do.

I didn't bother addressing his question. "If you get the signed agreement to us within a week we'll hold off on the other enforcement measures available to us."

" 'Enforcement measures'?" he spat, making no effort at this point to remain calm and civil. "What the hell do you mean by that?"

I was about to explain that we could arrest him and seize his assets—assuming we could track down his elusive plane, bus, and boat—but Nick raised a palm to stop me. He offered Brazos a smug smile of his own. "Your attorney can tell you all about it, *Winnie.*"

On hearing his secret nickname come out of Nick's mouth, Brazos knew for certain that the jig was up. He froze, his mouth hanging slack when he realized we had the power to expose him for the drugstore cowboy he was.

Nick chuckled. "See ya."

Without another word, Nick walked out of the room. I grabbed one last glimpse of Brazos, noting how immature and frightened he appeared. Also how dark his roots had become. Definitely time for a touch-up lest the public realize he was Italian opera progeny. Disillusioned, disappointed, and disgusted, I followed Nick out of the room.

Neither of us spoke until we were seated in the car.

Staring out the windshield, Nick asked, "Still nuts about that jerk? Still want to get down and dirty with him and have his babies and whatnot?"

"Nah," I said. "I'd rather put my steel-toed loafer in his nards."

Nick's head swiveled my way, a wide smile spreading his lips. "Now you're talking."

"Actually, I've got a better idea. Watch this." I pulled up my Twitter app on my phone and logged into my secret @ crazyaboutbrazos account. I typed a quick message.

Brazos Rivers at KDFW studio in Dallas right now!!!

I held my phone up and showed it to Nick, then hit the tweet key.

I pulled up the Brazos Rivers Fan Page on Facebook and posted the same information.

Nick snickered. "You're a damn evil genius."

He wasn't the first person to tell me that. The *genius* part didn't bother me, but I wasn't so sure about the *evil* part.

Screeching tires drew our attention. Two cars careened into the parking lot, one of them running up over the curb and sideswiping a holly bush as the driver took the turn much too fast. Three women leaped from the vehicles.

I rolled down my window and pointed at the Ferrari with its BRAZEN plate. "That's his car!" I called. "He'll be out in a minute."

As Nick and I pulled out of the lot, we passed a steady stream of crazed fans heading to the studio. The singer and his bodyguards were on their own this time. Tara Holloway was done with Brazos.

This river had run dry.

chapter twenty-five

$\mathcal{L}$eapfrog

Wednesday night, Nick and I watched Trish LeGrande's report about Brazos on the 10 o'clock news. His most recent fan attack was the lead story. Trish stood inside a recovery room at Baylor Medical Center, dressed in her usual pink.

"Country-western superstar Brazos Rivers and his team of bodyguards suffered minor injuries today when fans flocked to a studio where the singer was filming a commercial for Schweiger's Summer Sausage. Fans were allegedly drawn to the scene after the star's location was leaked on Twitter and Facebook by a fan using the alias 'crazyaboutbrazos.'"

The camera panned out, revealing Brazos lounging on a hospital bed next to Trish, his bodyguards spread about the room in chairs. My quick count tallied up three black eyes, two sprained fingers, a swollen nose, and an assortment of abrasions and contusions. Brazos had managed to escape with only a few scratches to his face and arms and bruised ribs. *Darn.*

"Was it wrong of me to have hoped he'd lose a toe or a

testicle?" I asked. "Maybe one of those waxed nipples he seems so proud of?"

"Nope," Nick said. "Seems fair to me."

Seemed fair to me, too. After all, Lu and I had risked our own safety to rescue the guy at the photo shoot, and I'd hurt my ankle trying to track him down at his parents' place.

The camera closed in on Brazos, his face filling the screen.

"Like I said before, I'm lucky to have such dedicated fans." He sounded less convinced this time. "They just get a little overexcited on occasion."

He offered viewers that seductive smile and those bright blue eyes that used to turn my insides to butter. Now, though, my insides stayed solid and unaffected.

I stared at the screen. "What did I ever see in that guy?"

Nick snorted. "Beats the hell out of me."

We flipped through the other news stations to watch their reports on the fan mob. I noticed that none of the other reporters had gained entry to Brazos's private room. All of them reported from outside the ER when the star was released. Had Trish charmed a doctor and finagled her way into the recovery wing? Or had Brazos willingly invited her in?

Only a short time ago I would've been crazy with envy. But now? Not at all. Trish could have that overrated, oversexed man-whore.

Friday night, Eddie and I were back on the trail of Russell Cobb. This time, rather than drive all the way out to Palo Pinto, we positioned ourselves in the airport's long-term parking garage where we found Cobb's Mercedes on the second level. I took a spot on the third floor where I had a partial view of his car—the front right fender, enough that I would be able to tell when it was moved. Eddie waited in his G-ride on the first floor. Given the near misses I'd experienced backing out last Friday, both of us had positioned our cars with the front end facing out so that we could quickly exit our spots.

A few minutes after eight, the headlights lit up on the Mercedes. I punched the button on my phone to call Eddie. "Cobb is headed your way."

"I'm ready for him."

I pushed the speaker button, sliding the phone into the windshield phone mount and keeping the line open so Eddie and I could stay in constant contact. I pulled out of my spot, going slow at first to ensure a reasonable distance between my car and the Mercedes. When I reached the exit line, Cobb was paying the attendant. Eddie idled directly behind Cobb. A Dodge sedan waited between me and Eddie.

Cobb completed his transaction and pulled out. Eddie drove up and handed the attendant exact change. Through my phone I could hear their exchange. Eddie declined a receipt and drove out, following Cobb.

I sat in my car, waiting impatiently and cursing under my breath as the driver of the Dodge and the attendant engaged in a conversation that seemed fairly involved. The driver was apparently having trouble coming up with the funds to pay his parking fee. He climbed about inside the car, emptying cup holders, the ashtray, and looking under the floor mats for spare change. *Jeez.*

"Cobb's heading to the north exit," Eddie said through the phone.

"I'll be on my way," I said, "as soon as the idiot in front of me scrounges up his fee."

I waited another full minute before shoving my gearshift into park, climbing out of my car, and marching up to the window of the Dodge. "I don't have all night. How much do you need?"

The disheveled guy at the wheel looked up at me. "Three bucks."

I handed a twenty to the attendant. "Here."

The attendant raised the arm and let the guy go. He drove off without thanking me. *Turd*.

I climbed back into my car, got my change, and drove as fast as I dared to the north exit. I put the pedal to the metal and a few minutes later I caught up to my partner and Cobb on the freeway. Eddie and I tag-teamed each other, taking turns being the lead car as if we were playing a vehicular form of leapfrog.

We followed Cobb east on 635 for approximately seventeen miles, then south on Central Expressway for a short distance. He took the Park Lane exit and turned into the prestigious Preston Hollow neighborhood that was currently home to former President George W. Bush. The houses here were generally large and pricey, ranging from lows in the $250s to upward of $5 million.

When Cobb turned down a street called Cavendish Court, I fell back even farther. Following him down the cul-de-sac would be too obvious. Instead, I pulled to a stop in front of a house and cut my engine and lights, using my night-vision scope to keep a close eye on Cobb. I kept Eddie informed through my phone.

"Hang back," I told him as I saw Russell Cobb exit his car and walk up to a house. "Cobb is going into a house on Cavendish Court."

"Is he carrying the cash envelope?" Eddie asked.

"I'm not sure. He's got a briefcase in his hand but that's all I can see."

There was no way of knowing whether the cash envelope was inside Cobb's briefcase. Too bad I didn't have Superman's X-ray vision.

A sliver of light shined out as the front door of the house opened inward. Given the angle, it was impossible for me to see who had opened the door to let Cobb in. The porch light next to the door illuminated the house number. I grabbed my tablet and typed the address into the Dallas County Appraisal District's Web site search function. According to the information that popped up, the house was valued at $467,000 and belonged to Harold and Trudy Craven.

I read the names out loud to Eddie. "You search Harold, I'll search Trudy."

A few seconds later, Eddie said, "All I'm getting on Harold Craven is his lousy score in some golf tournament and a Web site listing him as some big muckety-muck with Frito-Lay."

The potato chip manufacturer was one of the area's major employers and was headquartered in Plano, a Dallas suburb fifteen minutes to the north.

"You think Cobb is handling PR for Frito-Lay?" I asked.

"Could be," Eddie said, "though I'm not finding anything online that links the two. Got anything on Trudy?"

I typed Trudy's name into my browser and a long list of entries popped up. I pulled up the first one. "Looks like she's a state district court judge," I told Eddie. "You think that means anything?"

"I think it means she might be one of Cobb's clients."

Eddie could be right. After all, Cushings, Cobb, & Beadle handled public relations for several elected officials. Then again, if Judge Craven was one of Cobb's clients why would they be meeting on a Friday night, after regular business hours, at her house? Could they have some type of personal relationship? I asked Eddie whether he had any thoughts or theories about that.

"You know how busy judges are," he said. "Maybe Cobb's just trying to accommodate her schedule."

Could be. Eddie and I had spent enough time waiting our turn in busy courtrooms to know firsthand about overbooked dockets.

I tried searching Judge Craven's name again, along with the name of the PR firm. Sure enough, a couple of entries popped up, leading me to Judge Craven's now dormant campaign Web site. She smiled at me from the page. The flattering headshot depicted a fiftyish black-haired woman with straight hair cut in one of those chic, short, slanted styles that was mostly bangs. She smiled just enough to appear pleasant while maintaining a professional demeanor. The backdrop behind her consisted of legal casebooks with tan and red bindings, the *Southwestern Reporter,* third edition. An entry on the contact page advised those interested in arranging speaking engagements with the judge to contact Russell Cobb at Cushings, Cobb, & Beadle.

This lead appeared to be another dead end, like the seafood restaurant flyers. We could be totally wasting our time here. For all we knew, the buck stopped at Cobb, anyway. Maybe he and Larry Burkett were the only two involved. But what were they up to?

Cobb stayed only a few minutes before exiting the Cravens' residence with his briefcase again in hand. I ducked down in my car as he drove past, and let Eddie take the lead again. Cobb drove from the judge's house to a nearby restaurant.

Eddie parked in the restaurant's lot, while I pulled into the parking lot of a wine store a half block down.

My dashboard clock read 9:38. "Seems a little late for dinner," I noted.

Eddie's voice came through my phone. "Maybe he's meeting someone for drinks or dessert."

Again, Cobb carried his briefcase inside.

"I'll go in and scope things out," Eddie said, climbing out of his car. I heard a rustling sound as he tucked his cell phone into the inside pocket of his jacket.

A few minutes later, he emerged from the restaurant and returned to the line. "Cobb's meeting a client for drinks in the bar. He's spread his firm's brochures on the table." Eddie said he'd managed to snag a table nearby and overheard Cobb expounding on the many ways his firm could enhance the status of the client's medical practice.

We decided to call it a night. This felt like another pointless fishing expedition. We couldn't follow Cobb 24/7, and unless we actually saw him hand the cash over to someone we wouldn't get anywhere anyway. Our hard work didn't seem to be paying off. I hated it when that happened.

chapter twenty-six

A Sad Saturday

I spent the night at Nick's Friday night. Before Nutty's condition had deteriorated, Nick and I used to switch off sleeping at his town house and mine. Now, though, it seemed to make more sense to stay at Nick's, where Nutty would feel more at home.

I fixed Nutty a fried baloney sandwich, and Nick and I fed it to him by hand. The dog licked our fingers afterward in a show of gratitude.

"Ready for bed, boy?" Nick asked.

Nutty closed his eyes and released a long, slow breath.

"I'll take that as a *yes*." Nick gently scooped up his pet and carried him upstairs.

After giving the dog his usual good-night kisses on the snout, we went to sleep with Nutty lying on the bed between us, snoring softly. Both Nick and I had an arm draped over the dog. I found myself wondering if this is what it would be like if Nick and I married and had children. Would we one day fall asleep with our child cuddled between us?

When I woke the next morning, I noticed that Nutty was sleeping peacefully and quietly.

Too peacefully and quietly.

I put a hand to my mouth to stifle my gasp. *Oh, no. No, no, no!* Gently, I laid a palm on Nutty's side but felt no movement.

He wasn't breathing.

He'd passed in his sleep.

Hot, prickly tears sprang to my eyes and I had to fight not to cry out. As sad as I was to see Nutty go, Nick would be hit a hundred times worse. Rather than wake him, I decided to let him sleep in blissful ignorance until he woke on his own. Until then, I wept quietly into the back of Nutty's soft, furry neck.

When Nick stirred, I lifted my head.

He opened his eyes, his expression startled when he realized I was crying. He sat up immediately. "Are you okay?"

I looked from Nick, to the dog, and back again. "Nick—"

"Is he . . . gone?" Nick had yet to look down, as if he couldn't bring himself to face what he feared to be true.

I nodded.

Nick swallowed hard, closed his eyes, and pressed his fingertips to his eyelids for a moment. When he'd managed to compose himself, he retrieved one of Nutty's blankets from the floor. He looked down at his beloved pet, his eyes dark with emotion. Gently, he wrapped the dog in the blanket, leaving his face exposed. When Nick spoke, his voice was raspy with emotion. "I'll bury him in my mom's garden. He always liked digging there."

Silently, we dressed. Nick carried Nutty to his truck and laid him on the front seat between us. Tears continued to stream down my face as we drove to Bonnie's house.

As we came in the front door, Bonnie stepped into the

hallway from the kitchen. "Why, hello, you two! This is a nice sur—" She noticed the blanketed form in Nick's arms. "Oh, Lord. Oh, Nick. I'm so sorry, honey."

Nick cleared his throat. "Can you get me a shovel?"

"Sure, hon. Sure."

I followed Nick out back to his mother's vegetable garden. He laid Nutty on the grass next to the bed. Bonnie met us there a moment later with a rounded shovel. Nick took it from her and began to dig in an area where nothing was currently growing.

"Not there," Bonnie said. "Nutty used to dig up my peas. Made me madder'n hell, but he'd look up at me with those big brown eyes and I never could bring myself to punish him for it. Let's put him there."

The bare spot Nutty had dug up himself wasn't big enough so Nick began to dig up the adjacent pea plants, stopping once to rub the back of his sleeve across his eyes. "This dust is getting to me."

Bonnie and I exchanged glances. Nick wasn't fooling us.

While Nick dug, I sat on the ground with Nutty, keeping a hand on him as if to maintain a connection that could no longer exist other than in memory.

Bonnie went back into her garage. I heard the *tap-tap-tap* of a hammer, and she returned a few minutes later with a cross she'd fashioned out of white fence pickets. When Nick finished digging the hole, he picked Nutty up and laid him carefully inside. All three of us knelt down next to the hole and used our hands to gently cover the dog with earth. When we finished, Nick put the pointed end of the picket in the ground and eased the cross down into the dirt. Bonnie offered a short, simple prayer, put her fingers to her lips, then pressed them to the dirt on Nutty's grave.

Though Bonnie offered us lunch, we declined. None of

us felt able to eat under the circumstances. Nick gave his mother a hug and drove me home.

"You gonna be all right?" I asked Nick as he pulled to a stop in my driveway.

"Eventually." He was quiet a moment. "I'll call you later. I'm going to take my boat out."

I didn't bother pointing out that it was cold and overcast. I don't think he'd even noticed or that he'd care. He needed to be alone, to grieve, and there was no better place for him to do that than out in the middle of a lake on his bass boat. I wished I could comfort him, but I knew what he needed now was to be alone with his thoughts and his feelings and his memories, to confront his emotions unobserved and thus unrestrained, to let Nutty go in his own way.

I gave Nick a kiss on the cheek, squeezed his hand, and climbed out of the truck. I leaned back in before closing the door. "I loved that stinky old dog," I said, fresh tears in my eyes.

Nick emitted a sob that he tried to cover with a cough, and forced a soft smile. "Nutty loved you, too. Almost as much as your fried baloney."

chapter twenty-seven

Shoo Fly, Shoo

I spent the next few days trying to locate Brazos and his Ferrari, tour bus, plane, and boat. I had a sneaking suspicion that we'd never see a signed agreement and I wanted to keep tabs on him so I could swoop in for the kill when next Thursday came. Unfortunately, this task proved daunting.

I monitored the Twitter feeds, routinely checking the hash tag #brazosrivers to see if anyone had posted a sighting. No such luck. All I found was a bunch of chatter about the release of the Buckin' Bronco Boots ad, discussion about the bullet hole in the Dallas billboard, and chatter about how hot the singer looked on the stallion. I wondered if his fans would think he looked so hot if they realized the stallion was stuffed with poly fill. Kinda hard to get turned on by a guy sitting on an oversized Beanie Baby.

The singer's Facebook fan page was also devoid of useful information. Instead, there were just hundreds, if not thousands, of posts speculating on his new album and discussing his break from the Boys of the Bayou.

Not surprisingly, all of them were one hundred percent behind Brazos's decision to split from his backup singers and dancers.

Someone named Kirstie had posted: *You don't need the boys, BR. You are all MAN!*

From Elizabeth: *You're the star! The Boys were just riding your coattails.*

A post by Bree read: *Call me, Brazos!!! I'm willing!!! ;) (555) 678–2314*

Sheesh.

I added my own post. *Pay your damn taxes, jackass.*

The chances of Brazos actually reading my post were equal to my chances of being crowned Miss Lone Star State, but venting made me feel a little better.

I called Sierra to see if she might be able to offer some suggestions, but she wasn't much help. If Brazos wasn't on tour in the bus, he sometimes left it at his parents' house, or he sometimes took it traveling around the U.S. As for his boat, she said that he'd generally moved the vessel among the larger lakes in Texas, Arkansas, and Oklahoma while on vacation. He'd even taken it down to the gulf coast on occasion. Whether he'd continue that pattern knowing the IRS was now after both him and his assets was anyone's guess. He might have put the car, bus, and boat in locked storage somewhere, out of sight and out of reach. As for the plane, wherever it was, Brazos usually wasn't far away. Problem was, the plane was both large enough to go long distances and small enough to land at private airstrips. In other words, Brazos could be just about anywhere.

Argh.

The following Thursday morning came and I'd still received no signed agreement from Brazos nor any contact from his attorney, whoever she was. I tried calling the singer's cell phone number only to discover the service had been discontinued. Had he lost or broken yet another phone, or was he trying to make it harder for me to track him down? My gut told me it was the latter.

I phoned his parents. They didn't answer but I left them an emphatic message. "Call me back with Winnie's new cell phone number immediately or the next time you see your son it will be in jail."

Okay, so that was probably overstating the case. Even if I arrested Winthrop 7, as I'd come to think of him now, the judge would likely grant him bail and he'd be released in a matter of hours. Still, it couldn't hurt to give them a sense of urgency.

The last time I'd seen Sierra in person she'd shown me his planner, which revealed his schedule as completely open after the filming of the sausage commercial. I supposed it was possible that Quentin Yarbrough had booked another endorsement deal for the singer since that time. Might as well give the agent a call, right?

After a short wait, his receptionist put me through.

"I need to find Brazos Rivers." *Winnie the Shit* was more like it. "Do you know who his attorney is?"

"Sorry," Yarbrough said. "He's never given me that information. Brazos tends to share information only when absolutely necessary."

"Any chance he's got an upcoming engagement?"

"Let me check." Yarbrough was quiet for a moment, presumably looking through his file for Rivers. "No," he said a moment later. "He's got nothing in the pipes. And if he keeps demanding the moon, that's not going to change."

"He's turned down gigs?"

"Several," Yarbrough said. "He told me he won't consider anything less than half a mil from now on."

What an ego. The guy was popular, sure, but he wasn't the only fish in the sea. Or should I say the only fish in the *river*? "If something comes up, please let me know. Okay?"

"You got it."

Defeated, I rested my forehead on my desk. I'd been an absolute idiot to let Brazos string me along for so long. His plan had worked. He was on hiatus now, purportedly working on new songs for an as-yet-unscheduled tour, and nobody knew where to find him or his assets. It could be weeks before I tracked him down, months even. I wasn't sure I could handle that type of frustration. Besides, it was only another six weeks until my one-year anniversary with the IRS. Lu would be giving me a performance review, and my raise would be based on her evaluation. The year had been tumultuous up to this point, but overall my work had been successful. I'd put a number of tax cheats behind bars and collected significant sums for the agency. But if I let Brazos Rivers and the tens of millions of dollars he owed fall through the cracks, that failure would overshadow everything else I'd accomplished.

I couldn't let that happen.

I *wouldn't* let that happen.

Brazos was nothing more than an overgrown kid who, despite having traveled the world several times over, was not half as worldly and wise as he considered himself. Nevertheless, that incorrigible kid had bested me up to this point.

After allowing myself to wallow in self-pity for a minute or two, I pulled my head up off the desk, leaving a makeup smudge on my desktop calendar, and grabbed my purse. I doubted Brazos was at his parents' ranch, but I had to confirm that fact before going to the courthouse and seeking an order to obtain the Merriweathers' phone records. It was the only way I could think of to track Winthrop 7 down now. Surely the Merriweathers were in touch with their son. If their phone records provided his new cell number we could use triangulation to pinpoint his whereabouts.

A sticky note on Nick's door advised that he was out of the office for the rest of the day. Looked like I was on my own. *Ugh.* I was damn tired of making this drive. It was no longer exciting to drive out to the Brazos Bend Ranch. It was a grind.

Two hours later, I pulled up to the gate at the ranch and looked across the field at the luxurious house. There was no tour bus here today. No plane. No Ferrari. There were, however, more stuffed animals left along the fence, including three more teddy bears and, for some unknown reason, a white unicorn with a rainbow-striped horn.

I punched the buzzer on the keypad. *Bzzt.* There was no response.

I tried it again, holding it down longer. *Bzzzzzzt.* Still nothing.

Might as well go for broke, right? *Bzzzzzzzzzzzzzzzzzzzzzzzt.* If the Merriweathers weren't home, no harm done. If they were home, maybe the long, aneurysm-inducing sound would encourage them to respond to me. When nothing happened, I jabbed at the button multiple times. *Bzt. Bzt. Bzt.* I then went for a random pattern. *Bzzt. Bzt-Bzt. Bzzzzt. Bzt-Bzt-Bzt. Bzzzzzzzzt.*

I was beginning to get on my damn nerves, but there was still no reaction from within the house. Was nobody home? Or were Winthrop 6 and Marcella inside, attempting, once again, to avoid me?

I turned my engine off and sat there for a few minutes, my windows down, enjoying the day. It was almost March now, and today there was a hint of spring in the air. Before long, the tulips and hyacinths would be in full bloom.

As I sat there, many things went through my mind.

How stupid I'd been to let Brazos manipulate me, to believe the lies that rolled so easily off his tongue. How lucky I was to have Nick in my life. How Nick needed a couple of weeks to grieve, to get over the loss of his beloved Nutty, and then I'd drag him down to the animal shelter to pick out a new dog. That sweet old stinky thing had left a hole in my heart, too. It was about time to refill it.

The sound of a car driving up caught my attention. I turned my head, hoping to see Brazos in the Ferrari. Instead, a white cruiser with the gold and black Palo Pinto County Sheriff's Department logo pulled up. I raised a hand in greeting, but the deputy at the wheel failed to return the gesture.

As the stocky, white-haired man climbed out of his car, I climbed out of mine. "Hello, there."

"Whoa, now." He held up a palm. "Is that a gun on your hip?"

"Yes," I told him. "I'm with IRS criminal investigations out of Dallas."

"Dallas IRS?" He cocked his head, pondering my words for a moment. "What're you doing way out here?"

"Looking for Brazos Rivers. He owes Uncle Sam a dollar or two." Or three. Or 20 million.

I thought the sheriff might be amused, but the pinched expression on his face told me he was anything but.

He arched his back, stretching. Riding around in the cruiser all day had to be hard on the spine. He turned side to side, his vertebrae giving off a *pop-pop-pop*. "You got a search warrant?" he asked. "An arrest warrant?"

"No," I said. Not yet, anyway. "I was hoping to speak with his parents, see if I could get his new cell phone number."

He cocked his head and squinted his eyes at me. "You sure you're asking for professional purposes?"

What was this guy accusing me of? Abusing my position to get close to Brazos? Hell, if anything, I'd neglected my duties rather than overstepped my authority. Well, other than that little fence-climbing stunt I'd pulled last time I was out here. That feat of agility had pushed the boundaries.

Rather than answer his insulting question, I said, "Brazos has lied to federal agents. Multiple times. Now he can't be found. I'm just trying to track him down, is all."

He dipped his head. "I understand that. I also understand that these folks"—he lifted a chin to indicate the Merriweathers' house—"have a right to privacy and not to have their land trespassed upon. Unless you've got some type of warrant, you're no different than those stalkers that come out here looking for Brazos."

My mouth fell open. *No better than a stalker?* Was this guy shitting me? How dare he treat me like some pesky housefly, shooing me away. I was working here. On official federal government business.

"Let me guess," I said. "The Merriweathers made a substantial contribution to the sheriff's reelection campaign and now they've got the department in their pocket, officers coming out here at their beck and call to provide personal security services."

Just as I'd ignored his rude inquiry earlier, he ignored mine. "You best move along now," he said, resting his hand on the butt of his holstered gun, "or things could get ugly."

I knew then that it was inevitable. Things *would* get ugly. Maybe not today. Maybe not tomorrow. But no doubt about it, before this case was resolved things would get Marilyn Manson ugly. Fugly with a capital *F*. Totally and undeniably *butt* ugly.

"All righty then," I said, pretending to play nice. "You have a good day now."

The deputy stood there, watching, until I'd driven all the way down the road and turned to head back toward Dallas. The joke was on him, though. I turned around ten minutes later and drove past the ranch again, stopping to snatch the rainbow-horned unicorn for my niece as I headed toward Possum Kingdom Lake. *Neener-neener.* I'd driven all this way. Might as well see if the *River Rat* was docked along the lake or out on the water. Too bad I hadn't brought my long-range rifle. I could put a few holes in the boat, sink the darn thing, and snag Brazos when he swam to shore.

I spent the next four hours circumnavigating the lake, stopping at every public and private marina. I used my field glasses to scan the water. Again my efforts were for naught. There was no sign of Brazos's boat anywhere.

Where the hell was he? And where had he hidden his car, bus, plane, boat, and tushie?

chapter twenty-eight

A Deal with the Devil

On my drive back to Dallas, I found myself taking an exit into old downtown Grapevine. I had no idea where Brazos was, but Madam Magnolia might. Desperate times called for desperate measures, right?

I'd first met Madam Magnolia, a self-proclaimed "psychic consultant," when I'd been pursuing a case against a tax preparer who called himself the Tax Wizard. Not only did the Wiz make tax bills disappear by claiming illusory and ridiculous deductions, he performed magic tricks, as well. The Tax Wizard had subleased space from the psychic, occupying the front half of the small storefront while the Madam ran her business from the back. As it turned out, he was more senile than sinister. He'd escaped criminal prosecution and instead eased into the retirement he should have taken years before.

I parked along the curb in front of the building. Madam Magnolia's space was sandwiched between a women's clothing store and a cupcake shop. Purple curtains with gold fringe adorned the windows. Her name was spelled out in gold lettering across the glass of the front door.

According to the sign propped in the front window, the front half of her space was now home to an aromatherapist operating a business called Uncommon Scents.

I climbed out of my car and went inside, pushing aside the beaded curtain that hung just inside the door. The place had the same aromas of incense and patchouli that I remembered from last time, but now these scents competed with the smells of peppermint, jasmine, vanilla, and lavender. My nose twitched and wiggled involuntarily, experiencing an olfactory overload. I sneezed three times in quick succession before my sinuses gave up the fight and surrendered.

A skinny woman with short blond curls sat at a table, discussing the spiritual, emotional, and health benefits of various essential oils with a boxy redhead. They both looked up at me.

"Hello, there," said the blonde. "Can I help you?"

"I'm looking for Madam Magnolia. Is she in?"

The woman glanced at the antique wall clock. "This is her usual meditation time, but if you ring her bell she might be able to see you." She gestured to a small gold hand bell sitting atop a marble pedestal next to the thick curtain that led back to the psychic's digs.

I walked over to the pedestal. From behind the curtain, the faint sounds of someone chanting *ohmmm* met my ears. I picked up the bell and shook it gently. *Ting-a-ting-a-ting.*

A single green eye peeked out from between the two sections of the curtain that led to Madam Magnolia's chamber. A hand sporting gaudy, colorful rings on each finger emerged several inches below the eye. The palm turned upward and the index finger crooked twice, inviting me in.

I pushed the curtain aside and stepped into the dark room. The deep purple walls seemed to suck all light from the room. Not that there was much to begin with. The only illumination came from three pillar candles in brass candlesticks situated on a round table in the center of the room.

It took a moment for my eyes to adjust, but once they did I could see the black-haired Madam Magnolia now sitting on the far side of the table, her palms raised in either a trance or a sign of welcome.

"Hello, Tara," she said. "Please have a seat."

I slid into the wooden chair that faced her across the tabletop. As I did, my phone bleeped with an incoming text. "Mind if I check my phone?" I asked. "It could be work related."

She shrugged. "Make it quick."

"Or you could just tell me who's calling and why."

"What do I look like?" she said. "AT and T?"

I pulled my cell from my purse and checked the readout. The text was from Alicia, who must have been having a really bad day. All it said was, *How many days until April 15?*

I'd respond later. I set my phone down on the table. Nick and Nutty smiled up at me from the screen. Well, Nick smiled anyway. Nutty's mouth hung open and his tongue lolled out. Guess that was the closest thing a dog had to a smile, huh? Seeing Nutty gave my heart a painful squeeze. I pressed the button to turn off the screen and turned my attention back to the psychic.

"I knew you would be coming to see me," she said. "I sensed you were troubled."

"You did?"

She nodded.

Of course, trouble was pretty much a given for me, so it was an easy guess. I wasn't sure whether I actually believed in any of this stuff. In fact, I was 99.9 percent sure it was all a bunch of bunk designed to separate the

superstitious from their savings. Yet I couldn't deny that
Madam Magnolia had been right on the money when
she'd advised me before. She'd helped me track down two
separate targets in earlier cases.

"I need to find someone," I told her.

"Okay." She began to move her right hand in slow cir-
cles over the glass gazing ball on the table, as if warming
it up. "Who is he?"

She'd used the word *he*. Hmm. Had she sensed that the
person I was looking for was male? Or had she just made
a lucky guess? After all, she had a fifty-fifty chance of
getting it right. Part of me wanted to believe she had some
type of gift. Part of me thought my stopping by here had
been nothing more than an excuse to get a chocolate co-
conut cupcake from next door. Or should I go for the Italian cream this time?

"The man I'm looking for goes by the name Brazos
Rivers," I told her.

Her gaze snapped to my face and her hand stopped
moving, hovering over the ball. "The country-western
singer? With the blond hair and blue eyes? The one who
wears the chaps and silver spurs?"

"That's him."

She began moving her hand again, first in small cir-
cles, then in bigger ones. "I won't mind looking for him at
all. That sweet thing has got it going on."

Brazos might have it going on, but he was also young
enough to be her son. Maybe even her grandson. I didn't
point that out to her, though. The psychic was prone to
mood swings. If I made her angry, her visions might blur
or stop altogether.

"I'm getting something." She stopped moving her hand
and stared intently at the gazing ball. I did the same from
my side, but all I saw was the reflection of the flickering
candles in the glass and my eyes staring back at me.

There was a hungry look in my eyes, like they wanted a cupcake. A strawberry one, maybe? French vanilla?

"I see Brazos," Madam Magnolia said, a smile creeping across her face. "All of him."

All of him? "He's naked?"

"He's wearing his boots and spurs"—the smile grew even bigger—"but that's it." Still staring into the ball, she rubbed her lips together. "Damn, he's fine."

I leaned in, squinting, desperate to know what was under the hat. Brazos might be a liar, a cheat, and an absolute jerk, but he was still nice to look at, still worthy of a late-night fantasy in which he'd come to me, confess all his sins, and make up for them by writing me a check for the full amount of his taxes due and then screwing me silly. *Ugh.* Looked like Brazos still had a little hold over me, huh?

"I see another man now, too," Madam Magnolia said. "This one is just as fine as Brazos."

"What does he look like?"

"He's tall. Dark-haired. He's got a small scar here." She ran her fingertip over her cheekbone. "One of his teeth is slightly chipped."

There was no doubt about it. The scar and the tooth belonged to one man and one man only.

Nick.

A prickle of unease crept along my spine and the hairs on my neck and arms stood on end. Was this woman really seeing a vision? Or was she just making things up? Or had she simply noticed Nick's photo on my cell phone earlier?

"What are they doing?" I asked.

"Arguing."

Over me, perhaps?

"Can you tell where they are?"

"In a small bedroom," she replied. "The man with the

dark hair barely fits. His head is nearly touching the ceiling."

"Are they in a tour bus?" I asked. "A plane?"

"I can't tell," she said. "Uh-oh. Brazos took a swing at the dark-haired man. Got him right in the jaw. They're fighting now." A fresh smile crept across her face. "This is kind of hot."

I fought the urge to reach across the table and throttle her. The thought of Brazos hitting Nick made me furious. I didn't want anyone laying a finger on my man but me. The fact that Madam Magnolia was turned on by it ignited a hot anger in me.

"Wait." She ducked down, as if trying to get a better look. "Something's happened. The vision has become distorted." She put one hand on either side of the ball and shook it gently, as if it were a snow globe. "I don't know what's wrong. This has never happened before. It's blurry. I can only catch glimpses. It's like going through a car wash or trying to see through a windshield when it's raining so hard the wipers can't keep up."

She released the ball and sat back in her chair. "That's it. The vision's over." She stretched her open palm across the table. "That'll be one hundred dollars."

I reluctantly dropped five twenties into Madam Magnolia's hand, mentally chastising myself for wasting my money. I should've known better. I consoled myself with a lemon cupcake from the place next door, buying half a dozen more to take home with me.

There was nothing left to do at this point but see about getting a court order to require the phone company to give me access to the Merriweathers' phone records. Presumably they'd be in touch with their son and, once I determined what his new cell number was, I could get the marshals to use triangulation to track him down. The method had proven useful in a recent case involving a transnational criminal organization based in Tokyo that was selling counterfeit electronics. With any luck, the method could be used now against Brazos.

Friday morning, I placed a call to Ross O'Donnell, an attorney at the Department of Justice who regularly represented the IRS. I gave him the scoop on my investigation. He was nice enough not to point out what an idiot I'd been to believe Winthrop 7's lies.

Fortunately, Ross was available to meet me at the courthouse. He said he'd draft a quick order for Judge Trumbull to sign, assuming, of course, that she'd sign it. Trumbull was a left-wing liberal, a flower child from the sixties who believed in freedom, liberty, and limited police powers. Unfortunately, I was part of the law enforcement she was trying to limit.

I met Ross outside the doors to Judge Trumbull's courtroom. Ross was smart and persuasive, but was he persuasive enough to convince Trumbull to sign the order? I crossed my fingers.

We sat in the galley while she took testimony in a murder-for-hire case. The accused was a smallish white man with short hair and a stylish business suit. He appeared harmless until he turned the other way and I spotted the upper two arms of a swastika neck tattoo showing over the top of his collar. *Yikes!*

When the judge dismissed the jury for a break, she waved me and Ross up to her bench. Judge Trumbull was a round woman, with poufy gray hair and a set of jiggling jowls that made her look remarkably like a bulldog. She had a bulldog personality to boot. She looked intently from me to Ross. "I take it you two aren't just stopping by to say hello."

"No, Your Honor." Ross explained the purpose of our visit.

"Brazos Rivers?" Trumbull said. "Is he that cute young singer with the blond hair and the chaps and the silver spurs? The one that jingle-jangles all over the stage shaking his tight little tush?"

Ross looked to me for verification. He must not listen to country music or look at any magazines while standing in the grocery store checkout line or ever watch television. Seriously, Brazos Rivers was all over the place. Did Ross live under a rock?

"Yes, Your Honor," I said. "The chaps and spurs and all that? That's Brazos."

"He sure is a looker. And that voice . . ." She looked off, absentmindedly running her hand up and down the shaft of her gavel. Jeez. She was as bad as Lu and Madam Magnolia. Looked like Brazos's charms superseded any of their concerns about age-appropriateness.

Ross cleared his throat to get the judge's attention.

She turned back to him, her expression peeved. He must've interrupted a fairly steamy daydream.

"Would you like Special Agent Holloway to tell you more about this case?" he asked.

"She better," Trumbull replied, turning to me now. "You know I don't like to let you folks go digging willy-nilly into everyone's business. Convince me why I should let you have these phone records."

I gave her a brief history of my investigation, spinning the details a little in what I hoped would be a convincing way. "Mr. Rivers appears to have purposely misled the IRS to buy himself time to conceal his assets and to go into hiding."

Trumbull snorted. "Another way to look at it is that you failed on several occasions to take him or his assets into custody and let his cute little tush slip right through your fingers." She raised an accusatory brow. "And now you want me to make things easy for you."

My frustration got the best of me. "What do you want, Judge? Would you rather I had seized him and his bus the first time I saw him without giving him a chance to explain? Without the benefit of the doubt? Is that the kind of government you want?"

Luckily for me, Trumbull didn't take my outburst personally. "My, my. Someone's got a bee in her bonnet today."

And someone else was going to have a special agent at her throat if she didn't give me a ruling. "So? How about it? Can we get the order?"

"No can do, Miss Holloway. Brazos Rivers is too well-known to stay on the lam forever, if he even is on the lam. He'll resurface at some point and you'll get another chance to take care of things then." She banged her sex gavel. *Bang!* "Order denied."

Ross thanked the judge for her time while I fought the urge to scale her bench, grab her jowls, and shake her silly.

We left the courtroom, rode the elevator down to the lobby, and stepped outside.

I shook the attorney's hand. "Thanks for trying, Ross."

He shrugged. "You win some, you lose some. Good luck finding this guy."

"Thanks." I had no idea where to look. Perhaps I should take a cue from Madam Magnolia and look for him in a snow globe or car wash.

By then it was late afternoon and the sun was low in the sky. I decided to take a short walk down Commerce Street to clear my head, see if I could come up with a new strategy to nab Brazos Rivers and his assets, including his cute little tush. By the time I'd walked the five blocks between the federal courthouse at 1100 Commerce and the county courthouse at 600, I'd come up with no new strategies but I had worked up my curiosity. Vans from every local television station lined the curb in front of the courthouse and reporters stood on the steps, speaking into the microphones while their cameramen shot footage. Reporters at the courthouse was not uncommon, but it meant that something big was under way.

I continued on until I was at the bottom of the courthouse steps. Trish LeGrande stood on the top stair, her cameraman two steps below her. She wore a black suit today, though the hem, lapel, and sleeves were trimmed in her signature pink. Her butterscotch locks were swept up into a sleek updo.

She put her microphone to her glossy lips. "This is Trish LeGrande reporting from the steps of the Dallas County Courthouse where pretrial proceedings have just begun in a class-action lawsuit filed by north Texas farmers and ranchers against Palo Pinto Energy. The plaintiffs claim that benzene and other toxic chemicals used by the natural gas company in its fracking activities have leaked into their water wells, contaminating their water. Attorneys for PPE tell me that the company has waived its right to a jury trial. It will be up to the judge to determine whether the fracking activities caused damage and, if so, the dollar value of that damage. Attorneys for both sides expect the trial to take four or five days. Judge Craven's decision is expected to be rendered by the end of next week."

Wait.

Did Trish say *Judge Craven*?

I rushed up the steps, grabbing Trish by the arm. "Did you say Judge Craven will be deciding the PPE case? Judge *Trudy* Craven?"

Trish frowned—there was no love lost between us, after all—but she dipped her hand into the pocket of her skirt and pulled out an index card on which she'd jotted some notes. Her reporter's cheat sheet, I surmised.

Her eyes scanned the card. "Yes." She pointed at the

entry with a pink-tipped nail. "The judge's first name is Trudy."

Holy guacamole!

This tidbit was the missing piece of the puzzle. My mind quickly shuffled the puzzle pieces and assembled them to create a complete and vivid picture. Judge Craven was presiding over the PPE trial. PPE had waived its right to have a jury determine the case. Russell Cobb was in contact with both PPE and Judge Craven. Cobb had been secretly taking cash from PPE. Larry Burkett had taken pains to remove any connection to Russell Cobb from his records.

Yep, the picture was clear now.

PPE is bribing Trudy Craven to find in its favor in the class-action lawsuit. Larry Burkett is using his oil and gas profits to grease palms!

I realized Russell Cobb had likely been the one to set up the arrangement. He was probably getting a cut of the action. I also realized that the dumb thing in this situation might not be the luck. It might be me. Had I dug a little deeper into Judge Trudy Craven I might have learned on my own that she was presiding over the PPE case. Instead, I'd stopped digging too soon, assuming the fact that Cobb had performed public relations services for her was the only link she and Cobb shared. But I supposed there was no sense beating myself up about it. Regardless of how I'd learned this information, I knew it now.

Trish's reporter senses seemed to kick in, sniffing a potential story in the works. She narrowed her eyes at me. "Why did you ask about the judge?"

I lifted my shoulders in a mock shrug. "No reason."

I turned to go but was stopped by her hand on my arm now.

"When you ask a question," Trish said, "there's always a reason. What's up?"

I was tempted to taunt her in a singsong voice with, *I know something you don't know!* But then I realized *she* might know something *I* didn't. Brazos Rivers's current cell phone number.

"Tit for tat?" I suggested. "You might have something I need."

"What's that?" she asked.

"A current cell phone number for Brazos Rivers." Given that Trish had been the only reporter allowed into Brazos's hospital room after his latest fan attack, I had a sneaking suspicion the two might have something going on between them. A few days ago, that knowledge would have made me want to claw her eyes out. Now, however, not so much.

The spark of excitement in her eyes told me she had what I wanted. "If I give you his number, what's in it for me?"

"There's going to be some breaking news about one of my investigations soon," I said. "*Big* news."

"And it's related to the PPE trial."

It wasn't a question. She already knew. I nodded. "I'll call you when the shit hits the fan."

"And you won't call any other reporters? You'll give me an exclusive?"

For a woman who looked like a bimbo, she sure knew how to negotiate.

"Sure," I replied. "I'll give you an exclusive. As long as you won't say anything to anyone involved with the PPE case and you won't tell Brazos you gave me his cell number."

She held out her hand. "You've got yourself a deal."

chapter twenty-nine

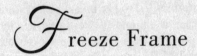

$\mathcal{F}$reeze Frame

I went into the courthouse, found the clerk's office, and asked for a copy of the petition that had been filed in the case against PPE.

The man working the counter reached over to a stack of paperwork in a plastic slotted tray and pulled out a document that appeared to be about thirty pages thick. "I've had so many requests for this petition I decided to keep it handy."

"Who's asked for it?"

"The usual." He stepped over to a machine behind him to run a copy. "Reporters. Attorneys working other cases against gas companies. Attorneys defending other cases against gas companies."

He finished running the copy, stapled it with a heavy-duty stapler, and returned to the counter. When I reached out to take it from him, he whipped it back, out of my reach. "You'll get your petition when I get my thirty-two dollars."

I pulled out my badge. "I'm a special agent for the IRS."

"And I'm a member of the cheese-of-the-month club. That and thirty-two dollars will get you a copy of the petition."

Sheesh. I pulled out my credit card.

Once our transaction was completed, I stepped aside to look the petition over. One plaintiff claimed that he'd been exposed to crystalline silica dust, resulting in respiratory problems. A female plaintiff claimed that the fracking activities led to her breast cancer. In addition to polluted water wells and the resulting health risks and costs of importing water, there were various other allegations. Several of the plaintiffs claimed that the seismic activity resulting from the drilling had cracked the foundations on their homes and caused their propane tanks to shift and leak. The plaintiffs cited numerous separate instances of run-of-the mill negligence, too. A plaintiff named Millard Blankenship alleged that PPE's crew had driven a truck over his septic tank, causing thirty grand in damage. Another alleged that PPE employees had failed to replace a fence they'd taken down when bringing drilling equipment onto the property.

Petition in hand, I all but ran back to my office at the IRS. Too excited to wait for the elevator, I ran up the stairs to my floor. Bad decision. By the time I reached Eddie's office to give him the news all I could do was hang on to the edge of his desk and wheeze, trying to catch my breath.

Eddie tilted his head. "Are you having an asthma attack? Or do you have some exciting news?"

"News," I wheezed out, my lungs gulping in air.

He tilted his head the other way. "I'm guessing it might have something to do with the PPE case?"

I nodded again, tossed the petition onto his desk, and fell back into his wing chair. He picked up the petition and thumbed through it, skimming the pages. When I finally caught my breath, I told him what I'd learned.

"Judge Craven? Taking a bribe?" Eddie shook his head and frowned. "Dang. I voted for her."

"What should we do?" I asked. "How do we prove that she's accepting money under the table from PPE?"

At this point, although I was 99.9 percent sure I was right about the bribe, we had no actual proof. We needed to amass incontrovertible evidence that Burkett had left the cash for Cobb, that Cobb had picked up the cash, and that Cobb had delivered the cash to Judge Craven. We had to prove all three steps in the process to win the case.

Eddie leaned back in his chair and stared up in thought at the ceiling. A moment later, he looked back down at me. "This sounds like a job for Inspector Gadget."

"You're right."

Inspector Gadget was one of our many nicknames for Josh Schmidt, a fellow special agent who was the office's tech guru. The guy not only knew computers and tablets inside out and backward, but he also had a slew of spy tools in his arsenal.

Eddie punched the button on his phone to ring Josh's office and put the device on speaker.

When Josh answered, I said, "Come down to Eddie's office, and bring all of your spy doohickeys and thingamabobs with you."

Eddie punched the button to end the call. "Doohickeys and thingamabobs? Are those technical terms?"

As amusing as Eddie sometimes found my country ways, I wasn't ashamed of my rural roots. "Yep. I hope he remembers the whatchamacallits and the gizmos and the doodads, too."

Eddie merely groaned in reply.

Josh appeared in Eddie's doorway. Josh was a short

guy, standing around five feet five. With his fair curls and baby blue eyes, he looked more like a Boy Scout than a member of federal law enforcement. He held a large cardboard box in his hand. "What's up?"

"You got plans tonight?" I asked.

"Kira and I are going to the movies."

"Cancel," I said. "We're gonna play spy."

At 6:30 that evening, I cut my lights, cruised up to the historical marker and climbed out of my car. Dressed in black boots, exercise leggings, and a hoodie, I was more shadow than person. One hand clasped a tiny digital video camera, the other a roll of duct tape.

The goats wandered up to watch, greeting me with a series of *baaas* that might as well have been sirens in the quiet night.

"Shhhhhh!" I tucked the duct tape under my arm, pulled a handful of raw peanuts from my pocket, and tossed them over the fence.

The goats quieted down, emitting only snuffling and crunching noises as they found the peanuts amid the dead, dry grass and ate them, shell and all.

Taking a quick glance left and right, I scurried up to the historical marker. I turned the camera on and shined my cell phone light onto the front of the historical marker, taking footage of the plaque. Once I'd documented the location, I affixed the camera to the backside of the marker, making sure the lens stuck out from the bottom so that it could record Burkett dropping off the cash envelope and Cobb picking it up.

I punched the button to begin recording and scurried back to my car. There were two cars in the lot at the feed store and a light on inside. Looked like the owner was doing some inventory. *Damn!* His timing stank.

Rather than hide out at the feed store again, this time I

drove down the road, just past PPE. I turned around and parked on the shoulder. I climbed out again, hurried to my trunk, and removed the spare tire. I leaned the spare against my front wheel, creating the illusion that my car had broken down and been abandoned on the side of the road. I slid down in the seat and pulled out a second video camera, this one a larger handheld model.

My chest vibrated with a rapid pulse as I waited, watching the PPE building for Burkett to emerge. At two minutes after seven, he came out the front door. I hit the record button and zoomed in on the man. Though the night was dark, the outside light next to the door of the headquarters provided enough light to show that Burkett had an envelope tucked under his arm.

I filmed him walking to his car, climbing in, and driving to the marker. When he turned off his headlights to drop the envelope, the camera attempted to refocus but it was too dark for it to pick anything up. Luckily, the smaller camera I'd attached to the marker would take footage to fill in the blanks.

Burkett turned his headlights back on and flashed them three times. He hooked a U-turn and headed back in my direction. Quickly, I positioned the camera on the dashboard, leaving it running. I ducked down in the seat so I wouldn't be visible from the outside.

My heart beat faster as I heard the sound of his car approaching on the highway. It began pounding when the car seemed to be slowing.

Burkett's car was so close now that his headlights lit up the top half of my car. I made myself as flat as I could on the seat. There was a crunch of gravel as his tires rolled across the shoulder, then the crunching ceased.

Holy shit! Has he stopped?

When I heard the sounds of Burkett switching his car into park and engaging the brake, I reached up, yanked the camera from the dash and the keys from the ignition, and scrambled to the passenger side. I tucked the camera against my chest and rolled onto the floorboard, pulling the hood over my head and my legs up in a fetal position, trying to make myself as small and invisible as possible. With any luck, I'd be too dark in these black clothes for him to make me out. If he shined a flashlight into the car, though, I'd be shit out of luck.

I heard footsteps in the gravel around my car and a *ping* as a stray pebble hit the bumper. Frantic, I squinted my eyes until they were mere slits. Given that I was facing the front of the car, I couldn't tell whether Burkett was looking in at me or not. But at least I didn't see any telltale signs of a flashlight playing around inside the car.

Approximately ten million heartbeats later, the sound of crunching footsteps sounded again, though this time they started loud and grew fainter. Burkett's car door slammed, the brake was released, and the gearshift engaged. The light that had filled the upper regions of my car moved off.

Thank God!

I gulped in air, realizing now that I'd been holding my breath. Tentatively, I peeked my head up over the seat. The red taillights of Burkett's Yukon grew smaller as he drove away, disappearing over a small rise.

I climbed into the seat, set the camera back on the dash, and pulled my night-vision scope from the glove compartment. Putting the scope to my eye, I took a look. Sure enough, the envelope had already been picked up from the marker while I'd been hiding from Burkett. I hadn't been able to catch the Toyota with my camera, but I hoped the one at the monument had picked it up.

I stuck the key in the ignition, started the car, and pulled forward. The spare tire flopped to the ground and I ran it over, my car bouncing for a few seconds before stabilizing. *Uh-oh*. Looked like the accounting department would be docking my next paycheck.

I'd made it only a quarter mile down the road before a patrol car from the Palo Pinto County Sheriff's Department came up from the opposite direction. When it passed, I spotted the same white-haired deputy who'd shooed me away from the Merriweathers' ranch sitting behind the wheel. In my rearview mirror I saw his brake lights flash as he slowed just past the PPE headquarters. Had Burkett called in to report the abandoned car? I could only hope the deputy didn't tell him the car had magically disappeared.

I slowed until the deputy's car, too, disappeared over the rise, then I hurriedly pulled aside and retrieved the camera from the marker.

When I set off again, I dialed Eddie on my cell phone. "Cobb's headed your way."

"We're ready for him."

Eddie and Josh were in the long-term parking garage at DFW. Josh had attached a tracking device to Cobb's Mercedes, one that would record his movements, showing he'd traveled from the garage to the judge's house. He also had a camera ready to take still shots of Cobb getting into the Mercedes. Eddie was parked near the entrance to the garage, ready to film Cobb as he arrived in and ditched the Toyota.

While the two of them would attempt to film continuous footage of Cobb traveling from the airport to Judge Craven's house, I would already be in position on her street, ready to document Cobb's arrival with the envelope containing the bribe money.

As I made the long drive back to Dallas, my cell phone rang. It was the U.S. Marshal's office calling. I jabbed the button to accept the call. "Did you track him down?"

After Trish had given me Brazos's new cell phone

number, I'd called the marshal's office and asked for their help. They'd agreed to try to find the singer for me.

"We found him," the male marshal said through the phone. "Problem is, he's south of the border."

"Mexico?"

"You got it," he replied. "Cozumel to be precise."

Out of the country, out of my jurisdiction. *Dammit!*

"Could you pinpoint a hotel or a beach or a restaurant?" Heck, I'd be willing to make a trip down there on my own dime, see if I might be able to slip a few pesos to a desk clerk in return for information about Brazos's plans.

"No such luck," the marshal said. "It looks like he's left his phone on his boat. The system shows its location as a quarter mile offshore."

Knowing Brazos, he'd probably dropped the phone into the gulf. *Idiot.* Didn't he have the sense to put his cell phone in his pocket? Nick was right. The guy acted like a spoiled adolescent.

"Thanks for the information," I said. "Can you keep checking every few hours and keep me updated?"

"Will do."

I tossed my phone into the cup holder and continued on into Preston Hollow. When I reached Judge Craven's neighborhood, I parked on one of the side streets, exchanged my black boots for sneakers, and climbed out of my car with the small digital video recorder.

Lest I pull a muscle, I walked around the block a couple of times to warm up and performed a series of stretches. My phone vibrated with an incoming text. It was from Eddie. *Cobb turning into hood.*

That was my cue. I clipped the recorder to the waist of my Lycra leggings, turned it on, and began jogging down the street.

I was halfway down Cavendish Court when Cobb's silver Mercedes eased past me. I slowed my pace to give him time to park and get out of the car. As I approached the judge's house, he was exiting his vehicle, his briefcase in hand.

Cobb glanced around as he made his way to the judge's door. Spotting me, he offered a friendly wave as I jogged past. I raised a hand and offered a smile in return. Looked like my ruse had worked. I put my hands on my head and slowed to a walk, pretending to be at the cool-down phase of my run, angling my hip in the hope that the camera would catch Judge Craven opening the door. Cobb slipped inside the house and the door closed behind him.

I stopped, ripped the camera from my waist, and clipped it to a barren rosebush that flanked Judge Craven's mailbox, pricking my finger in the process. The camera in place, I jogged off down the street, passing Eddie as he drove up.

I returned to my car to wait. Not two minutes later, Eddie texted me and Josh. *Cobb has left house.*

A half hour later, the three of us met up at my town house to look over the footage. While Josh set up his superexpensive, superfast Alienware laptop, I rounded up a couple bottles of beer for the men and poured a glass of moscato for myself. Hey, we'd earned them. Besides, it was officially after hours and we were on our own time.

Josh downloaded the digital files from each of the cameras and spliced them together into one continual stream. While the video quality wasn't bad, due to the angle at which Cobb had parked the Toyota, the camera I'd placed at the marker picked up only the first letter of the license plate. Once he'd turned off his headlights, there was only darkness and shadow and rustling sounds until he climbed back into the car and drove off. Cobb could not be readily identified.

"What do you think?" I asked. "Is that good enough?"

"I don't know," Josh replied. "How many Toyotas are there with license plates that start with the letter K?"

Eddie shrugged. "Let's see what else we've got."

We continued to watch the screen. The footage Eddie and Josh had taken at the airport parking garage was more promising. Eddie had been able to keep a constant bead on Cobb from the time he left the Toyota until he climbed into the Mercedes. Still, unless we could link the Toyota to the pickup at the historical marker, this footage would be useless. The same problem existed with the video we'd taken at the judge's house. The feed contained no solid proof that Cobb had concealed the cash in his briefcase and that he'd transferred the cash to the judge. Without a clear shot of Cobb carrying the cash into the judge's house and later leaving the premises without it, the video alone would not be enough for a conviction.

"What do we do now?" Josh asked, one hand clenching his curls. "Try again next week?"

"Practice makes perfect," I said. "On the other hand, I think Burkett's getting leery." I told them about Burkett stopping to check out my car. I turned to Eddie. "What do you think?"

"Hell," Eddie said, "I'm out of ideas."

We sat in silence, sipping our drinks and racking our brains.

Bingo.

The alcohol had loosened my brain enough to allow an idea to float free.

"Anybody want to buy Boardwalk?"

chapter thirty

*F*ull-court Press

Monday morning, I slipped into Judge Craven's court-room at the Dallas County Courthouse. Given that the case against PPE was a class-action lawsuit with dozens of plaintiffs, the place was as packed as the beer stand at the Dallas Cowboys' stadium during halftime. That fact worked in my favor, making my presence among the hundred or so others in the courtroom less noticeable.

On the off chance that Judge Craven might recognize me as the jogger who'd been running by her house last Friday night, I'd borrowed a reddish-blond wig from my boss, one I'd bought for her when she'd lost her hair to chemo a few months before. I'd also slipped on a pair of plastic dollar-store reading glasses. Though I'd selected a pair with the minimum magnification, the glasses none-theless distorted my vision. Everyone seemed very close, their pores enormous. The guy standing next to me had missed a spot on his chin when he'd shaved that morning, and the overlooked whisker looked as long as a cat's. Also, there was some type of small growth behind his ear that he really ought to get looked at.

Why was I in Judge Craven's courtroom? To listen to
the testimony, to keep tabs on the trial, to see if there
were any legitimate grounds for her to rule in favor of
PPE. There was always a small chance I'd been wrong
about the cash, that the PR man had kept every penny for
himself, and that Trudy Craven was in no way involved
with whatever was going on between Larry Burkett and
Russell Cobb. I highly doubted that, though. One trip
from the historical marker to Judge Craven's house could
have been written off as coincidence, but the fact that
Cobb had driven straight from picking up the cash to her
residence two Fridays in a row told me that he was playing delivery boy, acting as an intermediary between PPE
and the judge. It would have been far too risky for both
the judge and Burkett to deal directly with each other.
Heck, if I had to guess, I'd say it might have been Cobb
himself who'd negotiated this clandestine arrangement.
He'd probably realized he could do more to help PPE—
and get a bigger slice of the pie—by helping them buy a
favorable verdict than by writing up some one-sided PR
pieces and hope that someone would not only read them
but believe them.

My eyes surveyed the room. I recognized his wrinkled mug the instant I saw it. He sat at the defense table,
flanked by PPE's team of lawyers, two men and one
woman. All four wore business suits and serious expressions, though Burkett's was likely just for show. He had
this case in the bag. He was probably smirking on the inside.

If what I believed was true, that Judge Craven had
been paid to find in PPE's favor, the attorneys were mere
props in Burkett's stage play. I wondered if any of them
suspected that their client was up to no good, that he'd
bought the as-yet-to-be-rendered verdict. Judging from
the stacks of paper in front of them, the accordion files at

their feet, and the banker's boxes stacked behind them, I presumed not. The attorneys appeared to have spent a good deal of time gathering evidence and preparing for the case. All that work for nothing. And, when they received a verdict in their favor, they'd mistakenly believe it was their clever argumentation that had won the case when, in fact, their hollow victory had been purchased with dirty money.

At the other table sat the plaintiffs' primary attorney, a seasoned bigwig from one of the largest and most prestigious downtown firms. At his side was his second chair, a fortyish male attorney who appeared a little less seasoned but no less determined. With them were two women in their twenties, presumably junior associates getting their feet wet assisting with the paperwork and corralling the multiple witnesses.

In the front two rows of the gallery sat a bevy of reporters. Newspaper reporters. Television reporters. Radio reporters. Reporters for online news sources. Trish LeGrande sat among them, flirting with a couple of the more attractive male reporters. *Sheesh.* Wasn't Brazos Rivers enough man for her? Then again, she and the singer probably hadn't forged a deep connection. After all, he'd taken off for Mexico without her. Besides, Trish might look like a twit, but she wasn't stupid. She had to know she was merely another notch in Brazos's belt. Heck, he was probably just another notch in hers, as well.

The bailiff stepped in front of the vacant judge's bench and bellowed, "All rise."

Those who'd been lucky enough to snag a seat in the gallery rose. The rest of us gathered around the perimeter merely continued to stand.

The bailiff continued his spiel. "Dallas County district court is now in session. The Honorable Trudy Craven presiding."

Dishonorable was more like it.

Trudy Craven stepped out of her chambers. Her black hair slanted across her forehead, looking especially shiny today. Perhaps she'd used some of her bribe money on fancy hair products. She climbed up to her bench, spent a few seconds organizing her pens and papers, then looked down at the counsel tables. "Everyone ready to get started?"

The attorneys indicated their assent and she called the plaintiffs' attorney to make his opening statement. Fortunately, the guy cut right to the chase.

"This case is simple, Your Honor. Palo Pinto Energy contracted with the plaintiffs to extract natural gas from their properties. During the fracking process, PPE introduced a number of toxic chemicals into the substrata when disposing of the resulting wastewater. These chemicals seeped into the ground and contaminated the plaintiffs' wells, rendering the water unfit for consumption by humans or livestock. As a result, the ranchers were forced to truck in water for themselves and their livestock at enormous expense, in many cases spending amounts far in excess of the royalties they were paid by PPE. It is our contention that PPE did not properly dispose of the wastewater in that it did not inject the contaminated water deep enough into the earth."

With that he took his seat and the female defense attorney stood.

"Your Honor," she said, "this case is not nearly as simple as the plaintiffs' attorney would have you believe. First, the plaintiffs cannot prove that the levels of chemicals in their well water posed any health or safety hazard. Secondly, assuming that toxic chemicals did, in fact, contaminate their well water, the plaintiffs cannot prove that Palo Pinto Energy was the source of that contamination. Several other oil and gas companies drilled in the area and, as our experts will testify, any one of those other companies could have been the source of the pollutants. Finally, we will show that any well contamination was not due to improper disposal of the wastewater by PPE, but rather by defects in the wells themselves. Many were older wells that were improperly sealed, poorly maintained, or which had become compromised due to recent droughts in the area."

I had to give the defense attorney credit. She talked a good line. Heck, maybe she was even right. What did I know about oil and gas and fracking and water well maintenance? Diddly squat, that's what.

I spent the day listening to testimony from ranchers and farmers.

The first to testify indicated he'd become aware of the polluted water when the quarter horses he bred had refused to drink from their trough.

"Evidently they could smell something in the water I couldn't," he said. He went on to testify that he and his wife and young children later noticed an unusual taste in the water that came from their kitchen faucet. At the attorney's direction, he presented copies of bills for the service he'd had to hire to keep his livestock watered. "As you can see, it cost me a fortune to water my horses."

The second rancher to testify, a cattleman, had encountered the same problems with his water supply. What's more, his cows' reproduction rates had severely declined. The rancher suspected that chemicals in the water disrupted the cows' endocrine systems and thus caused infertility. Rather than continue to incur the steep cost of watering his cows, the cattle rancher had sold off his herd at a loss.

The third to testify ran a dairy farm. Concerns about chemical levels in the milk he produced led the dairy farmer to employ the services of a lab to test for contaminants.

"The lab found elevated levels of numerous chemicals in the milk and dairy products. Of course I couldn't sell polluted products." He'd taken a huge financial hit, too.

Of course the defense attorneys did their best to refute and minimize the plaintiffs' testimony, even going so far as to insinuate that global warming could be to blame for the failure of the cattle rancher's herd to reproduce. After all, what creature wants to climb on top of another when he's feeling hot and ornery? I half expected the defense lawyer to take stabs at the sexual orientation of the bulls or point out that the rancher's cows were visually unappealing or lacked personality. The defense also pointed out that the rancher was not an endocrinologist, and that his claims regarding his frigid herd were mere speculation. Personally, I thought he should check the cows' hooves for purity rings. Maybe they'd taken vows of chastity and were saving their virginity for their wedding nights. Then again, maybe standing up all day had reduced the blood circulation to my brain.

I returned to the courtroom Tuesday, arriving early enough to grab a seat on the back row. Today, research scientists testified on behalf of the plaintiffs regarding the levels of chemicals in the well water and soil. A petroleum engineer who'd been formerly employed by a gas company testified that he believed the source of the contamination was from PPE's activity. He offered maps and geological data and a bunch of scientific statistics to back up his assertions. Finally, two well inspectors testified that they'd examined the plaintiffs' wells and found them to be properly sealed and in good working order. Thus, they claimed, any contamination was not the result of defective wells.

The defense attorneys tried to poke as many holes in the testimony as they could, pointing out that the chain of custody for the water samples had not been adequately documented, raising doubts, however minor, about whether the samples were truly those of the plaintiffs. They also attempted to discredit the engineer by pointing out that he'd been fired from his job with the oil and gas company for alleged incompetence. The plaintiffs' attorneys were able to rehabilitate him to some degree when they asked about the circumstances of his termination.

"The company will tell you different," the engineer said from the stand, "but I was fired for being a whistle-blower. I informed people up the chain at the gas company that certain safety protocols were not being followed at the wells. I was trying to protect the men who worked at the well, to protect the company from liability, too, but they didn't see it that way. They said I wasn't a 'team player,' that I was overstating the risks, and they kicked me to the curb."

"What happened afterward?" the plaintiffs' attorney asked.

"One of the wells I'd specifically brought to their attention as a potential hazard blew out and injured three workers."

On conclusion of the engineer's testimony, the plaintiffs' attorney rested their case.

The plaintiffs' legal team had done a superb job. Had I been on a jury, I would've voted in their favor. Still, the defense team had scored some points, too, raised some doubts. Would the judge be able to rule in favor of the defense without raising eyebrows? I wasn't entirely sure.

Judge Craven called it a day. "We'll begin testimony from the defense tomorrow." She punctuated her words with a swift bang of her gavel. *Bam!*

chapter thirty-one

*B*each Bums

After I dressed Wednesday morning, I put in a call to the marshal's office.

"Any change in location?" I asked.

"No," they said. "We're still showing Mr. Rivers's phone located in the waters near Cozumel."

I thanked the man and hung up. Something didn't feel right about this. Brazos was a young guy used to being on the move. According to Sierra, he never stayed anywhere for long. Guys that age got bored easily. They didn't like to sit around and chill, they were always out looking for the next party.

I phoned Trish. "Have you heard from Brazos lately? Any chance he's got a newer cell number?"

"I don't know," Trish said. "I haven't heard from him since last time I saw you."

She didn't sound all that disappointed that Brazos hadn't kept in touch. Trish must be a realist, knowing that any dalliance she'd had with the star would be short and fleeting.

I pulled up Brazos's Facebook fan page. Nothing new

had been posted on Brazos's behalf since he'd fired Sierra. Looked like he hadn't yet found a new manager. Several fans had posted, though. Several said they'd spotted the singer in various nightclubs around Cozumel recently. One even posted a photo of her and the star on a patio trimmed in colored lights. Both held up margaritas, as if toasting the camera.

The last posted sighting was two nights ago. Where had he been since? In his boat sleeping off a hangover? Snorkeling? Lying on a beach somewhere wearing nothing but his cowboy hat, boots, and silver spurs? And as long as I was asking questions, exactly what was under that hat anyway? Inquiring minds wanted to know.

Having found nothing useful on Facebook, I pulled up Twitter and searched for #brazosrivers. I read through a number of useless tweets, mostly speculation about his new album and his breakup with the band.

I heard Brazos slept with 1 of the Boys' girlfriends.

Another tweeter replied. *Liar! He'd never do that!* As if she knew the singer and his moral code firsthand.

Others were less personal.

Hope he's writing more love songs.

Bought a pair of Buckin' Bronco Boots today. Gave me blisters.

Heard BR was seen with Pippa Middleton in London.

No way! He knocked up Miley Cyrus.

What a bunch of useless drivel. I powered through, pushing myself to read on. My patience paid off. A half hour in I hit pay dirt. "Woo-hoo!"

My unexpected cry scared Anne, who leaped from the bed and ran under it. Fraidy cat.

Alicia stuck her head out of my guest bath in the hall and pulled the foamy toothbrush from her mouth. "Did you find him?" she asked, her voice garbled by a mouthful of toothpaste.

"He's in Galveston," I said. "A fan spotted the *River Rat* anchored in the bay this morning."

I finished getting ready as fast as I could. I grabbed my ballistic vest, my raid jacket, and my handcuffs. Then I ran down the street to grab my favorite tool. *Nick*.

Too excited to knock, I used my key to let myself in. I found him sitting alone in his kitchen, finishing up a breakfast of frozen biscuits and sausage he'd nuked in the microwave. Nutty's food bowl still sat on the floor, a few stale kibbles in the bottom. The dog's blanket lay next to the bowl. It broke my heart that Nick hadn't yet been able to put those things away, to let his dog go. But I couldn't fault him. I knew I would feel the same way if I'd lost one of my cats.

"Come on!" I grabbed his plate from the table. "Winnie Seven is in Galveston. Let's go get 'im!"

"Galveston?" Nick stood and grabbed the remaining chunk of biscuit off the plate before I set it in the sink. "No kidding?"

"Nope."

He shoved the last bite into his mouth and mumbled something about rounding up his things.

A half hour later, Nick and I were headed south on I-45 in his pickup, pulling his bass boat on a trailer behind us. Fortunately, there was little midweek traffic on the interstate. We hauled both the boat and ass. If we were pulled over by a state trooper or a cop from one of the small towns along the way, we could pull rank and be back on our way in seconds.

Five hours later, we drove over the causeway into Galveston. It had been a few years since I'd last visited the island, which was a popular tourist spot given its proximity to Houston and its status as a departure port for cruise ships. As we drove through the historic downtown area, I admired the colorful Victorian houses, many of which had been constructed not long after the 1900 hurricane that had decimated the island and killed over six thousand people. The event, which was the most devastating natural disaster in American history, had led to the erection of the seventeen-foot-high and ten-mile-wide protective seawall. Unfortunately, even the wall was not enough to fully protect the island from Hurricane Ike, which hit in 2008 and wiped out several landmark hotels and restaurants positioned along the waterfront. The island had yet to fully recover.

Today, the island would be hit by Hurricane Tara. Yep, I planned to take this place by storm, arrest Brazos Rivers, and see justice served before blowing out of town.

On the drive down, I'd notified the marshals in Houston that I'd need a transport. I checked in with the office again by phone and was told two officers were waiting for us by a boat ramp. The agent on the phone provided an address and I plugged it into my cell phone's GPS app.

We found the public boat ramp not far from Stewart Beach, a popular family vacation spot with a beachfront water park and arcade. The beach was nearly vacant today, only a young mother walking with a toddler along the waterfront and a handful of seagulls stalking bugs along the sand. In the distance behind them was the platform of an offshore drilling rig and a large merchant vessel.

Two female marshals in uniform waited by an SUV in the parking lot. No doubt they'd volunteered for the assignment once they'd learned who they would be transporting.

Nick and I climbed out of his truck and introduced ourselves.

Both of the women teemed with excitement, their eyes sparkling.

"Is it true?" one asked. "You're going to arrest Brazos Rivers?"

Sheesh. She was clearly suffering from the same delusions about the man I had not long ago.

"Yes," I told her. "But trust me. He's not who he appears to be."

"Really?" asked the other. "Because he appears to be a total stud muffin."

The two shared a laugh. Nick rolled his eyes.

While the marshals waited onshore, I climbed into Nick's boat. He backed it down the ramp, then released the boat from the trailer. After quickly parking his pickup in the closest available spot, he hopped into the boat, pushed us back from the shore, and started the motor. With a final wave to the waiting marshals, we set out into the water, trolling out toward the cluster of larger boats anchored offshore.

Nick sat at the wheel while I sat in the passenger seat. The day was cool but bearable with my raid jacket on. The salty breeze that blew in off the water smelled of brine and seaweed, leaving a wet mist on our skin and tossing our hair. Nick's boat pitched gently up and down as we made our way over the waves.

"I wish I could get paid to do this every day," Nick said. "Think I could convince Lu that bass fishing somehow moved my cases along?"

"Not unless those bass owe some money to Uncle Sam."

A number of sailboats and large yachts were anchored in a designated no-wake area. Most had names painted on the back, the majority of which contained puns or irony or dirty sexual references. *Seas the Day. She Got the House. Wet Dreams. Buoys of Summer.* One sailboat read *Love to be Blown.* Another, the *Betsy Sue,* appeared to be named after the owner's wife.

Nick's boat had yet to be named.

I looked over at him and pushed out my lip in a pout. "How come you didn't name your boat after me?"

"I will," he promised. "I'll call her *Tara on the Seas.*"

"Jeez. Never mind." I picked up a red and white fishing bobber and tossed it at him, pegging him on the shoulder.

We scanned the boats, looking for the *River Rat.* The vessels, too big to come into the shallow waters around the docks, had smaller tenders or dinghies for the owners to use when coming ashore. The dinghies were missing from a number of the boats, indicating their owners had left their boats to venture onto the island. When we spotted the *River Rat,* however, we noticed its dinghy floating alongside, tethered to the yacht by a stretch of yellow nylon rope.

"He's aboard," Nick said, his intent gaze locked on the boat. "Boy howdy, this is going to be fun!"

I placed a call to Galveston PD, letting them know that federal law enforcement was on the water to make an arrest and requesting that they be prepared to provide backup via boat if necessary. After all, we had no idea how many people were aboard the *River Rat.* Brazos could be alone, or he could have his new band and an entire entourage of bodyguards on board. Maybe even some nubile young fans. Whether those on board would cooperate was another question. We special agents had learned to hope for the best but be prepared for the worst.

As we drew near, my eyes carefully scanned the boat, looking for signs of life. I saw none. What I did see, however, was an empty bottle of Bacardi rum lying sideways on a seat, along with a bottle of Jack Daniel's shoved under the railing and another of Jose Cuervo Especial tequila floating in the water next to the boat. A dozen beer bottles and cans were scattered about, too, some placed on tables or decks, others appearing to have been tossed aside. One of the beer bottles rolled lazily back and forth on the floor of the back deck, moving in synch with the waves, *rr-rr-rolling* from one side to the other, clinking up against the low wall at one side, then rolling across and clinking again as it rolled up against the other.

"What should we do?" I asked Nick. "Call out to him?"

"Nah," Nick said. "Why give them any warning?"

True. The element of surprise could give us an advantage. Judging from the number of alcohol bottles, Brazos was sure to have a bodyguard or two out here, maybe even all five of them. This wouldn't be a fair fight, if it came to that. My hope was that Brazos would realize the jig was finally up and that he'd peacefully surrender.

Nick turned off his motor and let momentum carry his boat the rest of the way. He reached out and grabbed the rail, pulling his bass boat up to the back and tying it to one of the metal cleats to keep it from drifting away once we boarded the *River Rat*.

My heart pumped wildly as we quietly climbed aboard, and I felt the warm surge of adrenaline flowing through my veins. We pulled our guns from our holsters and held them at the ready. Nick led the way, quietly moving toward the door that led inside the cabin. When he reached it, he looked back at me to ensure I was ready for whatever might face us on the other side.

I clenched my gun tighter and nodded.

He reached down and tried the handle. The resulting click told us that nobody had bothered to lock the door after their party last night. Some security team he had.

Nick slowly pushed the door open and stepped inside. I followed on his heels.

We entered what appeared to be a combination living and dining room of sorts, with built-in couches and tables situated along the right side and a galley kitchen along the left. Though the room had windows all along the top of both sides, the curtains were, for the most part, pulled closed, letting in only narrow shafts of light where they gapped.

The room smelled of booze, garbage, and cigarettes, underscored by the smell of stinky feet and male sweat. *Urk*. Three of the singer's bodyguards lay around the room, two on couches and one on the floor, all of them sound asleep. The bald one on the floor was snoring so loud he'd probably scared off every fish in a hundred-mile radius.

Nick and I exchanged glances, communicating wordlessly. My cocked head and raised palm said, *What should we do about these thugs?* His dismissive hand gesture and lift of his chin said we should let them continue sawing logs and focus on getting to Brazos.

At the far end of the room was another door, one which I suspected led to the sleeping quarters. Nick slunk forward, carefully stepping over the legs of the guard on the floor. I followed suit.

When he reached the door, he put out a hand and tried the handle. Again we heard the click of the latch releasing.

We stepped inside, locking the door behind us. A futile gesture, probably. The security team could easily kick the flimsy door in if they wanted to.

This room was even darker than the living area had been. The built-in shutters were closed and latched, letting only thin slivers of light through. Still, once our eyes adjusted, it was enough light to allow us to see with some help from my cell phone's flashlight app.

Brazos lay in the center of a jumble of sheets on a queen-sized bed. He was naked, other than his boots, spurs, and his cowboy hat, which lay askew across his crotch, providing just a glimpse of one ball, not enough for me to accurately judge the entirety of what lay under the hat.

Curled up next to him, her head on his shoulder, lay a tall, thin woman who looked to be in her early twenties.

Her long brown hair was as tangled as the sheets. She wore one of Brazos's concert tees, but no panties. The light from my phone illuminated her bare bottom. Her left butt cheek bore a tattoo, the words *I LOVE BRAZOS* under a full-color image in the singer's likeness, complete with the baby-blue eyes.

Nick chuckled and whispered, "I always knew the guy was an ass-face."

Nick stepped to one of the windows, strategically picking one directly in Brazos's line of sight, and threw open the blinds. "Rise and shine, Winnie boy. It's time to pay the piper."

chapter thirty-two

$\mathcal{S}$plish-Splash

"Whuh?" Brazos blinked against the bright shaft of light directed at his face and struggled to prop himself up on his elbows. The cowboy hat on his crotch slipped to the side.

I quickly threw open another set of shutters, the sun creating a virtual spotlight on his groin. I took a gander at his goods . . . *what little there was of them*. It might be time for him to pay the piper, but when it came to *his* pipe it was tiny. A piccolo.

"Wow," I said. "That's damn disappointing." I wondered how much I could get for my autographed copy of *Stud Farm* on e-Bay. The magazine had lost all its appeal.

Nick tsked in pity. "I told you he hadn't reached puberty yet."

Cutting us a dirty look, Brazos sat up and reached for his hat, using it to cover his crotch. "What the hell are you two doing on my boat?"

"We're taking you in," Nick said. "For tax evasion. Surely this can't be a surprise to you."

"Where are my men?"

Nick gestured to the door. "Out there, sleeping off what is likely one big-ass hangover."

The girl woke up then, emitting a shriek and sitting bolt upright when she realized two people with guns were in the room with her and Brazos.

"Are you pirates?" she shrieked.

Given that we lacked peg legs, eye patches, hooks for hands, or parrots on our shoulders, she should've realized she was off base. Also, we were not in Somali waters. But I'd cut the girl some slack. I supposed it was hard to think clearly when you'd been yanked from a deep sleep and probably had yet to entirely sober up from the preceding night's party.

"We're federal law enforcement," I said. "Don't move."

I turned to Brazos and pulled my cuffs from my pocket. "Winthrop Merriweather the seventh, you are under arrest."

"Who's Winthrop Merriweather?" the girl asked, looking at me.

Seriously, she couldn't glean the information from context? I squinted at her, trying to discern how much of her stupidity was natural and how much was alcohol induced. Judging from the bloodshot eyes blinking at me, I'd put the ratio at fifty-fifty, maybe sixty-forty. I cocked my head to indicate Brazos.

Nick was less proper and more direct. "He's the guy whose face is tattooed on your ass."

Her face scrunched in confusion as she turned toward the singer. "Wait. You're *Winthrop Merriweather*? I thought your name was Brazos Rivers."

"Brazos is his stage name." I proceeded to read Brazos his rights, motioning for him to stand. "You have the right to remain silent."

Our eyes met. His baby blues were ablaze with fury.

I continued. "You have the right—"

"Get the hell off my boat!" Before we knew what was happening, Brazos hurled his hat aside, leaped from the bed, and shoved me backward with both hands.

There was no time for me to react. My head snapped back, hitting the wall. Starfish swam around my peripheral vision.

Despite my brain-addled state, I could hardly believe what had just happened. Brazos Rivers, the man whom I'd idolized, whose every album I owned, whom I'd cheered on when he'd won his first, second, and third CMA awards, had just struck me.

Asshole.

With a primal roar, Nick rushed at Brazos. Though he had his gun in his hand, it was clear Nick preferred a more personal approach, to choke the life out of Brazos with his bare hands. I'd never before understood why men found a women's catfight so titillating but, as ashamed as I was to admit it, seeing Nick rush at Brazos, intent on killing the jerk to defend my honor, was kind of sexy.

The girl screamed and backed into a corner, while Nick and Brazos went at each other, falling across the bed and rolling over it, landing with a thump on the floor on the opposite side. Though Nick clearly had the upper hand, I figured I better jump in and put an end to the fight before someone got hurt. I'd taken only a single step in their direction when the door to the room came flying inward, followed by the stinky foot that had kicked it in. Two meaty hands grabbed either side of the opening, and the bald bodyguard propelled himself through, launching himself at Nick like a torpedo. He'd just grabbed hold of Nick's shoulders from the back when I tackled him from the side, slamming him against the wall.

Nick brought an elbow back and hit the guard behind

him in the face. The man's nose exploded in blood. Reflexively, he put his hands to his face, bellowing in agony and anger.

"We're federal law enforcement!" I yelled. "Stop fighting or we'll arrest you, too!"

The other two bodyguards peered into the doorway, their mouths gaping like fish on a line. They were smarter than they looked, though. Rather than risk a bloody nose, a bullet, or a trip to the lockup, they stayed out of the fray. One even went so far as to raise his palms in submission. If he'd had a white flag, or a mast for that matter, he would've likely surrendered the ship.

When the bloody-nosed guard grabbed Nick again from behind, Brazos took advantage of the situation to flee the room, his little-boy genitals swinging and his spurs jingle-jangling as he ran. Leaving Nick to handle the thug, I took off after the singer.

"Give yourself up!" I yelled as I chased him through the living room. "Or you'll be charged with resisting arrest, too!"

That ship had already sailed, but I figured I'd toss it out anyway.

Ignoring me, Brazos bolted out the back, scaring a trio of gulls who had perched on the rear railing. They flew off, cawing in alarm.

Brazos swung himself over the side of his boat and landed in his dinghy. The small boat bounced three times from the impact, and Brazos had to crouch down and hang on to the sides until it stabilized. He turned around now and reached for the motor to start it.

Where the hell did he think he was going in nothing but a pair of boots and spurs? Did he plan to motor to shore and run off down Seawall Boulevard, give the fishermen and the few tourists in town today a show? Or did he plan to set off for the open sea, maybe return to Cozumel?

It didn't much matter where he planned to go, because I was going to make sure he didn't get there. Before he could toss off the rope, I aimed my gun at the bottom of the boat and put three holes in it. *Bang! Bang! Bang!*

He glowered up at me. "You bitch!"

"Now, now. Is that any way to talk to the president of the Dallas chapter of your fan club?" Of course I planned to tender my resignation ASAP and tear up my official membership card.

In seconds, Brazos was up to his boots in salt water and the dinghy was sinking fast.

"My, my, Brazos Rivers," I said. "Looks like you're up a creek." I pulled my cuffs from my pocket. "Give me your hands. Let's get this over with."

"All right," he said, shaking his head. "You win."

He pulled himself up onto the back deck. But instead of holding his wrists out for cuffing, he charged at me once more. I should've known better than to believe his lies again.

Holy crap! What should I do? Shoot the guy? I'd gotten in big trouble for shooting a target before and ended up the subject of a criminal trial myself. Putting a hole in a boat was one thing, but if I put another bullet in a suspect, especially one as well-known as Brazos Rivers, I'd never live it down.

Luckily for me, I didn't have to make the decision. Having apparently rendered the thug useless, Nick hurtled past me, tackling Brazos full force on the deck. The two rolled around again for a second or two, like a couple of tomcats in a junkyard, then *splash!* They reeled off the deck and into Galveston Bay, boots, spurs, and all.

"Nick!" I ran to the edge of the deck, frantic. A brawl on the boat was one thing, but a fight in the water was another. One of them could drown, disappear under the murky green gulf water and never be seen or heard from again.

Winthrop's head bobbed up, his wet hair slicked to his head, exposing an inch-wide swath of dark roots now. The guy was way overdue for a touch-up. Sierra had probably scheduled his appointments when she'd still worked for him. Clearly, Brazos had no clue how to handle things on his own. He was a boy trapped in a man's body. A man's body with a boy-sized penis. He gulped air into his lungs.

Nick surfaced and wrapped his arm around Winthrop's head, like a giant squid grabbing its prey with its tentacles, pulling him down under again. All I could see now were flashes of color between the waves and the water the two were kicking up. *"It's like going through a car wash or trying to see through a windshield when it's raining so hard the wipers can't keep up."*

Whoa.

Had Madam Magnolia actually seen this vision? Or had she simply been making up excuses to give me vague, blurry, half-baked responses subject to all kinds of interpretation?

Regardless, I feared that if I didn't involve myself in this fight Brazos Rivers would end up a *drowned* river rat. The way Nick had taken Brazos down indicated that this wasn't just a professional matter, it was personal. Nick wasn't always in touch with his emotions, but at the moment they'd taken him over. He wanted to put an end to this man who had stolen his girlfriend's affections, who'd then assaulted that very girlfriend.

I shoved my gun back into my holster, looked around for anything I might be able to use as a nonlethal weapon. The bodyguard Nick had been scrabbling with stood in the doorway, a dirty sweat sock pressed up against his nose to stanch the blood. At least he'd given up the fight now.

My eyes spotted a round lifesaving device, a handheld

fishing net, and the top of a black bikini hanging from pegs. Nope, nope, and nope. *Aha!* A wooden oar hung from a rack next to the door. That would work. So would the pole with the hook on the end.

I grabbed the oar in my hand and held it like a fishing spear, attempting to take aim. Not easy to do when your target kept disappearing under the murky green water and resurfacing a few feet away. Nick kept getting in the way, too. The singer's bare ass surfaced. Then his foot, still wearing the boot and spur. Then a knee. Then a testicle. Finally, I had a clear shot at Winthrop's skull.

Bonk!

The singer went limp, unconscious. Realizing the man he'd been fighting was no longer fighting back, Nick let go of him and began treading water. Tossing the oar aside, I exchanged it for the hook, snagging Brazos under the armpit before he could sink to the bottom of Galveston Bay and be eaten by scavenger crabs.

I pulled him to the boat, reached down, and grabbed his arm, doing my best to tug him onto the deck. Not easy to do given that he was deadweight and his boots were filled with ocean water, adding several more pounds to the mix.

Nick quickly pulled himself up onto the deck to help me. In seconds, Brazos was sprawled out on the deck, his junk flopped to the side, as lifeless as a dead fish.

I cocked my head and eyed the thing. "It looks like a cocktail shrimp."

Nick raised a hand. "Stop, or I'll never eat seafood again."

I gestured to one of the bodyguards. "Bring me Brazos's hat." I feared that if we didn't cover his crotch, a seagull might also mistake his nether regions for a shrimp, swoop in, and try to fly off with it.

The man scuttled back into the boat, returning with the cowboy hat. I placed it over the singer's nards.

While the three bodyguards and the singer's latest conquest watched from the deck, I waved my arms and hollered to the police boat patrolling the perimeter of the anchored vessels. Nick pulled the water-soaked boots and spurs off Winthrop, and covered him with a beach towel. The outdoor temperature was far from freezing, but the ocean water was undeniably chilly. Besides, the guy had no body hair to keep himself warm.

I rounded up another beach towel for Nick and he wrapped himself in it. One of the bodyguards offered Nick a concert tee that looked like it would fit, but Nick refused it. "I'd rather die from hypothermia than wear that thing."

Brazos came to as the police pulled up and, putting a hand to the purple knot on his head, voluntarily climbed into their boat for a ride to the ambulance waiting on-shore. I phoned the two marshals, who said they'd follow the ambulance to the local hospital and take Brazos into custody on his release.

Nick let the bodyguard slide. The guy's nose had swollen to the size of a cucumber. He'd been punished enough. Besides, he'd only been doing his job. He said that when he'd tackled Nick he hadn't realized who we were, that we were members of law enforcement. Couldn't really fault him under the circumstances. Things had been happening so fast.

Now that their meal ticket was in custody and they were likely out of work, at least for the time being, the members of the security team helped us find the keys to the Ferrari among the clutter in the boat. According to them, Brazos had had the boat moved from Possum Kingdom Lake to Galveston shortly before I'd gone out to the ranch looking for him. The singer had driven the car down to the island and left it at the San Luis Resort, where he'd rented a suite. He'd then hired a captain and sailed down to Mexico, spending his days and nights boozing it up in Cozumel, scuba diving, and slipping his enchilada to as many local girls and vacationers as were willin'.

"Any chance y'all know where the tour bus is?" I asked. "Or the plane?"

Cucumber nose said Sierra had taken care of storing the bus and plane before Brazos had fired her, but ever since, the remaining members of his staff had been forced to help out. "The bus is in an RV storage lot in Ardmore, Oklahoma," he said. "I drove it there myself. Damn near wrecked the thing."

"Don't you need a commercial license to drive something that big?" I asked.

He lifted one meaty shoulder. "Beats the hell out of me." He went on to say that Brazos had him move it late at night when the bus would be less likely to be noticed, and that he'd instructed him to cover the bus in tarps so it couldn't be readily identified by the others who stored their RVs and campers at the site.

One of the other bodyguards chimed in now. "Last I heard the plane was at the municipal airport in Amarillo."

Obviously, Brazos had again tried to hide his assets from us. *Jerk.*

We locked up the boat, waited while the girl put her clothes back on, and gave the bodyguards and the girl a ride to shore in Nick's bass boat. The girl was a local, so she took off on foot. If I were her, I'd stop by the medical clinic and be tested for STDs. Then I'd jump on my phone and start calling tabloids, sell the rights to my story to the highest bidder. I could see the headlines now. THE HAT COMES OFF! BRAZOS RIVERS EXPOSED.

chapter thirty-three

$\mathcal{F}$ast Car

Once Nick's boat was back on the trailer, Nick and I climbed into the cab of his pickup with one member of the security team. The other two climbed into the bed.

We drove to a nearby tourist shop so Nick could buy some dry clothes. Meanwhile, the bodyguards got on their phones and called up the former Boys of the Bayou to see if they might be interested in employing their security services. They were in luck. Armadillo Uprising agreed to take them on. The former Boys even bought the men bus tickets from Galveston to Austin, where the band had decided to establish its home base. A smart move. With its South by Southwest and Austin City Limits music festivals, the live music industry in Austin was booming.

Nick emerged from the surf shop wearing a pair of knee-length swim trunks covered in sharks, along with a pair of cheap flip-flops, and a T-shirt that proclaimed him to be an EXPERT BIKINIOLOGIST.

I rolled my eyes. "Really? You had to pick that one?"

"Sure." He shot me a wink. "It makes me sound smart."

"Yeah, right."

We dropped the bodyguards at the bus station and drove over to the San Luis Resort. We'd obtained the key to Brazos's suite from his boat. Nick and I stepped inside to find the place thoroughly and utterly trashed. Lamps lay on the floor, their shades smashed. Curtains had been pulled from their rods and sat in crumpled heaps on the floor. The mattresses lay askew, halfway off their box springs.

"My God," Nick said, "Hurricane Ike did less damage than this."

It looked like a party had taken place in the suite. More liquor bottles were strewn about here, including a shattered bottle of Smirnoff Wild Honey vodka on the floor of the kitchenette, surrounded by sharp shards of glass. Wet bathing suits and towels littered the floor, giving off the funk of stale salt water and mildew. Three moldy slices of petrified cheese pizza floated in three inches of water in the clogged bathtub. I used a toothbrush to pull a pair of black lace panties from the drain.

Obviously, there was truth to the rumors after all. I couldn't believe I'd once fantasized about a man who'd do something this stupid and boorish and juvenile. But I supposed I shouldn't be too hard on myself. I'd been in love with a fantasy version of Brazos, one that I'd embellished and polished and perfected in my mind. Nothing wrong with that, necessarily. We all need a little fantasy, don't we? Our own Prince Charming to dream about? But what I was getting now was a big dose of raw reality. Also, a fresh whiff of something that smelled like vomit coming from the second bedroom. *Urk.*

"I'll call the front desk," Nick said, "let them know Brazos won't be back. And to send a whole crew of maids."

"This place doesn't need housekeepers," I replied. "It

needs a hazmat team. Or a wrecking ball. Or some gasoline and a match."

While Nick made the call, I checked the drawers and closets. I found two spare pairs of boots and spurs. I confiscated those. Heck, regardless of the shame the singer had now brought upon himself, the boots would likely fetch a pretty penny at a government auction. We'd use the proceeds to offset his long-outstanding tax bill. I also found a couple pairs of jeans I suspected belonged to Brazos, along with two western shirts and a leather jacket.

Nick picked up a hotel notepad from the bedroom desk, took a look at the scribbles on it, and chuckled. "Looks like Winnie was writing a new song. Get a load of this. 'Hop aboard my train, girl, it's coming into town, my caboose is loose and my engine is hot.' Looks like he had trouble rhyming the last verse. He's got a bunch of crap marked out."

Nick held the paper out so I could read it. Brazos had lined through "baby, give me what you got," as well as "you know I want you, want you a lot."

"Ugh. That's horrible." I took the paper from Nick. "But I bet this scrap of paper is worth something."

Nick arched a brow. "Still think the guy's a poet?"

"No. I think he's a poser. An oversexed, man-whore pretender."

Nick chuckled. "I knew you'd come around."

Nick and I rode the elevator down to the parking garage. The Ferrari was parked on the first level.

"Gotta say," Nick said as we approached the car, "she is a thing of beauty."

That she was. I couldn't wait to put my ass in the seat, grip the wheel, and open her up. Like I said, my federal badge was like a get-out-of-jail-free card. Still . . .

"Heads up," I said.

When Nick looked up, I tossed him the car keys.

A big smile brightened his face as he snatched them out of the air. "Are you kidding me? You're going to let me drive it first?"

"Why not? You've helped me out a lot in this case." More precisely, he'd tried to take it over. But that was water under the bridge at this point. What was important was that Brazos was in custody, his assets had been located, and nobody had been seriously hurt.

Nick unlocked the car and we climbed in.

He moaned in pleasure as he settled into the seat. "This thing cradles your ass."

He was right. "It's like sitting in butter."

After taking a quick look around the dash, he reached out his hand to turn on the stereo. The strains of opera streamed out of the speakers.

"What the hell is this crap?" Nick said. "Bonnaduce?"

"Danny Bonnaduce was the redheaded kid from *The Partridge Family,*" I said. "I think you mean Pavarotti."

"Whoever the hell it is," Nick said, "I'm not waiting for the fat lady to sing. This is over. Now." He punched the button to eject the CD, yanked it from the player, and tossed it over his shoulder. He tuned the radio to a country station. Ironically, the DJ was playing a Brazos Rivers song. "Whaddya know," Nick said. "I do want to get fast and filthy."

He started the engine. It purred like a kitten with a full tummy.

He backed out of the spot and headed to the exit for the parking garage. "Listen to that engine. I'm going to open this baby up and see what she can do."

"You realize you only get to drive as far as the boat ramp, right?" I told him.

He slammed on the brakes, throwing both of us forward until the seat belts snapped us back. "What did you just say?"

"I can't drive your truck all the way back to Dallas," I said. "I don't know how to drive something that's pulling a trailer."

"That's a lame excuse," he spat.

"Your boat is your baby," I reminded him. "If I put so much as a tiny scratch on that thing you'd never forgive me."

"True." He looked up in thought. "In that case, we might have to take a little detour on the way to the boat ramp. That is, *if you're willin'*."

"Oh, yeah," I said, giving him a grin. "I'm definitely willin'."

Nick zipped out of the garage and headed down the island, away from the developed area. Midweek there was virtually no traffic on this stretch of road and we could see a full mile ahead. He pushed down on the accelerator, then pushed down some more. The needle on the speedometer eased up to eighty, ninety, a hundred. When it reached one hundred twenty, he held it steady, unrolled the windows to let in a blast of ocean air, and tossed his head back. "Yee-ha!"

A mile later, he pulled onto a secluded stretch of beach and cut the engine. "You know what would be even better than driving this Ferarri?"

"What?"

"Making love in it." He wagged his brows. "Few people have had the opportunity to ride in a car like this. Even fewer have fooled around in one. What do you say? Want to knock one out?" He made a fist and faked a punch, making a clucking noise with his tongue.

I was willin' to do that, too. "Why not?"

Unfortunately, the thought of fooling around in a Ferrari was much sexier than the actual process. There wasn't much wiggle room in the cab. Eventually we realized the only way to make things work was for me to be on top. Even that didn't work very well. Every time Nick thrust into me, I ended up hitting my butt on the steering wheel and activating the horn.

Honk.

Honk.

Honk.

Hoooooooonk!

We eventually gave up, climbed out of the car, and finished on the hood with a dozen voyeuristic seagulls scolding us. *Caw! Caw! Caw!*

When we finished, we climbed off and gathered our clothes.

I glanced over at Nick. "You've got the Ferrari emblem imprinted on your ass."

He looked back over his shoulder, shrugged, and gave me that smile that never failed to warm my heart. "Totally worth it."

chapter thirty-four

Played by a Pup

The arrest of Brazos Rivers hit the airwaves like a freight train. His mug shot made the front page of virtually every newspaper in the nation, and the story was the lead on both the local and national evening news. Fortunately, given that I'd returned to Dallas immediately after he'd been taken into custody—well, immediately after Nick and I finished having sex on the beach—I'd managed to avoid the media frenzy. The local police in Galveston and the two female marshals had been interviewed extensively, and appeared thrilled to have been involved in taking down such a notorious, and sexy, target.

When I arrived at the office Thursday morning, Brazos had racked up another $2,191.78 in interest and my voice mail box had been flooded. It took me a full twenty minutes to listen to my messages. Reporters had called with request after request for interviews and information about Brazos and his tax woes. I jotted down their names and phone numbers and handed the list to an intern, instructing him to call them back with the name and phone number of the IRS public relations officer. As much undercover work as I did, I'd just as soon keep my name and face out of the news. Especially now that I was getting so close to busting Larry Burkett, Russell Cobb, and Judge Craven in their "justice for sale" scam.

At least I *hoped* I was close to busting them. It dawned on me as I headed to the courthouse that the preceding Friday could very well have been the final payment from Burkett to Judge Craven. After all, the payola couldn't be expected to go on forever, right? At some point the bill for the verdict would be paid in full.

On the other hand, who in their right mind would make full payment on something that had yet to be delivered? Maybe the payments would continue, at least until immediately after the verdict was rendered. Hell, I didn't know. Criminals didn't follow an established protocol. It wasn't like there was a rulebook to follow. Things could go either way.

My mind briefly toyed with what my options would be if I were unable to bring this case to a resolution tomorrow night. I supposed I could initiate an audit of PPE. After all, the cash withdrawals would show up in the bank statements. And I could easily prove that no such entity as Ector Oilfield Supply existed. But I feared it wouldn't be enough. Burkett could plead the Fifth, refuse to share any more details. I'd be able to prove he'd sucked cash out of the company, and I could deny him the deductions for the illusory drill bits, but without evidence proving what was actually done with the cash it was unlikely I could sustain a criminal tax evasion case.

As for maintaining a case against Cobb, the *K* on his Toyota license plate might not be enough to implicate him in picking up the cash at the marker. Plus, given that Judge Craven was a client of his, the two could easily explain his visits to her house as meetings to discuss her PR needs. After all, she was probably planning to run for another term once her current one expired. Defense attorneys were experts at poking holes in evidence and, without more, this case would look like a dartboard at an Irish pub once they were through with it.

We needed solid evidence. Video footage that couldn't be denied or reinterpreted. A paper trail.

We need to catch them red-handed.

The plan I'd devised last week over my glass of moscato had to work. If it didn't we might be shit out of luck.

As I sat in the courtroom Thursday afternoon, listening to a chemist testify on behalf of the defense that the levels of toxins in the plaintiffs' wells were too small to be of real concern, my resolve returned. Many of the plaintiffs had thought the gas leases and the royalties they'd earn would help put food on their tables, pay their mortgages, send their kids to college. Instead, they'd found themselves forced into financial ruin by PPE.

Several had moved off their properties due to the health and safety concerns. Though they'd listed their properties with Realtors, none had been able to sell their homes and land, even at giveaway prices. Several of the ranches had been foreclosed on by the banks, leaving the plaintiffs homeless and with bad credit to boot.

When the plaintiffs' attorney cross-examined the chemist, he posed a litany of pointed questions. *Hadn't he barely graduated from college a mere five years ago, having earned only a 2.1 GPA? Hadn't he had trouble finding stable employment since? Hadn't he been paid to testify on behalf of the oil and gas companies in thirteen other fracking trials? Hadn't his paper minimizing the safety risks of fracking been rejected by scientific journals due to a lack of thorough research and substantiation?*

Clearly, his so-called expert opinion had been bought,

too. *Sheesh.* Brazos had sold out to the music market. Judge Craven had sold out to a gas company. So had Cobb and this guy. Was everyone for sale? It sure seemed that way.

When testimony concluded at the end of the day, the defense rested.

"I have some smaller matters to hear in the morning," Judge Craven said, looking down at the attorneys. "I'll have my verdict for you at one o'clock tomorrow afternoon." With that, she banged her gavel—*bam!*—gathered up the notes from her bench, and disappeared through the door to her chambers.

Late that afternoon, I let Nick drive the Ferrari from the IRS to the federal auto impound lot. It was the least I could do for the man who'd tolerated my silly celebrity crush. Well, maybe *tolerated* was too strong a word. *Suffered through* was perhaps more precise. Either way, I figured I owed him. I'd unintentionally hurt him, stepped on his feelings, made him look and feel like a cuckold. Letting him drive the car was small recompense, but at least it was something.

At the attendant's direction, Nick pulled the car into a spot in the warehouse where the upscale vehicles were maintained for safekeeping. Reluctantly, he climbed out, emitting a loud, long sigh as he handed the keys over. "It was fun while it lasted."

I scooted over into the passenger seat of Nick's truck.

He climbed in and took the wheel, taking one last, longing glance back at the Ferrari. "I'm going to miss that car. She was one sweet ride."

"If you want a sweet ride," I said, sending my best seductive grin his way, "I'll take you on one."

A smile tugged at his lips. "Now you're talking."

Nick drove out of the impound lot and headed down the surface street.

"Get on I-30," I told him.

"Why?" he asked.

"Because I said so."

He cut me a narrow-eyed look, mumbled something about being pussy-whipped, and drove onto I-30. When we reached the Hampton Road exit, I told him to take it. A few blocks later we pulled up to the SPCA, the same shelter where I'd adopted my two cats a few years back.

"What are we doing here?" he asked. "I thought we were going to have sex."

"We are," I replied. "But first we're getting you a new best friend."

Nick turned the key to stop the engine and slumped back in his seat, staring at the building in silence. After a few seconds, he cleared his throat. When he spoke, his voice was soft and full of raw emotion. "No dog will ever be able to replace Nutty."

"I know that," I said. "It doesn't have to. But you need a new best friend."

His jaw flexed. "I'm doing just fine."

What a liar. I didn't bother pointing out that his emotions were obvious. He was grieving and sad and lonely. I understood there would always be a place in his heart that only Nutty had been able to fill, but that didn't mean there wasn't another spot a new dog could occupy, right?

I shrugged. "We're already here. No harm in going in and taking a look, right?"

"I suppose not." Nick exhaled a long breath. "But I don't want any pressure from you. Got it? I don't think I'm ready for this."

I raised my palms to indicate my agreement. "Understood."

As we climbed out of his truck, we could hear the sounds of dogs barking over the rush of traffic on the elevated highway ramp behind us. High-pitched yips mixed with baritone woofs, with a sprinkling of mid-range arfs in between. One even bayed, howling as if he were a wolf under a full moon rather than a mutt under an overpass.

Nick held the front door open for me and I stepped inside.

"How can I help you?" asked the curly-haired woman manning the front desk.

"He's looking for a dog to adopt," I said.

Now it was Nick's turn to raise a hand. "Hold on, now. Let's not get ahead of ourselves. I'm just here to take a look. That's all."

The woman looked from Nick to me.

"His old dog just died," I explained.

"Ah," was all she said, but her eyes told me she knew what Nick was going through, why he seemed reluctant. She stood and put a hand on his shoulder. Her gesture was probably intended to be an act of compassion and comfort, but I couldn't help but think she'd taken advantage of the situation to cop a quick feel of Nick's muscles. Heck, I would've done the same in her situation. Nick was every bit as handsome and sexy as Brazos Rivers. More so, even. Nick was tougher, an alpha dog. I supposed that would make me his bitch, though, huh? Not sure I liked that.

The woman removed her hand from Nick's shoulder and gestured for us to follow her. "Come this way. I'd be glad to show you around."

She led us back to the dog area and we made our way slowly up and down the rows, looking over the dogs available for adoption. A high-energy spotted terrier jumped up and down in one cage as if his legs were springs and he were a canine jack-in-the-box. A lazy black Lab lay on his side in another, yawning and stretching out his long legs as we passed by. In a third, a white Eskimo dog sat on his haunches, using his back leg to scratch behind his ear.

Nick stopped in front of a cage that housed what had to
be the ugliest dog I'd ever seen. Her feet appeared two
sizes too big for her bony body. Her tail drooped. Her
hair was a mottled mix of gray, black, white, and tan,
with a number of thin spots, too, her pinkish skin showing through.

"Mange?" I asked.

"No," the woman said. "Her fur was severely matted
when she was brought in. Some of her hair fell out when
we brushed her."

I guessed I shouldn't fault the dog. If not for my hairdresser saving me with the weave, I'd have a sparse spot
in my hair now, too.

Nick eyed the dog, who cowered at the rear of her
enclosure, her back to us. "What's her story? Was she a
stray?"

The woman nodded. "Animal control found her near a
school, nearly starved to death. It looked like someone
had dumped her there."

When Nick knelt down, the dog flattened her ears and
cast a glance over her shoulder, fear in her blue eyes.

"How could anyone have dumped a pretty thing like
you?" Nick said in a soft, soothing voice.

Pretty? The dog was anything but. Still, those blue
eyes held some appeal and once she put on some weight
and her fur grew back she probably wouldn't look so
pitiful.

The dog turned away, scooting herself into the back
corner as if trying to make herself disappear. Poor thing.

"Hey, wallflower," Nick called to her, refusing to give
up on the beast. "Give me a chance, huh?"

She cast another glance back at him, this one a little
less fearful, maybe even curious. With her big feet, bad
hair, and less-than-friendly demeanor, others looking for
a new pet probably hadn't given her a second look. No

doubt she wondered why Nick hadn't yet moved on to the next cage. Though I felt sorry for the dog, I was wondering the same thing myself.

"She's not well socialized yet," the woman said, "but we're working on it."

"That's okay," Nick said. "I always did like girls who played hard to get."

True. When I'd first met Nick I'd been in a serious relationship with another guy. Nick had been patient, though, pecking away at my defenses until I finally surrendered, breaking things off with Brett and starting a new relationship with Nick.

"What kind of dog is she?" I asked.

"She's an Australian shepherd mix," the woman said. "We've guessed her age to be around two years."

"Can I go inside and take a closer look?" Nick asked.

"Sure. Just be careful. Approach her slowly."

Nick lifted the latch to the enclosure and stepped inside, closing it gently behind him. He bent down so he'd be at the dog's level. "Come on, sweetie. Come say hello." He held out a hand for her to sniff.

I knew she'd come around. No female could resist Nick's charms forever.

Sure enough, the dog turned her head and extended her snout. Her ears pricked up and her brown nose twitched as she gave Nick's hand a thorough sniff.

When she finished the sniff test, he reached up under her chin and gave her a scratch. "See? I'm not so bad, huh?"

The end of her tail gave one tiny wag, so small I might've missed it if I hadn't been watching the two so closely.

"I saw your tail move," Nick told her. "You're warming up to me, aren't you?"

The tail wagged again, unmistakably this time, hitting the concrete floor with a *thump-thump-thump*.

"Want to come home with me?" Nick asked.

The woman beside me emitted a soft giggle. I knew exactly what that giggle meant. *If the dog won't come home with you, heck, I will!*

"How about it?" Nick asked the dog. "Want to be my girl?"

She extended her snout again and licked his hand.

"All right, wallflower," he said, reaching out now to rumple her ears. "We've got a deal."

A twinge of jealousy crimped my gut. Ridiculous, I know, to be envious of a dog, but I couldn't help myself, even if this whole thing had been my idea in the first place.

Nick stood. "I'm going to call you Daffodil. What do you think about that?"

The dog's tail wagged fully this time. She must've liked her new name. I thought it was a little goofy, but at least it was better than Nutty.

An hour later, Nick and Daffodil and I were in the pet supply store, looking over the collars. He'd tried a dozen on the dog.

"Which one do you think I should get?" he asked. "The blue one brings out her eyes, but the purple one with the polka dots is cute, too."

The dog looked from one of Nick's hands to the other, as if she couldn't make up her mind, either.

"You're not fooling me," I told her. "I know dogs are color blind." I returned my attention to Nick. "Get them both," I suggested. "No girl likes to wear the same thing every day."

"Good idea."

We emerged from the store a half hour and a hundred dollars later. Daffodil was now the proud owner of not one, but two new squeaky toys, one in the shape of a rubber chicken, the other a porcupine. She also had a case of gourmet canned dog food and three different boxes of crunchy treats. Nick had even bought her a new doggie toothbrush.

By the time we arrived at Nick's place, Daffodil was wagging her tail, running back and forth between us on the seat of the truck, and yapping happily. We climbed out of the truck and she hopped to the ground, prancing around Nick's front yard like the prom queen now instead of the wallflower.

I shook my head. "That dog totally played you."

"You think?" Nick said, though the smile on his face told me he didn't care whether the furry creature had manipulated him. When she ran back to him, he knelt down and scratched her behind the ears. "I think I'm in love with you already."

I felt a twinge in my heart on hearing his words. We'd been together quite a while now and he hadn't told me he was in love with me, yet he'd had this mutt for only a couple of hours and was already proclaiming his love for her. I couldn't help but be a little miffed.

Nick cut a glance my way. "No need to get jealous," he said, a smile playing about his lips. "I think I'm in love with her, but I *know* I'm in love with you."

My heart began pounding in my chest. *Had he just . . . ? Did he say . . . ? Could he . . . ?* My lungs had stopped taking in air and it took everything in me to wheeze out a simple, "Do what?"

Nick chuckled and his whiskey eyes locked on mine. "I love you, Tara."

My heart spun in my chest like the bottle on the deck. "You do?"

"Is that such a surprise?" He exhaled a long breath. "Why do you think I've been so pissed off about your crush on that no-talent twerp we busted?"

Moments ago I'd wanted to choke the life out of Brazos.

Now I found myself choking up. "You love me, Nick? Really?"

"Well, duh. I put up with all of your crap, don't I?"

After all I'd put Nick through, acting like such a twit about Brazos and dismissing his feelings, he could still love me? That really said something.

Happy tears filled my eyes. "Oh, Nick!" I threw my arms around his neck and hugged him tight, fearing I might float away otherwise. "I love you, too!"

We held each other for a moment. I'd never felt so content, so fulfilled, so thoroughly and utterly *whole*. Brazos might be overrated as a songwriter, but he'd got that part right.

"I hate to put an end to this," Nick said, stepping backward. "But I better get some food in that dog before she starves to death."

I rolled my eyes. "You are such a man." More than three consecutive seconds of intimacy and they began to freak out. Still, I'd take what I could get. Besides, those three seconds were so damn awesome they'd hold me over for a really long time.

chapter thirty-five

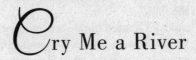

$\mathcal{C}$ry Me a River

Winthrop Merriweather VII was treated for a minor concussion at the hospital in Galveston, kept overnight for observation, and released into the custody of the two female federal marshals. They'd transported him from the island to the federal detention facility near Dallas, where he awaited his bail hearing scheduled for later this morning.

On my drive to the office Friday morning, I thought about Nick and what he'd told me. *He loves me.* Although I supposed I'd known it on some level, it sure was great to hear him say it out loud. I'd had the warm fuzzies ever since. I'd even found myself doodling the name Tara Pratt on a fast-food receipt in my car. *Sheesh.* I was like a schoolgirl, huh? Still, the name had a nice ring to it. And speaking of rings, I wondered whether there might be one in my future and what it might look like. But perhaps I was getting way ahead of myself here . . .

I arrived at the office to see Nick situating a framed photo on his desk. I ventured into his office. The five-by-seven photo was a snapshot of Daffodil that he must have taken last night. The rubber chicken hung limply from her mouth. She looked up at the camera, her head cocked at an adorable angle.

I was many things, but adorable was not one of them. How could I compete with that?

I frowned, green with envy. "You don't have a photo of me in here, but you've got one of your dog?"

Nick shrugged. "If I want to see you, all I have to do is look across the hall."

"Gee. Thanks." I treated him to a raspberry.

"You've got no one to blame but yourself," he said. "You're the one who made me go to the animal shelter."

True. And I was glad he had a new canine companion, even if it did mean I'd be sharing Nick's affections. I'd just have to get over it, huh?

I glanced at my watch. "Ready to go?"

"Hell yeah."

Nick and I met up with Brazos and his attorney at the federal courthouse. A group of fans was gathered in the hallway, alerted by someone who'd spotted the singer entering the building. When they spotted Brazos coming up the hall, they flocked to him, offering him more flowers, teddy bears, and phone numbers, all of which he promptly dropped into a trash can after entering the courtroom. Knowing what I knew now, I felt sorry for those girls. Their attention and dreams were being wasted on a guy who wasn't worthy of them.

Fortunately, Judge Trumbull had ordered her bailiff to keep the fans out of her courtroom. The last thing we needed right now was some crazed fan attempting to avenge Brazos by attacking the IRS agents who'd brought him down.

Winthrop VII's attorney was one I'd dealt with before, in a case against men running a mortgage fraud scheme. Jacqueline Plimpton was young, black, and thin, a graduate of Harvard Law School with a zeal for the courtroom and an ego nearly as big as Brazos Rivers's had been.

While he'd maintained his usual sparkly demeanor in the hallway with his fans, in the courtroom Brazos looked defeated. His shoulders were slumped, his normally dazzling eyes were dull, and his gaze was cast downward. He looked every bit the overgrown child that he was. At least he didn't appear to be pouting. Maybe finally having someone put him in his place had been good for him. Maybe he'd bounce back from this experience having learned a few things. Maybe he'd be wiser from here on out, less juvenile, more responsible. One could hope, huh?

The Merriweathers had come to court to support their son. They appeared simultaneously concerned and peeved, though they seemed more irritated at their son than the IRS.

Today, the judge would set bail for Brazos. I only hoped her infatuation with Brazos wouldn't impede her judgment as much as mine had.

"Your Honor," Ross O'Donnell argued on behalf of the IRS, "Mr. Merriweather should be denied bail. He's a clear flight risk. He's already traveled out of the country when he knew federal agents were looking to arrest him."

Of course, he'd come back into the U.S. not long afterward, which either meant his trip to Cozumel, Mexico, had been for pleasure only and not an attempt to evade arrest, or that the captain he'd hired had a full-payment-in-advance policy and Brazos had only paid for a week of services. If I had to hazard a guess, I'd say his return to Galveston was for the latter reason.

Judge Trumbull looked from Ross to Plimpton, letting her eyes linger for a moment on Brazos as they swept past him. Her eyes twinkled with awe and a flirtatious smile played about her lips, but at least she wasn't pleasuring her gavel today.

The defense attorney was more than happy to oblige the judge with a rejoinder. "Mr. Rivers no longer has the means to leave the country. The IRS has seized his car, his tour bus, his boat, and his private plane."

It was true. Once the security team had told us of the whereabouts of Brazos's mobile assets, we'd contacted agents in the collections department to solicit their help in seizing the vehicles and vessels. Everything was now housed at the impound lot, in preparation for public auction. The only thing Brazos purportedly had to his name were the clothes on his back, the boots and spurs on his feet, and his teeny-tiny wiener. *Neener-neener.* However, we also suspected he might have a foreign bank account he had yet to divulge.

Plimpton continued to argue the singer's case. "Mr. Rivers is far too well-known to be able to escape. Every time he goes out in public, a fan posts the information on Facebook or Twitter. You saw the fans in the hallway. Brazos has nowhere to hide, even if he wanted to. It would be impossible."

"Speaking of Galveston," Trumbull said, "what exactly happened down there?"

I suspected her question was more a matter of personal curiosity than a need for the information.

Ross gestured to Nick, inviting him to explain.

Nick stood to address the judge. "Agent Holloway and I boarded the *River Rat* to look for Winthrop. We found him asleep in bed. When—"

"What was he wearing?" the judge asked Nick, though her eyes were on Brazos.

Yep, definitely personal curiosity.

"He was wearing his boots, his spurs, and his hat," Nick said.

"That's all?" she asked, her voice husky with lust. Her eyelids drooped and her lips parted as she seemed to be picturing Brazos in his naked glory, which, in reality, wasn't all that glorious once you went south of his belly button. Seriously, his thing looked like it should be slicked up with tartar sauce. Judge Trumbull gripped the heavy end of her gavel with both hands, the handle sticking straight up between them, creating a phallic effect. "I heard something on TV about a concussion. Tell me about the arrest, how he got the head injury."

As Nick explained how he and Brazos had gone at each other on the boat, and then in the water, the judge's gaze went from Nick to Brazos and back again. She sucked her lip into her mouth and worked it as she listened, apparently visualizing the two attractive men fighting each other, probably pretending they were fighting over her. Obviously, the visual her mind created was getting her hot and bothered. But who could blame her? I'd gotten a little hot and bothered, too. I half expected the judge to take a personal recess, go back to her chambers and stick some ice down her pants to cool herself off.

When Nick finished, the judge gave herself a moment to finish indulging in her erotic courtroom fantasy, then sat up, all business now, and turned to Plimpton. "Honey, your client needs a wake-up call. A swift kick in the rear, too, but looks like Agents Pratt and Holloway have already taken care of that. You better set him straight."

The judge looked directly at Brazos now, pointing her gavel at him. "Don't you ever lay a hand on a federal agent again, you hear me? These folks put their lives on the line every day and they don't need some overblown choirboy taking potshots at them. If I ever hear of you pulling a stunt like that again, I won't just throw the book at you, I'll beat you with it first."

With that, she set his bail at $2 million.

"Your Honor," Plimpton argued, stepping forward. "That's much too high!"

Trumbull snorted. "That kid's got platinum albums falling out of his ears. You trying to tell me he can't afford to post bond?"

A defendant would be out of pocket only 10 percent of the bond's cost, with the bail bondsman posting the remainder. Surely Brazos could scrape together two hundred grand.

"That's exactly what I'm saying, Your Honor." Plimpton went on to say that Brazos was essentially broke. Evidently his decision to fire Sierra and the Boys of the Bayou hadn't been entirely out of animosity. He'd run out of money to pay them.

The judge frowned. "Where the hell has all of his money gone?"

Brazos's head hung a little lower. For the first time since he entered the courtroom, he spoke. "Booze. Expensive hotels. Travel. Dinners at fancy restaurants. Not just for me, but for my crew and friends and some of my fans, too."

It dawned on me then that Brazos, who'd been isolated as a child and never attended school with other children, probably had no idea how to develop and maintain a friendship. He'd attempted to buy his friends, to impress them with his money. And where had all of that gotten him? Penniless and imprisoned.

Plimpton handed the judge copies of statements from Winthrop's paltry bank account, the one I already knew about. She handed a copy to Ross, as well. Ross, in turn, showed it to me and Nick. The statement showed a current balance of only $43,147.65. A mere pittance given what the star had earned over the years.

"Is this it?" I asked. "There are no foreign accounts? No investment accounts? Just this checking account?"

"That's all," Plimpton said. "Those documents show everything Brazos has to his name."

The judge looked at the Merriweathers. "You didn't teach your son how to handle his money?"

Mr. Merriweather, who'd remained silent up to this point, stood in the gallery. "We tried," he said. "Obviously we weren't successful."

"Didn't he buy your ranch?" I asked.

Mr. Merriweather shook his head. "That's just rumor. My wife and I paid for the ranch with money we received when we sold our syrup business." He returned his attention to the judge. "Winnie's not much more than a kid, Your Honor. He's barely twenty-two. I hope you'll take that into account."

Trumbull chuckled. "You want me to ground him? Order him to remain in his bedroom and take away his TV privileges?"

"Couldn't hurt," Nick said. "Can you order him to keep his pants on, too?"

The judge pointed her gavel at Nick. "Hush, Agent Pratt. If there's going to be any trash talk in my courtroom it's going to come from my mouth and my mouth only."

Nick ducked his head in acquiescence. "I'll keep my thoughts to myself, Your Honor."

Eventually bail was reduced to $1 million, the Merriweathers promised to keep a tight rein on their son, and Winthrop VII promised to behave. Plimpton informed Ross that she wanted to discuss a negotiated plea deal, and the two of them headed out to the Department of Justice to work out the details.

Nick and I returned to our offices at the IRS, walking side by side in silence. Though we loved to see cases resolved, there was always a certain reflective period after finally nabbing a target, a time when we looked back on the case, mulled over what went right and what went wrong, what we might do better next time, what we had accomplished and what we had yet to achieve.

We stopped in the hallway between our two offices, our gazes locked.

Nick reached out to take my hand and let out a long breath. "I guess we're all done with Brazos Rivers now."

"Yep," I said, offering Nick a smile and a squeeze of my hand. "He's water under the bridge."

chapter thirty-six

*A*nd the Verdict is . . .

At half past noon, I rounded up Eddie and Josh and we
headed over to the county courthouse together. All of us
wanted to be there when Judge Craven issued her verdict.

The courtroom was packed even tighter today, and we
had to squeeze to get inside. My view of the judge's bench
was blocked by a tall rancher, but I had a view of Larry
Burkett's head from behind. Jeez. Even the back of his
neck was wrinkled. The guy was a walking testimonial
for sunblock.

My eyes scanned the room, noticing that there were
several armed deputies in the courtroom. Probably a precautionary measure in case anyone upset by the verdict
decided to cause a scene.

The bailiff ordered us to rise as Judge Craven entered
the room. Again, it was a moot point for the vast majority
of us, who stood around the perimeter of the room.

As the judge took her bench, Eddie, Josh, and I exchanged glances. Would she rule in favor of PPE? Or
would she do the right thing and rule in favor of the plaintiffs?

The speculation among the media was that the plaintiffs would claim victory. The defense attorneys talked a good line, but the testimony and evidence their witnesses had offered hadn't stood up well to scrutiny and had been pulled apart under cross-examination.

I squirmed, managing to slip into a small gap in front of the tall rancher from where I could see the judge now. After she settled in, she got right down to business.

"I have carefully reviewed the evidence in this matter," she said, her voice matter-of-fact, "and have come to the following verdict. With respect to the allegation that PPE employees caused damage to the septic tank on the property owned by Millard Blankenship, I find that the evidence supports a determination of negligence and hereby award the plaintiff damages in the amount of thirty thousand dollars."

Murmurs erupted from the crowd.

The tall man behind me said, "You got that right, judge."

I suspected he might be Millard Blankenship.

The judge continued. "With respect to the allegation that PPE failed to replace a fence it had removed in order to move its equipment, I also find for the plaintiff. Judgment is awarded in the amount of three thousand four hundred dollars and sixty-seven cents."

She continued on, awarding small amounts to several plaintiffs for alleged structural damage to their homes from the earthquakes, but denying relief to others, citing insufficient evidence. The impression she gave was that she'd carefully considered the evidence relevant to each particular claim and had attempted to issue fair and impartial rulings. But had she actually done that? Or was she, like Brazos Rivers, just putting on a show for the crowd?

I mentally calculated. Though Judge Craven had found

against PPE in the majority of claims so far, the damages she'd awarded totaled less than eighty grand, a mere pittance in the grand scheme of things. I suspected she might have ruled in the plaintiffs' favor on many of these smaller claims in an attempt to appear unbiased.

The real meat of this matter, however, was the pollution of the wells and the resulting health issues and devaluation of the plaintiffs' land. I listened, eager to hear her rule on those particular claims. Of course I suspected what she'd say, that PPE wasn't responsible, that the company had no legal liability to compensate the plaintiffs for the damage they'd suffered.

Judge Craven ventured on. "I find that the plaintiffs' wells were indeed contaminated by toxic chemicals in quantities that posed significant health and safety issues to the plaintiffs and their livestock, and that those chemicals were more than likely the cause of the health issues suffered by the plaintiffs."

What?

Eddie, Josh, and I exchanged glances again, this time perplexed glances. We certainly hadn't expected the judge to agree with the plaintiffs' scientific expert on this point. We'd expected her to find that the levels of toxins were within acceptable limits. After all, there was no clear standard or agreement within the scientific community regarding what levels were safe and when the line was crossed.

Was Judge Craven going to rule against PPE? Had I been wrong all along, wasted three days in this courtroom when I could've been working on my other investigations? Had I been wrong about PPE buying her off?

I had lots of questions. And, very soon, I'd have the answers.

Judge Craven looked down at the notes in front of her, as if afraid to meet the plaintiffs' eyes. "I do not find, however, that the plaintiffs proved that it was more likely than not that the contamination was caused by the negligence of PPE."

The judge's use of multiple negatives made her words difficult to comprehend, and it took a moment for the crowd to interpret her speech. Even I had to repeat her words in my head in an attempt to decipher them. She'd ruled in favor of PPE, right? Yep. She had.

A rancher in the galley hollered, "Speak straight, judge. What are you telling us about the wells?"

Judge Craven swallowed hard. "On all other claims, I find in favor of the defendant."

There was a short pause as her words sank in, then the room exploded in noise. The sound in the courtroom now was not mere murmuring as before, but rather was an absolute uproar.

Many in the room cried foul. Well, actually what they cried was, *"Bullshit!,"* which is Texan for *foul.*

Behind me, Blankenship huffed. "This can't be! Is that judge out of her ever-loving mind?" When those around him agreed that she very likely had lost her mental faculties, Blankenship posed the question to the judge herself, hollering over the din of the crowd. "Judge Craven, have you lost your marbles?"

A female plaintiff burst into tears, pointed an accusing finger at the judge, and shrieked, "This is wrong! You know it is!"

Both Blankenship and the woman were quickly escorted from the courtroom by deputies. When two men pushed their way through the crowd and stormed toward the judge's bench, they, too, were intercepted by armed officers. Both were shackled and led from the room, but handcuffs didn't stop their shouts.

"How can you live with yourself?" hollered the first.

The second directed his shouts at the room in general. "Big oil has the government in their pockets!"

Having rendered her verdict, endured a nasty verbal assault, and only narrowly avoided a probable punch in the nose, the judge banged her gavel one last time. *Bam!* With that, she turned and hightailed it through the door to her private chambers, taking her guilt and shame with her.

chapter thirty-seven

$\mathcal{B}$alloon Payment

By the time we made it out of the courthouse, reporters were already in place on the steps, interviewing the disappointed plaintiffs. Larry Burkett and his attorneys were escorted past by law enforcement who were probably less eager to protect their charges than to simply avoid a brouhaha.

Trish stood with the woman who'd been led from the courtroom. "Can you tell our viewers how you feel about Judge Craven's decision?"

"I feel like I've been violated!" the woman cried. "Like the world's been turned on its head! It makes no sense. None at all!"

An especially zealous reporter was able to stop Burkett and his attorneys for a quick comment. The lead defense attorney said, "The plaintiffs were simply unable to prove their case. Those contaminants could have come from any number of oil and gas companies. Judge Craven's decision was fair and right."

And expensive. Still, the bribe had cost PPE only a

fraction of what it stood to lose had she ruled against the company.

As I walked back into my office at the IRS, my cell phone vibrated in my pocket. I pulled it out. The readout indicated Katie Dunne was calling. I punched the button to accept the call. "Hi, Katie."

"I have to talk fast," she said. "The crew supervisor stepped outside but he'll be back soon."

"Sure," I said. "Shoot."

"Mr. Burkett just called from his cell phone on his way home from Dallas. He said PPE won the trial?"

"Yep," I said. "I was there when the judge gave her verdict. It was a total fiasco. Deputies had to haul a couple of the ranchers off in handcuffs."

"Oh, no." Her voice sounded feeble, weak. "I can hardly believe it." After a moment's pause she seemed to gather her wits. "Mr. Burkett told me to withdraw fifty grand in cash today. He told me that since PPE won the trial he's going to step up production and that the company will need an extra-large order of drill bits."

Katie's call confirmed what I'd suspected. That now that the verdict had been rendered, a final payment would be made, like a balloon payment on a loan, a bonus of sorts.

"Thanks, Katie." Knowing the shit might hit the fan tonight, and that Burkett might possibly think Katie had something to do with it, I said, "Do you have somewhere you and Doug can take your kids and dog tonight? A place where Burkett can't find you?"

Katie sucked in air. "Do you think we're in danger?"

"I think people do bad things when they find themselves in trouble," I said. "Burkett may put two and two together and realize you were the one to tip off the government. It can't hurt to play it safe."

"One of my high school friends lives in Weatherford," she said. "We can stay with her."

"Good. I'll be in touch."

At six-thirty that evening, after affixing a camera to the historical marker, I bent over and tiptoed across the pasture in Palo Pinto, the one that had once belonged to the illustrious George Webb Slaughter, hoping to blend in with the goats that surrounded me and nibbled at my hair and jacket. I was tempted to shoo the pesky beasts away, but I realized they provided good cover. If I hunched down among the herd I could blend in, remain virtually unnoticeable.

When I was within twenty yards of the fence, I stopped and squatted behind a scraggly mesquite tree to wait.

I watched the PPE headquarters through my night-vision scope, gently pushing the goats away when they mouthed it. "This isn't food," I told them. "Stop it."

A few minutes after seven, the door to the building swung open. Burkett exited with a thick envelope in his hands. It didn't look any bigger than the envelopes he'd used for the previous cash transfers, but he'd probably had Katie get the cash in larger bills this time.

I lowered the scope while he went to his car, knowing the headlights would blind me if I didn't. He pulled out of the parking lot and headed my way.

My pulse grew more rapid, warming me from head to toe, and adrenaline caused my lungs to work faster, too. My breath hung in the cool air, like a beacon marking my location. I sat back on my butt and curled my legs up in front of me, lowering my nose to my knees to prevent the cloud of steam from giving me away.

Baaaa.

A gray and white goat called right next to my ear. I was tempted to push him away but was afraid to startle the herd and possibly catch Burkett's attention. The goat seemed to sense my annoyance and decided to incite me further by raising his tail and dropping a load of tiny turds right next to my foot.

I stared the goat right in his horizontal pupils. "Seriously? You had to do that right now?"

He pulled his head back and butted my upper arm, knocking me sideways before waltzing off.

Burkett's Yukon came up the highway, slowing as he approached the marker. As he pulled over, his headlights played across the pasture, lighting up a moving swath that started forty yards away and headed rapidly in my direction. With any luck, the light would sweep quickly across me and continue on.

Alas, luck was not with me that night.

When Burkett pulled to a stop, his headlights were aimed directly at me. I felt like an actor in a spotlight. One who had forgotten her lines and froze.

Holy shit.

Surely he had to see me, right? Or did my dark clothes and the scraggly tree and the goats milling about provide enough cover? I wasn't sure, but instinct told me to hold my hands up over my head as if they were horns. When the goats around me *baaed,* I channeled Old MacDonald's farm from my kindergarten years and *baaed* along with them. *Baaa. Baaaaa.*

I hoped Burkett wasn't armed. I didn't want to die, especially out here in the middle of nowhere in a pasture with goat poop on my shoe.

Burkett cut his lights. I waited for the inevitable, for him to call me out, or shoot me, or spot me and simply drive off with the cash. But he did none of those things. Rather, he scurried up to the historical marker and dropped his envelope at the base.

Looks like we're still in business.

His dirty deed done, he rushed back to his car, started his engine, and flashed his lights three times, giving the signal to Cobb, who waited down the road.

The instant Burkett had completed his U-turn I was in motion. I snipped the barbed wire fence with wire cutters, slipped between the severed strands, and crab-scrambled up to the marker. In the distance, a car began heading up the road toward me. No doubt it was Cobb in the Toyota.

I pulled a decoy envelope out from under my hoodie and exchanged it for the envelope Burkett had left. I'd just made it back through the fence when Cobb pulled up, cutting his lights.

Rather than risk being spotted fleeing across the pasture, I flattened myself on the ground and lay as still as possible, hoping he wouldn't notice me. The goats meandered up, nibbling at my clothing again, but at least they surrounded me, obscuring any view Cobb might have had. It probably appeared as if they were snacking on dried tufts of grass.

Leaving his car running, Cobb exited the vehicle, snatched the envelope, and was back in the driver's seat in less than seven seconds. The guy had his moves down. As they say, practice makes perfect. He'd had seven months of practice with this routine.

He slid the car into gear and took off, driving thirty yards or so before turning his headlights back on.

I turned onto my back and looked up at the sky, releasing a relieved breath as the tension snaked out of my muscles. Out here, where there was little interference from lights, the sky was darker, the stars more bright and beautiful. Too bad I couldn't stay for a while and stargaze. But I had work to do.

I got to my feet, bade my goat friends good-bye, and

hurried back across the pasture to the G-ride I'd left on the dirt road a half mile away.

Once I was back in my car, I turned on the interior light, tore open the end of the envelope, and poured the money out onto my seat.

Whoa.

I'd never seen so much cash, not even when I'd worked the half-price night-crawler sale at Big Bob's Bait Bucket back in high school. We'd been busy that day. Anglers had come from all over the tricounty area to stock up on discounted worms.

The cash from the envelope included five straps of hundred-dollar bills, each strap holding one hundred bills. Ironically, for dirty money, the bills looked surprisingly clean and crisp, as if they'd come straight off the printing press at the Bureau of Printing and Engraving. I thumbed through a stack and, for some unknown reason, held the stack to my nose and sniffed it. I don't know why. It just seemed like the thing to do. The bills smelled of paper and ink. No big surprise there.

I slid the bills back into the envelope, slid the envelope into my glove compartment, and locked it inside. The money secured, I texted Eddie and Josh.

Pickup complete. Get ready. He's headed your way.

chapter thirty-eight

Fifty Grand of Green in Pink, Yellow, and Blue

I drove from Palo Pinto back to Dallas at lightning speed, leaning forward in my seat as if that would somehow make the car go faster. When I reached Preston Hollow, I parked my car three blocks away from the judge's house and continued to her residence on foot.

Looking around to make sure I wouldn't be spotted, I positioned myself behind an electrical box across the street, armed with both my Glock and the high-resolution camera Josh had given me. As wound up as I was, I had a hard time being still.

I'm ready for action.

Now.

Twenty long minutes later, Cobb's Mercedes pulled up to the judge's house. He hopped out with his briefcase in his hand, his usual MO. He scanned his surroundings, but only looked left and right, failing to look behind him, where I was hidden.

I snickered to myself. Criminals were never as smart as they thought they were. What I wouldn't give to be a fly on Trudy Cravens's wall when she and Russell Cobb realized their final payment consisted of fifty grand in Monopoly money. I had no idea how they'd planned to spend their dirty earnings, but they wouldn't get very far with the pink, yellow, and blue currency. Just for grins, I'd also stuck the get-out-of-jail-free card in the envelope, though I'd written VOID across it in red Sharpie, a little inside joke.

Cobb went to the door, rang the bell, and was promptly admitted, as usual. I saw Eddie and Josh advance toward the house on the street, using parked cars and brick mailboxes for cover as they filmed the goings-on at the Cravens' house.

Cobb had been inside less than a minute when the front door opened again, and he exited without fanfare, taking quick steps to his Mercedes.

What?

Why didn't he look enraged or upset? Why wasn't he ranting and raving and stomping his feet? For all he knew, Larry Burkett had duped him, filling the envelope with play money instead of the real thing. Why was he acting like nothing was wrong?

Cobb started his car, made a loop at the end of the cul-de-sac, and motored off, free as you please.

Eddie, Josh, and I met up in the middle of the street.

"What the hell?" Eddie said. "I expected the two of them to hit the roof. Where are the fireworks?"

Josh shifted his camera in his hands. "You think they didn't check the envelope yet?"

We had little chance to speculate. Where Cobb's red taillights had disappeared around a corner only thirty seconds before, headlights now came up the street. Fast.

"He's back!" I cried.

We scattered, rushing back to our places.

Cobb's Mercedes screeched to a stop in front of Judge Craven's house. He leaped from the car and barreled up the walkway so fast he had no time to notice the three special agents closing in. Before he could even knock on the front door, Trudy yanked it open once again.

Cobb stopped on the porch as she held up her hand. In her fingers were a stack of pastel pink, yellow, and blue bills and the voided get-out-of-jail-free card. "What the hell is this?"

Click-click-click. I made my way up the walk, snapping photos in rapid succession. As much as I prided myself on my sharpshooting skills, I had to admit it was nice to take shots with a nonlethal weapon for a change.

Josh closed in from the left with his video camera. Eddie swooped in from the right with his badge and gun in his hands.

Judge Craven spotted us advancing, her furious expression turning first to confusion, then to shock as she realized she'd been caught red-handed. Well, pink-, yellow-, and blue-handed, anyway.

Following Trudy's startled gaze, Cobb turned around, instinctively stepping backward as we approached. "Who are you? What are you doing here?"

Trudy went to slam her door, but by then Cobb had put a hand on the doorjamb to steady himself. All she managed to do was crush his knuckles before Eddie rushed forward and shoved the door open. Cobb shrieked in agony and grabbed his injured hand with the other, in the process dropping his car keys to the sidewalk. They landed with a clink.

I shoved the camera into the big front pocket on my hoodie and yanked my gun from the holster at my waist. "Put your hands up!"

"For God's sake!" screamed Cobb, still clutching his hand. "My fingers are broken!"

"All right," I said. "Sit down, then." What a baby. I hadn't made that much fuss when I'd been stabbed by a chicken at a cockfight. But that's a whole other story.

Cobb dropped to his butt on the front stoop.

Judge Craven was surprisingly more resistant. She ran back into her house, tossing the play cash into the air, the Monopoly money fluttering to the floor behind her like it was ticker tape and she was leading a parade.

"Josh!" I called. "I'm going in! Keep an eye on Cobb."

"Okay." He pulled his gun, holding it with both hands and aiming it downward. The guy was a whiz with technology, but he stunk with weapons. He had the gun in relatively the right position, though if he fired now he'd accidentally shoot himself in the foot. I made a mental note to remind him later to point the gun slightly away from himself when he was in a holding position.

I followed Eddie into the house. A bewildered Mr. Craven stood in the living room, his mouth gaping.

"Where's your wife?" Eddie demanded.

"Who the hell are you?" the man demanded right back.

"IRS!" Eddie shouted. "Now tell me where your wife is!"

The man frowned in confusion. "IRS?"

"Criminal tax enforcement," I said. "Your wife's in some trouble. You will be, too, if you don't tell us where she is."

The man gestured toward the hall. "She ran down there."

"Don't move," Eddie told him as we inched toward the hall.

"Come out now, Judge Craven!" I hollered.

The woman had spent years in the legal field. She ought to have the sense to cooperate with law enforcement. By attempting to flee she was only getting herself in deeper doo-doo and adding to her potential charges and sentence.

Eddie and I looked down the hallway. There were three doors that led off the corridor. All three were closed.

Eddie and I took a stand along each side of the first doorway. I reached out a hand, grabbed the knob, and threw the door open. We peeked inside, finding a half bath with nobody inside.

We repeated the process at the next door, finding what appeared to be a guest bedroom. I fell to the floor and took a quick look under the bed, while Eddie checked the closet.

"She's not under the bed." I put a hand on the footboard and leveraged myself back to a stand.

"Not here, either." He stepped away from the closet.

We hurried to the third door and threw it open. When we peeked inside, we saw Judge Craven struggling to get up onto the open windowsill.

"Stop!" I shouted, stepping into the room.

Trudy seemed to realize she'd never make it out the window. She slipped down the wall and turned to face us. When she began to raise her hands, relief surged through me. Looked like she was giving up now. *Thank goodness.*

Unfortunately, I was wrong. Trudy grabbed a tube of lilac-scented foot lotion from her bedside table and hurled it at me. I ducked and the tube bounced off my shoulder, tumbling to the floor. When I looked up again, a lamp was coming my way. I dodged to the side and managed to avoid it. *Thwack!* It slammed into the wall, bending the shade and breaking the bulb.

She aimed her next projectile, a paperback thriller, at Eddie. As far as weapons go, it was a poor choice. What did she think she was going to do, kill him with a paper cut? He turned sideways and the book hit him in the upper arm, causing no damage, before it, too, fell to the floor. Good thing she didn't read those big hardbacks. A bookmark fell out of the book. Hoped she'd be able to find her page when she resumed her reading in jail.

Judge Craven hurled a TV remote at us next. As it hit the doorjamb, the TV turned on and the battery compartment broke off, spilling two AA batteries onto the floor. Ironically, the station was tuned to the news, the reporter talking about the PPE case.

This was getting ridiculous. At least the bedside table was clear now. She was out of things to throw.

Guns aimed at Trudy, Eddie and I eased toward her.

"Put your hands up!" I ordered.

Trudy reached over to the nightstand, grabbed the drawer handle, and yanked the drawer open. She stuck her hand inside and whipped out a pistol.

"Duck!" I screamed to Eddie when I realized what Trudy had in her hand. "She's got a gun!"

Bang!

A bullet sailed over me and Eddie. I turned back, expecting to see a hole in Trudy's bedroom wall. Instead, she'd put a hole in her husband. He stood in the doorway, hanging on to the edge as if for dear life, a look of shock on his face. His striped button-down bore a hole in the right shoulder, a hole that was rapidly losing blood.

"Trudy?" His voice was hardly more than a whisper. "Why?"

He slid down the door frame, leaving a bloody smear along the trim as he crumpled to the floor.

"Harold!" Trudy screamed, dropping her gun to the floor and rushing to the doorway.

As she knelt by her husband, I grabbed her hands and yanked them up behind her, slapping my cuffs on them.

"No!" she cried, wriggling and struggling against the shackles. "I need to help my husband!"

I grabbed her arms and pulled her back away from him. "Haven't you helped him enough?"

I grabbed a towel from the couple's bathroom and pressed it to Harold's wound while Eddie called 911 to summon an ambulance. Three minutes and approximately two pints of blood later, two EMTs rushed into the bedroom. The first stepped on the tube of lotion, sending a lilac-scented squirt of white cream onto the carpet. The other inadvertently stepped on the television remote, ending its life with an audible crunch.

The paramedics hurriedly loaded Harold Craven onto a gurney and rolled him out to the waiting ambulance.

Trudy Craven and Russell Cobb were taken away by marshals. While Cobb maintained a poker face and said not a word as he was loaded into the car, Trudy sobbed and cried, "I never should have gotten involved! I never should have taken the money!"

"Gee, you think?" I snapped before slamming the door on her.

chapter thirty-nine

Things That go Boom in the Night

"Two down, one to go," I told Eddie and Josh as we stood in the Cravens' driveway.

With our two targets in Dallas now in custody, the only thing left to do was drive back out to Palo Pinto to arrest Larry Burkett. We had incontrovertible proof now linking his payments to Judge Craven and the dirty verdict. Time to snag his sorry ass and book it.

I turned to Eddie. "Think you and I can handle things on our own, let Josh get a late start on his date?"

"Sure," Eddie said. "No sense all of us driving out there."

"Great," Josh said. "See ya.'" He jogged off in the direction of his car.

Eddie drove to Palo Pinto while I navigated. I'd plugged Burkett's home address into my GPS app and we followed the directions out to his ranch. It was a damn good thing we had the help. Besides the fact that there was no moon and the night was pitch-black, the area was also devoid of landmarks. If not for the computerized voice telling us where to go, we would've gotten lost out here.

Burkett's property was fenced and gated, but the gate was only latched, not locked. Eddie drove onto the property, strategically parking at an angle behind the Ram pickup and the Cadillac that were parked in the driveway, blocking them in. You never knew when someone might jump into a car and attempt a getaway.

Eddie and I climbed out of the car and met on the porch of the sprawling, single-story ranch house.

"I don't see the Yukon," I said.

A detached garage sat at the back of the driveway. I walked over to it, stepping up to a window on the side. The illumination from my cell phone's flashlight app revealed a series of makeshift plywood tables and enough tools to supply a construction crew three times over, but no SUV. "Looks like Burkett's converted his garage into a workshop."

It also looked like he might not be home.

While the garage was dark, lights were on inside the house and we could see movement through the sheer curtains in the front windows. At least one person was inside. Eddie and I approached the door cautiously. He stood back a few feet while I rang the bell.

The porch lights came on and a woman's voice came from the other side of the door, her tone suspicious and tentative. "Who is it?"

I couldn't fault her for not opening the door. After all, the Burketts lived on an isolated stretch of country road. The situation was perfect fodder for a horror movie.

"Special Agents Tara Holloway and Eddie Bardin with the IRS," I replied loudly, realizing a visit from the IRS was probably every bit as horrifying to many people as an ax murderer, maybe even more so.

The door opened a crack. Two eyes peered out over the safety chain. Eddie and I flashed our badges at the eyes, which merely blinked in reply.

"Are you Mrs. Burkett?" I asked.

"Yes?" It was both an answer and a question.

"We're looking for your husband," Eddie said. "Is he home?"

"Why are you looking for Larry?"

I was tempted to say, *We'll ask the questions here,* but I knew from experience that a person could catch more flies with honey than vinegar. Of course I couldn't exactly offer this woman honey, but I could be as polite and direct as possible under the circumstances. "We need to talk to him about the PPE trial."

After a slight hesitation, she said, "He had to go out to one of the wells. There was some type of problem with the equipment."

Eddie leaned to the side to better see Mrs. Burkett. "Do you know where the well is?"

"Yes," she said. "He wrote it down for me."

She slid the chain out of the slot and opened the door fully. Picking up a notepad from a table in the entryway, she held it out to us. The note indicated he'd gone out to a well located on a property on FM 919, not far from the tiny metropolis of Gordon.

We thanked her for the information and returned to Eddie's car, driving out to the property, arriving in just under twenty minutes. While the owner's house sat a full half mile back from the road, the gas well was situated closer to the highway. The gate to the acreage stood open. The Yukon was parked next to the well, the front of the vehicle angled toward the gate. Not only were the headlights on, but the cab was lit as well. A man was visible in the cab. Though it was impossible to identify him with any certainty from this distance and with the headlights causing interference, I assumed the man was Larry Burkett.

Eddie and I drove up closer, leaving fifty yards or so

between our car and Burkett's SUV, giving ourselves a buffer zone in case he was armed. We climbed out and crept carefully toward the Yukon. Both of us had drawn our guns, the earlier events at Judge Craven's house having made us anxious.

"Mr. Burkett?" I called out loudly as we approached the truck. "We're federal agents. We'd like to talk to you."

The man in the car didn't move.

"I don't think he heard you," Eddie said.

"Mr. Burkett?" I called even louder, now only a dozen feet from the vehicle. "We're fed—"

I stopped in my tracks.

That wasn't a man in the cab. It was a fifty-pound bag of dog food wrapped in a man's jacket with a hard hat sitting on top of it.

Eddie must've noticed it, too. "What the hell?"

Before we could process the information, an odd hissing noise came from the well fifty feet away. A small flame shot up from the ground, followed by a louder hiss, followed by a larger flame. In the distance beyond the well, a dark shadow fled through the field.

"It's a setup!" I screamed. "Run!"

Eddie took off running across the field with me following two steps behind. We'd made it only a hundred feet when *BOOM!* A fireball erupted from the well. The percussive effect of the explosion slammed into me, sending me tumbling forward. An instant later, the flames scorched my back. Eddie had been thrown to the ground. On instinct, I dove on top of him, covering him as well as I could with my body.

If either of us were to go up in flame tonight, I'd rather it be me. Eddie had a wife and kids who needed him. I had Nick and my cats but no children depending on me. At least if I died here tonight, I'd die knowing Nick loved me. That was something, right?

We lay there for a moment, both of us screaming in sheer terror as the flames licked over us. Those fortune cookies had been right. Things had definitely heated up for us. Given the line of excruciating pain across my ass, I surmised that the hem of my jacket had caught fire and spread to my pants. When the initial burst of flame subsided, I rolled off Eddie and kept going, spinning across the pasture like a kid rolling down a hill, hoping to douse the flames that seared my skin.

When I'd rolled a dozen feet or so, I stopped, lying on my stomach and looking back over my shoulder. Smoke rose from my scorched ass. Farther back, the well shot a geyser of flame hundreds of feet into the air. The Yukon was fully engulfed.

Eddie and I scrambled to our feet and ran toward the house. A middle-aged couple stood on the front porch, their mouths gaping, a scared, squirming dachshund clutched in the woman's arms. I recognized them as plaintiffs in the PPE class-action suit.

"Have you called for help?" I hollered as we approached.

"Yes!" the woman cried. "It's on the way!"

A minute later, sirens sounded in the distance and flashing lights lit up the night sky, competing with the fire from the well. The first responders pulled through the gate and across the field, driving up near the well.

Eddie and I stood with the couple on their porch while the local fire department worked to extinguish the fire. We questioned the couple about the well, whether they'd seen Larry Burkett on their property tonight, but they'd been inside watching television since dinnertime.

The wife shook her head and clutched her dog even tighter. "We didn't notice a thing."

When the shock of the explosion waned, the blistering pain across my behind became unbearable. I looked back to see parts of my bare, blistered butt showing through the seat of my pants. The woman was kind enough to give me a bathrobe to wrap around myself.

When the fire was extinguished, Eddie and I were able to return to his car. The vehicle bore scorch marks but at least it still started. The Yukon, on the other hand, was a mere metal skeleton.

The firemen wore masks, but Eddie and I had to settle for lifting our shirt hems to our noses and breathing through the fabric, hoping it would filter out any toxic chemicals. The effort was likely futile, and we both knew it, so we breathed as shallowly as possible and moved quickly.

I glanced around and shook my head. "What a waste."

"Yeah," Eddie agreed. "And that bastard wanted to waste us, too."

"I can't sit," I said. "My butt hurts too much."

Eddie opened the back door of his car for me. "Lie down back here. I'll get your ass to the ER."

chapter forty

*R*ump Roast

Eddie drove me to the nearest hospital in Mineral Wells. While he waited in the lobby and phoned Nick, Josh, and Lu to give them the news, the doctors took a look at my backside in the ER. The shit had definitely hit the fan. As promised, I phoned Trish from the hospital bed and told her about Judge Craven's arrest and the explosion. She was thrilled to be the first reporter with the inside scoop.

"You're lucky," the physician told me as he cleaned my wounds.

I cringed, clenching my eyes closed and fisting my hands against the pain. "Funny, I don't feel lucky." I might've been embarrassed if I wasn't in such agony.

"These are second-degree burns," he said, "but they cover only a small area. It could've been a whole lot worse."

The doctor prescribed a burn ointment and three days' worth of painkillers. He was kind enough to give me the first dose before sending me on my way.

When I stepped into the waiting room, I found Nick and Lu sitting with Eddie. All three stood as I waddled in, trying my hardest not to use my glutes.

"Tara!" Lu grabbed me by the shoulders and looked into my eyes. "You all right?"

"I will be," I said, "once the painkillers kick in."

Now that he'd verified that I'd survive and recover fully—eventually—Nick treated me to both a hug and his mischievous grin. "I always thought you had a smoking hot ass. Of course, this wasn't exactly what I had in mind."

I rolled my eyes. "Har-dee-har-har."

Eddie gave me an intent look. "I know what you did out there, Tara," he said quietly. "Thanks."

I shrugged. "You'd do the same for me if our situations were reversed, right?"

"Oh, sure." He nodded vigorously. "No doubt about it. Mm-hm." He followed his snide remarks with a whistle, darting his eyes about.

"Jackass," I said, though he wasn't fooling me. Eddie and I had been through too much together, knew each other too well. I knew my partner had my back, would never leave me hanging.

Lu had ridden out to the hospital with Nick. Assured that Nick would get me home and look after me for the next day or so, Eddie said he'd drive Lu back to Dallas.

The pill kicked in and I slept blissfully on the drive back to the city, lying on my side on the seat of Nick's truck, his comforting hand on my shoulder. When we reached his place, he scooped me up in his arms and carried me inside, taking me up to his bed. He laid me gently on top of the comforter.

Daffodil had followed us up the stairs. She propped her front paws on the edge of the bed, sniffing my charred skin with her cold, wet nose. Seeming to sense I was hurt, she hopped onto the bed and licked my face.

I ruffled her ear. "You're a good girl, Daffy."

With that and a big yawn, I slipped away into la-la land.

chapter forty-one

osers

Eddie and I were chatting over coffee in the office kitchen the following Monday when Viola came in to fetch a fresh cup for herself.

"Well, well," she said, "if it isn't original recipe and extra crispy."

Eddie groaned. "At least that's a new one."

After the explosion, our coworkers had seized the opportunity to razz us. One had posted photos of the two of us on the bulletin board with the caption "The Hottest Team in the IRS." Another had affixed a sticky note to the microwave that read, "Out of Order. Use Tara Holloway's Ass." I couldn't walk down the hallway that morning without someone asking if I was "fired up" or sniffing the air and asking, "Does anyone else smell barbecue?"

The next few weeks were a flurry of activity as the Brazos Rivers and PPE investigations came to their conclusions.

Larry Burkett had returned to his house the night of the explosion and was arrested there. The marshals who'd apprehended him came by the IRS office to give us the play-by-play.

"We dragged his sorry ass out of bed," the first marshal said, smirking. "He was in his pajamas. We didn't let him change."

"Of course he denied any involvement," said the second marshal. "He claimed he didn't even know there'd been an explosion, that the battery in his Yukon had died when he was checking on the well and that's why he'd left the SUV there."

Of course nobody believed him. Clearly he'd left the car there to lure us in.

"He asked about you two," the first noted. "Wanted to know how you were doing."

I raised a brow. "His conscience was finally getting to him?"

"Hell, no. When I told him you'd both survived with only minor injuries he cursed."

Burkett wasn't the first tax evader to be disappointed by my survival. Dare I hope he'd be the last?

When later asked about the funds, Burkett claimed he'd been unaware of the cash withdrawals Katie had made from the PPE accounts. Nobody believed that either. He was charged not only with bribery and tax evasion, but also with attempted murder for rigging the well to explode when Eddie and I arrived.

Though Cobb wasn't talking, we speculated that he'd had his lawyer place a quick call to Burkett after his arrest. Burkett had likely put two and two together and realized that the jig was up and we'd be coming for him now that we had Judge Craven and Russell Cobb in custody.

Michelson and his son identified Cobb in a lineup as the man who'd bought the Toyota from them. The evidence against him was insurmountable. He'd go down with the judge and Burkett. Unlike his coconspirators, however, he'd been released on bail. Since he'd committed no violent acts and had benefited the least from the crime, taking only a skim off the top, the judge went a little easier on him. No doubt he'd be looking at a year or two in prison, though. The other partners in his PR firm had promptly disassociated from him, reinventing themselves as Cushings & Beadle Branding.

John Craven spent three days in the hospital, but was expected to make a full recovery from his gunshot wound. Despite everything that had happened and even though his wife had hidden the illicit funds from him, he continued to stand by Trudy. Part of me thought he was an exceptionally devoted husband. Another part of me thought he was an idiot.

Burkett's son took over the helm at PPE. The class-action lawsuit against the gas company was promptly retried in another court. Although the defense attorneys found a more respectable scientist to testify on PPE's behalf in the second trial, the judge nonetheless found in favor of the plaintiffs on every claim. Given the size of the judgment, it was unclear whether PPE would be able to remain in business. At any rate, if the company stayed viable, Burkett's son vowed to clean up the company's act, to ensure that all health and safety regulations would be carefully followed, and to do whatever it could to minimize the environmental impact of its drilling activities.

Both Katie and Doug Dunn left their jobs at PPE. Thanks to a recommendation letter from me, Katie landed a new job with the U.S. Department of Housing and Urban Development in Fort Worth. The position had much more upward potential than her dead-end job at PPE, and offered better benefits than Mr. Burkett had provided. Doug took a new position with the Fort Worth water department. They sold their mobile home and bought a small brick house in the western part of the city, trading in their country life to become city slickers—or at least suburban slickers, if there was such a thing.

Jacqueline Plimpton and Ross O'Donnell worked out a plea deal for Brazos Rivers, who'd finally stopped lying and resisting and decided to cooperate. He'd spend nine months in jail and be forced to complete two hundred hours of community service. No doubt photos of him spearing trash on the highway would make the front pages of the tabloids.

His record company was under strict orders to send the singer's royalty earnings directly to the IRS until his taxes, penalties, and interest were paid in full. Ironically, the attention brought about by his arrest increased sales of his songs threefold, which would allow Uncle Sam to recoup the amount due much quicker. When I last checked, we'd already garnered a cool $3 million.

The plane sold for $2 million at auction. The Ferrari went for $350,000. The sale of the tour bus to Armadillo Uprising brought in another hundred and fifty grand. Heck, the boots brought in $2,000 a pair, the singer's trademark silver spurs a cool $5,000. Of course I'd never sell the spur he'd given me at the photo shoot. They were my own personal memento, a reminder to keep my head out of the clouds and never again to let my personal feelings affect my professional judgment.

In late March, just when I thought I'd finally catch a breather, Lu traipsed into my office and plunked an enormous stack of files on my desk. "Got some fresh cases for you."

She didn't bother giving me time to voice a protest before traipsing right back out.

"What are they?" I called after her.

"Charity fraud," she called back. "And someone posing as an IRS agent."

I pulled a few files off the top of the stack. The cases

were something new for me. With charity fraud, people pretended to be collecting for worthwhile causes when in actuality they were playing on people's emotions and keeping the ill-gotten profits for themselves. Despicable, huh?

The case at the bottom of the stack was something new, too. Someone in the Dallas area had indeed been posing as an IRS employee, making phone calls, sending threatening letters and e-mails. As Brazos had once said, why would anyone in their right mind pretend to be an IRS agent? One glance at the file told me why. Under the ruse, the culprit had tricked people into providing their Social Security numbers, birth dates, and bank account information. Armed with this data, the perpetrator had emptied the victims' accounts. The file documented over twenty-five victims in the last six months, over $85,000 stolen.

They say imitation is the sincerest form of flattery, but in this case the imposter was only making the IRS look bad. Many of the victims seemed to think the guilty party could actually be someone within the IRS.

Could it be true? Was one of my coworkers abusing their position to access personal data and steal from taxpayers? Or was the perpetrator someone on the outside with the savvy to successfully sell themselves as an IRS employee?

Looked like it was time to get to work and find out.